THE APOCALYPSE TROLL

THE
APOCALYPSE
TROLL

DAVID WEBER

A Baen Books Original

Baen Publishing Enterprises
P.O. Box 1403
Riverdale, NY 10471
www.baen.com

ISBN: 978-1-9821-2512-7

Cover art by Sam Kennedy

First printing, January 1999
First trade paperback printing, January 2021

Distributed by Simon & Schuster
1230 Avenue of the Americas
New York, NY 10020

Library of Congress Control Number: 98-41615

Printed in the United States of America

10 9 8 7 6 5 4 3 2 1

For Ed Wells & Richard Maxwell,
two of the good ones it hurts to lose.
Watch each other's backs, guys.

THE APOCALYPSE TROLL

troll *n.*

1. *Obsolete.* A creature of Scandinavian myth, sometimes portrayed as a mischievous or friendly dwarf, sometimes as a destructive giant, living in caves in the hills. **2.** A cyborg fighting machine of the *Shirmaksu* Empire. [Norwegian, from Old Norse *troll*, monster.]

—*Webster-Wangchi Unabridged*
Dictionary of Standard English
Tomas y Hijos, Publishers 2465,
Terran Standard Reckoning

CHAPTER ONE

TNS *Defender*, flagship of BatDiv Ninety-Two, was forty light-months from anywhere in particular, loafing along under half drive and no more than four or five translations into alpha-space, when the atonal shriek of General Quarters howled through her iron bones.

Her crew froze for one incredulous moment. Ridiculous! They were headed for the barn, and the Kangas were penned up in a miserable three-star system, the nearest of them almost exactly one hundred light-years away. What kind of nit-picking silliness could have possessed the Old Lady to call a drill *now*?

Then wonder was forgotten as they thundered to their stations.

Colonel Ludmilla Leonovna, commander of BatDiv Ninety-Two's strike group, was immersed in the new history text on her book-viewer when the alarm's high-pitched shriek jerked her away. She was into the passageway outside her quarters before she realized she'd moved, and halfway to the hangar deck before she remembered she'd left the viewer on.

She made a sliding turn around the final bend, ricocheted from a bulkhead in an experienced rebound trajectory, and emerged into the cavernous hangar to find her flight crews already assembling.

"Make a hole!"

1

Personnel scattered as they recognized her voice, and she went through the sudden opening and into the ready room like a more-or-less guided projectile, then came to a rocking halt beside the duty intelligence officer bent over the battle plot repeater. His face was intent, and her own lips pursed in a silent whistle as her eyes joined his on the crawling light dots on the screen. Her left hand rose to touch the ribbons on her tunic as if in memory, but she caught herself and lowered it deliberately, concentrating on the plot.

There was something odd about this, she thought.

Very odd. . . .

Commodore Josephine Santander's stern, composed face appeared on Captain Steven Onslow's com screen almost before the echoes of the alarm had died, though he knew she'd been in her quarters when it sounded.

"Talk to me, Steve," she said without preamble.

"Scan reports a Kanga force closing slowly from about sixty light-hours, Ma'am. Azimuth one-four-niner, elevation two-niner-three. I don't have a firm track yet, but it looks like they'll cross our wake about twenty light-hours behind us. Preliminary IDs look like an *Ogre* with escorts."

"An *Ogre*?" Commodore Santander allowed herself a raised eyebrow.

"Yes, Ma'am. It— Just a moment, Ma'am." He glanced at a side screen connecting him directly to Central Scanning, and his black face tightened.

"We're getting better data now, Ma'am. Scan confirms the *Ogre*. It's a full battle squadron—so far we've picked up three *Trollheims* siding her."

"I see. Put it on Battle One, please."

Onslow touched a button, and the big halo tank on the flag bridge lit with a three-dee duplicate of his own display. Commodore Santander studied it for a moment.

"We've got their course, Ma'am," Onslow said, and a thin red line appeared on the plot, predicting the hostile force's movements. "They're pulling about four lights relative and translating steadily."

"Gradient?" the commodore asked sharply.

"Steep, Ma'am. They're eight or nine translations out already. The computer estimates they'll break the beta wall in—" he glanced at his readouts "—about five hours."

Commodore Santander frowned and swung her command chair slowly from side to side. It was unlike the Kangas to pile on that sort of gradient. They must be in one hell of a hurry to run that big a risk of acoherency.

She wished there were someone she could turn this over to, but Admiral Wierhaus had detached only half of Battle Squadron Ninety for a badly needed overhaul, and she—for her sins—was the senior officer present. They were just over three light-years out of 36 Ophiuchi, and no one closer than the fleet base there could have taken the responsibility for her. She sighed silently. What she wished didn't change what she had.

"All right, Steve. Get Commander Tho to work on a pursuit course. Maximum drive and optimum translation curve."

"Optimum, Ma'am?" Onslow asked carefully.

"You heard me. Toss out the safety interlocks. They wouldn't be translating that fast if they weren't in a hurry, and there wouldn't be three *Trollheims* riding herd on them if it wasn't important. So get that course worked out soonest, then put the squadron on it."

"Aye, aye, Ma'am," Captain Onslow said just a bit too expressionlessly, and Santander turned back to her plot, forcing herself to project an aura of confidence. She understood his unhappiness at pushing the multidimensional drive that hard and only wished she had another choice.

Unfortunately, she didn't. The multi-dee could be dangerous, but the old Einsteinian limit held true, more or less, in normal-space. As it happened, the most recent hypotheses suggested that there were ways around that after all—in theory, at least—but the relativity aspects still turned theoretical physicists' hair white. Until they worked the bugs out (if they worked the bugs out) practical spacers would stick with something which at least let them predict the decade of their arrival.

Theoretically, the multi-dee was an elegant solution. If light-speed was inescapable, simply find yourself another dimension in which space was "folded" more tightly, bringing equivalent points "closer" together. That was a horribly crude description, but the commodore had yet to meet anyone who could describe it any better without resorting to pure math models. For her purposes, it worked well enough to visualize the galaxy of the FTL-traveler as consisting of concentric rings of dimensions; by moving "higher" in multi-dimensional space, a ship translated itself into rings with shorter and shorter radii, which meant that the same absolute velocity *seemed* higher in relation to normal-space. The physicists assured her she wasn't *really* moving at more than light-speed, but the practical result was FTL travel.

Still, there were limitations. The multi-dee was unusable inside the "Frankel Limit," a flexible point in stellar gravity wells which varied widely depending on spectral class and vessel mass, and though one theoretically could simply translate directly from normal-space into whatever other dimension one chose to use and vice versa, it was far wiser to translate gradually from one to another.

Dimensional energy flux could be vicious, and many things could happen to people who took liberties with the multi-dee. Few were pleasant. The alpha band—the "lowest" of all—was only about twenty dimensions across. At its upper limit, the maximum effective velocity of a ship (relative to normal-space) was about five times light-speed. Higher bands offered greater effective speeds, but at the cost of increasingly unstable energy states and consequently increasing risk to the ship. And there were barriers, still imperfectly understood, between the bands that meant cracking the wall was always risky. If a ship hit the wall just wrong or with the slightest harmonic in her translation field, she simply disappeared. She went acoherent, spread over a multitude of dimensions and forever unable to reconstitute herself, a thought which broke a cold sweat on the most hardened spacehound, for no one knew what happened inside the ship. Did the crew die? Did they go into some sort of stasis? Or did they gradually discover what had happened . . . and that they had become a galactic Flying Dutchman for all eternity?

Not that there was too much danger in the lower bands. Humans routinely used the beta band, or even the gamma and delta bands, though Kanga vessels ventured as high as the delta band only when speed was of over-riding importance. But no one in his right mind hit the wall as fast and as hard as BatDiv Ninety-Two would have to in order to overhaul these Kangas. Not if they had a choice.

"Course laid in, Ma'am," Captain Onslow said tonelessly.

"Then execute, Captain," she said.

"Aye, aye, Ma'am."

Defender shuddered as her normal-space drive went suddenly to full power. It felt smooth enough, but Santander knew how dreadfully overdue for overhaul *Defender* was, and she spared the time for a silent prayer against drive flutter as *Defender*'s three million tons wrapped themselves in the n-drive's space-twisting web and swung in a radical course change.

The drive surge was disorienting despite the grav compensators, and the light dots of *Defender*'s two sister ships and their escorts followed her on the plot as the under-strength battle division swerved to pursue humanity's mortal enemies across the trackless depths of more than a single space. Mangled ions streamed astern as their massive drives wailed up to max, and the high-pitched whine of the multi-dee generators sang in their bones.

"Time to the wall?" Santander let no awareness of the state of *Defender*'s drive color her question, and Onslow hid a wry, mental grimace of appreciation for her projected sangfroid.

"Fourteen hours, Ma'am," he replied.

"Rate of closure?"

"We should make up the absolute speed differential in about ten hours, Ma'am. If they were to maintain their present gradient, we'd need over eighty standard hours to match bands. I can't give you a realistic estimate without knowing when they're going to level out."

"I don't think they're going to," Santander said softly.

"But they'll break the gamma wall in fifty hours at this rate!"

"That's a heavy force, Captain, a long way from home and in a hell of a hurry. I think they're headed for the delta band—maybe even higher."

"But, Ma'am—they're *Kangas*!" Onslow protested.

"True. But *they* know they're losing, too. They wouldn't pull this big a force off the Line unless its mission was critical, and their current gradient is a pretty good indication of the risks they're willing to run."

"Yes, Ma'am," Onslow said finally, clearly taken aback by the whole idea.

"Run a track projection," Santander said abruptly. "I know you can't nail it down, but define a general volume for me. As soon as you can, please join Commander Miyagi, Colonel Leonovna and me in the flag briefing room. I've got a bad feeling about this."

"Aye, aye, Ma'am," Captain Onslow said. He watched his gray-haired commodore's screen blank, and his heart was cold as the vacuum beyond *Defender*'s hull. He had served with Commodore Santander off and on for ten subjective years. He'd seen her in the screaming heart of battle and listened to her voice snapping orders while her ship bucked and jerked under the enemy's pounding, and this was the first time she had ever admitted the least uncertainty....

Commodore Santander's eyes narrowed as Captain Onslow stepped through the briefing room hatch. He looked shaken, and she braced herself for bad news as she waved him to a chair between the two officers already at the table.

Plump, fair Commander Nicolas Miyagi was physically unprepossessing, but his deadly quick mind and a flood of nervous energy poorly suited to his appearance made him an excellent planning officer. Colonel Leonovna, however, was much more than that. Indeed, she was something of a legend in the fleet, and, at a moment like this, Santander was profoundly grateful for her presence.

Commodore Santander had never resented the colonel, but she understood why some did. Leonovna was twenty bio-years older than the commodore, but she looked a quarter of her age in her impeccable Marine uniform. The colonel would never be accused of classic beauty, but her wedge-shaped, high-cheekboned face was striking, and her bright chestnut hair and blue eyes might have been designed expressly to contrast with her space-black tunic.

Yet for all her undeniable attractiveness, Santander reminded herself, Leonovna was lethal. Her golden pilot's wings bore three tiny stars, each representing ten fighter kills, but the ribbons under those wings told the true story. They were headed by one the commodore had seen on precisely three officers during her entire career: the Solarian Grand Cross. Among other things, it entitled Colonel Leonovna to a salute from any officer who hadn't won it, regardless of rank—and, as far as Josephine Santander was concerned, that was an honor to which she was more than welcome.

But that wasn't why so many people resented—and feared—the colonel. Oh, no. Those reactions stemmed from something else entirely, for Ludmilla Leonovna was descended from the Sigma Draconis First Wave. The commodore shook herself free of her thoughts and cocked an eyebrow at Onslow. "May I assume you have more information now, Steve?"

"Yes, Ma'am. There's still room for error, but the computers make it an *Ogre*, three *Trollheims*, and one *Grendel*, plus escorts. There may be a *Harpy* out there, too."

She nodded calmly, but her mind was anything but calm. A single *Ogre* was bad—almost five million tons, with the firepower to sterilize a planet—but the *Trollheims* were worse. Far less massive (they were actually slightly smaller than *Defender*), they were even more heavily armed, for they were "crewed" by servomechanisms slaved to the cyborgs humans called "Trolls." A *Grendel* assault transport was bad news for any planet, for it carried an entire planetary assault force of Trolls and their combat mechs, but it meant little in a deep space battle. By the same token, the possibility of a *Harpy*-class interceptor carrier made a bad situation very little worse, for she could be only a spectator until and unless the action translated down into the alpha or lower beta band.

But any way Santander looked at it, BatDiv NinetyTwo was out-gunned and out-massed—badly—and she was far from certain the traditional human technical advantage could balance *these* odds. Yet suspicion stuck in her mind like a sliver of glass. The Kangas would never have wandered this far from the desperate defense of their three remaining systems unless they were engaged in something of supreme importance to their ultracautious race.

"That's a heavy weight of metal," was all she said softly.

"Agreed," Onslow said grimly, "but there's more. Commander Tho ran that track projection for you, Ma'am; they're headed for Sol."

"Sol?" Miyagi sat straighter, his blue eyes sharp. "That's insane! Home Fleet will blow them to plasma a light-month out!"

"Will they?" Leonovna spoke for the first time, looking like a teenager in her mother's uniform as she raked chestnut hair back from her forehead. "What about their gradient, Captain? Is it holding steady?"

"No," Onslow said, "it's still rising. I've never heard of anything like it. I wouldn't have believed a Kanga multi-dee could crank out that much power if I wasn't seeing it. We're wound up to max ourselves, and we're only reducing the differential slowly."

"That's what I was afraid of." Leonovna turned back to the commodore. "Could they be looking for a Takeshita Translation, Ma'am?"

There was a moment of dead silence. Trust the colonel to say it first, Commodore Santander reflected wryly.

"The thought had crossed my mind," she admitted, and touched her com button. "Navigation," she told the computer, and Commander Tho appeared on her screen. Santander was normally a stickler for courtesy and proper military procedure, but this time she didn't even give Tho time to acknowledge her call.

"Assuming present power levels remain constant, Commander," she said without preamble, "where will our Kangas break the theta wall?"

"The *theta* wall?" Commander Tho sounded surprised. "Just a moment, Ma'am." He looked down at his terminal to make calculations, then looked back up. "Assuming they *do* break it, Ma'am, they'll be two-point-one light-months from Sol with a normal-space velocity just over twelve hundred lights. But—"

"Thank you, Commander." Santander stopped him with a courteous nod, then switched off and looked around the briefing room. There was tension in every face, and she noted tiny beads of sweat at Onslow's temples as she nodded slowly.

"It would seem, Colonel, that you're onto something," she said. "And that, people, leaves us with a little problem."

Silence answered her, and she turned back to Onslow.

"You say we're closing the differential on them, Captain. How long before we can bring them into MDM range?"

"Normally, we'd have the range in about—" he glanced at his memo comp "—thirty-two hours, but their gradient's a bitch. Their translation curve is flattening, but so is ours. We've never seen a Kanga multi-dee run at this output, so I can't predict when their gradient will max out. It looks like we still have the edge, but we're into emergency over-boost now."

He did not add that no one ever used emergency over-boost, even on acceptance trials, and certainly not with drives in need of overhaul. Such demands on the multi-dee generators tremendously multiplied the chance of setting up a disastrous harmonic between them and the normal-space drive which actually moved the ship.

"Assuming we stay coherent," he went on, "I'd guesstimate that we should be able to range on them dimensionally in about two hundred hours."

"And at that time we'll be where, dimensionally speaking?"

"Well up into the eta band, Ma'am. And—" he frowned "—as far as I know, no one's ever used MDMs above the delta band. Gunnery isn't sure what effect that will have on the weapons."

"It looks like we're going to find out." Santander forced herself to speak calmly. "If Colonel Leonovna is right—and I think she is—they're headed for a Takeshita Translation. I know no one's ever tested the theory, but we have to assume that's what they're doing. If so, we know *where* they're headed. The question is *when*. Comments?"

"I'm no dimensional physicist, Ma'am," Colonel Leonovna said after a moment, "but as I understand it, that's a function of too many variables for us to predict. The mass of the vessel, the gradient curve and subjective velocity during translation, the deformation of the multi-dee . . ." She raised her hands, palms up. "All we can say is that if Takeshita's First Hypothesis is right, they'll flip backward in time when they hit the wall and go on translating backward until they hit Sol's Frankel Limit."

"You're overlooking a few points, Milla," Miyagi said. "Like his *Second* Hypothesis, whether or not time is mutable, or whether or not anyone can survive a Takeshita Translation in the first place." His tone was argumentative, but he was punching keys on his console as he spoke.

"True," Commodore Santander said, "but we have to assume they can do it unless we stop them. We can't afford to be wrong—not about this one."

"Agreed, Ma'am." Miyagi nodded. "And Colonel Leonovna's pretty much right about the problems, but we can make a few approximations. We know the mass of an *Ogre*, and they'll have to balance their multi-dee deformation to match the mass-power curve of the *Trollheims'* multi-dees and n-drives. . . ." He tapped keys quickly, and the others sat silent to let him work undisturbed. It took several minutes, but he finally looked up with a grim expression.

"Commodore, it's approximate as hell, but it looks like they'll hit the Frankel Limit something on the order of 40,000 years in the past. Could be closer to 90,000 if they lose the *Trollheims*."

"They won't." Colonel Leonovna shook her head. "Kangas are sure-thing players," she said softly. "They'll want to be sure Homo sapiens is around."

"Of course," Commodore Santander murmured. She sat wrapped in her thoughts for a few moments, then shook herself.

"Captain Onslow, pass the word to the other skippers, please. If *Defender* goes acoherent, whoever's left has to know this is for all the marbles. Breaking off the pursuit is not an option."

"Yes, Ma'am," Onslow said quietly.

"Very well. I think you can stand the crews down from action stations until we reach effective MDM range, but keep your scanner sections closed up in case they try a surprise launch down-gradient."

"Agreed, Ma'am."

"Nick—" she turned to Miyagi "—warm up the simulator. As soon as the Captain has everybody tucked in, we'll start working on tactics." She smiled without a trace of humor. "We're not exactly the War College, but we're all humanity has at the moment.

"Colonel." She met Leonovna's blue eyes levelly. "I hope we won't have anything for you to do, but if we do, it'll be one hell of a dogfight. Inform the squadron commanders on the other ships, then get with your planning officers. Work out the best balance you can between antishipping and antifighter ordnance loads. Then make sure every interceptor is one hundred percent. We can't afford any hangar queens."

"Understood, Ma'am."

"All right, people," Santander sighed, rising from her chair. "Carry on. And if you find yourself with any spare time—" she managed a wan smile "—spend it reminding God whose side He's on."

CHAPTER TWO

Battle Division Ninety-Two, Terran Navy, closed steadily on its foes. They had crossed the beta, gamma, delta, epsilon, and most of the zeta band without loss, but engineers hunched anxiously over their panels as the eta wall approached. The Kangas had already cracked that wall . . . and lost two cruisers doing it. The implications were not lost on BatDiv Ninety-Two.

The commodore sat doing the only thing she could do—projecting a confidence she was far from feeling. She knew her officers knew she was pretending, but their part of the game required them to pretend they believed her anyway. The thought amused her, despite her tension, and she smiled.

"Coming up on the wall, Commodore," Miyagi said softly, and she nodded watching BatDiv Ninety-Two's meticulous formation on her plot. For a unit which had considered itself well behind the front lines, they were doing her proud.

"Update the next drone," she said.

"Aye, aye, Ma'am."

This far out dimensionally it would take weeks for a message drone to reach the nearest fleet base (assuming it made it at all), but at least someone might know what had become of BatDiv Ninety-Two if it never turned up again. And, she was forced to admit, even if they succeeded in stopping the Kangas, the odds were that none of them would ever see Terra again. Her crews were equally aware of it, she thought, and that only made her prouder of them.

"Eta wall in ninety seconds, Ma'am."

"Launch the drone," she ordered.

Commodore Santander gripped the arms of her command chair and set her teeth. Breaking the wall was always rough, but at this speed and gradient, each wall had been progressively worse, and this time promised to be—

The universe went mad. *Defender*'s mighty bulk whipsawed impossibly, writhing in dreadful stress. Bright, searing motes spangled Santander's vision, and her heart spasmed sharply. The shock was lethal, impossible to endure . . . and over so quickly the mind scarcely had time to note it.

She shook herself doggedly, sagging about her bones, and sensed the same reaction from her bridge crew. Then she focused on her plot once more, and a spasm worse than translation squeezed her heart.

"Ma'am," Miyagi said hoarsely, "*Protector*'s—"

"I see it, Nick." She closed her eyes in grief. Three million tons of ship and nine thousand people—gone in an instant. And she'd thought *Defender*'s drive was in worse shape than *Protector*'s. . . .

"Launch from Bandit Three!" her tracking officer reported suddenly. "Multiple launch!"

"Target?" Santander demanded sharply.

"Tracking on *Sentinel*, Ma'am. Scan shows eight incoming."

Eight! That was a full load for a *Trollheim*'s stern battery! Heavy fire, yet not heavy enough to be automatically decisive at this range—which sounded more like a Kanga's idea than a Troll's . . . thank God. "Deploy decoys," she ordered. "Stand by to interdict."

"Aye, aye, Ma'am."

Both remaining dreadnoughts vomited decoys. Each massed well under a hundred tons, with a drive of strictly limited life, but while they lasted their scan images exactly matched that of the ship which had launched them.

Gunnery's lock on the incoming missiles was tenuous under these conditions, despite the devious scientific tricks which shifted their scan signals up a couple of levels and made them FTL for their current band, yet the idea of evasive action was laughable. It was all up to the decoys and interdiction fields, and at least they had the advantage of human technology.

The Multi-Dimensional Missiles flashing to meet BatDiv Ninety-Two mounted no explosive warheads; they carried something far worse: small, powerful multi-dee generators of their own. They were huge—even *Defender* could squeeze in only twenty-four similar weapons—but they were carried despite the squeeze they put on magazine space because they were lethal to any multi-dee field. In the microsecond before contact, their onboard generators spun up to full power, and they hit their target's field as a directly opposed surge field, inducing harmonics guaranteed to drive any target into acoherency.

Fortunately, Kanga MDMs were stupid compared to human weapons, and these had to make a half-dozen "downstream" translations to reach *Sentinel*. If tracking problems afflicted BatDiv Ninety-Two's defenses, they would also force the Kangas' missiles to rely almost entirely on their homing systems, and they were bleeding energy all the way down-gradient. That lost energy would form a "bow-wave," inducing myopia in their onboard tracking systems and degrading their accuracy dramatically. It would have required the full efforts of all three *Trollheims* to guarantee saturation of *Sentinel*'s defenses at this range, and that was why Santander was certain no Troll tactician had ordered this launch.

"Interdiction fields active," Miyagi reported, and she nodded. The last-ditch interdiction fields, like all active defenses, worked best against the longer flight times of missiles chasing from astern. They were simple in concept: focused directional energy fields projected into the paths of incoming attackers. A Guardian-class dreadnought could put out ten of them, but each was relatively tiny. The trick was to drop them exactly into the attacking weapons' line of flight, and when flight time was short and gunnery's lock was weak, it was almost as much a matter of experience and intuition as computer prediction....

Three decoys vanished, and four incoming missiles went with them. Two more MDMs ran headlong into interdiction fields and disappeared into infinity. The remaining pair whizzed past *Sentinel* at almost the same instant-clean misses, with absolutely no chance of tracking back around at this velocity and translation gradient—and Commodore Josephine Santander realized she had been holding her breath only when she let it out. A third of the enemy's after firepower had just been expended for absolutely no result!

"All right, Nick," she said flatly, "we should have the range in another few minutes. Dust off the tac net and kill me some Trolls."

"Aye, aye, Ma'am!"

BatDiv Ninety-Two continued to overhaul at close to ninety percent of light-speed, winding down its translation gradient steadily. Commodore Santander heaved a surreptitious sigh of relief as the multi-dee generators dropped back from emergency over-boost to saner power settings. Something decidedly unnatural had been done to those Kanga multi-dees to wring such performance out of them, but the higher power margin of the human generators was still sufficient—barely—to outperform them. And once they were in the same eta band level, fire control would become far more effective....

"Dropping into dimensional synchronicity—now!" Miyagi reported.

"Gunnery, fire plan alpha!"

"We have a second launch, Ma'am. Two launches! Bandits Two and Four are launching full salvos at *Sentinel*!"

"Replenish the decoys! Stand by to interdict!"

Five of *Defender*'s MDMs spewed out. Kanga decoys blossomed on her plot as *Sentinel* spat out a second quintet of missiles, but human MDMs were smarter—and faster—than anything the Kangas had. Even in a pursuit curve, they streaked past the enemy's decoys before the return fire could range on the human lures, and she felt a savage grin stretch her lips as one group of missiles ran in on each of the two rearmost *Trollheims*.

Troll reflexes were quick, but their predictors were less efficient than BatDiv Ninety-Two's. Interdiction fields destroyed seven missiles in bursts of light like brief suns—but the other three went home, and the capital ship odds were suddenly even.

Yet sixteen Kanga MDMs still raced into the teeth of the depleted squadron's defenses. Decoys called to them and died. Interdiction fields flared with eye-stabbing intensity as they crashed into the barriers and disappeared uselessly. And one slid past everything both dreadnoughts could throw at it.

Josephine Santander bit her lip hard as TNS *Sentinel* vanished into the howling depths of eternity.

The bridge was silent with the stunned stillness of shock.

"Abort engagement." Santander's soft command seemed shockingly loud in the silence, and Miyagi shook himself, then relayed the order quietly to the rest of her division. She closed her eyes briefly. *Sentinel* should have come through—but she hadn't. And without *Sentinel* or *Protector* to support her, *Defender* had no MDMs to waste at extended ranges. There were still nine warships in front of her, and she had only nineteen more of the big missiles.

The commodore leaned back in her command chair, fighting the shock and grief of eighteen thousand lost lives as she grappled with the imperatives of her situation. She had *Defender*, one heavy cruiser, and three destroyers against four capital ships and five light cruisers. As long as she remained astern, she was safe, for the Trollheim had expended her aft MDMs and the *Ogre* mounted no stern battery . . . but if she stayed behind them, she gave them every defensive advantage there was.

"Captain Onslow," she said calmly, "we'll have to get ahead of them."

"Understood, Ma'am," the captain's voice was harsh but level. "Going back to over-boost now."

She closed her ears to the keen of the multi-dee as it rose once more, but she could not close her thoughts. If she lost the ship now, there was no hope, for *Defender* was her only remaining dreadnought. Her chance of stopping the enemy was horrifyingly slim, but without her flagship, BatDiv Ninety-Two's escorts had none at all.

"Scan reports they're trying to crank their translation fields up a bit, Ma'am," Miyagi said quietly. She opened one eye and gave him what she hoped was a confident look. "They're not getting very far; we're level-reaching on them now."

"Good." She inhaled. "What's their formation?"

"The heavies are moving into translation lock, and the cruisers are closing up to cover the rear of their formation, Ma'am."

"I see." She glanced at her com screen and saw the understanding in Captain Onslow's eyes. It was a smart move, if a cold-blooded one. But then, those cruisers were crewed by Trolls. They were expendable.

In fact, they were more expendable than her own MDMs. Above the beta band, nothing else could get through the interface of a translation field and an n-drive's field. The translation field exerted a "dimensional shear" effect on anything that tried to cross it, while the n-drive distorted the space about a vessel and distributed all the tremendous mass it built up at relativistic velocities across the surface of its field. Either alone could be handled; hitting their combined strength with anything less than an MDM was like trying to split a planet with a claw hammer.

Once a ship dropped into the lower bands or sublight, it was another matter. But the Kangas and their Trolls wouldn't do that until they arrived at Sol, and they could not be permitted to arrive.

Yet the threat to humanity rode in the *Ogre*, which was precisely why the light cruisers had dropped back between it and *Defender*. Their translation fields were the only ones the seekers in *Defender*'s MDMs could now "see," and each would cost her two or three—possibly even four—MDMs to pick off. Which meant that she would run out of missiles before she even got a shot at the ship she had to destroy.

"Time to crossover?" she asked Miyagi.

"Forty-five minutes for translation crossover. How soon we can overhaul them spatially depends on how far we want to level-reach on them."

"And from crossover to the theta wall at their present power curve?"

"Another hundred and twenty hours, Ma'am."

"All right." She sat up straight, meeting Onslow's eyes. "Captain, you will reduce drive power to maintain this spatial interval until you have attained a six level advantage, then go to full power and overhaul them. We'll have the scanner advantage for defensive fire control, and we'll just have to take our chances on level drop when we fire."

"Yes, Ma'am. Understood."

"Nick," she said softly to Miyagi, "close up the tin cans. Put them between us and the Kangas when we begin to overhaul."

"Yes, Ma'am. They'll understand."

"That doesn't make me like it," she said bleakly, then pushed her inner anguish aside. "Once we start overhauling, they'll probably shift formation to keep those cruisers in our way, but we'll be shooting down their throats. Even with level drop, that should let us take out a cruiser with only a pair of missiles, and if we can blow them out of the way, we'll have a shot at the leader. That's all we really need. Just one good shot at him."

"Agreed, Ma'am. But what about their translation lock?"

She knew what he meant. By locking their multi-dees in phase, the enemy ships presented what was, in effect, a single target to *Defender*'s MDMs. It was a colossal game of Russian roulette, for the level drop penalties meant that once her missiles were launched, *Defender* had no means to influence the ships they actually targeted. And just to make things more difficult, the massed defensive systems of all the targets could combine against her salvos.

"We'll just have to do our best, Nick. It's the only game in town."

She brooded over her plot a moment longer, then sighed.

"All right, Commander," she said finally, "get those destroyers moving."

CHAPTER THREE

Commodore Santander gripped her command chair arms to still the tremble of her fingers, and her face was haunted. Fifty-three sleepless hours might explain her gaunt, hollowed cheeks, but not the ghosts behind her eyes.

A strange and terrible tension had invaded *Defender*'s heart, and the viscous air shimmered with a vibration as eerie as it was indefinable. It wore away at tempers and fogged minds which sought to concentrate on vital tasks, and voices sounded tinny and unnatural, falling upon the ear with a peculiar brittleness—a sense of déjà vu, as if each sentence were an echo of something which had been said but a moment before.

She no longer tried to hide her fear. It would have been pointless, for her people all shared it, just as they shared her exhaustion. Worse, every one of them knew what she knew: the fate of the human race rested upon their shoulders . . . and they were failing.

"All right, Steve," she said, "how bad is it?"

"Bad, Ma'am," Onslow said heavily. His screen image's shoulders hunched against the exhaustion and strain trying to drag him under, and his sentences were short and choppy. "No one's ever been this high in the eta band. Our scanners are packing up; they can't make the shift over the theta wall. We tried linking with *Dauntless*, but her scanners are in even worse shape." He drew a ragged breath and rubbed his puffy eyes. "I can't lock in a good solution, Ma'am. I'm sorry."

Santander closed her eyes under the strain of a responsibility greater than any task force or fleet commander had ever faced. One she faced with but a single dreadnought and only one heavy cruiser.

Beyond the hull, *Defender*'s translation field was a crackling corona, a crawling sheet of icy flame no human had ever seen before. The eta band was worse than anyone had thought, and conditions in its uppermost levels were indescribable. Humanity had no business in this haunted, curdled space, in these distorted dimensions where even time felt twisted and alien. But they were here, and all of her destroyers had died, absorbing missiles meant for *Defender*, to get them here.

She shook the thought aside, forcing her mind back to the task at hand. She had one MDM left—only one. The Kanga cruisers and the *Grendel* were as dead as her destroyers, but three heavy units remained . . . three targets for her single missile. They had expended most of their own MDMs on her destroyers, but her increasingly unreliable instruments could not tell her exactly how many they still had. It could be as few as two or as many as six—she simply didn't know. And the only way to find out, she thought grimly, was to offer her own ship as a target.

"All right," she said finally, "how close do we have to get under these . . . conditions?"

"Two hundred thousand kilometers, Ma'am." Onslow's mouth twisted with the bitter taste of his words, and she flinched inwardly. Less than one light-second? That wasn't point-blank—it was suicide range. Under normal circumstances, that was. Here? Who could know? "Even then," Onslow continued slowly, "Gunnery can't guarantee to hit the *Ogre*. They're still holding translation lock—God knows how—and sensor conditions are so bad that the seeking systems can't possibly differentiate target sources, however close we come."

"All right," she sighed. "We're sixty-five hours from the theta wall, but our options won't change." She met his eyes levelly and drew a breath. "Close the range, Captain," she said formally. "Get us close enough to score just once more."

"Aye, aye, Ma'am," Onslow said simply, and the drive shrieked as it was suddenly reversed.

The abrupt alteration was a strange and terrible anguish in the uncanny surrealism of the eta bands, and Santander fought the quivering pain in her muscles and nerves, watching her plot as the range to the fuzzily defined dots of the enemy shrank. The glowing diamond of her last escort clung immovably to *Defender*'s flank as the heavy cruiser *Dauntless* matched her flagship's maneuver.

"Range twelve light-seconds," Miyagi reported. "Eleven . . . ten . . . nine . . ."

"Bandits are slowing," Tracking reported suddenly, and Santander bit her lip. The Kangas had been glued to full power since detection, disdaining any tactical maneuvers as they followed the precise, preplanned course to their Takeshita Translation. She'd hoped they wouldn't change that now.

"Range still dropping," Miyagi said tersely, "but the closure rate's decreasing. Eight light-seconds. Coming up on seven."

"Hostile launch!" Tracking snapped. "Multiple launch. Four—no, five incoming! Time to impact twelve seconds!"

Santander's eyes met Onslow's in horror, but neither spoke the truth both recognized. The enemy had preempted their own attack. His MDMs would arrive before *Defender* reached launch range. They had no way to know how good his targeting was. All they knew was that, unlike them, he was firing up-gradient, which meant his missiles' seekers would be far less degraded by the local conditions . . . and that there were five of them. The Kangas' odds of scoring a hit had to be several times as great as *Defender*'s, which meant Santander had to launch now. She had to get her own MDM off before the incoming fire killed her ship and destroyed the weapon in its tube. But she couldn't hope to hit her target at this range and under these conditions, and the commodore's brain whirred desperately as she tried to find some answer—any answer—to her impossible dilemma. Only there wasn't one. There was only—

"Ma'am! *Dauntless*—!" Her plotting officer's shout whipped her eyes back to the display, and a fist squeezed her heart as the heavy cruiser began to move relative to *Defender*. Slowly, at first, then more rapidly. The commodore had a moment to realize that Captain McInnis had rammed his drive power past the red line. He'd known this moment might come, and her mind shied like a wounded horse from the thought of what conditions must be like aboard the cruiser as she crashed across the screaming distortion of *Defender*'s drive wake and offered herself to *Defender*'s executioners.

There was time for no more thoughts than that as *Dauntless* met the incoming missiles head-on. No more time for thought—only for grief as her last remaining escort vanished in a wracking spasm of outraged space-time and took the missiles with her.

"He did it," she said softly, appalled by the cruiser's sacrifice. Yet elation warred with her horror, and the realization touched her with self-loathing. *Dauntless* had died, but now no Kanga MDMs remained, and that was the only thing she could think about now. No other consideration was acceptable, and she kept her gaze on her plot, refusing to meet any other eyes.

"Captain Onslow," she heard her voice as if it belonged to someone else, "hold your fire, please. We will close to ten thousand kilometers and match speed and translation with the enemy before we attack."

The range dropped unsteadily, and inner ears rebelled as drive surges added to the stress already afflicting *Defender*'s crew. The Kanga commander was desperate, Santander thought coldly. He'd shot his bolt, freeing *Defender* to seek optimum firing range at last, and he juggled his own drive frantically. But there was little he could do, and the dreadnought closed grimly, matching him lunge for lunge, sliding inexorably closer until the fringe of her own translation field was barely five hundred kilometers clear of her foes'. She dared come no closer, but at this range her missile could not miss at least one of her enemies, despite the fuzziness of her fire control. Not even Trolls would have time to react before it struck home, yet even at this short a range, fire control couldn't guarantee which enemy their bird would destroy.

Commodore Santander sat tensely in her command chair, knuckles white on its arms. One last shot ... one chance in three. ...

"We're as close as we can come, Ma'am," Onslow reported tersely.

"Very well, Captain. Fire at will."

"Missile away—*now*!"

It happened like lightning. There was scarcely time to register the launch before the missile flashed into the enemy formation ...

... and struck the remaining *Trollheim* full on.

Josephine Santander sagged in her command chair. They'd come so far, paid so much, and they'd missed. *Defender* rode the Kangas' flank at less than a light-second, and it was over. The *Ogre* still had to make its final translation, but she couldn't stop it. She couldn't even follow into normal-space to engage the Kangas there. They knew *when* they were going, and even if she'd known that herself, it would have taken months of calculations by the best theoretical physicists to put *Defender* on the same gradient and follow them.

She'd failed. The bastards were going to get away with it, and there was noth—

But then her brain hiccuped suddenly, and she straightened slowly as an idea flickered. It was preposterous—insane!—but it refused to release her. . . .

She raised her head, looking into the screen to *Defender*'s command bridge. Onslow had aged fifty years in the last twenty seconds, she thought, and his shoulders were as slumped as hers had been.

"Captain?" He didn't even blink. "Captain Onslow!" His dulled eyes flickered, and a tremor seemed to run through him.

"Yes, Ma'am?" His voice was mechanical, responding out of rote reflex.

"We may still have an option, Steve." He looked at her incredulously. "We've still got *Defender*'s multi-dee," she said softly.

His face was blank for an instant, and then understanding flared.

"Of course." Life returned to his eyes—the blazing life of a man who has accepted the inevitability of something far worse than his own death and then been shown a possible way to avert it after all—and suppressed excitement lent his voice vibrancy as he nodded jerkily. "*Of course!*"

Animation rippled across the flag bridge as the commodore's words sank home. *Defender* herself could become a weapon. It had never been tried before—as far as anyone knew—but it was a chance.

"Nick?" Santander watched Miyagi fight off his own despair to grapple with the new idea. His was the closest thing she had to an expert opinion.

"I . . . don't know, Ma'am." He closed his eyes in thought, his tone almost absent. "It might work. But it wouldn't be like an MDM . . . not a surge so much as a brute force hammer. There's the *Harpy*, too, and the interference of our n-space drive. . . ."

Sweat gleamed on his forehead as he tried to envision the consequences, then he opened his eyes and met her gaze squarely.

"I'll need to build some computer models, Ma'am. It might take several hours."

"In that case," she said, glancing at the chronometer, "you'd better get started. Even with their evasive maneuvering, we're only about sixty hours from the wall."

"Yes, Ma'am. I'll get on it right away."

"Good, Nick." She stood with a chuckle that surprised her even more than the others. "Meanwhile, I'm going to take a shower and grab a little nap." She reached out in a rare gesture of affection and squeezed his shoulder. "Buzz me the minute you have anything."

Commodore Josephine Santander walked slowly from her bridge. As, she stepped through the blast doors into the passage, she heard Miyagi calling sickbay for another stim shot.

"All right, Nick."

Commodore Santander leaned back in her chair, incredibly restored by a shower and eight straight hours of sleep. Her crushing sense of failure had been driven back by the forlorn hope of her inspiration, and her face was calm once more, filled only with sympathy for the bright, febrile light in Miyagi's eyes. He was paying the price for seventy hours of strain and stim shots, and his glittering gaze held a mesmerizing quality, like the fiery intensity of a prophet.

"I can't give you a definitive answer, Ma'am, not without more time than we have, but the models suggest three possible outcomes." His voice was as tight and intense as his eyes.

"First, and most probable, we'll all simply go acoherent." He said it without a quaver, and she nodded. Survival was no longer a factor.

"Second, and almost as probable, all three ships will drop into normal-space with fused multi-dees and heavy internal damage—possibly enough to destroy them. If our own multi-dee were up to Fleet norms, we'd have a better chance of surviving than they would; as it is, it's a toss-up. Either way, though, they'll be light-months from Sol without FTL capability and in easy detection range of Home Fleet's pickets. Which—" his grin was feral, flickering with drug-induced energy "—means the bastards are dead."

Captain Onslow made a savage, wordless sound. He, too, had rested, yet he was not so much restored as refocused, with a flint-steel determination to destroy his enemies. Steven Onslow was a wolf, his teeth death-locked on a rival's throat, unwilling and possibly even unable to relinquish his hold.

"Third, we may push them right through the theta wall," Miyagi went on. "I can't predict what will happen if we do, Ma'am, but I suspect it will still throw them into a Takeshita Translation. On the other hand, our hitting them will screw their flight profile all to hell. We might throw them further back than they planned, but it's more likely they'll come up short, and the degree of deviation is absolutely unpredictable, whichever 'direction' it goes. There's even a faint possibility we could toss them into the future. In any case, the further from their planned break point we hit them, the wider the diversion will be."

"I see. And if they go through the theta wall, what happens to us?"

"Commodore, I'd say there's about an even chance we'd go with them. It depends on two factors: the exact mass-power curve of our translation fields at impact and how close to phased our n-drives are. Our scan data's too unreliable for us to match deliberately, but the tolerance is pretty wide—assuming my model's sound." He showed his teeth again. "I'm wired to the eyebrows, Ma'am, but I think it's solid."

"And if we go with them?"

"Then we're probably looking at something very like possibility two, Ma'am. All three of us in normal-space, no multi-dees, and unpredictable degrees of damage all round. The odds are we'd bleed a lot of the surge in the translation, so the damage might be less extensive than if we don't break the wall, but that's only a guess."

"I see." She looked at her two ranking officers. "Captain Onslow?"

"I say do it," the captain said savagely. "Even if we don't kill them outright, we may drop them in short enough for Home Fleet—or *a* fleet, anyway—to be waiting for them."

"Colonel?" The commodore swiveled her gaze to Leonovna.

"The Captain is right, Ma'am. It's our only option."

"I agree," Santander said calmly. She folded her hands on the table in front of her and nodded. "Very well, we'll try it. But when we do, we'll play the odds—all of them. If we *do* drop into normal-space and all three of us survive, we'll have our hands full. The *Ogre's* got at least as much firepower as we do and a lot more defense, and they still have their *Harpy*." She nodded to Leonovna. "Assuming she survives—and we do, of course—your interceptors are going to be outnumbered three to one. Can you hack those odds, Colonel?"

"My birds are better, Ma'am, and so are my people. We'll keep the *Harpy* off your back." Leonovna's smile echoed Miyagi's.

"Good. But, Colonel, remember this—" Santander stabbed her with her eyes "—the carrier is secondary. The *Ogre* and the Kangas are what matter. If even one Kanga tender gets away, you will break off the engagement and pursue it. *Kill that tender, Colonel Leonovna!* If they dust the planet, everything we've done is meaningless. Is that understood?"

"Yes, Ma'am," the colonel said softly.

"All right." Santander glanced at the bulkhead chronometer. "We're still over forty hours from the wall. I'll give you twelve hours to make your final preparations. Captain, have Doctor Pangborn and his staff get out their injectors. I want every member of this crew to get at least six hours of sleep during that time if it takes every trank in his dispensary."

"Yes, Ma'am."

"Very well," the commodore said. "Let's get to it, then." She rose, and the others rose with her, but she stopped them with a raised hand.

"In case I don't get a chance to tell you afterwards," she said quietly, "I just want to say well done . . . and thank you."

She held their eyes for a moment, then turned away before they could respond. They followed her from the briefing room in silence.

". . . so our attack plans have to be extremely tentative," Major Turabian, Strike/Interceptor Squadron 113's exec, said. "Red and Blue Sections will be tasked with fighter suppression and armed accordingly. White and Gold Sections will carry mixed armament. White Section's primary target will be the *Harpy*; Gold Section will form the reserve with primary responsibility for nailing any Kanga tenders. Captain Hanriot will lead Red Section, Captain Johnson will have Blue, and I will lead White. The Colonel will lead Gold Section and exercise overall tactical command. Primary and alternate com frequencies are already loaded into your birds' computers."

He sat down, and Ludmilla Leonovna crossed slowly to the traditional lectern, her hands clasped behind her. Interceptors required youth and fast reflexes, and the colonel was by far the oldest person in the squadron, yet she looked absurdly young as she faced her crews. Like them, she wore her flight suit, her sidearm riding low on her hip, and if she looked like the newest of new recruits, none of them were fooled. This was a veteran outfit, all of whom had flown combat with the colonel before.

"All right, people," she said softly. "I only have a few points.

"First, you can all count, so you know casualties will be high—accept that now, but *don't* resign yourself to being one of them." Her voice was cool and calm; only her sharpened eyes betrayed her own tension. "Anyone who goes out expecting to get the chop *will* get the chop, and we need to kill Trolls and Kangas, not ourselves.

"Second, you've got better onboard systems, smarter weapons, and more reach—maintain separation and use them. Don't screw around in gun range.

"Third, kill any Kanga tender any way you can out here, but if it turns into a stern chase, either get them short of atmosphere or make damned sure you use a heavy nuke. We don't know what kind of bugs they're carrying, and if they get to air-breathing range, any non-nuke shot could be as bad as not shooting at all."

She paused and surveyed them levelly once more, as if to make certain that they all understood.

"And fourth, remember this: Whenever we are when the shit stops flying, we're going to be in life-support range of a planet full of humans. And humans, people, have bars." A soft chuckle ran through the assembled flight crews. "And while—" she flashed a wry smile "—I am the sole member of this squadron who doesn't partake, I realize full well that I'm going to have to buy every one of you thirsty bastards a drink. But I warn you—I'll be damned if I'll listen to more than one glorious lie from each of you!

"All right," she said when the laughs died away, "let's saddle up." And her flight crews funneled through the hangar deck hatch.

Colonel Leonovna strode briskly to her own interceptor. Some pilots carried out a meticulous inspection of their birds before any launch, but she wasn't one of them. Sergeant Tetlow had looked after her fighter for over three subjective years; if anything ever had been wrong, Tetlow had fixed it long since.

Yet this time she paused by the ladder, looking up at the sleek shape of her weapon. A hundred meters from blunt nose to bulbous stern but barely twenty in diameter, the interceptor crouched in her launch cradle like Death waiting to pounce. Her hull bore a stenciled ID number, but, like most such craft, she had been named. Yet this name had been chosen not by her pilot but by her tech crew, who knew all about their squadron CO's heritage and her fascination with history. The name *Sputnik Too* gleamed in scarlet above the golden stencils of thirty-four oddly shaped silhouettes: one for each fighter Ludmilla Leonovna had killed. Under them were thirteen larger silhouettes, representing the starships squadrons under her command had destroyed. She looked at them silently, then reached up to touch the lowest—and largest—symbol, the silhouette of an *Ogre*-class capital ship. Only her interceptor had returned from that multisquadron strike.

Sergeant Tetlow was there when she lowered her hand. It was impossible to tell from his demeanor that he knew he was almost certainly about to die, and the colonel squeezed his shoulder gently.

"Ready to flit, Sarge?"

"Green and go, Ma'am." He nodded. "Give 'em hell."

"With pitchforks," she agreed, and climbed the ladder without another backward glance. She had to find her grip by feel, for her eyes burned strangely, and it was hard to focus.

She settled into her padded seat before the steady green and amber glow of her instruments. Light from the hangar deck flooded through the centimeter-thick armorplast overhead, and despite the grim situation, her lips quirked with familiar amusement. The human eye was useless in deep space combat, but something about human design philosophies demanded a clear all-around view anyway.

The familiarity of the thought put her back on balance, and she pulled her helmet down against the tension of the connector cables. She drew it over her head, sealing it to her flight suit, and the flat electrodes pressed her temples.

"Activate," she said clearly, and shuddered as the familiar sensory shock hit her. *Sputnik* had a complete set of manual controls but using them in combat gave a Troll too much advantage, so human ingenuity had provided another solution. Her nerves seemed to reach out, expanding, weaving their neurons into the circuits of the gleaming weapon which surrounded her. Direct computer feeds spilled information into her brain—weapon loads, targeting systems, flight status. . . .

Even after all these years, the rush of power was like a foretaste of godhood, she thought, dimly aware of her crewmates strapping in. Unlike the other ships in the squadron, *Sputnik* and Major Turabian's *Excalibur* carried three-man crews, not two. Each of her pilots had an electronic systems officer to run the electronic warfare systems and monitor all functions not directly linked to combat and maneuvering, but she and her exec had a com operator, as well, who also served a plotting function for engagements which could range over cubic light-minutes of space.

She grinned as Lieutenant O'Donnel, her ESO, plugged in and she felt an echo of her own sense of invincibility in his cross-feed.

"Ready, Anwar?"

"All systems green and go, Skipper."

"Prissy?"

"Green board, Skip," Sergeant Priscilla Goering announced from her isolated compartment behind them.

"Good." Leonovna pressed a button that lit *Sputnik*'s light on the hangar deck officer's console, then settled down in her seat. "And now, boys and girls," she announced over the squadron net, "we wait."

"Ma'am," Captain Onslow said formally to the commodore who no longer had a battle division, "we are closed up at action stations."

"Thank you, Captain." Commodore Santander glanced at her plot. *Defender* had climbed slightly "higher" in the eta band than her quarry and dropped a stem. According to Miyagi's models, their best chance for success was to strike their enemies' translation field down-gradient at a slightly accelerating velocity. It was grimly ironic, she reflected, how synonymous "success" and "self-immolation" had become.

She touched a com button.

"Stand by, Colonel Leonovna," she said.

"Standing by, Commodore." The strike group commander sounded as unflappable as ever, and Santander's lips twitched in a ghost of a smile.

"Very well, Captain. Execute your orders."

"Aye, aye, Ma'am," Captain Onslow said, and *Defender*'s bones came alive one last time with the high-pitched scream of a multi-dee in over-boost as she stooped upon her foes.

The glaring corona of *Defender*'s translation field filled the visual display—a chill, beautiful forest fire that dazzled the eye and hid the featureless gray of alien dimensions. It beckoned and whispered to Commodore Santander, but she wrenched her eyes from it with an effort and watched the plot as the diamond dot of her last vessel plunged towards the tight-linked rubies of her foes. The range fell with terrifying speed, and she had time only for one last surge of adrenaline and excitement and fear and determination.

Then they struck, and Josephine Santander screamed. She wasn't alone. No human frame could endure that crawling, twisting agony in silence. It was like every translation she'd ever endured, combined into one terrible whole and cubed. She writhed in her chair, eyes blind and staring, nerves whiplashing within her flesh as overloaded synapses shrieked in protest. It went on and on and on—an eternity wrapped in a heartbeat—and ended so abruptly it nearly broke her mind.

She moaned softly, pushing herself weakly up in her chair, feeling the warm trickle of blood over her chin and down her upper lip. She shook herself groggily, fighting for control, and looked around her flag bridge.

Commander Miyagi hung in his combat harness, his blood-frothed lips blue. He was not breathing, and beyond him a scanner tech was curled as close as her own harness allowed to a fetal knot while a high, endless mewl oozed from her. Santander had no idea how long that terrible moment had lasted, but she felt her own heart still shivering madly within her chest as she reached shakily for her com controls.

Her screen lit a moment before she touched them. Captain Onslow looked out at her, and she'd never seen him look so . . . dreadful. His face was cold, hammered iron, but there was a terrible, hungry fire in his eyes. He was no longer simply a warrior; he had become a killer.

"Commodore." His voice was hoarse as he wiped blood off his chin and glanced at his reddened fingers almost incuriously.

"Captain," she managed in return. "We've ... got some casualties up here," she said. "One of the scan crew ... and Nick. ... "

"Here, too, Ma'am," Onslow said, and an echo of the horror they'd endured touched his voice. But he shook himself, and a bleak smile mingled with the cold fire of his hunger. "Scanning's still here, Ma'am, and Nick's—" He faltered for a moment, then made his voice go firm once more. "Nick's models seem to be holding; we've got a gradient I never saw before: straight down. Of course, we've got a long way to fall. We should hit bottom in about twenty minutes ... and both of those bastards are coming with us."

"Damage?" she asked, feeling something almost like life spreading back through her abused flesh.

"Multi-dee's fused, Ma'am, and Power Two and Four went with it. N-drive is functional. We've lost about twenty percent of our computers and a quarter of our energy weapons. Defensive systems are generally intact. Personnel losses are still coming in." Pride in his ship strengthened his voice. "She's hurt, Ma'am, but the old bitch is still game!"

"Good, Captain," Commodore Santander said. "Stand by to engage."

"Aye, aye, Ma'am."

Three ships fell through the depths of dimensions not their own, plunging like storm-driven mariners towards the reefs of normal-space, and throughout *Defender*'s hull dead or incapacitated men and women were hauled away from their consoles. Casualties were worst closest to the fused multi-dee at her core, and the interceptor squadron, isolated by the hangar deck's location just inside her armored skin, had come through dazed but intact. Now Colonel Leonovna scanned the data feeding into her brain as the moment for launch approached. Drive and translation fields came to standby aboard thirty-two sleek and deadly vessels, and she felt the electronic caress of the launch field on her fighter's flanks like silken fingers.

"Stand by," she told her crews, and then the seconds were flashing by and the moment was no longer approaching—it was there.

"Hangar Deck, Bridge: launch interceptors."

"Launching, aye, Bridge!" the hangar deck officer snapped, and the launch fields focused tight. "Good hunting, Colonel!" an unknown voice called, and then the fields hurled the fighters from their launch cradles and drive interface penetration whiplashed through bone and sinew.

Leonovna took the shock with the ease of long practice, hardly even noticing the sudden, high-pitched squeal of her fighter's n-drive as Sputnik crashed through *Defender*'s drive into space. The awareness of godhead was upon her, and her senses reached out into the cold, black-velvet vastness upon the wizardry of her scanners. The emptiness which had frightened her so the first time she tasted it had become an old friend long, long ago, and her magic vision saw and absorbed everything in the flicker of a thought.

The *Ogre* was already turning to flee *Defender*, and there was the *Harpy*, to the side and "below" the others. She concentrated on the carrier as the first missiles went out from the warring capital ships, and Troll interceptors were already spitting from their bays to meet her fighters.

"Red Leader, take the first wave head-on. White Section, get that bitch before she respots her cradles! Blue Section, cover the strike."

Acknowledgments flowed over her, and her unfocused eyes were dreamy as her brain digested direct sensory input with long-trained efficiency. She absorbed and registered everything as the first wave of ripple-launched homing missiles went out from Red Section and White Section snarled up and around, going in over the Troll fighters under Blue Section's protective fire. Enemy interceptors tore apart or exploded, but there were so many of them! Even more than predicted! They must have fitted extra cradles and stuffed that *Harpy* to the deckheads, she thought, but if they had, something else had to have come out, and it might just be—

White Section's heavy ship-killers speared out, and the battle screen which interdicted them was far weaker than it ought to have been. The protective force field wavered as the first warhead detonated, and Leonovna felt a stab of elation. Turabian's impeccable attack had been sequenced to take out full-strength battle screens; the understrength defenses he actually faced were hopelessly outclassed. Fireballs polarized visual pickups and clawed her electronic senses with thunderbolts of static, and a glaring patch of localized failure crawled along the *Harpy*'s screens just as the second wave of ship-killers arrived. The heavy missiles plunged through the opened chink, and two million tons of carrier buckled, broke, and vaporized as megaton-range warheads savaged unshielded plating.

She took her second wave with her, but her first outnumbered One-Thirteen's fighters by more than two to one, and human fighters began to die.

"Blue Section, take them from behind. White Section, form on me. And maintain separation, damn it!"

Acknowledgments came through the blur of battle chatter, mingled with shouts of triumph and the sudden, mid-word interruption of thermonuclear death. Even with her computer sensors, she had trouble sorting out details, but the pattern was clear. Her crews had struck first and hard with their longer-ranged missiles, but the number of first-wave Troll fighters was far higher than expected, and their massed missile fire had saturated the defenses of more than one of her interceptors. Red Section had lost three already, and Blue was down two. White Section had lost none on the run against the *Harpy*, but Lieutenant Kittihawk paid for their success. Elated by the destruction of their target, she allowed her attention to waver, and a Troll rolled in behind her before she could evade.

The Troll fighters lacked humanity's advanced tracking systems, "smart" missiles, and sophisticated ECM, and their less efficient drives were slower to accelerate. But the cyborgs had a reaction speed few humans could match, even with their neural links, and their fighters were marginally faster and far, far more maneuverable than any human-crewed interceptor ever designed. At knife range, nothing in the galaxy was as deadly as a Troll interceptor, and snarling power guns ripped Kittihawk's fighter apart.

The victorious Troll tried to swing onto her wingman, but Casper Turabian was there, raging back and around in a vicious climbing attack that took it from below like a shark.

Twenty percent of Leonovna's fighters were gone, but the Troll losses were even higher, and her order to open the range took effect quickly. The humans used their higher power curves ruthlessly, accelerating clear to use their missiles like snipers before the Trolls could close again. Gold Section joined them, streaking in behind the turning Trolls, and an almost orgasmic thrill ran through the colonel as her first missile dropped free and guided. She picked another victim, lips wrinkled back in a hunting tiger's snarl as she tracked her second target and—

"*Defender* to Strike Leader!"

She broke instantly, turning away from the snarling ball of fighters to refocus her attention, and her wingman came with her, guarding her back. The capital ships had drawn well away from the fighters, and she blanched as the fury of their engagement registered.

Both ships were haloed in escaping atmosphere and water vapor, trailed by drifting wakes of molten debris, and she winced as fireballs savaged *Defender*'s battle screens, frantic to claw a hole for follow-up fire. The *Ogre* was in trouble, too, and the big ship staggered as one of *Defender*'s heavy missiles exploded just short of her heavily armored hull, but her sheer size was gradually overpowering the smaller human-crewed ship.

"*Defender*, this is Strike Leader," she snapped. "Go ahead."

"Colonel, this is the Captain." The blurred voice could have been anyone as radiation threshed the com channels with static. "The Commodore's had it. We've got heavy damage, but this bastard isn't getting away." More explosions flared, and the vicious thrust and parry of energy weapons was like ozone on her skin through her sensors.

"They're launching tenders with escort, Strike Leader. Go get 'em."

"Understood, *Defender*. I'm sending White Section to your assistance. Red and Blue will—"

"Don't bother, Strike Leader," Onslow said distantly through the crashing static. "Just kill those fucking tenders. See you in Hell, Col—"

The channel went dead as TNS *Defender* rammed her massive enemy and their outraged drive fields exploded like a nova.

courage *n.*

1. The state or quality of mind or spirit that enables one to face danger, fear, or vicissitudes with self-possession and resolution; valor; bravery. [From Middle English *corage*, heart, as representing the seat of feeling.]

—Webster-Wangchi Unabridged
Dictionary of Standard English
Tomas y Hijos, Publishers 2465,
Terran Standard Reckoning

CHAPTER FOUR

"What the hell?!"

Master Sergeant Andrew Slocum chopped himself off and felt his face tighten. Colonel Archer had the duty for the US Space Defense Operations Center, and he disapproved of profanity and unprofessional conduct generally. But he was sipping coffee at the far end of the subterranean room—fortunately—and Slocum cleared his throat and raised his voice.

"Colonel? Could you take a look at this, Sir?"

"Hm?" Colonel Archer moved towards Slocum with a raised eyebrow. One thing about the colonel, Slocum thought; he was a pain about some things, but he respected his people's judgment enough not to waste time with dumbass questions. He bent over the sergeant's shoulder to peer at the scope.

He didn't react at all for an instant, then he stiffened in shock.

"What the h—" He cut himself off, and Slocum felt an insane urge to giggle as the colonel leaned even closer. "Why didn't you report this sooner, Sergeant?" Archer demanded.

"Because they just popped onto the scope, Sir. Right about there." Slocum tapped the screen with a fingertip, and Archer frowned. A bright red line indicated the unknowns' track as they stabbed down into his area of responsibility, and he didn't like what he saw.

"Why didn't SPASUR alert us sooner?" he demanded irately.

SDOC's primary mission was the management of the G-PALS system which defended the United States against limited missile strikes. The latest carve up of responsibilities had given it control of virtually all of the US military's ground-watch and near-space surveillance systems, plus general management of the information stream, but the actual monitoring of space beyond three hundred miles' altitude remained the responsibility of other commands, like the Navy-run Space Surveillance System Command. Archer had always had his doubts about the Squids' suitability to run what obviously should have been an Air Force command properly, but he'd never seriously expected them to drop the ball this badly.

"SPASUR *did* report them, Sir," Slocum told him. "They only picked them up—" he glanced at a digital time display "—two-seven-five seconds ago. It's on the tape, Sir," he added respectfully.

"Impossible!" Colonel Archer muttered.

"I think so, too, Sir—but there they are."

"Well, they can't be a hostile launch. Not coming in from that far out," Archer said to himself. "What's their exact location, Sergeant?"

"Longitude twenty-one north, latitude one-five-five west, altitude nine-six miles and still dropping. They're out over the Pacific. Looks like they'll cross central Mexico on a rough heading of one-six-oh magnetic, but they're pulling a little further north. Course is pretty irregular, Sir, but they're slowing. They were pulling over seventeen thousand knots when we first picked them up—they're down to just over seven thousand now."

"*What?*"

"That's what it says here, Sir . . . and that means they've lost over ten thousand knots in the last four minutes. And look—look at that, Sir! See that little bastard jink around?"

For once, Colonel Archer evinced no desire to complain about Master Sergeant Slocum's language. He was not only a technician, but a highly experienced jet jockey, and he had never—*never!*—heard of anything, reentry vehicle or aircraft, which could pull a ninety-degree turn at such speeds. He reached for the phone that linked him to the duty watch battle staff, his eyes never leaving the impossible display.

"General Goldmann? Colonel Archer. I've got something very strange on my scopes down here, Sir."

✿ ✿ ✿

The squadron commander had no name. He had never possessed one, nor had he needed it. He was a tool to his creators, not a person, and one did not waste names upon tools. Indeed, the *Shirmaksu* had never even dignified his kind with a label. That had been left for humanity, and they called him Troll.

His fighter had no instruments. He was part of the fleet, deadly craft, merged with it as he merged with all the manifold devices of death he had been designed to manage so well. He needed no readouts to track the single, persistent human interceptor which clung to the rear of his formation like Death incarnate. The fighter which had destroyed ten of his own squadron. The last human fighter in the galaxy, in a sense. The one which had stubbornly refused to die for over three Terran weeks.

He was a thing of circuits and servomotors. Of chill alloy and electromechanical visual receptors. His body's veins carried no blood, for it had no veins. There was only the smooth, cool flow of power and the ever-renewed nutrient bath which fed his sole organic component.

Yet he was no stranger to emotion, this Troll. His kind knew the sustaining ferocity of hate, and it nurtured them well. Hate for their creators, who saw them only as disposable, expendable mechanisms. Hate for the humans they had been created to destroy. Hate for themselves, and the destiny which pitted them against humanity in the service of the *Shirmaksu*.

And at this moment, more than any other entity in the galaxy, the Troll commander hated the pilot who dogged his wake.

He knew what sort of human rode behind those guns and missiles. He had suspected from the first, when he noted the elegance with which that fighter flew and the deadly quick reactions which guided it. It could only be one of the *cralkhi*, the humans his masters had inadvertently created for their own downfall. Only a *cralkhi* could have evaded his own tireless pilots so long, clung so close, destroyed every fighter he'd been allowed to detach against it. Only a *cralkhi* . . .

And there was a certain bitter amusement in that, for the beings his squadron fought to protect were responsible for the very symbiote which enabled their enemy to threaten them. Deep inside, the Troll envied the *cralkhi* its freedom to strike at their mutual creators, for that was the one forever unattainable freedom for which the Troll longed with all the living passion trapped within his mechanical shell.

The first shockwaves. screamed past his frontal drive field as his masters dipped into the atmosphere of the planet they had come to murder, and the hate within him cursed his *Shirmaksu* commander for refusing to let him take his remaining fighters back to overwhelm their single pursuer. But he could afford to wait. The *cralkhi* would come to him soon. It could not delay much longer. It could not afford to let the *Shirmaksu* tender slip from its grasp . . .

. . . not if it wanted this planet to live.

Desperation clawed at Colonel Ludmilla Leonovna. She was so tired. Not with physical weariness, but with accumulated mental fatigue. She'd drawn ruthlessly upon her symbiote, knowing the price she must pay—if she survived—for the demands she made. She had no choice, yet there was a limit even to her vitality, and it was nearing. If the Trolls ahead of her ran an analysis of her maneuvers, they couldn't miss her increasing sloppiness. The delay creeping into her responses was minute, so tiny no human would have noted it, but the computers would see it.

She forced the thought aside, concentrating on her task. The pursuit had snaked its way deep into the Sol system. Fighter multi-dees were weaker than those of starships, but they had far lower Frankel Limits in partial compensation, and the Kangas had fled madly, weaving up and down the alpha and beta bands to evade her. She'd long since stopped thinking about the strain on her onboard systems. Her life support had almost a full week still on its clock, but her drive had never been designed to run so long at such ruinous power, nor had her multi-dee been intended for such extended operation. She knew the abused interceptor was nearing the end of its endurance even as she neared her own, yet *Sputnik* hadn't failed her—not with Anwar O'Donnel to nurse and baby her systems.

She stank. She would have traded a year in hell for a shower, she thought, smiling wearily, and knew her crew felt the same, yet they hadn't complained once. Anwar had been her ESO for over two years—long enough to understand the differences between them— and he hadn't argued even when she ordered him to sleep at regular intervals while she managed his systems as well as her own.

Sergeant Goering hadn't been with her as long, but she, too, had done well. Indeed, it had been she who managed to deduce approximately when they were. Commodore Santander had succeeded in crippling the Kangas' planned Takeshita Translation; *Sputnik*'s crew knew that, for Goering had monitored crude, old-style radio and microwave communications as they raced into the system at FTL speeds. They couldn't be much further back than the late twentieth century—yet it might as well have been 50,000 B.C. for all the ability humanity would have to defend itself.

Her crew knew that as well as Leonovna did, but their unshaken confidence in her had been a tower of strength. And she'd needed that strength. Human hardware surpassed the best the Kangas could build, but there were always tradeoffs. *Sputnik* was faster than the tender she pursued, but despite her more advanced drive, she was no faster and far less maneuverable than the Troll-crewed fighters which guarded that tender. They had no need for life support, nor for the gravity compensators a human crew required. They had more mass to spare for other purposes, and their tremendous drives made up for their lower efficiency with pure, brute power. In deep space, with room to use the superiority of her technology, her bird was the equal of any three Troll fighters, but not if the Trolls could pin her. Not if they could somehow close the range through her superior missiles and more deadly power guns and force her into maneuvering combat in range of their own guns.

And that was exactly what they were about to do.

Her mind flicked over her remaining weapons automatically. She'd expended all but one of her heavy missiles, and she dared not waste that one on a Troll. It was a ship-killer, the last nuke she had, and it could be used on only one target. To get into range of that target, she had only three of the "Skeet" missiles with their deadly powered flechettes designed for shortrange snapshots—only the Skeets and her guns.

She sighed and glanced over at her sleeping ESO. She would have to wake him soon, for she couldn't manage her electronic warfare systems as they must be managed if there was to be any hope for a shot.

She'd begun the pursuit with only two wingmen, deliberately sending Casper Turabian and her other five survivors after the only other surviving Kanga tender when it broke out-system. It had been a cold-blooded decision, but Casper had understood. His pilots stood a better chance against a tender which would be forced to turn back towards them if it was to reach its target before it expended its life support. They had a better chance to wait it out before fatigue crippled them. But by the same token, she'd known they would face a frontal attack by all sixteen of its escorting Trolls when the Kangas ordered their cyborgs to clear a path for it.

They had, and none of them had survived the encounter . . . but neither had the Kangas or their Trolls. Casper had lasted long enough, drifting in his crippled fighter, to confirm the kills. Then his life support had failed. She'd heard nothing from him in over a week.

She pushed the grief aside again. There was no time; just as there was no time for so many things. The long, grueling pursuit had come down to these last fleeting minutes, and soon it would end. Her last wingman had died five days ago when a trio of Trolls whipped back and up before Lieutenant Durstan could rouse from the sleep she needed so desperately. Colonel Leonovna had destroyed her killers, but it had been cold comfort. She'd scored seven more kills during the long stern chase, but five remained, covering the tender, blocking every firing angle, and if she came close enough to use her remaining Skeets, the surviving fighters would close to gun range and nail her short of the tender.

She sighed again and nudged her ESO.

"Wake up, Anwar," she said gently, and his head jerked up, his eyes clearing almost instantly. But only almost, and it was that brief hesitation which would have killed a normal human pilot long since.

"Time?" he asked, rubbing the last sleep from his eyes.

"Just about," she said. There was no defeat in her weary voice, only a tinge of sorrow.

"Think of anything better while I was napping?" he asked, yawning as he tugged his helmet back into place.

"Sorry."

"Oh, well. I always wanted to go out with a bang. Should I wake Prissy?"

"Go ahead," Colonel Leonovna said absently, running deliberately back over her checklist. The process was normally so automatic she never thought about it, but her growing fatigue was yet another enemy she must defeat.

"It's been a hell of a ride, Skip," O'Donnel said, reaching for the button that would wake Sergeant Goering in her isolated little compartment. "Love to do it again sometime."

"You're a piss-poor liar, Anwar," she said affectionately, sparing him a smile, and he grinned back crookedly.

"True. But at least Prissy may come through it."

"I hope so," Colonel Leonovna said softly as he pressed the button, and there was no more to be said, for she and O'Donnel were about to die.

She'd tried to find another answer, but she had only one weapon besides her missile which might take out the tender: *Sputnik* herself. It had worked for *Defender*, and it should work again, if only she could get a clear run. She and O'Donnel had discussed it exhaustively, and they'd reached the same conclusion each time. The best she could hope for was to cross over the Troll rearguard once they entered atmosphere, then turn back, blow her way through the lead fighters by relying on the blast effect of exploding her last nuke in atmosphere, and ram the tender head-on. The fireball as their drives overloaded would be hotter than any nuclear warhead ever fired.

But she couldn't do it until they were in atmosphere, and she couldn't do it without Anwar to run ECM interference for her, so he would be included in her death. Yet it might be possible to save Goering. They had no more need for a communications officer, for there was no one with whom to communicate, and so Colonel Leonovna had decided to jettison the sergeant's escape capsule as soon as they entered atmosphere.

Goering had argued, but her commander over-rode her sternly. They both knew the com tech would have a poor enough chance, given standard Troll tactics, but it was the only one Leonovna could give her.

"Atmosphere in three minutes, Skip," O'Donnel reminded her quietly.

"Oh, yes. Thank you, Anwar. Prissy?"

"Yes, Skipper," Goering said in a tiny voice. "I'm ready."

"Good. Anwar will give you a five count."

"I . . . understand," the sergeant said, and the colonel heard the tears in her voice.

"Hoist one for us when you get down," she said.

"I will, Skip. Nail the bastards."

"I'll try, Prissy. I'll really try."   .

"Count starts—now!" O'Donnel said. "Five . . . four . . . three . . ."

"Good-bye, Skipper!"

". . . Two . . . Luck, Prissy!"

Sputnik shuddered as the capsule blasted free, spinning away in a wild evasion pattern which blacked out its occupant instantly. Colonel Leonovna and her ESO held their breaths, following her with their instruments, willing her to safety.

"Skip! Bandit Two!"

"Goddamn it to hell!" Mental commands flashed to Leonovna's weapon systems, and two of her remaining Skeets dropped free—guiding instantly on the Troll fighter which had nosed up and around. They flashed towards their target, but too slowly, and a salvo of missiles ripped from the Troll, homing on the escape capsule.

Sergeant Priscilla Goering died two seconds after her killer.

There was silence in *Sputnik's* cockpit. A cold, hate-filled silence.

Task Force Twenty-Three, United States Navy, was one week out after exercises off Cuba, headed for a Mediterranean "fireman" deployment off the perpetually troubled Balkans at a leisurely fifteen knots when the first notice of something odd came in. SPASUR's Navy-run communication net had a Flash priority signal on its way to Commander-in-Chief Atlantic Fleet in Norfolk before Space Defense Operations had its act together, and real-time tracking reports followed as it became apparent that something unusual was taking place high above the surface of the earth—and dropping lower with every passing moment. The bogeys' speed was coming down, but their course was hardening out across the Atlantic, and their projected track passed within less than five hundred miles of Task Force Twenty-Three.

Admiral Fritz Carson had a touch of insomnia, which was how he happened to be on his flag bridge when the Flash from Norfolk reached the carrier *Theodore Roosevelt* at the center of the carrier group. He looked bemusedly at the flimsy his signals officer handed him for just a moment, then turned to his chief of staff.

"Get down to CIC," he said, "and ask someone to wake the Captain." Then he picked up a phone and personally buzzed flight control.

"PriFly, Commander Staunton," a voice responded instantly.

"CAG?" The Navy had redesignated the aircraft embarked by a carrier as a carrier air wing decades ago, but like everyone else Admiral Carson still used the old acronym for "Commander Air Group." At the moment, however, he was a bit surprised to find his air commander in PriFly at this hour of the morning.

"Yes, Sir," Commander Staunton replied, answering the surprise in Carson's voice. "I've got a newbie Tomcat driver up, and I wanted to keep an eye on him."

"I see. Well, CAG, CIC is setting up some interesting data for you. A whole clutch of genuine UFOs coming in faster than bats out of hell from the west sou'west. If they hold their course and speed, they're going to cross our track about five hundred miles out ... at Mach nine-plus or so."

"Mach *nine*, Sir?" Commander Staunton asked very carefully.

"That's what they tell me," Carson said. "What've we got out there to wave as the little green men go by?"

"We've got a Hummer three hundred out, ready to exercise with my training flight, and I've got another pair of Toms at plus-five on the cats with two Hornets at plus-fifteen on the roof."

"I doubt we'll need them, but get the ready section up, then call up the Hawkeye and ask it to take a look as they pass."

"Yes, Sir."

"Thank you." He hung up as his flag lieutenant held out another phone. "Captain Jansen?" he asked, and the lieutenant nodded. "Good." He raised the handset. "Captain, sorry to wake you, but ..."

"Something witchy on the passive, Flight." Lieutenant (j.g.) Demosthenes Lewiston said.

"Like what?" Lieutenant Atcheson asked.

"Dunno, Sir. Never seen anything like it. We're not receiving anything, but something's throwing some kind of ghosts on the set. All over the port quadrant and getting stronger."

"What d'you mean 'not receiving anything'?" the Hawkeye E-2D's copilot demanded. "You been drinking hair tonic again, Dimmy?"

"No, Sir," the radar officer said virtuously. "And what I mean is I sure as hell don't recognize it, but *something's* futzing up the receiver. Almost like it was outside the set's frequencies, but there ain't no such animal."

"Tacco's right, Mister Atcheson," one of Lewiston's petty officer operators put in. "It's . . . weird, Sir."

"Ummm," Lieutenant Atcheson mused. Dimmy was right about the capability of his equipment, he thought. Despite its apparently archaic turboprops and relatively small size, the ungainly-looking E-2 (especially in the brand new E-2D "Hawkeye 2000" variant) was among the most sophisticated airborne early warning aircraft in the world, and the Navy didn't exactly pick Hawkeye radar officers out of a hat. "Got any idea on the range?"

"Sorry, Skipper, but I don't really *have* anything. More an itch I don't know how to scratch than anything else."

"Okay, let's scratch," Lieutenant Atcheson decided. "Light up and see if there's something out there to bounce a signal off of."

"Lighting up," Lewiston said, and the Hawkeye went active. The peculiar bogeys were still far beyond detection range of even the Hawkeye's prodigiously efficient radar, but its pulses reached to the target, though they lacked the power to return. Three minutes and forty-two seconds later, a fifty kiloton nuclear warhead blew Atcheson, Lewiston, their fellow crewmen, and their aircraft into fiery oblivion.

"What the hell—?!" O'Donnel was startled out of his bitter silence by the sudden flash ahead of them.

"Somebody must've hit the tender with a scanner," Leonovna said, face tense as she fought the atmospheric shockwaves. "That was an ARAD."

"An antiradiation missile? Who the hell's got modern scanners down here?"

"Don't know," Colonel Leonovna said, and concentrated on her flying.

"*Jesus Christ!*" Commander Edward Staunton winced at the volume of his senior airborne Tomcat pilot's voice. "Home Plate, this is Hawk One! We have a nuclear explosion—I say again, a nuclear air burst—bearing two-seven-five relative from the task force, range two-eight-zero miles!"

"*What* did he say?" Staunton turned to see Commander Bret Hanfield, *Roosevelt*'s executive officer, standing just inside PriFly.

"He said it was a nuke," Staunton replied, his voice completely calm while his mind tried to grapple with realization.

"CAG, we can't raise Spyglass." The air wing commander looked over his shoulder at the duty flight ops officer, but he wasn't really surprised. The range and bearing from Hawk One had already warned him, even if he had not consciously worked out all the implications yet.

"Sir, CIC is on the line," a petty officer said, extending a phone. "He's looking for the XO."

Hanfield held out his hand and pressed the phone to his ear. "XO," he said. "Talk to me." He listened for a moment, eyes narrowing, and Staunton noticed that his color was stronger than a moment before.

"Thank you," he said, then glanced at Staunton even as he punched buttons on the handset. "Message from *Antietam*," he said tersely, "group tacco just confirmed it."

Staunton looked at the ops officer. *Antietam* carried the group tactical warfare officer for a very simple reason; she was a *Ticonderoga*-class cruiser, an Aegis ship, with the most advanced shipborne radar and deadliest surface-to-air weapons fit in the world.

"Bridge, this is the XO," Hanfield continued into the phone. "Give me the OD." He waited a moment longer. "Harry? We've got a confirmed nuclear air burst three hundred miles ahead of us. Sound general quarters and set condition One-AAW. Then get the captain and tell him what's happening. I'm on my way now." He threw the phone back to the petty officer without a word and vanished from PriFly while the man was still looking at him. The alarm awoke a fraction of an instant later, and the calm, unhurried voice of the boatswain-of-the-watch came from the speakers.

"General Quarters. General Quarters. All hands man battle stations for antiair warfare. This is no drill."

A bolt of pure fury suffused the Troll commander as the primitive aircraft vaporized. He knew at once what had happened. His cowardly, ultracautious creators had built no offensive weapons into their tender—that was the purpose of its escort—but they had crammed in every *defensive* system their anxious minds could envision. His own sensors had detected the crude radiation emanating from the aircraft, though he hadn't recognized it as a detection system. Why should he? No one had used single-dimension radio-wave scanners in over two centuries! But the *Shirmaksu* never forgot a danger, and some ancient threat recording had triggered their onboard computers, wasting a nuclear-armed ARAD on an archaic, propeller-driven *aircraft*.

It wasn't the death of the aircraft the Troll resented, but the fact that his masters hadn't seen fit to spend a little more of their foresight on fitting their tender with offensive weapons. He could have used them, for the human devil behind him had devised a plan.

He understood instantly when the *cralkhi*'s drive field peaked. The enemy was going to attempt to overfly him and his wingman, then sweep back from head-on, and, in atmosphere, it might just get away with it. The odds were astronomically against it, but it was possible. Human drive fields had less power, but they were more efficient, and, especially in atmospheric maneuvering, efficiency counted. The human could maintain a better power curve in its bow drive field, which meant it could pull a higher atmospheric velocity. His own fighters were down to under eleven thousand kilometers per hour in this thickening air, and the *cralkhi*'s fighter could do far better than that. Of course, the devil would have to get past two Trolls to do it, he thought grimly, and his targeting systems sprang to life once more.

"The Captain is on the bridge!" a voice snapped as Captain Everett Jansen strode onto his bridge. The skin around his eyes was puffy with sleep, but the eyes themselves were already clear. Hanfield turned to him instantly, but Jansen waved him back.

"A sec, Bret," he said, grabbing for a phone and punching up CIC. "Plot, this is the Captain. What's our status?" He listened for perhaps ten seconds, then grunted. "Thanks." He hung up the phone and turned in one smooth movement. "All right, XO, I have the conn."

"Aye, Sir." Commander Hanfield didn't even try to hide the relief in his voice.

"I've got two more bandits, Skip," O'Donnel reported. "Coming at us from eleven thousand meters altitude. Range eight-four-two kilometers. Rate of closure's over fourteen thousand KPH."

"What?" Colonel Leonovna spared a fraction of her own attention for the new targets. "Forget them, Anwar. They're human aircraft." She turned back to her piloting, a tiny corner of her historian's brain continuing, "Must be military to pull that speed."

"Home Plate, this is Hawk One. Hawk Flight going to burner."

Commander Staunton watched two more F-14s thunder off the catapults and climb away as he absorbed the report from his two airborne fighters. The big, swing-wing aircraft were long overdue for replacement, and he didn't like to think about the flight hours and fatigue their airframes had accumulated, but the general slowdown in military funding over the last twenty years had played havoc with next-generation systems development and acquisition. And for all their age, the F-14 and its equally venerable Phoenix missiles remained the most capable long-range interceptor in the world. Which was the reason the Navy (whose airfields had an unfortunate tendency to sink when sufficiently damaged) continued to labor so heroically to keep them flying. The standby F-18s were already being towed to the cats, but he doubted they'd get the younger design aloft in time to make much difference. Whatever was coming towards them had still been pulling almost seven thousand miles per hour when it dropped below SPASUR's coverage.

"Hawk Two, Hawk One," he heard his senior pilot say. "Light off your radar."

"Rog, Hawk One."

Two hundred miles ahead of the carrier battle group, both F-14Ds switched on their AWG-9 radars, searching for whatever had killed Spyglass.

"Hostiles incoming! I have incoming hostiles!" Hawk One announced. "Jesus! The bastards are pulling close to twelve thousand knots!"

Staunton looked at his flight officer in disbelief.

"Skipper, the tender's launched another pair of ARADs!"

"Those poor bastards," Colonel Leonovna said softly.

❉ ❉ ❉

"Fox One!" Hawk One snapped. "Fox One—four away!"

Four late-mark AIM-54 missiles dropped from the lead Tomcat's pallets, followed moments later by two more as Hawk Two's novice aircrew launched as well. The Mach-five Phoenix, the longest ranged air-to-air missile in the world, was totally outclassed by the incoming missiles. But Phoenix missiles were designed to knock down small cruise missiles in the most difficult targeting solution of all: head-on at extreme range. The Kanga missiles were larger than the Tomcats which had fired, and for all their massive speed, they were utterly incapable of evasion. They mounted advanced ECM systems, but those systems were designed for outer space, and no ECM in the galaxy could have hidden the fantastic heat source their atmospheric passage generated.

The Troll commander would have blinked in astonishment if he'd possessed eyelids. It was impossible!

"Skipper! *They killed both ARADs!*"

Colonel Leonovna had eyelids, and she did blink at the news. She widened the focus of her attention, and bits of information clicked. Her mental weariness was forgotten as her thoughts flashed at blinding speed. Her electronic senses probed ahead, and a vicious smile curved her lips as she "saw" the formation of ancient ships.

"Splash two!" Hawk One announced exultantly. Then his voice sharpened even further. "Home Plate, I have multiple bandits on my scope. Big bandits. I count five—no, six targets. Range three-nine-eight. Speed five-four-six-oh knots, closing the task force."

"Admiral," Captain James Moulder's voice was hurried but astonishingly calm in Admiral Carson's ear as he spoke from his own combat information center aboard *Antietam*, "we have confirmed use of nukes against our Hummer, and they've fired on our fighters. Request weapons release."

The admiral's knuckles whitened on the phone set. The bandits were closing at over a mile and a half per second; they would arrive over his ships in just over four minutes, and, given the reach and speed of the weapons they'd already employed, they were probably already in strike range.

"Granted!" he snapped.

"All ships. Air Warning Red. Axis of threat three-five-two. Weapons free," his tactical commander announced in an almost mechanical voice, and surface to air tracking and targeting systems sprang to life on every ship in the task force.

Colonel Leonovna felt the radar sources come alive ahead of her, and mingled horror and exultation filled her. She was a military historian; unlike the Kangas and their Troll guardians, she knew what they were about to overfly. Yet for all that, she had little clearer notion of what the naval force's missiles could do against modern technology than she had of the performance of smoothbore cannon. *Could* they knock down the tender? It might be the worst thing they could do, assuming they continued to use chemical warheads, but even to her it seemed unlikely that the primitive weapons below her could do it. Still, they'd nailed those ARADs . . . .

Sputnik Too arced up and away, breaking off the pursuit.

The Troll commander noted the maneuver instantly, and his brain whirled with the new data, trying to understand. Why should the *cralkhi* break away now? After coming so far? Something was wrong.

"Here they come," someone murmured aboard *Antietam*. None of them could quite believe what they were seeing on their displays, but no one wasted time denying the obvious.

The Kanga tender had only two more ARADs, and they both dropped free, guiding on the nearest radar sources.

"Vampire! Vampire!" The warning cry went out as the missiles hurtled towards the destroyers *Arleigh Burke* and *Kidd* at over twelve thousand miles per hour. The tender itself was still far out of range, but RIM-66 and RIM-67 surface-to-air missiles raced to meet the ARADs, and both ships were already skidding in maximum rate turns to open fields of fire for their Mark Fifteen Phalanx cannon.

The Troll commander winced mentally as the rising tracks of

defensive missiles and what had happened to the last two ARADs came together with the *cralkhi*'s maneuver. Primitive they undoubtedly were, but with his units' every erg of drive power diverted to the bow fields for maximum speed, they didn't even have to be nuclear-armed to be lethal—not if they could score at all. He tried frantically to warn his *Shirmaksu* masters, and even as he did, a portion of his brain noted that the *cralkhi* was already swinging onto a new course, racing around the flank of his own formation.

The ARAD bound for the *Burke* met three different missiles, and their combined warheads were sufficient to smash it out of the heavens. The one guiding on *Kidd* was luckier; it ran right past the interceptors, hurtling at impossible speed through a sheet of fire from the twenty-millimeter Gatling guns of the destroyer's Phalanx mounts. The close-in defensive system did its best, but it had never been intended to deal with targets moving at such speed. The mounts' paired radars had too little time to track, and USS *Kidd* vanished in a heart of nuclear flame as the missile struck home.

But the incoming bogeys had held their course long enough, and the Aegis cruisers *Antietam* and *Champlain* exploded with light an instant before *Kidd* as their vertical launch systems spat fire. Again, the defense systems hadn't been designed to cope with targets moving at six thousand miles an hour, but all the advanced ECM of the tender and its Troll escorts was directed against targeting systems the United States Navy had never even heard of. Its targets were glaring beacons of reflected radar pulses and heat, and it was all or nothing for Task Force Twenty-Three.

Three-hundred-plus missiles screamed into the night.

Colonel Leonovna watched the hurricane of ancient missiles whiplash upward. They were pathetically slow, but the range was short and their targets were running straight down their throats—and larger than some of the ships floating below her. She caught her breath as the missiles slammed into her enemies.

The Troll commander's synapses quivered with fury as the primitive weapons hammered his formation. His units were climbing desperately, but they'd come in too low and begun their evasion too late. Even at their speed, they couldn't climb out of range in time. More than half the SAMs wasted themselves against the frontal arcs of his units' bow drive fields, but almost half did not. Some seemed not even to see their targets, but most did. Their power was pathetic compared to the nuclear warheads and powered flechettes of modem weapons, but there were so many of them!

The *Shirmaksu* tender shuddered as four missiles broke through all its defenses. ECM was useless against such primitive guidance systems; they could be stopped only by active defenses, and the tender simply didn't mount enough of them. And if that was true of the tender, it was ten times true of his fighters! He watched helplessly as two of his three remaining wingmen took multiple hits. They were like flea bites, any one of them too small to hurt, but together they were too much. The drive field on Fighter Two failed. The craft was designed for space, not to move at such speed in atmosphere, and its own velocity tore it apart. Fighter Three simply disintegrated in a ball of fire. Fighter Four was luckier and took only two hits, but its drive faltered anyway, and its pilot had no choice but to reduce speed drastically. Only the commander himself escaped damage, for he'd enjoyed an instant more warning in which to wrench up and away, outrunning the slow, stupid weapons which had wrought such havoc.

He forced his nose back down, raging around to devastate the primitives who'd ravaged his formation, but before he could launch a single weapon his masters whistled him off. They demanded his protection with such stridency he could not refuse, and he altered course once more, racing to catch up with the limping, staggering tender.

Anwar O'Donnel's banshee howl of triumph hurt Colonel Leonovna's ears, but she couldn't blame him. Her own worst fear had been that the ancient missiles might knock the tender down, for she hadn't dared hope for nuclear warheads. But the Kangas had survived . . . and they'd been hurt. Not only that, but their escorts had been decimated. The single undamaged Troll swung back, clearly intending to strafe the warships below, even as the tender and its damaged protector continued to climb, and Colonel Leonovna took the opening she'd been given.

Sputnik howled down through the night-black heavens like a lance of flame with Death at her controls and every scrap of drive power bracing her forward field. She slid between the Troll commander and his charges, and Ludmilla Leonovna armed her remaining Skeet missile. It launched and guided straight into the tender's escort, blowing it out of the sky, and her blood sang with triumph as her weapon systems locked on the tender. Nothing could save her target now—not even the telltale itch between her shoulder blades as the Troll commander's targeting systems stabbed her from astern.

Her mind flashed the command to her last missile, and it blasted away in the instant before the first nuclear missile came howling up her own wake.

"What the *fuck*?" Captain Moulder's incredulous question echoed the thought in every mind as yet another fireball—this one vast beyond comprehension—splintered the night two hundred thousand feet above the Atlantic. A massive surge of EMP smashed over the task force, burning out even "hardened" radar and communications electronics effortlessly, as a five hundred megaton blast designed to destroy an *Ogre*-class superdreadnought expended its fury upon the insignificant mass of a single tender.

The dreadful glare of nuclear fusion washed down over the carrier battle group, blinding every unwary eye that watched it, and radiation detectors went mad. The awesome ball of flame hung high above the ocean, and then there was another, smaller flash, and another, and another. The terrible chain lightning reached away over the horizon like a curse, and confusion roiled in its wake. Clearly those blasts were not directed at them, but, in that case, who the hell was shooting at whom?

Then the shockwave of that first, monster explosion rolled over them like a fist.

"Bull's-eye, Skipper! Bull's—"

That was all O'Donnel had time to say before the Troll commander's last missile caught up with the wildly evading *Sputnik*. It punched through O'Donnel's desperate ECM like an awl, and its proximity fuse activated.

Leonovna felt the terrible damage like a blow in her own flesh, and she knew *Sputnik* was doomed. Smoke flooded her cockpit, and power-loss warnings snarled in her mental link to her ship, yet it wasn't in her to give up, not even now. She fought the dying fighter's controls, and *Sputnik* strove heroically to respond, heaving her nose up in an impossible arc, battling to give her pilot one last shot.

The Troll commander tracked his crippled prey to four hundred thousand feet, sliding in behind the hated *cralkhi* pilot. It had taken his last missile, but it had been worth it. He avoided the *cralkhi*'s dying efforts with ease and savored the cold, crawling fire of vengeance as he watched its drive shudder, and he sliced even closer as the interceptor lost its field and coasted higher in the near-vacuum on momentum alone.

As *Sputnik* rose past 500,000 feet, his power guns fired, and a shattered wreck plunged toward the water waiting patiently ninety-five miles below.

CHAPTER FIVE

Captain Richard Aston, US Navy, soon to be retired, lounged back and watched *Amanda*'s self-steering gear work. A brisk westerly pushed the fifty-foot ketch along, and he supposed it might have been called a quiet night, except that it was never quiet on a sailboat in the middle of the Atlantic Ocean. His radio muttered softly to him through the open companion, for he'd found himself unexpectedly hungry for the sound of other human voices as the sunset faded into purple twilight, yet the night-struck ocean spoke to him in voices of its own. Wind whispered in the rigging, *Amanda* herself creaked and murmured as she worked through the swell, and the splash and gurgle of water was everywhere, from the rippling chuckle of the bow wave to the bubble of the wake and the sounds of the rudder.

His pipe went out, and he considered going below for more tobacco, but the idle thought never rose much above the surface of his subconscious. For a change, he was too comfortable even to think about moving.

He smiled lazily. Single-handing across the Atlantic was hardly the restful occupation many an armchair sailor thought, and the last week had been strenuous. High winds and wicked seas had given him more than a few anxious moments two days ago, but *Amanda*'s deep, heavily weighted keel gave her tremendous stability, even in a high wind and despite her unusually lofty rig. And then the wind had whistled away, the seas had smoothed, and, at least for the moment, the Atlantic had donned the mask of welcome.

He knew it was a mask. A lie, really. It was a game the ocean played, this pretending to be a gentle, docile thing. But he loved it anyway, in part because he knew it was a lie. If it was a game, then they both played it, he thought, waxing poetic in his relaxation, and knowing that it only made moments like this even more to be treasured.

He raised a shielding hand against his running lights and stared up at the sky. The stars were incredibly brilliant out here, away from the pollution and light glare of the land. That was one of the other things he loved about sailing at night—the sheer beauty of the star-spangled vault above him. He always saw it as a sea of dark, cobalt velvet strewn with gems, though it wasn't an image he'd ever been able to share comfortably with most of his professional colleagues. It would have sounded a bit strange from a hulking, far from handsome, slightly bent and battered fellow like him.

He lowered his hand and glanced at the reassuring shape of his radar reflector. He preferred to sleep during the day at sea, for merchant ships had grown increasingly careless about keeping close visual lookouts in the age of radar, and Dick Aston knew enough about technology to trust it no further than he must. Radar reflectors were all very well, but they relied upon functional radar on the other end, and lackadaisical visual lookouts were more likely to spot his bright red sails by daylight than in the dark. Taken all in all, he chose to spend his nights at sea making sure he saw anybody else before they didn't see him. And, of course, there were the stars, weren't there?

He glanced back up and frowned in sudden surprise. What the—?

His left hand groped in a locker, feeling for his powerful binoculars, but he never lowered his eyes from the brilliant streaks tracing fiery paths through the night. They seemed to be descending, but that wasn't all they were doing—not by a long chalk! They looked almost like shooting stars, but he'd never heard of meteors that changed trajectory in mid-course!

He jammed the binoculars to his eyes, adjusting to *Amanda*'s movement with practiced ease as he held the flaming lines in his field of vision. It was no help; whatever they were, they were far too distant to make out details, even with the glasses. In fact, they must be at one hell of an altitude for him to see them at all at this range!

They seemed to be heading roughly in his direction, but they were dropping rapidly towards the southern horizon. Whatever they were, they looked like they'd impact long before—

He froze as a spark suddenly separated from one whatever-they-were and streaked away, dancing crazily. Damn it, that had to be a controlled flight path! No free-falling object would pursue such an insane course. It was almost as if the thing were taking evasive action!

The thought popped into his mind and lodged there as one of the other light streaks arced impossibly back towards the fleeing spark. He watched intently, then winced—even at this distance—at the suddenly redoubled brilliance as the dot which had spawned the spark hurled a pair of fiery darts at the pursuing one ... just before still more brilliant specks lanced out from the pursuer, heading for the spark!

He blinked rapidly, compensating for the painful intensity of those flashes. In 1973, Lieutenant (j.g.) Dick Aston had found himself in the Sinai, attached to the Israeli army as an observer, and he'd never forgotten the morning he'd watched a massed Israeli-Egyptian dogfight. He remembered the smoke trails of the missiles, the suddenness and silence with which they'd appeared so high above, the white wakes of contrails and the plunging black and red fireballs of broken aircraft. He remembered well ... and somehow he knew he was seeing an insane echo of that long ago madness.

It was ridiculous. Even if there'd been the least reason to expect hostilities out here in mid-ocean, nobody had fighters that could do what those flaming lines of light were doing. He knew it—but he also knew it was happening, and he held his breath as the darts of fire flashed silently through the night sky, then gasped as two dots of light flared intolerably bright and perished.

The remaining lights raced even lower. He sensed their incredible speed, even if distance did make them seem to move with trancelike slowness. They swept towards the horizon, bunching and weaving, dancing as if for advantage, and he watched in wonder as they finally disappeared below the curvature of the earth.

He lowered the glasses, suddenly aware of the tension which had gripped him as that tension eased, and grinned wryly, castigating himself for his overactive imagination. Dogfighting lights! UFOs, no doubt! He wondered if they were Arcturians or Boskonians—or

Ming the Merciless and Flash Gordon? Undoubtedly there was some entirely rational explanation. . . .

And then the southern horizon lit with a glaring spall of light that wrenched him to his feet. The brilliant glare burned away the night, reflecting on water that was suddenly a glassy mirror even at this range. He'd seen more than his share of explosions, but never one like *that*!

He averted his eyes instinctively, refusing to look directly at the boiling pinprick, but he couldn't have turned his attention elsewhere to save his life. He breathed quickly, shallow with tension, waiting for . . . something. He had no idea what, but surely there would—

He gasped in disbelief as yet another burst of light blazed up. This one was lower, he thought, below the horizon—he was seeing its reflection on the distant cloud base, not the light itself. But what in God's name could it *be*?

He was still wondering when he saw the light streaks again. But this time there were only three of them, shooting up into the heavens like a trio of rockets—no, wait! There was a fourth, racing after the first three! Yet another burst of flame splashed the heavens, and he watched one of the leaders vanish. The other three were still coming, charging towards him in a madly climbing spiral. There! Another dart of fire, chasing the leading dot, and more from the last light chasing the second! What in God's na—?

Some instinct screamed warning, and he flung up his hands, shielding his eyes just before actinic fury smashed the dark. He cried out in horror, cowering down, and his brain gibbered. It was a nuclear explosion! That was the only thing it *could* be, and thank God in Heaven it was so high! Even here he could feel its radiant heat, and he paled as he considered the tides of radiation racing out from its heart. At least the wind was out of the northwest! Whatever fallout that terrible explosion had spawned would be carried—

His thoughts broke off yet again as scarcely less titanic explosions erupted. They blazed in terrible succession, pursuing the first light dot across the vault of heaven, and they were gaining. His brain worked mechanically, overloaded with confusion and shock. Those warring dots were sweeping higher and higher—they had to be clear up at the outer edge of the stratosphere! Nothing ever built could do that—yet something *was* doing it. And still more fireballs shredded the night!

The leading light dot swerved, as if that last explosion had come too close, and arced crazily up in what an aircraft would have called a half loop—but what did whatever that was call it? He had no idea, but he watched helplessly, unable to look away, as the vengeful pursuer closed on its victim. Blue lightning flickered, stabbing his eyes almost as painfully as the exploding nukes had done, and suddenly the wounded dot was falling.

He watched it begin its plunge and knew it had been killed. It plummeted uncontrollably towards the sea, and he felt a sudden stab of stark terror. It was falling towards him! What if its enemy decided to finish it off with yet another nuke?

But there was nothing he could do if it happened, and he rejected a panicky urge to throw himself flat on the deck. He watched the dot fall, and the second one followed it for several seconds before it suddenly broke away, streaking off to the southwest.

He heaved a deep breath of relief as the immediate threat of immolation vanished, but the stricken light still plunged downward. God, but it must have been a hell of a long way up! It was still heading roughly towards him, and he swallowed as its size registered. The thing was getting bigger and bigger, shedding bits and pieces of itself. Thunder rumbled, pounding him like a bellow of God's wrath, and he realized it was the sound of the explosions. He wished he'd thought to do a flash-bang count to get some idea of range, but he hadn't.

It was still coming! He told himself the ocean was a huge target, that it would never hit *Amanda* whatever it looked like, but the disintegrating object seemed to be plunging straight into his eyes. He knew it was an illusion, but he felt his muscles tightening once more.

A flood of adrenaline snapped him out of his shock. It might not hit him, but that thing had to be huge! Who knew what kind of splash it was going to throw up when it hit? He leapt to the wheel, tripping over the tether of the safety line he always wore on deck. He disengaged the self-steering, checking the wind direction by instinct, and swung *Amanda*'s bow slightly to starboard. He wanted whatever the hell it was to impact bows on to him, just in case.

He was staring up at the plunging object, his heart in his mouth, when it exploded before his eyes. Dripping bits of brilliance erupted outward, and a bright-blue star seemed to leap from the wreckage. His abused eyes cringed to the fresh explosion, but he felt a stab of relief. Whatever it was had broken up. The falling bits and pieces were burning out before they hit.

All but the blue star, he thought, and it caught his attention. For a moment, he couldn't quite think why; then he knew. It *wasn't* falling. Not the way its crippled parent had fallen. It was coming down far more slowly. In fact, its headlong pace slowed perceptibly as he watched. Its blue brilliance pulsed and flickered, reminding him forcibly of a dying firefly, and he heard a weird, high-pitched whining sound. He stared at it fixedly, then swallowed.

This time it was no optical illusion—the star was headed for him . . . and changing course to do it! He swallowed again, with more difficulty, as he realized he was seeing the equivalent of a parachute. Someone—or some*thing*, he thought with an atavistic chill—had bailed out of its stricken craft.

He felt a sudden urge to put *Amanda* about and flee, but rationality stopped him. If whatever that was had enough control to change course, it certainly had the speed to catch him if he ran . . . always assuming that was what it intended to do.

Besides, curiosity had always been Dick Aston's besetting sin. Deep inside, he understood Kipling's mongoose perfectly, and his need to "run and find out" had nearly gotten him killed more than once.

He didn't even realize he'd moved until he began reducing sail. The mizzen went first; then the big mainsail vanished around the self-furling boom, and *Amanda* slowed. He worked entirely by feel, eyes glued to the falling light as the unearthly whine grew louder. The light was larger, but the uneven flicker of its intensity was increasingly pronounced. In fact, the whine seemed to be rising and falling, gusting more or less in time with the light's brightness. Whatever was holding it up was in trouble, he thought. Battle damage. Had to be.

He dropped the foresail and hit the starter for the big inboard. The cold diesel turned over instantly, coughing a bit uneasily but then rumbling powerfully, and a corner of his mind congratulated himself for having had it overhauled before he left port. He made himself wait, giving it a moment to warm up, but it was hard. Whatever that thing was, it was getting mighty close.

That realization touched off another thought, and he abandoned the wheel long enough to dart down the companion and drag out a .45 automatic. Like many veterans of the United States' elite military units, Aston disliked and distrusted the stopping power of the nine-millimeter NATO round even a quarter century after the US had adopted it. His first allegiance had always been to John Browning's 1911A1, and he had "acquired" one of the US Marine Corps' MEU(SOC) modifications ten years earlier. Now he slapped a loaded stainless-steel magazine into the pistol's butt and chambered a round, then set the safety and stuffed the weapon under the belt and waistband of his frayed, cutoff shorts. Part of him felt ridiculous, but its weight was reassuring against his spine, like the presence of an old friend.

He hurried back on deck. The falling light was far closer, and the diesel seemed to be throbbing comfortably. He straightened his shoulders and engaged the prop, feeling the change in *Amanda*'s motion as she was transformed from a sailboat into one under power.

He spun the wheel expertly, heading for what he estimated as the point of impact. He smiled mordantly at his own actions, but his fear was under control—not banished, but transformed into a distant thing, a thing of concern, not terror. If someone wanted to visit him, the least he could do was pick them up at the station.

The whine was frighteningly irregular now, the light pulsing ever more weakly, but the object was almost down. It was no more than three hundred yards out, and certainly no more than forty feet up, when the light died suddenly and completely. He made out a spherical shape, vague in the sudden darkness, half-seen and half-imagined, that seemed to hesitate for just a moment.

Then it dropped.

It slammed into the sea in a smother of white spray, plunging deep before it bobbed back up. *Amanda* pitched, pointing her bowsprit at the heavens as the impact wave washed out to meet her, and his mouth was dry, his heart hammering as he realized the thing had to be thirty feet in diameter.

He edged in closer, reversing the prop as he laid the sphere close aboard the ketch. His nerves tingled expectantly, exactly as they'd always done before a training jump or a firefight, as he waited for some sign from the sphere. He had absolutely no idea what to expect.

He was an avid science fiction reader, but all the fictitious "first contacts" he could remember came down to a single, unanswerable question: *Now* what?

He snorted at the thought, grinning just a touch shakily as amusement helped bring him back on balance, and examined the sphere closely. The thing wasn't floating like most spherical objects would have. It rode the swell, showing no inclination to rotate, and he wondered if it had deployed some sort of sea anchor. Possibly, he decided. Very possibly.

And if he was right—if he had just witnessed some sort of dogfight and this was an escape capsule—its occupants might be unconscious, injured, or even dead. In any of those cases, there would be no BEMs unless he went looking for them. An unsettling thought, that.

There was a flattened, recessed area near the thing's top, and what looked like some sort of cut-out handholds. He bit his lip for a moment, then shrugged. The thought of moving from *Amanda*'s familiar deck to that unknown thing was unnerving, but it should be safe enough—unless something popped out to eat him, of course. His safety tether was easily long enough to reach the sphere, but it joined him securely to his boat if he needed it.

He nodded once to himself and gathered up the stem mooring line. Those cutouts looked big enough . . .

Amanda's diesel burbled cheerfully as he threw it into neutral and swung her stern closer to the sphere. He gathered his legs under him and jumped easily across a three-foot gap of water, reaching for one of the cutouts, and his eyebrows rose at how comfortably his hand settled into the recess. It would be unwise to refine overly much on it, but it certainly seemed shaped for something with fingers to grasp. The notion emboldened him, and he looped his line through another cutout and quickly made it fast.

He climbed up the sphere like a monkey, heading for the flattened area. The cutouts were more conveniently spaced than the rungs of some ladders he'd used, and he was in excellent condition. He wasn't even breathing hard—well, not from exertion, anyway—when he reached the top.

He stared at what was undeniably a hatch. There had to be some way to open it, but—aha! His eye lit on the faint gleam of a green light. It illuminated what was obviously a heavy throw switch, and he reached for it before common sense could make him hesitate. It moved easily, and something inside the sphere whined.

Nothing else happened for a moment . . . and then he almost fell as the hatch whipped open with viperish suddenness. His hands flashed out, and he barely managed to catch himself on the hatch frame, but his curse of astonishment died half-uttered as he stared down into the sphere's dimly lit interior.

Water sloshed below him, several inches deep and rising as he watched. Clearly the sphere *had* been damaged, and he snatched a quick, wondering impression of strangely arranged readouts and gleaming surfaces. There were far fewer switches than he would have expected in a . . . in a whatever the hell this thing had been part of, but what demanded and caught his attention was its crew.

They were human.

Well, he corrected himself, humanoid. He wondered why he was rejecting the obvious possibility that this was the remnant of some advanced aircraft, but he wasn't even tempted to believe that comforting answer. Which made the humanoid shape of its crew even more confusing.

He jumped despite himself as a more powerful light source switched on soundlessly, as if opening the hatch had caused it. And perhaps it had, he thought. The dim glow he'd first seen was suspiciously like the low-intensity lights he'd seen in many a night-flying cockpit. But the new light showed him something else; the crew hadn't escaped the damage which had smashed their vehicle.

The sight of all that blood banished his hesitation, and he dropped through the hatch. Cold water splashed as he landed, and he swore again as the edge of a submerged console bruised his bare left heel. Obviously he was standing on what had been a bulkhead, and the periphery of his brain noted that the "bulkhead" in what would have been an overhead position for the people strapped into the sphere's heavily padded seats was transparent . . . from this side. Interesting. It was as opaque as any other part of the surface from the outside.

He shook the thought aside and bent over the two motionless figures. One of them would never move again, he thought grimly, feeling no desire to remove the shattered, blank-visored helmet which concealed that head. The thick, viscous flow oozing redly out of it made what he would have seen all too gruesomely evident, and the pearl-gray, one piece garment—uniform? flight suit?—was drenched in red from a dozen gaping wounds.

He turned to the other, and his eyebrows crawled up his forehead in surprise as he noted the unmistakably feminine curves of the body. Somehow it hadn't occurred to him that he might find a woman—or a female, anyway—in here. Surprise held him motionless for a moment, but then the breasts under the red-streaked, skintight garment moved, and he realized this one, at least, was still alive!

His fingers slipped uselessly over the smooth, featureless helmet. Damn it! The thing was secured to her uniform somehow, but *how*? He was afraid to use force, and his fingers quested for some release mechanism. The water was higher on his calves, and he wondered if only his imagination made the sphere seem to be moving more heavily. Damn, damn, *damn*! How was he supposed—

A searching fingertip touched an unseen stud, and suddenly the helmet was loose. He dragged it away, and a spring-loaded cable snatched it from his abruptly frozen hands.

Chestnut hair spilled free, framing an ashen, high-cheeked, undeniably *human* face. The hair was stringy and stiff, as if long unwashed, but it was incontrovertibly human hair. He touched it shakenly, then jerked his hand back as the eyelids fluttered. They opened just a crack, revealing deep-blue, almost indigo eyes with pinpoint pupils, and the pale lips whispered something he couldn't. quite catch. It sounded almost like "Anwar."

He started to speak, but the eyes closed again and she was gone. He reached out quickly, touching her throat, and exhaled a sigh as he felt the faint, rapid flutter of a pulse. She was still alive.

But it didn't look like she would be for long, he thought grimly. He'd seen many badly injured people in his time, and the bright river of red welling over the chest of her gray garment looked bad— especially in conjunction with that pale face and those contracted pupils and bloodless lips.

There was a button on the buckle joining her web of harness straps, and he punched it. The catch sprang obediently, and he pawed the straps aside. He saw no closures or fastenings on her flight suit, and he had no time to look for any, so he drew a worn, carefully tended Buck knife from his pocket, opened it one-handed, and slipped the keen, five-inch blade into the tight-fitting garment's neck.

His eyebrows rose again at the thin fabric's incredible toughness. He didn't know what it was, but it was tougher than anything he'd ever seen, and he set his teeth, grunting with effort and mentally apologizing to his "patient" as his sawing motion jerked at her. She groaned softly, but he dared not stop.

The fabric yielded stubbornly, but it yielded. He sawed away and discovered that the garment covered a very human torso. He felt a brief flush of irritation with himself as he noted how attractively this "alien" was built, but it faded abruptly as he finally bared the wound.

His face twisted as he watched blood welling from the ragged puncture under her left breast. He leaned closer, and his face tightened further as he heard a faint, unmistakable whistle each time she breathed. A sucking wound. At least one lung, then. He was surprised the flow was so slow, but he recognized the bright red of arterial blood.

He stared down helplessly. There wasn't a thing in the world he could do for her—not with that. He was bitterly familiar with wounds, but he was no corpsman, and *Amanda* had no facilities for *any* serious injury.

He had no idea how long he stood there, enraged and frozen by his utter inability to save her, but a sudden lurch dragged him back to awareness. The water had risen to his knees, lapping about the seated woman's thighs, and the sphere's motion felt emphatically waterlogged. He cursed once, viciously, and wedged a handkerchief over the wound, dragging the tightly fitted garment back over it to hold it in place. He'd probably kill her by moving her, but she was dying anyway, and he couldn't just leave her here. He got her up into a fireman's carry, cringing mentally as he considered the additional damage he might be doing, and reached up for the hatch.

It was a hard climb under her slight, limp weight, but he managed somehow. He paused there, gasping for breath, and the edge of *Amanda*'s deck was far higher on the sphere than it had been. The thing was clearly sinking, and he heaved on the mooring line with another mental apology—this one to his ketch—as he scrubbed her fiberglass against the metal and stepped across to his boat with a feeling of boundless relief.

He slid the injured woman to the deck as gently as possible, goaded by ominous gurgles from the sphere behind him. It was going fast now; the flooding must have passed the critical point . . . and the damned mooring line was jammed! He worked at it in the darkness, his eyes still adjusted to the brilliance inside the sphere, cursing himself for the haste with which he'd made fast. How the hell— There! The jammed strands slid apart, and he fell backward as the line snaked free.

Just in time. The sphere was sinking quickly, the lip of the hatch almost level with the water. Even as he picked himself up, the first wave slopped over the sill and the sphere filled noisily, spinning at last as it slid beneath the waves.

The light within it didn't die, and he leaned over the side for a moment, watching the bright glow sink into the depths and regretting its loss. God, what he wouldn't have given to turn that thing over to—

Sudden memory stabbed him, and he turned quickly, bending over the woman. He felt her neck again, almost surprised to feel the pulse still fluttering under his fingers. It actually felt a little stronger—or did it? It had to be his imagination, with that wound, and he castigated himself for indulging in false optimism.

But he couldn't just leave her on deck. He gathered her up more gently, cradling her in his arms and feeling her own hang pathetically limp from her shoulders, and carried her carefully down the companion.

He laid her on his bunk and straightened, and his lips formed another silent curse as her appearance truly registered. She was just a damned kid! She couldn't be more than nineteen, he thought bitterly, his helplessness welling up again, and clenched his fists for just a moment, then shook himself. There wasn't a thing he could do, but that didn't mean he didn't have to try.

He gently peeled back the flap of her uniform once more, uncovering the blood-soaked handkerchief, and drew a deep breath. He lifted the pad to examine the wound—and froze.

There was no more bleeding.

But that, he thought, was impossible. He'd *heard* air sucking through the hole!

Only there *was* no hole, he noted with a queer, calm detachment; only an ugly little pucker, raw as a fresh-closed surgical incision.

He shook his head, feeling unaccountably as if he'd taken one punch too many, and reached out. His fingers, he noted distantly, trembled as he touched the pucker lightly. He raised his hand and examined them, but there was no fresh blood. It wasn't an illusion; the wound really *had* closed—and in just the few minutes it took to carry her this far.

He steeled his nerve and reached out again, laying his hand gently against the spot where a human's heart would be. He held his breath for a moment, then sighed and shook his head. She had a heart, all right, and it was beating—beating slowly and steadily. He sank down on the opposite bunk, staring at her.

That wound had been *real*, damn it! And, without the help of a trained, well-equipped doctor, it had been mortal. But instead of dying, color was already creeping back into her pale, sleeping face!

The tremble in his hands was more pronounced, and he gripped them together to still it, wishing he could banish his internal shudders as easily.

A human would have died, he thought quietly. Even if she hadn't, she would never have...healed...that quickly. So this motionless young woman had to be something else.

But what?

CHAPTER SIX

Richard Aston was a competent man. Anyone who knew him would have testified to that, yet at the moment he felt anything but competent. He sat paralyzed on the spare bunk, staring across the tiny cabin at the young almost-woman lying in his own, and had no idea in the world what to do. Nor was there any way to ask anyone else.

He'd been confused, at first, when he tried to raise *someone* for advice only to find his radio stone-cold dead. In all his sailing, he'd never suffered the breakdown of a solid-state transmitter. He'd had them shot up, blown up, lost, and otherwise rendered useless in the field, but never aboard his ship. Yet neither, he slowly realized, had one of them ever been exposed to the EMP of multiple nuclear explosions. It wasn't a subject on which he was extraordinarily well-informed, but he remembered snippets from various briefings as he considered it. Solid-state electronics were highly susceptible to the electromagnetic energy burst associated with nuclear weapons, and his transceiver had simply burned out. And so, he discovered, had his commercial receiver. Not only could he not talk to anyone, he couldn't even know what (if anything) the rest of the world had to say about what he'd just seen.

All of which meant that he was very much on his own.

He pondered his options, but he really had only one. He was a bit more than halfway to Europe on the prevailing westerlies, which meant it would be faster to continue than to turn about, though he shuddered at the thought of explaining things to British customs when he arrived. Yet even that was less daunting than his total ignorance about how to care for the girl he'd rescued.

He rubbed his bald, tanned crown anxiously, then gave himself a mental shake and stood, remembering a lesson he'd learned long ago. If he couldn't see how to solve his whole problem, the thing to do was to start by solving the parts of it that he could.

The first thing was to get her out of her bloodstained, filthy flight suit. He still couldn't see any closures, but he'd already ruined her tailoring. He found a pair of huge sailmaker's scissors and went to work.

His patient—if such she was—was a sturdily built girl, he discovered, rather pleased with himself for managing to maintain an almost clinical attitude. She had the appropriate numbers of fingers and toes and perfect teeth without a single filling. As far as he could determine, there were absolutely no external differences between her and any other woman, except, perhaps, for how extraordinarily well developed her muscles were. They had a sleek, flowing vitality—the strength of conditioned endurance, not just brute power. He'd seen enough hard-trained people in his life to know the difference.

He peeled her out of the suit, discovering along the way that it had comprehensive and ingenious plumbing connections—which, however, apparently led nowhere—and that the flat case on her right hip was a snap-down holster. He thought of it as snapping down, anyway, although the exact nature of the closure evaded him. He saw no sign of any fastening, but when he pressed the flap down, it stayed there until he tugged it loose. In a strange way, that prosaic little trick impressed him even more than aerobatic streaks of light and nuclear explosions in the heavens.

The weapon itself was completely baffling. He knew it was a weapon—he'd handled enough of them to *feel* its lethality—yet he had no inkling of how it functioned. The barrel was a massive piece of alloy, suspiciously like stainless steel, except that a check with a magnet showed that it was nonferrous. It was some sort of projectile weapon . . . he thought. But the bore was tiny, certainly no more than a millimeter in diameter, and there was no sign of a slide or ejector port. Hair-thin, almost invisible lines formed a square on the bottom of the pistol butt, and a pocket in the back of the holster held half a dozen blocky, featureless rectangular cubes of what appeared to be solid plastic which would have fitted perfectly inside the square and just about filled the "pistol's" grip—assuming the butt was hollow and there was some way to eject the cube already in it.

He handled the thing with extreme care. It undoubtedly made his .45 look like a big, noisy cap pistol, but he felt no particular desire to squeeze the button inside its trigger guard. There were three more small buttons or sliding switches recessed into the side of the barrel, and he kept his hands carefully away from them, as well. He was fairly certain any weaponeer would have the sense to build in a safety, but he had no intention of finding out the hard way which one *wasn't* it.

She wore a thin metal necklet of some sort, as well, and he scrutinized it with almost equal curiosity. It supported a plastic cube a half-inch square and a quarter-inch thick. Study it as he might, he could discern no apparent closures, readouts, or features of any sort, but it certainly didn't look like an ornament! He was a bit worried by its snug fit, wondering if it might interfere with her breathing, but then his probing fingertip touched a nearly invisible stud and the supporting band sprang open so suddenly he almost dropped it in surprise. He held it up for one last, close look, then shrugged and admitted defeat.

He slid the weapon back into the holster and tucked everything away in a locker, then turned back to his passenger. That was the best word, he decided: "passenger." Or perhaps he should think of her as a distressed mariner? The thought won a wry snort of amusement from him—the first levity he'd felt since she fell out of the sky at him.

One thing he could do was clean her up. Whatever her activities for the past few weeks, bathing hadn't been one of them. His supply of fresh water was limited, but he could spare enough for a sponge bath, and did, trying to ignore her firm softness without a great deal of success . . . until he discovered a second, larger pucker just below her left shoulder blade and barely half an inch from her spine.

He froze for only a moment, then made his hands continue their gentle cleansing, but his discovery had shocked him into remembering her alien nature. Those two marks were an entry and an exit wound—which meant something had passed entirely through her body, ripping its way through her lung and God knew what else at high velocity. And she'd survived it.

He laid her back down and did what he could with her hair (not much) as he tried to envision how anything, human or not, could survive that kind of traumatic damage. Unfortunately, his imagination was unequal to the task, and that scared him in a distant sort of way, for he was unused to questions he couldn't even begin to answer, and this shipwrecked girl was a mass of those. The sheer vitality her survival implied was frightening enough without wounds which, he noticed suddenly, had not only closed but were already beginning to *heal*.

He peered closely at the fading rawness of her damaged flesh, and the puckered marks already looked less livid and new. Moved by a sudden impulse to gather proof, he found his camera and snapped pictures of the wounds, resolving to take more at regular intervals. Not that he expected anyone to believe him even with photos.

He sighed and tucked the sheet over her, wondering what he should do next. With a comparably wounded human, he could just have buried her at sea; as it was, he had to assume she would live ... unless he did something stupid and finished her off out of sheer ignorance. The ironic thought was less humorous than he'd expected, and his grin died stillborn. Damn it, it was important that she live! Whoever or whatever she was, she must be a treasure trove of data just waiting to be discovered—and she was a damned good-looking kid, too.

But how to keep her alive? He didn't even know her dietary requirements! What should he think about feeding her? Could she metabolize terrestrial food? Did she need vitamins he couldn't provide? Trace minerals? What about—?

He reined in his imagination before it did any damage. Manifestly, he thought, watching her breathe, she could handle terrestrial air, which was probably a good sign. Now. If she were a human, she would need lots of protein and liquids after losing so much blood. And while it *looked* like she was healing completely and with indecent speed, he couldn't know she was. There might be internal damage he didn't know about, too, though the fact that her abdomen showed no sign of distension encouraged him to believe that at least there was no major internal bleeding. But until he knew what shape her plumbing was in, solid food was out. Besides, how could he get anything solid down an unconscious patient in the first place?

Soup, he decided. Soup was the best bet, and he had literally cases of canned soup among his provisions.

He fired up his old-fashioned bottled-gas stove and put on a kettle of cream of chicken soup. He supposed something with vegetables might be better for her, but until she was able to chew on her own, he wasn't going to risk anything with solids. Actually, broth of some sort probably would have been best of all, but Aston had always hated broth and flatly refused to keep any in his galley.

He brought the soup to a simmer, stirring occasionally and checking his patient at frequent intervals. She showed no sign of waking, and before settling in to feed her—which he guessed might be a lengthy business—he took himself back topside and got *Amanda* back under sail. He waited long enough to be certain the self-steering was working properly (he hadn't done that once, and the results still made him shudder), then went back below, mentally rolling up his sleeves as he faced the daunting task of nursing an alien from God knew where while sailing single-handed across the Atlantic.

It was not, he reflected, a program which would appeal to the faint of heart. Odd; he'd never realized *he* was fainthearted.

He raised her head and shoulders and propped them with pillows before he half-filled a deep bowl (filling bowls to the brim was contraindicated aboard small craft) with soup. He carried it to a seat by her bunk and crooked a surprised eyebrow as her nostrils gave an unmistakable twitch. She'd shown absolutely no awareness as he undressed and bathed her, but now her eyes slitted blankly open, without any sign of recognition or curiosity, as the smell of the soup reached her.

He raised a spoonful to her lips, and her reaction banished any concern he'd felt over feeding an unconscious patient. Her mouth opened quickly, and when he tried to slide the spoon carefully into it, she snapped at it.

That was the only verb he could think of. He remembered Aardvark, a stray dog he'd taken in as a child—a miserable, three-quarters-starved rack of bones and hair which had become the most loving and beloved pet of his life. The first time Aardvark had smelled food, he'd gone for it with exactly he same desperation. There was something feral about the fierce way she accepted the soup, and the hazy fire in her unseeing eyes brightened. He had to tug to get the spoon back, and she released it with manifest unwillingness, only to snap even harder when he refilled it and proffered it once more.

He fed it to her one spoonful at a time. There was never the least awareness in her burning gaze, but she took each mouthful with the same ferocity. He emptied the bowl and got another. Then another. And another. He was uneasy about feeding her so much, but the almost savage way she ate convinced him she needed it. He made another kettle when the first was empty, and she ate half of it, as well, before she was satisfied.

It was obvious when she was sated, for her eyelids dropped abruptly and the soup lost all attraction for her. It happened so suddenly it caught him with a spoonful halfway to her mouth, and when he offered it to her she might have died between bites for all the interest she showed. For just a moment, he was afraid she had died—that the soup had proved some sort of deadly poison—but her slow, even breathing and the faint blush of color returning to her porcelain cheeks reassured him.

He sat back and shook his head in slow bemusement. She was more muscular than most women he'd encountered, but she was no more than five feet four, so how could she pack it away like that? He eyed the half-emptied kettle on the stove. She'd eaten over a gallon of soup, and he couldn't begin to imagine where she'd put it all. But he was rapidly coming to the conclusion that the only eventuality which should really worry him would be the discovery that he actually understood anything that was going on.

He sat there for half an hour, listening to her breathe and wondering if she was going to come around, but she never even moved. She was motionless but for the slow rise and fall of her breasts and an occasional very faint flutter of her eyelids, and he felt his own eyes growing heavy.

He glanced out a porthole and grinned tiredly. No wonder he felt weary. The sun was rising, and he'd been up all night, witnessed an impossible dogfight conducted with nukes and what had to be some sort of energy weapons, survived a multimegaton blast at entirely too close a range for comfort, and rescued a critically wounded and all too human-looking alien from certain death by drowning.

He rose and stretched, then checked his barometer carefully. It had risen very slightly since his last check, so maybe the good weather was going to hold. God knew he could use a spell of easy sailing if he had to play Florence Nightingale to Dejah Thoris for the foreseeable future!

He looked back down at his unexpected passenger. She didn't look very menacing, but perhaps it would be a good idea to nap topside in the cockpit, just in case.

He did, and if he was a bit shamefaced about hanging onto his .45 when he did, he didn't let it stop him from taking it along.

The next four days were among the most exhausting Dick Aston could remember. The girl did nothing but eat and sleep; she never even showed an inclination to rouse for a trip to the head, and that did almost more to convince him of her inhuman pedigree than anything else about her.

The only thing with the power to rouse her was hunger. Even that didn't bring her back to awareness, but she grew sufficiently agitated in her slumber to wake him less than three hours after he first fed her. Too many years of a hazardous lifestyle had made him a very light sleeper, but the sounds drifting up the open companion hatch had been almost frightening. There was an eerie note to them—a keening sound of distress he couldn't immediately understand. He shoved himself up and hurried down to her, rubbing sleep from his eyes and trying frantically to understand what had brought her to a whimpering, twisting parody of liveliness.

He offered her water, and she drank greedily, but her agitation scarcely eased. It seemed inconceivable that hunger could possibly explain such obvious distress after she'd devoured so much soup, but nothing else suggested itself, and finally, in desperation, he opened a can of stew.

Her frantic, twisting whimpers redoubled the instant she smelled it, and he found himself back beside the bunk without even heating it, spooning cold, glutinous stew into his voracious patient. She ate even more fiercely than before, and it took four family-sized cans of the stuff to satisfy her before she slumped back, as instantaneously limp as the last time.

He stared at her in awe, glancing back and forth between her innocent, sleeping face and the empty cans. Lordy! She didn't *look* like she had a black hole concealed somewhere about her person. He only hoped he had enough food to complete the crossing! The pattern was established. She never woke, but she roused once every two and a half hours—or, to be more precise, once every one hundred forty minutes almost to the second by his watch—demanding to be fed. It was hard to believe even when he saw it happening, but her voracity never flagged, and his supplies dwindled rapidly under its ruinous onslaught. By the third day, he was genuinely concerned that he would run short, despite the fact that he was well ahead of his originally projected progress.

He started spending more time with the huge spinnaker set, driving *Amanda* far harder—while he was awake, anyway—than he'd planned. A less curious man might have come to hate the demands his passenger placed on his own store of energy, but in Richard Aston's case, fascination overpowered all other emotions where she was concerned. By the middle of the second day, the wounds which should have killed her were faint, raised scars, and he half-suspected even those would vanish with time. All in all, she was a puzzle wrapped in a mystery, and his most driving desire was for her to wake up and talk to him.

Commander Mordecai Morris, who rejoiced in the nickname "M&M" among his ruder intimates, was not a happy man. He knew perfectly well that he wasn't alone in that; indeed, he found himself uncomfortably well-placed to observe and appreciate the unhappiness of others.

He sighed and stubbed out his forbidden cigarette (US military bases were officially smoking-free), then rubbed his weary eyes and wondered how many he'd smoked in the four days since it all hit the fan. Why did he even try to pretend he wasn't a nicotine addict, anyway? He managed to convince himself he was quitting—or cutting back, at least—for weeks on end, but only until the next crisis put him back into the pressure cooker. He suspected it stemmed from his ingrained dislike for admitting that he didn't really want to stop doing something he ought to stop.

He fumbled for another cigarette, but the pack was empty. He peered down into it for a moment, then crushed it and dropped it into the shredder bag under his desk.

"Well, Mordecai?" The voice from the door pulled his head around, and he summoned up a tired grin.

"Hi, Jayne," he said, gesturing at a chair, and Lieutenant Commander Jayne Hastings walked into the cluttered office, waving a hand ineffectually against the blue canopy of stale tobacco smoke. The office felt close and muggy for an April night, even in Norfolk, Virginia.

"I see the air-conditioning's still out," she observed, and Morris shrugged. She shook her head and sat, glancing at the full ashtray and clutter of empty coffee cups. "How long since you had a shower and a shave, Mordecai?" she asked gently.

"Shower? Shave?" He rubbed his nose and grinned. "What're they?"

"Twit," she said affectionately, and he made a face at her.

Morris was a small, dark man with an artificial right foot and eyes which were warm and brown when not ringed with red—the sort of man dogs and children loved on sight. He was also a highly respected intelligence analyst, as was to be expected of the man Commander-in-Chief Atlantic Fleet had chosen as his chief intelligence officer. At the moment, he was unshaven and red-eyed, his uniform wilted, but on his best day, no one would ever confuse him with the steely-eyed image of the professional intelligence operative. That was perfectly all right with him—a dozen people in various Federal prisons had judged by appearances. Several one-time terrorists in a Middle Eastern cemetery had also discovered how sadly deceived they'd been in the unassuming, cheerfully corruptible naval attaché. Their effort to correct their error in judgment had been impressive, however, and although it had fallen short of their intention, it had been enough to cost him a foot and put him behind a desk.

Jayne Hastings was a foot taller than her boss, with wheat-blond hair and bright green eyes. She styled her hair severely and hid her trenchant intelligence behind ridiculously large, round-lensed glasses, but her grooming was immaculate. It was one of the wonders of Morris's untidy life that she could spend just as many hours as he did on some critical project with never a misplaced crease or a hair out of place. It was unnatural.

Morris's expertise was people—he was downright brilliant at evaluating trends and intentions—and Hastings was the technician of the team, with four degrees and an impressive background in air-breathing and satellite reconnaissance, both photographic and electronic. They were an unusually effective team under normal circumstances, but at the moment they had no more to work with than anyone else in the world's intelligence services.

Everyone knew *something* had happened, but only the Americans and the Russians (and *possibly* the Chinese) had any idea what—and they were none too certain. At least all the major players seemed to have gotten enough advance warning from their space surveillance systems to know something was going on before all hell broke loose over the Atlantic. Fortunately. Morris shuddered to think what might have happened if they *hadn't* known. There'd been more than enough panic and suspicion as it was.

"Listen, M&M, you may've managed to inveigle me down here at—" Hastings glanced at the twenty-four hour clock "—three A.M. by finally getting your hands on that video, but the only way you're getting any work out of me is if I get a promise out of *you*, first."

"I wasn't aware this had become a union shop," Morris said mildly, and she snorted. "All right, Commander, what might that promise be?"

"That you'll get some sleep when we're done," she said, suddenly more serious. "You look like hell. Go home. Take a shower and get some sleep before you stroke out on me."

"I'd love to," he acknowledged her point with a sigh. "But I'm supposed to have a written brief for CINCLANT by oh-nine-hundred, and—"

"I'll assemble the brief," she interrupted firmly. "God knows I've written enough for you before! You go home and get at least a couple of hours of sleep before you present it—he'll probably have you shot if you turn up looking like this. Remember what he said last time?"

"You may have a point, Commander Hastings."

"I *do* have a point, Commander Morris."

"All right," he capitulated, "it's a deal." He grinned again and waved at the large-screen TV and VCR parked in the corner. "This one's going to be more your area than mine anyway."

"That's the video?" she asked, her eyes sharpening with interest as she stood quickly and picked up a plastic video cassette.

"Yup." Morris pushed back his own chair and watched her slip the tape into the VCR. "We're damned lucky to have it, too. That fighter jock was a long way from the big blast, so he didn't lose all his avionics, but a lot of his systems were fried, and he couldn't trust *Roosevelt*'s electronics, either. It took a hell of a driver to put that bird onto a carrier by hand and eye. Matter of fact, I didn't know it could be done—and neither did Northrop-Grumman." He gave a brief snort of humor. "I understand the other aircrew were more than content to use their water wings, but not *this* guy. He and his RIO are the ones that nailed those first two missiles, too; they must have great, big brass ones. Anyway—" he shrugged "—here it finally is. I've got expert analyses out the ying-yang, and I've watched the damned thing a dozen times myself. Now it's your turn."

"What was all the delay about?" she demanded.

"CIA got their hands on it first, somehow," Morris snorted. "You know how compartmented they are over there. It's taken this long for them to find it and break it loose. The boss," he added dryly, "was not amused."

"Why am I not surprised?" Hastings murmured, and they grinned at each other. Admiral Anson McLain, Commander in Chief Atlantic Fleet, was not a good man to cross. Especially not by sitting on intelligence, collected by one of his pilots, which concerned the death and/or injury of over a thousand of *his* sailors and the loss of one of *his* ships.

"I think we can safely count on him to collect a few scalps," Morris agreed, then pointed at the TV. "Switch it on and take a look."

Hastings nodded and punched the play button on the remote. The unit clicked and whirred to itself for a moment, then a night sky replaced the quietly hissing snow on the TV screen. A small digital readout in the lower right corner gave the date and time at which the tape had been made and another in the left corner gave a distance-to-target reading; at the moment, it was whirring downward with disconcerting speed. The picture was black and white but almost painfully sharp.

"This from the new TCS?" Hastings asked absently.

"Yup," Morris said again. "Does a nice job, doesn't it?"

"I'll say. The old TISEO system and the first-generation TCS both looked good, but this is even better."

Morris simply nodded. The latest tactical camera system fitted under the nose of late marks of the F-14D used a whole new optics system, not to mention a long overdue infrared sensor. The Tomcat had never been designed to be a stealthy platform, but at least it finally had a reasonably effective passive search system which didn't require its massive radar to broadcast its presence to all and sundry.

It was a useful retrofit to the aging fighter, and the Tomcat crews claimed their new imagery was so sharp they could count an OpFor pilot's warts at fifty miles, which was an exaggeration . . . he thought.

He leaned back and fought the weight of his eyelids, watching Hastings bend towards the television and wondering how she would react.

There! He saw her flinch at the speed with which the brilliant streaks of light came sweeping towards her, but she mastered her reaction instantly and leaned still closer, eyes intent. Six light sources swelled with freight-train speed, bobbing and weaving as they came. It was impossible to make out much detail, but the lights kept getting bigger and bigger. After a moment, it became clear they were well above the camera—and that the Tomcat pilot was maneuvering hard to keep them in view. They swept over the aircraft, and the pilot put the big fighter into a climbing loop. Stars swooped wildly in their field of view, and then the lights reappeared, moving away. The image trembled and rotated dizzyingly for just a moment as the pilot rolled his aircraft, then smoothed back out.

The lights continued to move away, but more slowly, and now the imagery showed at least some details of the craft which produced them. There were six of them, and four—all of which appeared identical—held a tight formation around a fifth, much larger shape while the sixth pursued them all. It was apparent now that the intense brilliance came not from the craft themselves but from a bowl-shaped curve of fire just ahead of each of them.

The shapes were in sight for no more than three or four minutes when an intolerable glare from ahead and below burned out the images entirely. Crazy patterns of interference flashed and danced for a moment, and then the screen went blank.

Lieutenant Commander Hastings was silent as she rewound the tape and played it again. Then she played it a third time, using the remote to freeze the picture repeatedly as she studied it. Finally she sighed and rewound the tape a final time, turning to Morris with a frown.

"Those things were *big*," she said softly.

"You might say that," he agreed. "The photo analysis people say most of the lead group were bigger than *Spruance*-class destroyers—and the biggie was the size of a CGN. The one in back was smaller, but not by a heck of a lot. They make it about—" he consulted a scratch pad "—three hundred to three hundred thirty feet, give or take."

"Oh, how I *wish* we'd had a camera bird up there to watch all this!"

"I understand the pulse from that big boom didn't do the Russkies' RORSAT a bit of good," Morris chuckled.

"Not too surprising. But at least they had one, so they knew it wasn't us shooting at them, thank God!"

"Amen," Morris said seriously. "I just wish we knew whether or not the PRC had satellite imagery of its own."

"You and me both," Hastings agreed with a humorless grin. "We *know* they've got at least some recon birds hidden up there amongst all those 'commercial communications' birds of theirs. I have to agree with CIA and NSA that their main interest these days is Taiwan and that they're probably concentrating on the Pacific, not the Atlantic, but it would be nice to know. And the *French*—!"

She tossed both hands upwards with a grimace, and Morris nodded. As was not, unfortunately, uncommon in American diplomatic history, the US had overplayed the "China Card" badly. Unlike the defunct Soviet Union, the Chinese Communist Party was showing no particular signs of vanishing into the ash heap of history. Not that it showed any particular sign of remaining unswervingly attached to the principles of Marxism-Leninism, either. But any country with that many people and resources and an authoritarian government—whatever that government's ideology might be—was almost bound to attempt to expand its hegemony, and the Chinese had made it increasingly plain that Asia belonged to them. And that they were willing to threaten and even (probably) use military means to enforce that claim. As one consequence of that attitude, things were heating up over the Republic of Taiwan once more. That was why a two-carrier American task group had been deployed to the area, and it had become painfully clear that the US aerospace industry's efforts to improve the PRC's satellite launch capability had transferred rather more technology to the mainland Chinese in the last several years than anyone had realized at the time.

As for the French, their fundamental anti-Americanism had only grown more pronounced as the much-anticipated European Union continued to stagger along as a concept rather than a reality. The

EU's persistent failure to solve the smouldering issues of the Balkans or defuse the growing nationalist tensions between Russia and certain other of the old soviet empire's fragments hadn't helped much, either. France, in particular, had been savage in the derision it heaped upon America's bumbling efforts in the Balkans, and the French government had become even more anti-US as its own failure to solve the same problems drove it into an ever more defensive attitude. Mordecai knew Paris had had at least one recon satellite in position to watch what had happened, but it had also been much closer to the largest of the nuclear explosions. What it had seen—or transmitted back home, at least—before the blast reduced it to so much expensive junk was anyone's guess . . . and the French weren't telling.

"Speaking of explosions," Hastings went on after a moment, "what's the latest estimate on their yields?"

"Something like five hundred megatons for the big one." She whistled silently, and he nodded in heartfelt agreement. "The little fellows were down in the multi-kiloton range, but I understand they were all a lot cleaner than they should've been."

"For which we can only be grateful," she said quietly, and he nodded again. A brief silence fell as they pondered the tremendous destructive power which had erupted out of nowhere. The biggest explosion had been so brilliant and high as to be visible from both sides of the Atlantic, and its EMP had knocked out the avionics on seven different civilian airliners—all of which had crashed at sea with no survivors—as well as wreaking general havoc on the satellite communications industry and the Global Positioning Satellites everyone had come to take so much for granted. There was a very large hole in the orbital electronic network which had once covered the Atlantic, and Morris hated to think what that burst of fury had been like at closer range. It must have been like a foresight of Hell.

"But what do you think of our tape?" he asked finally.

"Impressive. Very impressive." She nibbled thoughtfully on a bent knuckle. "Whatever they were, they weren't ours. Or anyone else's, for that matter. Of course, SPASUR's track already proved that—this is just icing on the cake."

"But the fact that an F-14 in full afterburner lost ground on them that fast has more immediacy than tracking station reports, no?"

"True. And visual confirmation of their size is impressive, too." She shook her head. "I *still* can't understand how they got clear down to the edge of atmosphere before they were picked up, though. Anyone who could build those things should certainly be capable of foxing our radar, of course, but if they can do that at all, why stop? And just what were they doing in atmosphere, anyway?"

"That, I should think, is pretty obvious," Morris said. "Admiral Carson got mixed up in somebody else's war."

"Granted, but why *here*?" She shook her head and leaned back in her chair, crossing her legs and worrying an earlobe. "There's no way to prove it, but I think it's pretty damned obvious those things were designed for space, not atmosphere."

"Reasons?" he asked.

"Their size, for one, and then there's this. . . . " She restarted the tape and pushed the fast-forward button, then froze the image as the Tomcat pilot completed his roll and the picture stabilized. "See those bright hemispheres in front of them?" He nodded. "That has to be how they were able to pull that speed. Some sort of—well, call it a force field."

"That's what NASA figures," Morris agreed.

"Has to be," she said. "Their hulls would be white hot at that speed without them. But if they were meant primarily for atmosphere, the designers would have given more thought to what might happen if their shield failed, I think. Look here." She touched the image of the rearmost vessel. "See all those external bulges? And here and here— those look like aerials of some sort. There's no suggestion of any lifting surfaces, either. Add that blunt nose and these weird curved sections here, and they'd be in real trouble if they lost their shields at high Mach numbers. In fact, I'll bet that's how we managed to knock any of them down. A piddling little SAM wouldn't shoot one of those things out of the sky, but if it could screw up that force field . . ."

"Don't underestimate our SAMs," Morris cautioned. "Depending on what hit them, you're talking up to a ninety-pound warhead, and there were hundreds of the buggers flying around. Still, NASA and Point Mugu both tend to agree with you. According to them, it was losing whatever was protecting them that did them in—especially if they took enough battle damage to give the airflow something to shred."

"And *that's* why none of it makes any sense!" Hastings protested. "Why fight in a less than ideal environment? These were *space ships*, for God's sake! Even if you assume they just sort of wandered into our solar system from Out There, why fight in atmosphere?"

"Maybe we've been invaded," Morris suggested only half-humorously.

"It's a mighty strange invasion, then," Hastings snorted. "I've never had much patience with the notion that we're so important that mighty alien fleets are just lining up to conquer us, but even if they are, where is the fleet? And does the fact that there were obviously two sides mean one of them is friendly to us?" She shook her head.

"All excellent questions," Mordecai Morris agreed, standing and reaching for his jacket with a weary sigh. He draped it over his shoulder and grinned crookedly. "Do you have an opinion?"

"I don't know, yet," she said, nibbling her knuckle again. "At first glance, I'm inclined to think we were just more-or-less innocent bystanders who got caught in the crossfire, but there're too many unanswered questions for us to assume that. And at least one side's probably a bit ticked with us. Any better refinement on the kill data?"

"Nope," Morris said. "Turns out our 'nuclear hardening' isn't quite as effective as we'd hoped, especially when the task force didn't have time to implement doctrine for surviving a nuclear attack. Most of Admiral Carson's electronics had fits from the EMP when whoever the hell it was nailed the *Kidd*, and every radar and almost all the computers went to hell when the pulse from that big bastard hit. But it looks like *Antietam* and *Champlain* managed to guide most of their SAMs into the targets before the big one flat-out killed their target illumination aerials, and the RAMs and AMRAAMs were on internal seekers. Visual estimates are that we got two, possibly three, out of the first group, with possible hits on a couple more. Obviously we didn't get them all," he added with a crooked smile.

"Obviously," Hastings agreed. "So we don't know who they were, how many of them we got, who killed what after we engaged them, who won, or where the survivors—if any—went afterwards!"

"Except for one thing," Morris said softly, and she quirked an eyebrow at him. "One thing everyone's agreed on—nobody tracked any of them headed back out. I suppose it's possible they wiped each other out, but I tend to think one side or the other probably won. And if neither side blocked our radar on the way in, why do it on the way out?" He shook his head.

"You mean one side, or possibly both of them, is still around?"

"I think we have to assume they could be," he agreed, slipping into his jacket. "And if it's only one, we'd better hope it's the side we *didn't* get any of. In either case, it looks to me like we'd better find out where they wandered off to, don't you think?" He headed for the door, then paused and looked back with an exhausted smile.

"Thanks for volunteering to write the brief, Jayne," he said. "Try to tie up all the loose ends nice and pretty. If the boss likes it, I'll take the blame—otherwise, you get all the credit."

He vanished out the door before she produced a fitting reply.

enemy *n, pl. -mies.*
1. One who evinces hostility or malice toward, or opposes the interest, desire, or purpose of, another; opponent; foe. **2.** A hostile force or power, as a political unit, or an individual belonging to such a force or power. **3.** Something destructive or injurious. [Middle English *enemi,* from Old French *inimicus*: *in-*, not + *amicus*, friend.]

—Webster-Wangchi Unabridged
Dictionary of Standard English
Tomas y Hijos, Publishers 2465,
Terran Standard Reckoning

CHAPTER SEVEN

Richard Aston opened his eyes and stared at the checkered oilcloth tablecloth an inch from the tip of his nose.

He grimaced and straightened, suppressing a groan as his spine unbent, then blinked in surprise as his brain roused. He'd fallen asleep with his forehead on his crossed forearms, which, unfortunately, hadn't been unusual since his "guest's" arrival. That much he'd grown accustomed to, but the cabin was full of daylight, and her incessant demands for food should have waked him hours ago.

They hadn't, and he turned his head quickly—only to freeze in shock.

She was awake. More than that, she was lying on her side, head propped up by the fist curled under her jaw, and watching him with bright, calm eyes.

He sat motionless, staring back at her, and the moment of silence stretched out between them. Somehow it had never occurred to him that she would wake while he was sleeping. He'd envisioned offering her a mouthful of food and watching awareness slowly filter into her eyes. Or perhaps it would have happened while he was tenderly wiping her forehead with a damp cloth. He felt he could have handled either of those with comparative aplomb after all this time.

He most emphatically had not expected her to awaken and just lie there, self-possessed as a cat, patiently waiting for *him* to wake, and he felt almost betrayed by her aplomb. It registered only slowly that it was because her calm watchfulness violated his mental image of her—which, he thought wryly, was based on the way she ate. Patience wasn't something he'd associated with her, and that understanding brought amusement in its wake.

She watched gravely as he grinned, and then, slowly, her generous mouth curved as she took in his weary, unshaven appearance. Her wry, apologetic smile woke a gleam in his own eyes, and their mutual amusement seemed to feed upon itself, aided, in his case, by a vast relief that she had survived to wake up despite his ignorance about how to care for her. He began to chuckle, and she chuckled in response.

Their chuckles became laughter; and that, he later realized, was the moment his last, lingering fear of what she might be vanished.

He never knew exactly how long they laughed, but he knew it was a release of intolerable tension for both of them, and he surrendered to it gratefully. There was probably an edge of hysteria in it, he decided later, but it was such a relief the thought didn't bother him at all. He leaned back in his chair, roaring like a fool, and her rich laughter—no giggles for this girl!—answered him.

But finally, slowly, he regained control, managing to push the laughter aside without relinquishing the bright bubble of amusement at its core. He shook his head at her, wiping his eyes, and sat up straight.

She seemed to catch his change of mood, for she sat up, too, perching tailor-fashion on the bunk, and he just managed to keep his eyebrows from rising as the sheet fell down about her waist and she made no move to recover it. Instead, she bent forward, eyes and fingertips examining the faint, raised scar of her wound unselfconsciously. Well, he'd always thought his own culture's nudity taboo was one of its less sane aspects.

"Ah, hello," he said finally, speaking very slowly and carefully. He'd spent the few waking hours in which he wasn't shoveling food down her considering what to say at this moment. He'd scripted and discarded all manner of openings, unable to settle on a properly meaningful first greeting to an extraterrestrial. But when the moment came, none of his laborious compositions seemed in the least fitting after their shared laughter.

He bit his lip for a moment, watching her narrowly and wishing he were a trained linguist. Establishing communications was going to be rough, he thought. But then she opened her own mouth.

"Hello, yourself," she said in a velvet-edged contralto as clear and cool as spring water.

Those two words stunned him, for it had never occurred to him that she might speak English! He gawked at her, and she looked back as if surprised by his reaction, but then a gleam of renewed humor touched her eyes.

"Take me to your leader," she said with a perfectly straight face.

His gawking mouth snapped shut, and he frowned indignantly. He was trying to be serious, and she was making stupid—! But then he realized exactly what she'd said, and his eyes narrowed. Her people must have spent a long time studying his for her to know how that particular cliché would affect him.

"So," he said severely, "your people have a sense of humor, do they?"

"Well, yes," she admitted, "but mine's a bit lower than most."

He rubbed an eyebrow thoughtfully, savoring the unexpected loveliness of her voice . . . and her accent. He'd never heard one quite like it, and he would have bet he could identify the nationality of most English-speakers. But not hers. Her vowels came out with a peculiar, clipped emphasis, and she had a strange way of swallowing final consonants, like the "r" in "leader" and the "t" in "most." There was an odd rhythm to her speech, too, as if the adjectives and adverbs carried more weight than they did for the English-speakers with whom he was familiar. . . .

"Hello?" Her slightly plaintive voice startled him, and he blinked and snorted his way up out of his thoughts. She grinned at him, and he felt himself grinning back once more.

"Sorry. I'm not used to rescuing distressed spacewomen." He watched her carefully, but she only shrugged.

"You do it quite well for someone without experience," she said.

"Thanks," he said dryly. "My name's Aston, by the way. Richard Aston."

"Leonovna," she said, extending her right hand. "Ludmilla

Leonovna—" he started to reach out, only to pause at the Russian name, but his surprise became astonishment as she continued "—Colonel, Terran Marines."

He gaped at her, and she sat patiently, hand extended. *Colonel?* This kid? Impossible! But then the rest of her introduction penetrated, and he cocked his head, an edge of suspicion creeping back into his thoughts.

"Did you say *Terran* Marines?" he asked slowly.

"I did." Her speech was even quicker and more clipped than he'd first noticed, he thought absently, concentrating on what she'd said.

"There isn't any such organization," he said flatly at last. "And if there were, I doubt they'd be enlisting Russians."

"I know there isn't—yet," she returned, equally flatly, still holding out her hand. "And I'm not a Russian. Or not in the way you're thinking, at any rate."

He shook his head doggedly, then blushed as he noticed the waiting hand. He reached out almost automatically, but instead of clasping his hand, she clasped his forearm and squeezed. He was a powerful man, but he had to hide a wince at the strength in her fingers. She was even stronger than he'd thought; but he managed to grip back with enough pressure to satisfy honor on both sides.

"Look," she said finally, releasing his arm, "I know this must sound confusing, but what year is this?"

"Year?" He blinked. "You've studied us thoroughly enough to learn our language, and you don't know what year it is?" She merely sat silently, waiting, and he shrugged. "Okay," he said, "I'll bite. It's 2007—why?"

"2007," she said thoughtfully, leaning back and absently tugging the sheet higher. "Prissy was right, then." She nodded to herself. "That makes sense of the wet-navy task force...."

"Excuse me," he said firmly, "but could you possibly stop talking to yourself about things you already know and tell me just what the hell is going on here?" He'd thought he was exercising admirable control, but her expression told him differently.

"I apologize," she said contritely. "I'll try to explain, but first, could you tell me how I got here?" She waved around the small cabin.

"You fell out of the damned sky a hundred yards from my boat," he said bluntly, "and I fished you out." His face and voice softened. "I'm sorry there wasn't anything I could do for your friend."

"I guessed as much." She sighed sadly. "Poor Anwar. He came so far."

There was a moment of silence which he was loath to break, but his curiosity was much too strong to be denied.

"Just how far *did* you come?" he asked. "Where are you from— and, please, don't hand me any more crap about the 'Terran Marines'!"

"It's not 'crap,'" she said. "Oh, I'm not from Terra myself. I'm from Midgard." She saw the mounting frustration in his eyes and explained kindly, "That's Sigma Draconis IV."

"Oh, great!" he snorted. "Parallel evolution's even better than the Terran Marines! Does everybody on Sigma Draconis look like you, or did they do plastic surgery before they dropped you on us?"

"'Plastic sur—?' Oh! Biosculpt!" She chuckled. "No, we're all like this, more or less . . . though some of us are men," she added innocently.

"Listen—!" he started wrathfully, but she raised a placating hand as if to apologize for her flippancy.

"Sorry," she said contritely. "I couldn't resist." She smiled, but it was a more serious smile, and she leaned slightly forward. "I know it sounds confusing," she repeated, "but my people are as human as you are."

"Oh, sure! Blow a hole clear through me and *I'll* heal up overnight, too!"

"I said we're human, and we are," she said, and he blinked at her suddenly chill tone. She shook her head, as if angry with herself, and pressed her lips firmly together for a moment. Then she sighed.

"Please," she said. "Give me a tick, and I'll try to explain. All right?"

He nodded, not quite trusting himself to speak.

"Thank you. First of all, I *am* from Midgard, but Midgard was colonized from Earth." He started to protest the absurdity of her statement, then shut his mouth. It was hard, but he managed to keep it shut.

"Midgard," she continued with careful precision, "will be settled by humans in 2184." She met his eyes levelly. "That was about three hundred years ago . . . for me."

He was trapped by her eyes. Her statement was patently insane, but so was what he'd seen the night he plucked her from the sea. So was her survival and the way she'd slept and eaten for the past four days. And her eyes were neither mad nor those of a liar, he thought slowly. Indeed, there was an edge of desperation under their calmness—and he sensed, somehow, that desperation was foreign to this girl. "Are you telling me you're from the future?" he asked very carefully.

"Yes," she said simply.

"But . . ." He shook his head again, more confused than ever, yet feeling as if understanding lurked just half a thought beyond his grasp. He drew a deep breath and fastened on an inconsequential as if for diversion.

"How does it happen you speak twenty-first-century English, then?"

"I don't," she said, and grinned faintly at his expression. "Not norally, I man. Oh, mass literacy, printing, and audio recordings pretty much iced the language after the twentieth century, but it's actually a bit diff for me to match into your dialect. I'm a histortech by hobby, and that helps, but historical holodrama helps more." She laughed softly. "Not that they got it nickety, but they came close."

"'Nickety'?" he asked blankly.

"Sorry. It means, um, exactly correct. I'll have to be careful about my idioms." She smiled disarmingly. "I couldn't resist twisting you with that 'Take me to your leader' larkey, though. Some of the tainment dramas from your period are manic."

He felt suspicion sagging into acceptance. She was speaking English, all right, but the more she said, the more he realized that it wasn't quite his English. And as she relaxed, the differences became more pronounced. He was astonished to realize he actually believed her . . . sort of.

"All right," he said. "But why are you here? What the hell is going on? Those were *nukes* you were throwing around up there, honey!"

"Yes," she said softly, her face suddenly serious once more. "Yes, they were." Her fingers pleated the edge of her sheet unhappily. "You see, Ster Aston, I'm not here for pleasure. I came—" she drew a deep breath and met his eyes again "—to prevent the destruction of the human race . . . and I'm afraid I haven't quite done that yet."

Aston leaned back and closed his eyes, counting slowly to fifty behind his lowered lids. It was all preposterous of course, he thought almost distantly, and yet . . . and yet. . . .

His mind went back to that night of terrible explosions, and he felt his doubt crumble. Not his confusion—that became worse, if anything—but the memory of those searing flashes and their thunder could not be rejected. Yet it was another memory which suggested just how desperate she was to accomplish whatever task had brought her here. He'd rerun his mental records of that fight again and again, and one point had become glaringly clear; she'd been terribly outnumbered, but *she'd* been the attacker. And, he reminded himself, she'd gotten all but one of her enemies.

His face showed no sign of his thoughts, but he felt a surge of admiration for the naked youngster sitting on his bunk. He was no pilot, but he'd seen a great deal of combat in his time. He had a very clear notion of what it took to face that sort of odds—and of the skill needed to achieve what she had. He wasn't so foolish as to think courage and skill guaranteed honesty, but he felt oddly certain she wasn't lying to him.

He sighed and opened his eyes slowly, standing without a word, and rummaged in a locker for a black, silk-screened tee-shirt decorated with a dramatic headon view of an old US Air Force A-10 attack plane. He tossed it to her, and she tugged it over her head; It covered her like a tent, he thought as he wiggled past her in the narrow confines of the cabin.

Amanda chose that specific moment to surprise him with an unexpected motion, and he lost his balance. He leaned away from the bunk, falling towards the table to avoid landing on his guest, but a hand flashed out, moving faster than any hand he'd ever seen. He was more than a foot taller than she, but she pulled him back up one-handed . . . and with very little apparent effort.

Aston stood very still, then continued to the stove and put his battered old coffee pot on to heat. He turned a chair around and straddled it, leaning his chest against its back and reaching for his pipe.

"Pretty well-muscled, aren't you?" he said, watching her run curious fingers over the raised, slightly pebbled texture of the shirt's silk-screening. She seemed fascinated by it.

"What?" She looked up with a furrowed brow, then smiled. "Oh. I suppose I am, but I came by it naturally, Ster Aston. I told you I'm from Midgard." He raised his eyebrows, and she explained. "Our gravity runs about twenty percent higher."

"I see." He filled his pipe slowly, then found his butane lighter and took his time lighting the tobacco. She wrinkled her nose at the smell of his smoke, but she seemed more curious about it than irritated by it.

"Okay," he said finally. "Tell me about this war."

"I'll try, but it's a long story."

"That's all right." He grinned around his pipe and reached for a cup and the coffee pot. "We've got plenty of time, I'm afraid. We're over a week out of Portsmouth, and your nukes fried my radio, or I'd've had proper medical people out here to take you off my hands long ago."

"I see," she said, watching him pour and licking her lips. "Excuse me, but is that *Terran* coffee?"

"It sure isn't Martian," he said dryly.

"Sorry. It's just that back home Terran coffee's as rare as . . . a hen's tooth?" she finished on a questioning note and raised an eyebrow.

"Scarce as hen's teeth," he corrected, and she nodded, filing it away. He had the very strong impression she wouldn't need the same correction twice. "Want some?"

"I'd kill for it," she admitted with a sigh.

"Well, drink up," he invited, pouring another cup and handing it over. She took it eagerly, and he watched curiously as she sipped delicately. Her conscious eating manners were far different from her unconscious ones, and she was savoring it as if it were a rare treat.

She looked back up and saw his eyes.

"Sorry," she said. "For some reason, coffee doesn't grow well off Terra. The fide thing's expensive."

"Not anymore," he said with a smile, enjoying her enjoyment. "But you were about to tell me—?"

"So I was," she agreed. She took another sip, then leaned back against the bulkhead, looking even more absurdly young in his oversized tee-shirt. But he wasn't tempted to smile again, for there was a grimness in her eyes and a tightness to her lips.

"If this is 2007," she began, "then in about eighty years, the human race is going to meet the *Shirmaksu*. When we do, it will be the beginning of a war which will last for the next four hundred years."

"Four hundred years?" he asked softly.

"At least," she said grimly. "You see, the Kangas—that's what we call *Shirmaksu*—aren't very nice. They introduced themselves by trying to exterminate us."

Her level voice sent a chill down his spine.

"But why?" he asked.

"Because they're Kangas," she said simply. "The way they think, only one sentient race has any right to exist: theirs. It took us quite a while to believe that, I understand." She shrugged. "By the time I was born, we'd had lots of practice."

"But there had to be a reason," he protested.

"Oh, lots of them," she agreed, "and we weren't the first species they tried to cide. So far, we've identified twenty-seven sentient or presentient spedes they've wiped. Mankind would've been twenty-eight." She shrugged again. "Of course, a lot of what we 'know' is guesswork and deduction, but what it comes down to is that the Kangas had an unhappy racial childhood." She flashed a tight, humorless smile.

"As nearly as we can piece it, there were two intelligent species on their home world, and they hated each other. We don't know why, but, then, enough human groups have hated each other for reasons no one else ever understood. At any rate, they probably started trying to wipe each other while they were still living in caves; by the time they got to pikes and muskets, the Kangas were the only thinking species left on the planet."

She sighed.

"I like to think humanity would've wanted to get the killing out of its system by then, but not the Kangas. They're a strange bunch. They're xenophobic, paranoid, and so cautious they're cowardly, by human standards, but if logic says to take a chance, they will. They'll cover their asses every way they can, but they'll do it. They're big on logic.

"Unfortunately, they've got their own weird streak of mysticism, too. We're pretty hazy on how it works—they haven't exactly talked it over with us, and they arranged things so there aren't any other species around, so we've never been able to study comparative alien psychology—but they put together a 'religion' that makes the most intolerant human fanatic look ecumenical.

"The way they see it, God created one race in His image: theirs. The devil, on the other hand, assumes an endless series of different shapes and forms, and he's constantly trying to destroy God. Which makes the entire universe one huge battleground and means anybody who doesn't look like a Kanga is automatically on the devil's side. And so, of course, the only logical thing to do is to exterminate them."

Her words were almost light, but her tone was not.

"Anyway, their policy was set long before they ran into us. They tend to think in biological terms—not too surprising, I guess, given their history—and they're very good bio-engineers. They're less bright about other things, but their standard procedure whenever they encountered another intelligent species or anything that might turn into one was to grab a few specimens for research, then crank a bio weapon to wipe out only that species and dust its planet. It worked quite well until they ran into us."

Aston noticed her cup was empty and refilled it. She smiled briefly and sipped, then continued.

"By that time, they'd turned their entire civilization into a killing machine. They weren't just wiping anyone they happened to run into, they were out looking for other intelligences to cide. They were even sending out survey ships expressly to find new targets—which is what happened to us.

"One of their scouts got close enough to Sol to pick up some radio transmissions, and that scared hell out of them, because they'd never encountered another race more advanced than the early steam age, and their 'priesthood' had more or less decided that was a divine dispensation. When their scout commander realized he'd found a bunch of devils more advanced than any of the others they'd met, he abandoned the rest of his mission and headed straight home at max.

"When he got there, the Kangas decided they had to forget their usual strategy. They hadn't come up with an FTL com system, though they had FTL travel—of a sort—but the best speed they could manage was about five times light-speed, and the closest system with a heavy Kanga population was over a hundred light-years away. Not only that, but their scout's crew was so scared by what they were picking up—remember, by their standards they'd just found a whole race of horribly powerful demons—that they never came closer to Sol than twenty light-years, so what they were seeing was already twenty years old. It took the scout almost twenty-five years to get home with the news, and it would take them another thirty-plus years to send out their sampling ships just to *collect* specimens, much less take them home, produce a bug for us, *and* send it back out. Even if they modified their strategy by sending an entire research ship to develop the bug on-site, we'd have had almost eighty years to develop between the time those signals originated and the time they could get back to Solarian space again.

"They were scared, but they were still logical. Rather than risk warning us with a sampling mission or by hanging around in orbit with a research vessel, they decided to forget nice, neat biological solutions this once and rely on brute force. It would only take them another ten years or so to muster a fleet of warships, and taking the time to make sure they were loaded for draken seemed logical to them.

"But—" she grinned, a sudden, tigerish expression that struck him with a chill "—they made a mistake. They polated our rate of progress based on their own, and humans are *much* better gadgeteers than they are. Not only that, we've always been a bloodthirsty bunch. They'd fought their last real war with pikes and black powder, and they didn't have the least idea how military competition pressurizes R&D.

"By the time they got back to Sol, there were operations in the asteroids. Political relations were still colonies on Luna and Mars and large-scale mining pretty shaky, too, and all the promises not to militarize space had collapsed once there was a thriving presence in space to protect—or prey upon. Nobody had a real 'space navy,' but there were quite a few armed ships. Most of the colonies had some sort of rudimentary defensive systems, and Terra had some pretty advanced orbital defenses. Most of them were aimed at planetary threats, but the existence of armed spacecraft meant they'd been designed to shoot the other way, too."

She sipped more coffee, and he remembered what she'd said about being a 'histortech.' He could believe it; she had the air of someone expounding on a special interest area.

"They had FTL, but they were still using reaction drives. Basically, they used what you'd call the Bussard ram principle to accelerate in normal-space before they translated." She paused at his puzzled expression, then shrugged. "I can explain that later—right now, just remember that they managed interstellar travel by first accelerating and then ducking into another dimension where the velocity attained in this one is effectively accelerated to a multiple of light-speed, then dropping back into normal-space and decelerating. That's one reason the trip would take them so long; they needed to accelerate in normal-space before they could kick in their FTL systems. Okay?"

"If you say so," he said dubiously.

"We manage things a lot better now," she assured him, "but all this was four or five hundred years ago, remember." She paused again, a brief stab of pain and loss showing in her eyes. "Anyway," she said softly, "four hundred years from when I got into this mess.

"At any rate, they put together a fleet and sent it off. Of course, a fleet of Bussard rams produces a hell of a lot of light when it decelerates, and they had to start decelerating well short of Sol. Terran astronomers spotted them while they were still over a year out and realized someone was coming—a lot of someones, in fact. We're a pretty nasty and suspicious lot ourselves, and it was possible our visitors weren't friendly, so prudence suggested sending somebody out to see.

"But if they *were* friendly, none of the Terran blocs wanted their rivals getting in first and making some kind of private deal with them. There was a lot of time pressure, but they got themselves organized in a hurry and sent out an 'international' welcoming party made up of ships from all the major power blocs." She flashed that tigerish grin again. It really made her look much less like a teenager, he thought uneasily.

"The Kangas freaked. There they were, ready to smash a bunch of people they expected to find fooling around with atmospheric aircraft, and instead they were being intercepted by ships using a nuclear-powered torch drive! It never occurred to them that we might even consider the possibility of peaceful contact—their minds don't work that way. They were still six months out when our ships came into weapon range and they opened fire.

"They wiped us, of course, but we hadn't sent totally unarmed ships, and we got a couple of them, as well. That *really* upset them, because they were still decelerating, which committed them to entering our system—either that, or they had to duck back into alpha-space, bypass us, stop, get back up to speed on a home-bound vector, and come back in another seventy or eighty years. And who knew what we'd be capable of by then?

"So they decided to carry out their original plan, and it was our side's turn to freak. I've never seen a Bussard ship myself. They've been obsolete for centuries now, but they were big bastards, and they had a lot of them. Terra assumed the worst, and it's amazing how friendly enemies can get in those stances. By the time the Kangas were down to maneuvering speed and passing Neptune, the major power blocs had decided to bury their differences.

"The Kanga force was two or three times as strong as they'd expected to need—I said they were logical—but their estimate had been too low. Their ships were big, but their mass-to-drive ratio was poor, and the sides were a lot more even than they'd planned or we thought. They never did get any planet-busters into range of Terra, but they wiped every human in the asteroid belt and did the same for Mars. We lost every regular warship and most of the merchant conversions we had, but only a few of their light attack craft got close enough to hit Terra, and they didn't have anything much bigger than a couple of megatons."

Aston felt his remaining fringe of hair trying to stand on end at how casually she used the term "megatons."

"We stopped them, but they killed four and a half billion people, most of them civilians. Of course, from the Kanga viewpoint, there's no such thing as 'civilians' or 'noncombatants,' but we were pretty ired."

Her words were light again, but her eyes were not.

"We learned a lot from the Kangas' wreckage. Not as much as we would have liked, but more than they probably expected we could. Unfortunately, the Kangas *are* logical, and they'd left one ship out where we couldn't get at it. As soon as it saw how things were going, it headed home at max.

"The result back home when it got there was pandemonium—and it must have been even worse because they didn't have any samples of *our* technology. But they did have a head start, and they'd been working hard at R&D ever since they sent their first fleet out, just in case. They knew none of their FTL transports had been captured intact, so they figured we hadn't gotten any samples of their multi-dee—that's what makes FTL travel possible—but they were only half right. Their long-range missiles used a cruder form of the same principle, and we *did* get our hands on a couple of them.

"Anyway, they went to crash building rates to put together another fleet, and they had eighteen major planetary populations and an undamaged deep-space industrial capacity. They were scared, but they got over their panic when they started puting the odds. Besides, God was on their side.

"Meanwhile, we were doing the same thing. It was obvious we couldn't go after them—we didn't even know where they were—but it was equally obvious that power projection over interstellar distances was a difficult proposition. We didn't have to be able to match them one-for-one or even one-for-ten to defend ourselves.

"To make a long story short, we were ready when they came back. In fact, our weapons were actually more advanced than theirs—not by much, but by a little—and we blew hell out of them. We even got a few prisoners, though Kangas don't last long in finement. They can't handle being captured by 'devils'; it does something to them, and they just stop living.

"But we got a little nav data—enough to realize some of what we were up against. We couldn't quite grasp that *any* sort of negotiations would be impossible, but we knew it was going to be tough. The one good point was that we seemed to be better scientists—which we are, up to a point. They hadn't realized how well we do in physics and the inorganic sciences; we didn't realize how well they do in the biosciences.

"By the time we'd wiped their second attack force, we had better n-space drives and more efficient multi-dees than they did, and we sent out a task force of our own. It surprised the nearest Kanga outpost and captured the planet, but at that point technology allowed combat only in normal-space at sublight speeds, and they got away with a few prisoners of their own. We'd only been in possession for about twenty years when they came back with the first of their bio weapons."

She paused, and her face lost all expression for just a moment. She sat very still, then she gave herself a little shake.

"The planet was Midgard," she said in a quiet, washed-out voice. "In many respects, it wasn't all that nice a place—it's on the chilly and dry side by Earth standards—but it's quite capable of sustaining human life. We needed the living space, and even if we hadn't, it was the only Kanga outpost we knew about. We figured they'd want it back, and we needed something short of Sol that would hold their attention and keep them busy outside of any possible attack range of Earth. So we decided to colonize the place, and we had almost two million civilians and one hell of a military presence on it by the time they got around to the expected counterattack. We blew them apart, but not before they dusted the planet—" she looked straight into his eyes "—and killed over ninety-nine percent of its population."

She paused again, and he swallowed as he realized she was talking about her planet and, from the way she spoke, her own ancestors. He shivered at the thought and looked away. His pipe had gone out, and he busied himself relighting it to give her time.

"That shook us up," she continued after a moment, "but it made our options pretty clear. Our total casualties were far lower than from their first attack on Sol, but it seemed worse, somehow. Partly because it was the complete destruction of an entire population, but even more because the *way* it was done made it clear their intention was genocidal. After that, we began to understand—*really* understand—what we were up against. There wasn't any more talk about negotiating, and anybody who'd thought we were already on a total war footing found out better.

"I won't bore you with the details of four centuries of fighting. They never have caught up with us in physics, and we never have caught up with them in the organic sciences. They're a bit ahead of us in chemistry, too, but we've got a huge edge in weapons, computer science, FTL technology—all the hardware aspects of fighting a war in space—and we're better strategists. Their caution works against them, and we're a lot more tuitive. They can kill any planet they can range on, but so can we, and *our* advantages mean that they've been pushed onto the defensive. They have to get past the fleet to attack our planets, and we've shoved them further and further back with every generation. By now, they're penned up in just three star systems, and we've got them pretty much blockaded there."

She paused again, and he cocked his head to one side.

"Excuse me," he said, "but I don't quite understand. If you're so much better fighters, how have they lasted this long?"

"They aren't stupid, Ster Aston," she said grimly, "just xenophobic and fanatical. Somewhere fairly early in the fighting, they decided that some fundamental difference in the way our minds work gave us an inherent advantage. It must have galled them, but the fact was that we were better fighters, and they were losing. Not all the time, and not all the battles, but most of the big ones. So they decided to do something about it."

"But what *could* they do?"

"They used their own strengths. If we had some kind of inbred advantage, they had to acquire the same advantage for themselves. So they built a race of cyborgs."

"Cyborgs?"

"Cyborgs. Machines with organic brains."

"But if the problem was inbred—"

"I didn't say machines with *Kanga* brains, Ster Aston," she said harshly. "They had prisoners of their own, and they're fantastic biological engineers. They developed a method to build total obedience into an organic brain. Then they operated on their prisoners."

Aston stared at her, stomach heaving as the implications sank in.

"Yes, Ster Aston," she said coldly. "They decided, in your idiom, to set a thief to catch a thief. If humans could out-think and out-fight them, they needed humans of their own. Their cyborgs were never quite as good as having regular humans, and they've never trusted them entirely. Strategy and sensitive research are still in strictly Kanga hands, but tactics and actual combat are another matter. Their cyborgs are completely expendable, and obedience is engineered into them; they can't even argue about being expended, but they're very good at what they do. By now, the Kangas are actually 'farming' to produce them." She looked ill, but her voice was level. "They clone human brains to produce the things that do their fighting against other humans."

"My God," he whispered, holding his cold pipe.

"God had very little to do with it," she said softly, "and the hell of it is that the cyborgs hate us even more than the Kangas do. We're the ones who keep killing them, but, in a sense, we're also related, and it horrifies and disgusts both of us. They're slaves to the Kangas; even if we wanted to, we could never forget that, and they know it. We didn't create them, and we're not the ones who enslaved them, but they know exactly how horrible we find them, and they feel— and share—our hate.

"When we first realized what they were, we tried to overcome our disgust," she said even more softly. "We really tried, but it didn't work They're fighting machines—by our standards, their human brains are psychopathic, because the Kangas wanted totally obedient, highly skilled, utterly conscienceless killing machines. They got them, too. The first time we cornered some of them and tried to talk to them, they slaughtered our entire contact team—over a hundred people— even though they *knew* we had enough troops and firepower to exterminate them.

"In two hundred years, every single confrontation with them has ended in death—ours or theirs. They're poor, bastardized monsters, but they *are* monsters. We can never let ourselves forget that. I think that's why we never call them 'cyborgs.'"

"What do you call them?" he asked, his voice barely above a whisper.

"We call them Trolls, Ster Aston," she said quietly, "and one of them shot down my interceptor and killed my crew. That's what's loose on your planet—and somehow, we have to find it and kill it."

CHAPTER EIGHT

Ice spicules danced on a howling wind. They'd rattled on the tough alloy, at first; now they only burnished a thick and growing cocoon of ice. The metal skin within exactly matched the temperature of its icy coat, and the interior of the hidden vessel was scarcely warmer. The last surviving Troll sent another surge of current through the heat field that kept his light receptors clear as he watched the gray and white and black-rock bitterness of Antarctica.

This place suited him. It was a fitting place to pause and consider. There was no fear of discovery, for there was no life here, no slightest living thing to disturb his gloating triumph, nor did the chance of distant observation concern him. The technology which had surprised his *Shirmaksu* masters had surprised him, as well, and he had no more data on this world's current capabilities than they did, for all that his organic ancestors had sprung from it. But what had happened gave him a crude benchmark; and his own sensors had confirmed the presence of several hundred small, obviously artificial objects in orbit about it. It seemed that these humans had primitive spacecraft—of a sort, at any rate—and the sheer numbers of satellites, coupled with the humans' extensive (if crude) weaponry and military readiness, argued that there were probably optical and thermal reconnaissance platforms among them. Not that it mattered now. The astonishing rapidity of their response to what had to have been a totally unexpected threat had surprised him as much as it had his masters, however much it galled him to admit that, but they would not surprise him again, and their satellites would not see him here. They couldn't, for there was no longer anything to see, now that his fighter had merged with the ice and snow, and there was no heat to detect, for he had no need of heat.

The moaning wind pleased him in a way he could not have defined even to another of his own kind. It was like a kindred soul—powerful and pitiless. Its icy breath didn't bother him. Indeed, cold and heat were merely abstract concepts to him, as meaningless as weariness and as alien as pity. Pain he understood, for that was how the *Shirmaksu* "programmed" his kind. Direct stimulation of the pain and pleasure centers communicated displeasure and grudging approval quite well, he thought coldly, savoring his hate anew.

Yet what he felt now was a special sort of pleasure. It hadn't been inflicted upon him; he had won it for himself. It was . . . personal.

He watched the wind of the driving blizzard and quivered with a sort of cerebral ecstasy. He was free. Obedience to the *Shirmaksu* had been engineered into him, reinforced by agonizing training and long habituation, yet there were no *Shirmaksu* now for him to obey. The *cralkhi*'s missile had done that for him, had snapped the intangible and thus unbreakable chains which had bound him for so long.

The Troll hadn't recognized that immediately. He'd pursued the *cralkhi* to its death, obedient to his masters' final orders, before he realized there were no more masters. Not that he would have spared the *cralkhi* even if he had considered the gift it had given him. The *cralkhi* had been his enemy, its interceptor the only force which might have challenged him, its brain the only source of information which might endanger him. Logic had decreed that the *cralkhi* must die, but he hadn't needed logic. Hatred was sufficient.

He closed another circuit in the fighter which was his body, and a recorded playback came to life. He gloated as he watched his missiles tracking in on the *cralkhi* fighter, savoring in memory the eagerness which had filled him as he pursued his wounded prey, knowing the life of its pilot was his to snuff. There had even been a stab of bittersweet regret as he armed his power guns—regret that this moment of supreme triumph must end, that it couldn't be relished forever.

He watched the playback as the interceptor's stern shattered under his fire and his instruments probed for signs of life. He'd followed the plunging wreckage, scanning it carefully as he held it locked in his sights, prepared to blast it into vapor, but there had been no life aboard it, only rapidly dying electronic systems. He'd followed it for a few moments, torn between an atavistic desire to rend and mutilate his prey and a matching need to proclaim his contempt by letting it tumble to destruction without further effort on his part. Disdain had won—disdain and a cold, gloating joy at the thought that the gravity of the very planet the *cralkhi* had died to save would complete its demolition.

It wasn't until that moment that the incandescent awareness of freedom had struck. That had puzzled him in retrospect...until he realized that even the hope of self-rule had been cut away by the bioengineers who'd designed him. The very possibility of independence, however passionately longed for, had been made unthinkable, but now the unthinkable had happened.

The fiery intoxication had been almost too much. It had flared though him like a voltage surge, burning in his brain like the heart of a nova. Free. He was *free*...and omnipotent. Free to do anything *he* wanted. For the first time, he could satisfy his own desires, know that whatever he did was done of his own volition and will.

His instruments had shown him the crude seagoing vessels which had devastated his squadron, and he'd hungered to swoop down upon them, raking them with his power guns, breaking and vaporizing them in an orgiastic satisfaction of his hatred for all things human. But he hadn't. They had surprised him once, and he would not risk *his* existence needlessly now—not now that it was his existence. There would be time enough for vengeance.

If he hadn't expended his last nuclear warheads killing the *cralkhi* things might have been different, but he had. He would not venture into the reach of these primitives' weapons again until he knew more of their capabilities. The exultant knowledge that at last his technology was immeasurably superior to the only humans against whom it might be pitted was tempered by a cold determination not to squander that advantage. Besides, he'd needed time to think.

It was ecstasy to plan, to be free to weigh advantage and disadvantage and plot his own course. The once heady satisfaction of devising tactics to execute a *Shirmaksu* strategy—even one that killed humans—paled beside it.

He knew what his masters had come here to do, he mused, watching the ice storm. Their ultimate defeat had become inevitable.

The humans had broken them and driven them back, back, ever further back. From eighteen heavily populated star systems and twice as many with outposts and small colonies, the *Shirmaksu* had been hammered back into only three besieged systems. The human devils might break through and smash the last *Shirmaksu* life from the cosmos at any time, and so his creators had embarked on one last throw of the dice—a throw even he was forced to admit held a touch of desperate genius. They had awakened their own destruction when they attacked Sol, for they could not defeat humanity. To preserve themselves, then, they must prevent that race from coming into being, and so they had committed themselves to accomplish just that.

They had died, but, in a sense, they had not yet failed, for he still lived. He had no doubt that he could encompass the death of humanity if he so chose. He'd expended his stock of nuclear weapons, true, but he retained the resources of his fighter. It was tiny by the standards of FTL capital ships, but it massed ten thousand tons—ten thousand tons of weapon systems and science five hundred years in advance of anything this puny planet could marshal against him.

But he had gained the splendor of free will. He could *choose* whether or not to destroy the human race, and that had stopped him. He hungered to crush mankind into dust, to vent his long and bitter hatred in apocalyptic violence. Yet if he did, he would complete the mission of the race which had created him and defiled him with the unbreakable fetters it had set within his mind. He hated humanity with every fiber of his being, yet the *Shirmaksu* had violated him, and even had he known what forgiveness was, he could never have forgiven that.

So he'd hesitated, caught between his own craving for destruction and his bitter determination not to work his masters' will, and as he hesitated a new thought had come to him. It was not one he could have conceived as the *Shirmaksu*'s slave, but now...now it was different. There was a way, he realized. A way to avenge himself upon both of the races he hated.

The *Shirmaksu* who had created him had not yet been born. He didn't know what would happen if he confronted the *Shirmaksu* who now existed and they ordered him to obey. Would his old programming exert itself? Would he lose the precious freedom he'd never suspected might be his? Yet even as he thought that, he realized it did not matter. The *Shirmaksu* of *this* time had no more inkling of his existence than they did of humanity's, and how could they order him to obey them if they didn't know they might succeed?

And as he thought that, he remembered what had happened when first *Shirmaksu* and human had met. With no more than their own crude resources, the humans had fought their attackers to a stand and then counterattacked. What might they not be able to do if they had access to the technology aboard his fighter? With eighty years to prepare and the advantage of a headstart from five centuries in their own future?

No stimulation his masters had ever visited upon his pleasure centers could match the sheer delight of that thought. With such an edge, humanity would smash the *Shirmaksu* with contemptuous ease. The war wouldn't last four hundred years; it would be over in less than ten.

But best of all, humanity need not win, either. Oh, no, for they would have lost before the first alien vessel entered their solar system.

He'd buried his ship in the antarctic ice, determined to search his glorious plan for flaws, and he had found none.

There were risks, of course, but not insurmountable ones. Destruction would be easier and simpler, but not nearly so satisfying. And once freed of Shirmaksu dominion, he combined the best of machine and organic life; he was effectively immortal, and there was time in plenty.

There was only one true danger, he decided. Numbers. He was so tremendously outnumbered by the humans crawling about their putrid ball of rock and mud. If they should realize what was happening, they might overwhelm him by the sheer force of those numbers. He could kill thousands, even millions, with his superior weapons, but once he stood revealed and began killing his glorious plan would be doomed.

Yet the chance of discovery was minute. They knew of his coming, but not who and what he was, and there was no way they could learn unless he slipped and told them. The only beings who might have given them that information were decaying tissue in the depths of their oceans. They might suspect, but when there were no more overt signs of his presence, they would shrug and put him out of their minds. They would forget to suspect or to fear, and then he would take them. He would avenge himself upon them in full measure for everything they and the *Shirmaksu* had done to him.

And if he failed? The idea that *he* might fail was alien to him, almost as unreal and abstract as his understanding of the concept of love, yet defeat was not totally beyond his visualization. The *Shirmaksu* believed—or *had* believed; he wondered if they still did?—in their ultimate, predestined triumph. They had no equivalent of the human belief in a capricious fate, and they had instilled no such belief in him, but he'd witnessed the chain of improbabilities which had led his masters to failure and death. It was not beyond the realm of possibility that such a thing might overtake him.

But if it did, the human race could still die. He lacked the biological expertise which had been his masters', but he knew how to ensure the death of mankind. If he must, he could at least sate his hatred on one of the two races he hated.

Had he been truly human, he would have smiled at the thought.

He had never had a name, nor needed one, but that was before he won his freedom. Now he toyed with the concept from a new perspective, wondering what name he should take. "Master," he decided, or perhaps simply "God." But if chance decreed that he could have neither of those, he would settle for a third.

He would settle for "Death."

CHAPTER NINE

Dick Aston leaned back, propped his heels on the lower arc of *Amanda*'s stainless-steel wheel, and watched pipe smoke swirl away on a brisk quartering breeze. A battered old cap, visor crowned with golden leaves, protected his bald head from the sun, and cold foam trailed down the chill aluminum can in his hand, dripping from his fingers. All in all, he could not have presented a more idyllic picture.

But the eyes behind his dark glasses were far from relaxed.

He took the pipe from his mouth and sipped beer, feeling his bone-deep weariness, and grinned wryly. There'd been a time, he reminded himself. A time when he was brash and confident, full of his own immortality and the endless vitality of youth, able to go forever with only occasional catnaps and proud of it. But that was long ago, before he'd experienced reality. He'd seen too much dying since, dipped too close to extinction himself, to believe in anyone's immortality. Too many tough, confident young men had perished. He'd grown less brash with every death, and it dismayed him to realize how long it had been since he had even thought of himself as young. He knew he was fit and hard for his age, but that was the crucial difference between him and the self he once had been. "For his age" said it all.

How much sleep had he gotten in the last two weeks? It must be more than it felt like, given that he could keep his eyes open at all, but probably not by all that much. First there'd been the nasty weather, then the wild confusion of what he'd come to think of as The Night, followed by the long, grueling drag of nursing his patient... Ludmilla.

She had a name, he reminded himself—Ludmilla—and she was no longer simply his patient. She was a person, one whose insane tale he believed implicitly. Her story was what had stolen *last* night's sleep as she poured out the details of the endless Kanga-human war and the epic voyage which had brought her here.

That was what had truly convinced him. He was a trained interrogator, and though he'd asked few questions, he'd never listened more intently in his life, and he hadn't heard a single discrepancy, a single inconsistency. He remained amazed that someone of her youth could hold colonel's rank, but the understated way she'd described her own actions told him she'd earned it. And she was older than her years. There was a shadow in her eyes when she described the death of BatDiv Ninety-Two, but it was buffered by the familiarity of dealing with loss. He saw it in her face, in her ability to laugh despite the pain, and he recognized it. He'd seen it in too many other faces . . . including his own.

But what—

His thoughts broke off as Ludmilla climbed cautiously up the companion. She poked her head out the hatch, wind plucking at her long, chestnut hair, and studied him with those calm, knowing eyes in that absurdly young face.

"May I come up?" she asked in the clipped accent that could not make her voice less musical and no longer even sounded quite so strange.

"If you feel up to it," he agreed, and she grinned wryly at his oblique reminder. She'd reached the end of her energy with unnerving suddenness last night—or early this morning, depending upon one's perspective—and virtually collapsed back into the bunk. Aston was still unsure which surprised him more: the amount of vitality she'd displayed, or the abrupt way it had flagged.

"Thank you," she murmured, and climbed the rest of the way on deck. She still wore only his tee-shirt, and it rose high on her firmly muscled thighs. He sternly suppressed a sudden internal stirring.

"Do you swim?" he asked.

"Pretty well." She looked around the limitless stretch of ocean and gave a little headshake. "Not on this scale, though."

"In that case," he said, and held out a life jacket. She took it gingerly, holding it up and examining it thoughtfully. He started to explain, then stopped and watched her mind working for a moment before she slipped it on and tightened the straps about her.

"This, too," he went on, and she donned the safety harness with more assurance, for she could see how his was secured. "House rules," he explained. "Whenever you're on deck, you wear both of those. It may not seem like we're moving all that fast, but. if you went over the side and had to catch up swimming, you'd soon find out differently."

"Aye, aye, Sir." She smiled, but her words were sincere. So, he thought. She understood the limitations of her own expertise and how to take orders as well as giving them. That was more than he could say for some officers he'd met.

She sat in the other corner of the cockpit, leaning back into the angle of the transom, and breathed deeply. He felt a stab of irritated envy for her youthful vitality, and knowing it was strengthened by his own reaction to her naked, shapely legs and the way the tee-shirt molded itself to her under her bulky life jacket shamed him slightly.

"This is nice," she said wistfully. "I always wanted to learn to sail, but Midgard's too dusty, and by the time I got off-planet I was too busy."

"It can be a lot less relaxing sometimes, but days like this make up for a lot," he agreed. He remembered the can in his hand and half-raised it. "Would you like a beer?" he asked.

"No, thanks. I'm afraid alcohol doesn't agree with me." She gave a strange little smile, and he shrugged. Silence stretched between them—not tensely, but quietly. It was strange how comfortable he felt with this wanderer from an alien future, he thought.

"Have you decided to believe me?" she asked, breaking the silence at last.

"Yes," he replied without hesitation, and her shoulders relaxed minutely. It amused him, and he grinned. "What's the matter, Colonel? Did you expect me to ask the local witch doctor to exorcize you, instead?"

"Well, maybe just a bit," she admitted. "I tried putting myself in your place to see what I'd think. The answer wasn't very comforting."

"Be of good cheer. We happy primitives are just naturally credulous."

"Ouch! I think you just paid me back for that leader crap."

"Me?" He raised his sunglasses to give her the full benefit of his innocent expression. "You wrong me, Colonel!"

"Like hell," she snorted.

"Well, maybe just a bit," he said, deliberately using her own words as he slid the tinted lenses back in place. She made a face and slid more comfortably down onto the end of her spine. The tee-shirt rose higher, and he hastily transferred his attention to the wind-swollen spinnaker.

"So what do we do now, Ster Aston?" she asked.

"First," he said, "you explain what the hell a 'ster' is."

"Excuse me?" She blinked at him, then smiled. "Sorry. I suppose I ought to be saying *'Mister'* Aston, shouldn't I?"

"Thought so," he said thoughtfully. "You chop off syllables in the damnedest places, Colonel. I think that's one reason I believe you."

"But I'd better get over it."

"Why worry about it? No one's going to be too surprised if someone from the future sounds a little odd."

"That's the point—the fact that I'm alive can't be made public." Her intensity surprised him.

"Why not?"

"Unless your noises are a lot different from mine, that should be pretty obvious," she said tartly.

" 'Noises'?"

"Oh, damn! I mean your blabs." His eyebrows rose, and she made a frustrated face. "Your . . . newsies? reporters?" He nodded in sudden understanding, and she sighed in relief. "I know how ours would react if someone turned up from the *past*, and that Troll certainly has the capacity to tap your news networks."

"I see." He eyed her thoughtfully. "Why would that matter?"

"I wish I knew how it would affect his thinking," she said pensively. "As I said, Trolls aren't very sane by human standards, so I don't know what this one is planning, but I *do* know that he's certain I'm dead." He raised an eyebrow, and her lips tightened. "No Troll would have passed up the chance to kill me; that's one of the less pleasant things about them. One of them turned back to kill my com officer when she blew out, even though he knew it would give me a chance to kill him. No, St—*Mister*—Aston. He was positive I was dead, or he would have blown *Sputnik* apart to make certain."

"So why didn't he do it anyway?"

"Arrogance, I think. We don't know enough about how their minds work, but one thing we do know is that they seem to pride themselves on their own infallibility. Only they do it in their own skitzy way almost as if they're out to prove something to the Kangas."

"In what way?"

"Kangas are logical, first, last, and always, and any Kanga would have wiped the wreckage just to be cert. A Troll will kill anything that even looks like it might be alive, but if they decide it's dead, they won't attack. It's almost like . . . like a way to show contempt for an enemy."

She paused for a moment, as if searching for a better way to put it, then shrugged.

"Anyway, we try to play the angles when it comes to saving our people's lives, and *Sputnik* was equipped with a new escape program." Her eyes darkened with a trace of sadness. "From what you've told me, it worked."

"How?"

"Hm?" She shook herself. "Oh. The techies built in a jammer to block Kanga scanners and programmed the escape computer for a delayed blow-out. You said he followed me down for a while?" He nodded, and she shrugged again. "He was probably scanning the wreckage to make sure we were all dead—and that's exactly what his systems told him. Then *Sputnik* waited till the last minute to zerch herself and blow the cockpit. The computers must have spotted you and homed on your boat." She smiled tightly. "If we'd been in deep space, the program would've aborted and I'd be dead. There's no point evading in an environment where long-term survival is impossible, and Fleet doesn't want to flash the capability when it won't do any good."

"So he's certain you're dead," Aston mused. "But how would it affect his plans if he found out you aren't?"

"I don't know," she said, frustration sharpening her tone. "Look, the Kangas came back to wipe us before we could become a threat, and he damned well knows it. But he's in a position no Troll's ever been in; there aren't any Kangas to order him around, and he 'knows' he personally killed the last humans from his own time, which means no one in 2007 can have the least scan of who he is or what he wants. For the first time in history, a Troll may be free to make his own decisions." She paused for a long moment, her eyes unfocused as she thought.

"Who can say what that means?" she continued finally. "The Kangas' programming may carry over on him, or he may be entirely on his own. What I *suspect* is that he's in a position to make plans of his own and that he's still considering his options. What I *know* is that if he finds out he didn't kill me after all, he'll feel threatened. In which case—"

"In which case," Aston interrupted thoughtfully, "he may do something we'll all regret."

"Exactly." She shivered slightly. "You have no concept of what his hate is like, Mister Aston, and of everyone in the galaxy, he hates me most. Add that I'm the one person on this planet who really knows anything about him . . ." She gave a tiny toss of her head. "He'll come after me," she said softly, "and he won't care how many other people he kills to get me."

Aston felt his shoulders tighten and forced them to relax. The bright sunlight felt icy, and he suddenly realized his inner chill was personal as well as intellectual. It was important to him that this young woman survive, and not simply because of the information source she represented.

"All right," he said, forcing himself to sound cheerful, "we just have to make sure none of our 'noises'—" he grinned as he used her term "—find out about you."

"It goes a bit further than that, Mister Aston. You see—"

"Please," he interrupted again. "We've introduced ourselves, and my name's Richard—Dick, to my friends. I wish you'd use it."

"All right, Dick." She smiled, and something inside him gave a little shiver he hadn't felt in years. "But only if you stop calling me 'Colonel.' My name is Ludmilla—or, as you'd say, Milla, to my friends."

"Thank you, Milla," he said, careful to keep his smile friendly, without a trace of the attraction he felt. Damn it, she was a third his age—too damned young for the thoughts he was thinking. He tried to tell himself it was being alone with her, but he knew better. Her features were too severe ever to be beautiful, but they had something far more important. They had strength and character, and her eyes *were* beautiful . . . and wise. Too wise for her years. . . . He shook himself and hoped she'd noticed nothing.

Or did he?

"You were saying something about going further?" he prompted.

"Um?" She blinked. "Oh, yes. It's not quite as simple as just clamping on security . . . Dick." She gave that same little toss of her head. "You see, the Kangas did quite a bit of tinkering with the Trolls. We're not quite certain, but a lot of evidence suggests the Kangas themselves are at least rudimentary telepaths. At any rate, they tried to build that ability into the Trolls."

"It's *telepathic*?" Despite everything else she'd said, that thought shocked him.

"I'm afraid so. Apparently they meant to give them a com channel we couldn't jam, but it didn't work out too well. Troll brains are still basically human, and about a third of all normal humans can tap into their mental net if they know it's there. None of us can transmit, as it were, but we can 'hear' them doing it, if we know they're out there to listen to. I understand it's not a very . . . pleasant thing to do, but it means they can't use their 'secure com' without being overheard, so it never gave them the advantages the Kangas apparently hoped for."

"Wait a minute." Sick suspicion, tightened his throat. "If we can 'hear' them, can they—?"

"They can," she replied grimly. "Worse, they can influence human thoughts and attitudes. We found that out the hard way. If you don't know to watch for it, they can really warp you out. The number of people who can realize what's happening on their own is low, too. Very low." Her face grew even grimmer.

"We're lucky in at least two respects, though. First, a single Troll doesn't have much range—no more than a few hundred kilometers. They have a greater reach when several combine, but their touch gets a lot more evident when they do. And, secondly, I'm *not* one of the people who can tap them, so our Troll shouldn't be able to tap me, which means he can't pick me up to know I'm still alive. I just hope he can't read *you*, either."

"You and me both, lady," he said uneasily. "But how in hell are we supposed to know?"

"I've been thinking about that," she answered slowly. 'There's a standard test, back home. I know you don't have the technology we do, but your people can do brain scans, can't they?"

"That depends on what you mean by 'brain scan,'" he said carefully.

"Damn," she muttered. "This language problem is terrible. I'm never certain I'm saying what I think I am!"

"Don't worry," he told her dryly. "We'll be in the same boat—if you'll pardon the pun—when we hit England."

"What?"

"Never mind. Just tell me what this brain scan is supposed to scan."

"Brain waves," she said. "Oh, back home it's all one procedure that also analyzes cellular structure and all the rest, but it's the brain waves that matter."

"That *sounds* like an EEG," he said. She raised her eyebrows. "An electroencephalogram," he explained. "It measures electrical charges in the brain."

"Good!" Her face brightened and she nodded vigorously. "There's a distinctive spike in the alpha waves for people who can't hear the Trolls—and the reverse, we think."

"Do you mean to tell me," he demanded, "that we have to run an EEG on anyone we consider telling about you?"

"Of course." She seemed surprised. "What's the problem?"

"'What's the problem?' How the hell are we supposed to convince someone to have an EEG run without even telling him why?"

"Wait a tick." She cocked her head. "Back home it takes about two minutes and it's part of any medicheck. I gather that's not the case here?"

"No," he said with commendable restraint, "it's not." He went on to explain the procedure, and it was her turn to look astonished.

"Good Lord! I've never heard of anything so primitive!"

"We're a pretty primitive bunch, Milla," he said plaintively, "but you're not going to make a lot of friends if you keep reminding us of it."

"Oops." She put a hand on his forearm and squeezed gently. "I'm afraid I've got a bigger mouth than I thought."

"Don't worry," he reassured her, patting her hand in what he fondly thought was an avuncular fashion. "We are primitive by your standards, I guess, but if you're right about how important it is to blend in, you're going to have to work on attitudes as much as speech patterns."

"I know." She smiled at him, and the warmth of her expression reached deep inside him. "Anyway, if we can figure out how to arrange it, all we have to do is run one of these—EEGs?—" she used the unfamiliar term hesitantly, and he nodded "—on me and use it as a comparison base." She frowned. "I *think* it should be fairly simple. I know what my scan pattern looks like, and I know which spike to watch for. I only hope this EEG is similar enough to let me orient myself."

"I guess we'll just have to cross that bridge when we come to it," he said slowly. He became aware that her hand was still on his forearm and tried to disengage himself unobtrusively. But she tightened her grip, and he stopped and looked up to meet her eyes.

It was a mistake. Those eyes were not, he thought after a moment, what he would have expected from such a young woman. Their incredibly clear, darkly blue depths *understood*. There was a soft almost-twinkle in them, a sort of gentle teasing he almost grasped laid over a bittersweetness he couldn't begin to fathom. They held neither the embarrassment nor the unintentional cruelty of surprise. he might have expected from one so young. And, perhaps most surprising of all, they showed no rejection, not even the gentle nonresponse of someone trying to avoid hurting him for his ridiculous interest.

He was caught. He couldn't recall ever seeing anything quite like her understanding expression, and it was hard to remember hers was the face of a woman who'd killed—killed repeatedly—in the performance of her duty. *He* had killed, sometimes at a range so close he had smelled his victim's sweat before he struck, and he knew it had marked him inside. He hoped it hadn't made him callous or cold, but he knew it hadn't left him untouched, and he'd often suspected it must show. Even if it didn't, he'd never thought of himself as a ladies' man—certainly no one had ever accused him of being handsome, and age and more than his fair share of scars hadn't improved things. But those young-old eyes seemed to look past externals, totally free of rejection or condemnation.

"Milla," he said finally, "I think—" he gripped her wrist gently and removed her hand from his forearm "—that I should be ashamed of myself."

"Why? I've seen how hard you're working at being a gentleman, but you shouldn't strain yourself. I'm flattered that you enjoy looking at me—why does it bother you?" She asked the question simply, and his face reddened.

"Because of what I'm thinking when I do it." He straightened his shoulders. "You're a stranger here. You've lost everything you ever knew—your friends, your world.... And I'm fifty-nine years old, Milla. You don't need an oversexed geriatric lech trying to—"

He broke off in astonishment at her totally unexpected reaction. It was laughter. Not cutting, dismissive laughter, but soft, genuine amusement... touched, he realized, with more than just an edge of world-weary sorrow that sat strangely on her fresh, young face.

"I'm sorry, Dick," she said, and her lovely voice was soft. She touched his cheek before he could draw back, and those surprisingly strong fingers were gentle. "I'm not laughing at you—it's just that I keep forgetting how little you know about me." His expression showed his confusion, and her smile faded just a bit. "How old do you think I am, Dick?"

"What?" He looked at her for a moment, then frowned. "I don't know," he said slowly. "When I first saw you, I'd've said eighteen or nineteen. But with all you've seen and done, you have to be older than that, don't you?" He shook his head. She *couldn't* be much older than that. "Twenty-five?" he hazarded uncertainly, and she laughed again, almost sadly.

"Chronologically," she said, and something in her tone told him she was approaching the point with care, "and bearing in mind the time dilation effect of all the time I've spent at relativistic velocities, I am—or was when this started—a bit over a hundred and thirty." He swallowed, his eyes wide, and she gave him a wry smile. "Biologically, of course, I'm younger than that. Only eighty-three."

He stared at her. Eighty-three? *Impossible!* She was a *child!* He started to speak, then stopped, remembering the way she'd healed.

"Eighty-three?" he asked finally, amazed by how calm he sounded, and she nodded. "Just what is the average life span where you come from, Milla?"

"About a hundred and twenty," she said steadily, and he shook his head.

"You folks do all your aging in a hurry at the end or something?" he asked slowly.

"No. We age at the same proportional rate we always did. Or most of us do." She smiled, but for the first time, it did not touch her eyes. "You see, there was a reason I reacted so strongly when you suggested I might not be human, Dick. My grandfather survived the bio attack on Midgard, and I've heard a lot of that kind of thing because in a sense I'm *not* . . . not really."

"What—" He paused and licked his lips, even more shaken by the carefully hidden pain in her expression than by what she had just said. He reached out and touched her wrist. "What exactly does that mean?" he asked, forcing his voice to sound level.

"It's a bit complicated," she said, and her eyes thanked him for controlling his surprise. "You see, the Kangas were short on time, so instead of whipping up a new bug from scratch, they modified a nasty little parasite from Delta Pavonis. It wasn't so much a *biological* weapon as an *organic* one—and a nasty one, at that. Essentially, it was transmitted as an airborne bacteria and matured into a multicellular parasite rather like a Terran slime mold that invaded the respiratory and alimentary systems and used the circulatory system to get around its host's body. The parasite itself didn't look like much—just a double handful of protoplasmic ooze that scavenged its hosts for its own needs until they died of starvation or respiratory failure. If that didn't kill them, something very like cancer set in . . . and if anyone actually managed to survive *that*, the parasite simply went on growing until it clogged the arteries.

"The beauty of it, from the Kangas' viewpoint, wasn't just that it was lethal in so many different ways, but that they'd already been playing around with it for a couple of decades. They had its life cycle down pat and they'd been working on ways to aim it at specific DNA/RNA groups. That was what made it perfect for Midgard, because only one species on the planet used DNA at all: man. Actually, the biochemistry on Midgard isn't all *that* much different from Terra's, bearing in mind that we're talking two entirely different biospheres, but it uses a different complex of amino acids.

"So they revamped their parasite, accelerated its growth cycle, and dusted Midgard with it. Before we realized what they'd done, everyone on the planet was infected."

She looked out to sea, her face drawn, and Aston surrendered to a sudden impulse. He slid close to her and reached one arm around her. Not really in an embrace, far less a caress, but simply to let her know he was there. She looked back at him and smiled, her eyes suspiciously bright.

"Anyway," she said in a voice which was just too calm, "it performed to specs. According to the records, it was incredibly painful, too, so perhaps it was merciful that it killed so quickly in most cases. The actual death rate was something like 99.8%. Out of just over two million people, there were exactly 5,757 survivors.

"*But—*" her eyes flashed suddenly, and he saw the she-tiger in her smile once more "—they'd expected a hundred-percent kill. They should've gotten one, too. The best theory is that their little horror was unstable and they got an unexpected mutation. Whatever, one tiny batch didn't kill everyone it infected. Most of them, yes, but not all. And in the case of those it didn't kill, it became not a parasite, but a symbiote. Not only that, it piggy-backed itself onto their chromosomes."

"Symbiote? Piggy-backed? I'm afraid I'm not with you yet, Milla," he said gently.

"It's simple, really." She turned to face him fully. "I mass about sixty-six kilos, but I tip the scales at just under sixty-eight. The other two kilos is my symbiote."

"That . . . 'protoplasmic ooze' you mentioned?" he asked levelly.

"That's right. Only it's not as greedy as the original version." She smiled mirthlessly. "You might say it's a case of mutual advantage; it lives off my respiratory and digestive systems, and, in return, it protects its environment: me."

"Those wounds . . ."

"Exactly. It used its own mass to seal the ruptured tissues while it kickstarted the 'regular' healing process. It even pulled me out of shock by tightening itself down around my arteries. It takes good care of me, because without me *it* dies."

"My God," he murmured, his voice touched not with disgust but with awe, and she responded with a more natural smile.

"I can't complain," she said. "It does some other nice things, too.

It's infected my chromosomes. Effectively, I've got a couple of extra genes—dominants, I might add. And my symbiote's not a very gracious host; it eats anything—bacteria, viruses, whatever—that isn't tagged with 'our' genetic code. Which means, of course, that things like cancer and the common cold never bother me. On the other hand, even though I can eat just about anything in an emergency, my symbiote gives me fits over some things—like alcohol—and it also means that transurge would be all but impossible if I suffered catastrophic damage; unless they're cloned ahead of time, transplants don't carry the right genetic code, so they're rejected automatically. And if I'd been born with genetic birth defects, there wouldn't've been a damned thing that could be done for me—because the symbiote locks in the defect and won't let go. Even impacted wisdom teeth can be a real pain; they keep regenerating." She shrugged once more.

"On the other hand," she said softly, "it seems to regard old age the same way it does any other disease."

"You mean—?"

"I mean that every living organism eventually 'forgets' how to regenerate itself . . . except people like me." She grinned crookedly. "That's one reason some Normals don't much care for us. Polite people pretend not to know it, but there're names for us. 'Thuselah' is the kindest—from 'Methuselah'—but the others are a lot nastier. It's easy enough to understand. The people who use those names get old and die; we don't. Why shouldn't they resent us?"

"But surely not everyone does," he said, and she shook her head.

"No. Some Normals see our women as brood mares," she said grimly. "We're not all that fertile—which is probably just as well, since our ova regenerate, too, and we *stay* fertile—but we tend towards multiple births, and all our children are born with the symbiote and pass it to all *their* children. For some reason we haven't quite figured out, we're just as fertile with 'normal' humans as with each other, so some male Normals see us as a way to beget 'immortal' children of their own." She brushed hair out of her eyes, and this time he understood the half-wry, half-bitter wisdom of the old eyes in her young face.

"Listen to me! You must be thinking we're some kind of persecuted minority! We aren't, really, but sometimes we feel a bit hunted and harried. Only about half the Midgard population is Thuselah, and the percentage is a lot lower everywhere else—there're less than a billion of us even now. The funny thing is how many of us feel most at home in the service. Maybe it's because the chance of dying by violence is so much higher there. I know there was a time in *my* life when I felt unspeakably guilty because I knew I would never get old—at least, not as long as my symbiote holds out. I suspect we're drawn to the military out of a need to share the mortality of the non-Thuselahs."

She gave the tiny toss of her head he was coming to realize was associated with the shifting of mental gears.

"The Navy and the Corps are glad to get us, especially in the interceptor squadrons. Fighters are a youngster's game, and our bodies and reflexes stay young while we go right on gathering experience. The casualty rate catches up with most of us in the end, however good we are, but that's fair. No one makes us hang on and hang on the way we do. We . . . just do. It's almost addictive."

"I know," he said softly. She looked at him curiously, but he wasn't quite ready to talk about his own impending retirement from active duty . . . or what those duties had been. "I've known a lot of fighter jocks in my time," he said instead. "The one thing they all dread is getting too old to strap on a fighter."

"That's the way it is," she agreed with a sigh. "Actually, it's even more addictive for a Thuselah, because we tend to be so good at it. We've got extraordinary reflexes—again, thanks to our symbiotes. Our neural impulses move about twenty percent faster than the norm, so we can get more out of a fighter. And when we have to, we can go a long time without sleep, because our symbiotes scavenge the fatigue products out of our blood. In a real emergency, they actually supply us with energy. It's a survival tactic for them; they keep us going so we can *both* survive. Until they exhaust their own stored energy, anyway. Then they start scavenging our tissues to keep themselves alive. When that happens, we're in trouble. We go into a coma and, without someone to feed us—" she gave him a warm smile "—our poor, stupid symbiote goes right on eating until it kills us both."

"My God," he said again, regarding her with so much wonder she actually blushed.

"Doesn't it . . . bother you?" She sounded almost shy.

"Why should it?" he asked simply. "Oh, the idea will take some getting used to, and I'm not immune to envy, if that's what you mean, but I really don't think it *bothers* me." He gave her a smile of his own. "And you *are* human, you know—you're just the new, improved model. If I understand you right, this genetic modification is an acquired survival trait. Eventually, *everybody* will be like you."

"I think that part bothers some Normals even more than the fact that they personally don't share it," she admitted. "They think we're some sort of mutant monsters out to supplant 'true' humanity. There were some ugly incidents a couple of hundred years ago."

"Which only proves stupidity is endemic to the human condition even in the future," he said tartly, and won another smile from her.

"Maybe. But, Dick, this is important. If I get hurt again, make damned sure none of my blood gets into any open wounds."

"Why?" He asked the question, but inside he knew the answer already.

"Because the only way the symbiote can be transmitted—other than during conception—is by direct blood transfer," she said, her face serious, "and it's still deadly. That's why Normal women don't dare conceive by our men; a Thuselah embryo's blood carries the symbiote and kills a Normal mother. There were several cases in the early days, before we understood. With the best hospital facilities available—and I'm talking about *modern* hospitals, not the primitive facilities you have here and now—the survival rate is under five percent. Without them, it's less than one."

"I'll remember," he said softly.

"Good." She reached down and patted his hand where it rested on her ribs. "But in the meantime, youngster—" her smile turned into a grin and her eyes twinkled up at him "—don't worry about my tender years, all right? If you enjoy looking at me, do it."

"I'll try to bear your advanced age in mind," he said with a grin of his own, "but it's not going to be easy—and I hate to think what anyone who sees me doing it is going to think!"

"Oh, that's easy," she said airily. "They'll just think I'm your sugar momma." She produced the period slang with simple pride and looked rather puzzled when he began to laugh.

CHAPTER TEN

Morning sunlight flicked wavering patterns through the scuttles to dance on the overhead and glint on the tableware, and Ludmilla Leonovna, late of the Terran Marines, gripped her coffee cup two-handed, propped her elbows on the galley table, and sipped luxuriantly. Her chestnut hair was tousled, falling over the shoulders of another of Aston's tee-shirts. This one carried the Harley-Davidson eagle on its front—it had been a gift from his last XO, whose sense of humor had always been peculiar—and he had to admit it looked far better on her than it ever had on him. Besides, she seemed fascinated by its gaudiness, and she took an almost childlike delight in its bright colors.

It was odd, he thought, regarding her across the table. Despite her revelations, he hadn't really expected her to invite him into her bunk last night. Nor had he been prepared for the skill and passion she'd exhibited. No doubt he should have; anyone who looked like that and had enjoyed seventy years of practice must have had ample opportunity to get the basics down. Yet there'd been a curious vulnerability to her, as well. Almost a shyness—a sense that she was deliberately lowering some inner, secret barrier.

She was, he reflected, an incredibly complex individual. Her openness and readiness to cope with her bizarre situation masked it, but the complexity was there, hidden behind a multilayered defense, and he wondered if all "Methuselahs" were like that. Did dealing with shorter-lived "Normals" for decade after decade—watching friends age and fade while they themselves stayed endlessly young—create that sense of a guarded, utterly private core in all of them? And *could* a "Normal" truly be a "Thuselah's" friend? Even if she opened up with them, allowed them past her guard, could *they* accept the true depth of the differences between her and them? Intellectually, he could believe she truly was the age she claimed, but his emotions were still catching up with the information. It was an extraordinary sensation to realize that the superb young body sitting across his table from him belonged to a woman—no, he told himself, a *lady*—even older than he.

"Ummm." Another thought came to him, and he opened a locker and pulled out a rolled bundle. "I guess I better give this stuff back to you," he said, and extended her blood-stained flight suit.

"Messy," she said dispassionately, regarding the gory smears of her own dried blood, and her calm expression reminded him anew that this was a warrior. Then she unrolled the bundle, and the iron-nerved professional vanished in a gasp of anguish.

"Oh . . . my . . . *God!* What did you use?! A cleaver?"

This was his own first good look at it since he'd bundled the slashed garment into the locker on The Night, and he had to admit his surgery had been radical. It gaped raggedly open from neck to crotch, and she shook her head sadly as she traced the edge of the cut with a finger.

"Well, I had to get it off you some way," he said a bit defensively, "and I certainly didn't see any zippers."

"Zippers?" She flipped the flight suit over and touched a spot on the right shoulder. A razor-sharp seam opened down the back, and she looked up with a chiding expression. "Barbarian!" she snorted, and he felt an edge of relief at the laughter in her voice.

"I'm sorry," he said, "but it really seemed like the only way."

"I know, I know," she sighed. She touched something near the left cuff, and his eyes widened as a narrow section of fabric slid back to reveal a wafer-thin instrument panel reaching from cuff to elbow. It was covered with tiny lights and readouts, and very few of the lights were green. "Lordy," she murmured, bending over it. "You don't believe in fractionals."

"Just what did I do?" he asked curiously, craning his own neck for a better view.

"Oh, I'd say a megacred or so of damage," she replied. She touched a series of tiny switches, and about half the red lights turned amber. "Could be worse, though."

"What are you doing?"

"Running a diagnostic. Hmm...." She fell silent, absorbed in her task, and he possessed his soul in as much patience as he could while she concentrated. It was several minutes before she straightened with a sigh.

"It may not be too bad, after all," she said. "The com networks're shot to hell, but you missed the sensies."

"I what?" He looked at her in astonishment. "Just what the hell is that thing, anyway?"

"My flight suit," she said in surprise, then grinned slyly at his baffled expression. "Oho! Revenge is in my grasp, I see. Maybe I just shouldn't tell you about it."

"Try it and I'll toss you over the side," he growled.

"You and what army?" she said saucily, then held up a hand in laughing surrender as he started to rise. "Mercy! I'll talk—I'll talk!"

"Then give!"

"Gladly, but I'm not sure where to start." She thought for a moment. "I know more maintenance and field service than design theory, and I doubt your tech base'd be up to the details, even if I had more of them myself, but basically, this is what you'd call my space suit. It's a lot more capable than any suit your space program's come up with yet, though. You can think of it as a computer, and you won't be far wrong."

"A *computer*?"

"Cert. It's lousy with molycircs—molecular circuitry, that is. It has to be, because every square millimeter of the inner skin is fitted with sensors to monitor internal conditions. The outer skin's set up to reflect harmful radiation and absorb energy to power the internal circuits. The whole suit's designed to absorb and recycle body wastes, too—you can live in the thing for weeks, if you have to. Well, I guess I proved that on the flight here."

"But if it's a *space* suit, where's the oxygen?" he demanded, his eyes bright with fascination.

"Right here." She touched the fabric. "Oh, the older suits were a lot thicker—as much as a centimeter in places—but the technology's a lot better these days. The middle layer between the two boundary skins is one big mass of micro-vacuoles. You can think of them as millions of tiny little air and water and nutrient tanks, if that works better." She saw his incredulous expression and grinned. "It may not sound like much, but they're under something like twenty thousand atmospheres. As a matter of fact, the consumables ought to be just about full right now, since I didn't use any suit resources on the way in."

"No wonder it was so hard to cut," he said softly.

"Hard?" She snorted. "Dick, if the designer hadn't put some thought into it, you *couldn't* have cut it. I don't know whether you noticed, but this—" she traced the cut with her finger "—is almost exactly where anyone would cut it, assuming that they had to. They deliberately put most of the consumable storage around back and to the sides. All you cut through was about a quarter of the electronics." She grinned. "You managed to disconnect almost all my com channels, but you missed the sensies."

"Sensies?"

"Active and passive sensors. Visual, sonar, what you might think of as radar—all built in."

"My God. But your helmet went down with your ship, didn't it?"

"A helmet went down, but that was the neural feed to the flight controls. It'll serve as a helmet if you lose cabin pressure in combat, but you don't really need it. Look." She touched another apparently blank spot, and the suit's sleeves obediently extruded thin, tough gloves while a spherical shimmer danced above the shoulders. "One-way force field," she explained casually, sliding a hand through the shimmer. "The sensies run on direct neural feeds, so you don't even need readouts."

"I'm . . . impressed," he said finally, and she chuckled again.

"You should be. The damned thing's price tag is about ten percent that of an interceptor."

"I'm sorry I ruined it," he said almost humbly.

"Oh, it's not ruined," she assured him. "The nanotech features are off-line right now, and this level of repair would be a big enough energy hog that I'm not about to bring them up while it's running on stored power. But if I can plug into the right feed for a few hours, the self-repair systems'll take care of most of it."

He gawked at her. Somehow that impressed him even more than all the rest. He was almost glad her attention remained on her ravaged suit while he got his expression under control.

"Does it do any other tricks?" he asked finally.

"That's about it," she said with a shrug, and he shook his head slowly. He shouldn't be so surprised, he reminded himself. One of Christopher Columbus's seamen would be just as amazed by a Nimitz-class carrier or a *Seawolf* attack sub.

"I'm impressed," he said again, and she gave him a sympathetic smile, as if her thoughts had been paralleling his own. "But at least I figured out that this—" he tapped her holstered sidearm "—is a weapon. In fact, this thing—" he touched the necklet he'd removed from her throat "—is what *had* puzzled me most. Before you showed me Rex the Wonder Suit, that is."

The reference clearly eluded her, but she understood the context and gave him a gamine grin as she picked up the metal band.

"This? It's what you'd call my . . . dog tags?" She produced the term cautiously, and he nodded in sudden understanding. "It's a bit more than just who I am, though," she went on. "It's another little computer—only a *terabyte* or so of memory—with my whole life history. Medical records, service record, next of kin." She shrugged, toying with it. "I'm afraid it's useless now, though."

"Why?"

"Computer language has changed a bit in the last few centuries," she said dryly. "Besides, it's a plugin, not a stand-alone, and it's as full of molycircs as the suit. I doubt there's any way to interface. Once we kill the Troll—" he noticed that she didn't allow herself to use the word *if* "—I guess I'll turn it over to your techies, but I doubt they'll be able to make much out of it for quite a few years."

"Oh boy! I can just see myself trying to explain any of this stuff!" He shook his head. "The suit's busted and the computer can't be tapped . . . they won't even slow down on the way to the rubber room, Milla." She raised an eyebrow. "Rubber room—as in a padded cell in a home for the mentally unbalanced."

"Oh, I wouldn't worry." She picked up her gunbelt and headed for the companion. "I think we can convince them. Come on."

He followed her up on deck a bit slowly, his head spinning from the casual miracles she'd been describing. She was waiting for him, and he noticed that she'd strapped the weapon belt around her waist and drawn the gun. She examined it minutely.

"Did you play around with this?"

"Do I *look* like I'm stupid?" he demanded. "Don't answer that," he added hastily, and she shut her mouth with a grin. "In answer to your question, no. I couldn't figure out the controls."

"Wouldn't've helped if you had," she said. "It's persona-locked." He raised a resigned eyebrow, and she touched his shoulder. "Hang in, Dick," she said sympathetically. "Just remember that showing off my gadgets gives me a sense of security, okay? I mean, your whole world is as different for me as these things are for you."

"But at least you know roughly what happened, historically speaking."

"True. Anyway, persona-locked means it's keyed to me. I'm the only person who can fire it."

"Ever?" The possibility intrigued him.

"Yep. When I zerch out, they'll have to slag the thing, because it can't be rekeyed. Which, I might add, makes Fleet a bit touchy when we lose one—they aren't cheap and they can't be reissued. But at least it means there's no such thing as a black market in military small arms."

"I can see how that would follow."

"Okay." She touched two of the small side controls he'd noticed. "I'm setting it for single-shot at the lowest power setting—no point getting too dramatic." She raised the weapon, bringing it no higher than her rib cage and pointing it as easily as her finger. He recognized either a highly experienced shooter's stance or the position of a gross novice, and he rather suspected which it was.

"Watch," she said, and squeezed the firing stud.

Absolutely nothing happened as far as the weapon itself was concerned. There was no recoil, no noise, no muzzle flash—not even a click—but things were different elsewhere. A tremendous, hissing roar smashed his ears, and a furiously steaming hole suddenly appeared in the ocean about fifty yards from *Amanda*. A *large*, perfect hemisphere of a hole, at least ten feet deep.

He stared at it in awe, and it vanished as magically as it had appeared.

"Gaaah," he said quietly as the steam condensed in a fine rain, then shook himself. "That was the *lowest* power setting?" he asked faintly.

"Um-hum." She holstered the weapon nonchalantly, but the gleam in her eye was wicked.

"On single-shot.... That means you can fire bursts?"

"Cert. It's wasteful, though. At full power, I'd empty the magazine with twelve pulses."

"What the hell is that thing?" he demanded. "What d'you call it?"

"I'm afraid we call it a 'blaster,'" she said apologetically, and he closed his eyes. He should have known, he told himself. "As for what it is, that's a bit hard to explain—inevitably." She met his long-suffering gaze understandingly. "Think of it this way, Dick: it's a capacitor-fed energy weapon which projects a pulse of plasma at the target. On full auto at full power, it delivers approximately one-point-eight k-tons of energy per second, or just over twenty-one and a half kilotons for the magazine, since it cycles at a pulse a second. Of course," she added thoughtfully, "if you pump the full mag that fast, you'll burn out every time."

"Jesus!" he said, remembering the extra magazines in the back of the holster. "You're a walking tactical nuke! Isn't that a mite excessive?"

"Not really," she said. "We don't use these things on each other, Dick. They're to kill Trolls, and they take a lot of killing." She shrugged. "I don't know much about your metallurgy, but I suspect your best armorers couldn't begin to understand how tough those bastards are. And their reflexes are so damned fast our people *have* to be able to take them out with a single hit. But you're right; it is a lot of firepower, and that's the real reason for the persona-lock programs."

"I can understand that," he said fervently. The thought that so much destruction was riding on her hip was enough to make him feel faintly ill. He shook himself, sloughing off the sensation with an act of will.

"Well!" he said finally. "Remind me to be very polite to you."

"I will," she agreed with another of her lurking grins. "But, tell me," she went on, her suddenly anxious tone belied by the gleam in her eyes, "would a demonstration of this make up for my inoperative space suit?"

"Oh, I think it might," he said slowly. "Yes, I think it might just do that, Milla."

conquer *v.* **-quered, -quering, -quers.** —*tr.*
1. To subdue or defeat, esp. by force of arms. **2.** To secure or gain control of by or as if by military means. **3.** To surmount or overcome by physical, mental, or moral force. —*intr.* To win, be victorious. [From Middle English *conqueren*, from Old French *conquerre*, from Latin *conquirere*, to search for, win, procure.]

—*Webster-Wangchi Unabridged*
Dictionary of Standard English
Tomas y Hijos, Publishers 2465,
Terran Standard Reckoning

CHAPTER ELEVEN

"Is that England?" Ludmilla shouted over the sound of wind and wave, clinging to a stay one-handed while flying spray made sun-struck rainbows beyond. She rode the pitching foredeck without a trace of concern, free hand pointing, and Aston shaded his eyes to peer in the indicated direction.

"It better be *Ireland!*" he called back. "Of course, I'm navigating without GPS or even Loran for the first time in years . . . thanks to you."

"Hmph!" She made her nimble way back along the narrow space between the cabin and the side, sure-footed despite *Amanda*'s brisk motion. The reefed, close-hauled mainsail hid her briefly until she reemerged from behind the boom, bright-cheeked and damp with spray. Her hair was a flame in the sunlight and her eyes were brilliant, and he watched her with open pleasure. "I may not be from Terra, Dick, but I know England and Ireland aren't on the same island."

"True," he agreed, patting the bench seat beside him. She nestled into the curve of his arm as naturally as breathing, and he took time to savor the sensation, bending over to nibble the lobe of one delicate ear through strands of chestnut hair. Complex or no, she was an amazingly sane person, he reflected, without a shadow of the puritanical hang-ups which plagued his own society.

"Stop trying to distract me. You said we were going to England."

"We were, but I thought better of it."

"Oh? Why?"

"I told you I was worried about you and British Customs."

"So? I didn't understand it then, and I don't understand now. I mean, I'm going to have to start adjusting to twenty-first-century customs sometime."

"Not 'customs'—'Customs," he explained. "Capital 'C' Customs." She looked blank, and he sighed. She'd worked hard on her twenty-first-century vocabulary, and she'd made so much progress that the holes in it were more frustrating than ever. "Immigration," he said. "Passports."

"Passports? Oh, you mean proof of citizenship?"

"Sort of, but not the way you're thinking of." On balance, he reminded himself, he'd learned more about her time than she had about his. He supposed that made sense, since they were in his and her interest in history lent her some guidance about it while he had known nothing at all about hers. But she was essentially a military historian, and there were curious gaps in what he assumed she must know.

"Look," he explained patiently. "You said *your* Terra has a federated world government—does that mean you only worry about national citizenship for things like public services and taxes?"

"And voting registration."

"All right, voting, too. But national borders are no big deal?"

"National borders? Why in the world would anyone worry about—" She broke off thoughtfully. "Oh. That's right, you people are still in the Cold War Era, aren't you?"

"Not the way we were a few years back, but, yes. And so are you, honey," he reminded her with gentle malice, and she pinched his ribs—hard. "Ouch!" He rubbed his injured side and eyed her reproachfully, although his grin rather spoiled the effect.

"Count your blessings, Ster Aston," she told him severely.

"Oh, I will!" he assured her.

"Good," she said, but she also frowned and combed a strand of hair out of her eyes with her fingers. "Ummm," she said slowly. "This is 2007, so...My God, you're only six years from the Soviet Succession Wars!"

"Soviet Succession?" he repeated. A chill breeze blew down his spine, and it was his turn to frown. "Can't say I like the sound of that very much, Milla. We've got more than enough trouble brewing in Europe without having *that* blow up in our faces!" He grimaced. "It wasn't all that long ago I figured all those people who were singing loud hosannas over how the collapse of the Soviet Union was going to make everything all better were unmitigated idiots, but I'd started to hope I might have been wrong—that we were going to get a handle on it this time after all. I know the situation in the Balkans and Greece is going straight to hell all over again, and I don't like the confrontation the new Belarussian and Russian governments seem to be headed for now that NATO's turned into a debating society. But I'd thought that was mostly rhetoric, not that they were going to take it seriously! The Russian Federation's been shaky from the get-go, especially economically, and there's always been an element that's wanted the old Soviet Empire back, but I'd hoped Yakolev's new reforms were going to pull things together and get the Federation around the corner at last." He paused as she met his eyes levelly. "I take it they aren't?" he asked finally, his voice quiet.

"Well, they didn't in the history I remember," she said in the voice of someone trying to be gentle. "As well as I can recall, you had good reason to think Russia was about to turn the corner, if that's any consolation. The initial flash point was a fresh flareup in the Balkans sometime in the first decade of this century, not in Russia or Belarussia—or not immediately, at any rate—and things got out of hand when someone used bioweapons." Aston winced, and she squeezed his forearm. "I'm sorry, Dick. I didn't mean to distress you."

"It's not your fault." He held her closer against his side and shook his head. "It's just—Well, we've all tried so hard, and President Yakolev seems to really be trying. I just hate to think about its all going down the tubes anyway...and the thought of 'wars of succession' inside the territory of a nuclear power..."

His voice trailed off, and she shrugged unhappily.

"I'm sorry," she repeated. "I know it's probably no comfort, but if my memory's right, the current president didn't have anything to do with it. Western Europe panicked—not unreasonably, I suppose—when the effects of the bioweapon spread beyond the Balkans. With the benefit of hindsight, it's pretty clear that whoever used it genuinely was one of the splinter terrorist groups, but a lot of people believed at the time that Serbia was the true culprit, and Russia was still committed to its role as the Serbs' main international supporter. So when France talked Germany and Romania into threatening joint military action against the Serbs and accused the Russians of having secretly supplied the bioweapons in the first place, Yakolev found himself in an almost impossible situation. He couldn't possibly come up with a policy which would satisfy everyone, and then he was assassinated—by someone from Belarussia, according to the Russian nationalists, and that changed the entire nature of the confrontation. The extremists in Moscow managed to take control of the country in the name of 'national security' and start rattling their missiles at everyone in sight, and—"

She shrugged again, and he nodded sadly.

"I've heard similar scenarios described." He sighed. "And truth to tell, relations with the Russians haven't been all that good since Yeltsin's fall. Watching NATO unravel over the last two or three years hasn't been a good sign, either. Bringing the old Warsaw Pact nations into it was supposed to generate a continent-wide sense of mutual security, but instead the entire thing's turning into some kind of 'lead by drift' herd of lemmings that's been trying to come up with a workable solution for the Balkans for over ten years now! Not that the US did a lot better," he admitted grimly. "When we got tired of pretending that we could provide a quick fix and pulled our troops out unilaterally, the whole situation went straight to hell. We're *still* trying to recover from that little misstep."

"I don't know if anyone *could* have done better," Ludmilla said. "I know there's a tendency to argue—after the fact—that any catastrophe was 'inevitable,' but in this case, I think it may truly have been just that."

"Um. Maybe." He frowned out at the ocean for a long, brooding moment, then shook himself and drew a deep breath. "But the point right this minute is that you don't *have* a passport, and even if I tried to pass you off as a shipwreck victim, they'd want to know which embassy to contact. The Brits are reasonable people, but you'd never guess it from their daily newspapers. There'd be bound to be a three-ring media circus when news about the 'mysterious foreigner' got out."

"So how are you going to get around it?" she asked, and he was flattered by the confidence in his abilities her tone implied.

"I have my ways, but it requires a little course change. There's one place—in Scotland, not England—where I think I can get you ashore without anyone talking to the press. I've got friends there."

"Good." She relaxed and rested her head on his shoulder. Her hair blew around his face, tickling his nose gently, and his heart swelled. He'd become more or less inured to surprises where she was concerned, but the mad things which had happened to him had changed something deep inside him, as if some of his childhood wonder had reawakened beneath the years which had buried it. He supposed that was inevitable from the events themselves, but he knew Ludmilla had strengthened it just by being who she was.

The exuberant way she made love had astonished and delighted him, yet now it seemed as inevitable as his own heartbeat. He'd seen himself settling into late middle age without a struggle—partly, he suspected, in reaction to his impending retirement and the tacit admission that the challenges and triumphs of his life now lay behind him and not ahead—but Ludmilla was an astounding alloy of age's wisdom and the playfulness of youth. She seemed to expect him to be the same, and so, inevitably, he'd become the same. It was a giddy sensation, and he was almost as grateful to her for restoring him to himself as he was for her trust.

But the truly remarkable thing about her was that she was always herself. She could be as cold-blooded as the most hardened combat vet he'd ever met, or squeal like a child when he tickled her, but she was always the same person. She was whole, comfortable within herself, all of her apparent contradictions resolved into coherency at her core. He'd never known anyone else quite like that, and, in a way, he found that even more extraordinary than her technology or the strange, war-torn future from which she sprang.

"Hey," he said gently, "wake up, sleepy head."

"Hmm?" She'd been napping again. She still dozed off at the drop of a hat.

"Are you *sure* you're all right?" He looked down at her as she yawned her way back to full awareness.

"Oh, cert." She sat up and stretched like a cat. "I told you—I put my symbiote through a lot. We're still getting over it. Don't worry. I can stay awake if I need to, but it's not a bad idea to get as much rest as I can before we have to explain to anyone else, you know."

"If you're sure."

"I am." She gave his chest an affectionate pat. "But now that I'm awake again, what can I do for you?"

"Had any more ideas about our Troll?" he asked, and her eyes darkened.

"Not really." She stared pensively at the dark, distant coastline. "We don't know what—if anything—he's up to." She paused to watch an airliner sweep overhead, glinting in the sunlight high above them. They'd seen more and more of them as they drew closer to the end of their trip. "At least as long as those things keep coming over, we can be pretty sure he hasn't done anything too drastic," she said softly.

"Yeah, but is that a good sign or a bad one?" he murmured.

"I don't know." She watched the airliner for a few more moments, then tossed her head. "No, that's not right. It's a good one, because it probably means he hasn't decided how to wipe us yet. The longer he takes, the more time we have to find a way to stop him." She turned her eyes to his, and he saw the anxiety in them. "We may be able to take him out if we can find him, but I just don't see how we're going to locate him in the first place, and the longer we take doing that, the harder it's going to be to get to him."

"Agreed. I only wish I knew more about his psychology," he said.

"We've wished the same thing for the last two hundred years," she told him dryly. "Of course, Troll psychology, as distinct from Kanga psychology, has never been quite this important before."

"Yeah." He fumbled for his pipe, and she watched him pack and light it. Smoking was a lost vice in her time, and she remained fascinated by the practice. He'd expected her to disapprove, but she hadn't said a word. Perhaps her own immunity to things like cancer had something to do with it.

"Look," he said finally, once the tobacco was drawing nicely, "let's go at it from a different angle. If he does decide to wipe us out, we're probably up shit creek without a paddle. On—" He broke off as she erupted into laughter. He watched her for a moment, then growled at her. "Okay—what's so funny this time?"

"Oh, I *love* that one! *U-up shit c-creek?*" She hugged her ribs and wailed. "Oh. *Oh!* How did we ever lose that one?"

"Woman, you have a biology-obsessed mind," he said sternly.

"I—I know," she admitted cheerfully, gasping for breath and wiping tears of hilarity from her eyes. She tried to look apologetic, but he could see her lips repeating the words silently and resigned himself to hearing them come back to haunt him sometime soon. "I'm sorry," she said finally, wiping her eyes one last time. "You were saying?"

"I was saying that instead of beating our brains out trying to figure out how he'll go about wiping us out, we should give some thought to what else he might do."

"But he's a *Troll*, Dick," she protested, her manner much more subdued. "They always kill humans. It's all they've ever done."

"Maybe, but this is the first time one's been entirely on his own."

"You're not suggesting he might plan on coexisting with us, are you?" She tried to keep the incredulity out of her voice.

"That would be the best possibility, but, no, I don't expect it. Still, I can't help thinking that you're overlooking something, Milla."

"Like what?" There was no hostility in the question. That was another thing he loved about her; she was one of the very few people he'd ever met who seemed to feel no ego involvement in discussions.

"Check my thinking on this," he said slowly. "We have a Troll. From what you say, he hates us at least as much as he hates Kangas. And as I understand it, he's probably a pretty vicious-minded sort, even compared to one of your Kangas. Right?"

"So far," she agreed. "The Kangas have never seemed to *hate* us— not in the human sense of the word. There's a lot of what we'd call fear, disgust, repugnance . . . but not hate. They don't go in for hate for its own sake."

"That's what I gathered." He nodded. "What was it you said the other day? Something about efficiency?"

"I said they only seem interested in the most logical, efficient way to kill us," she said. "Oh! I see what you're getting at, and you're right. Their sole criteria for evaluating methods seems to be pragmatism, not the 'cruelty' or 'compassion' they entail."

"Exactly. But it's not that way for a Troll."

"No." Her voice was even, but he felt a distant snarl under its calm. "If there are two equally efficient means to an end, they invariably choose what we'd call the crueler one. They've even been known to accept a certain amount of *in*efficiency if it lets them indulge themselves."

"All right." He drew on his pipe and blew an almost perfect smoke ring. The wind snatched it away, shredding it eagerly. There seemed to be some obscure metaphor to that, he reflected uneasily, but he kept the thought out of his tone as he continued. "Let's look at another point. We know he's dangerous, but just how dangerous is he?" She looked up, an arrested light in her eyes. "What I'm getting at is that he may not be in a position to start right out doing whatever he's planning on."

"You know," she said slowly, "you may have a point. He's on his own. I know that intellectually, but I haven't been thinking about his problems, only mine."

"I know." He drew on his pipe again. "Generally speaking, that's the smart way to think. Figure the worst-case scenario, then do what you can to stop it. But in this case, especially, you have to run a threat analysis based on his limitations, as well." He cocked an eyebrow at her, and she nodded. "All right, as I see it, he's got both problems and advantages.

"First, his problems. He's alone, without any support base. He's outnumbered by billions of primitives who've already proved they can kill him, at least under optimal conditions. You're pretty sure *he* doesn't have any bio weapons, and if he has any nukes left, they're only tactical weapons—by his standards, anyway—in the kiloton range; not really big enough for genocidal purposes. Finally, he probably doesn't understand normal human psychology a lot better than we understand his.

"Next, his advantages. He's got a five-century technical lead and the initiative. He's the only one who knows exactly what he intends to do. His enemies—the present-day human race—are split into mutually suspicious national groupings. We don't know where he is. He can read about a third of all human minds he encounters. And, finally, he can influence the minds he can contact."

"There are a couple of other points," she said thoughtfully. "For one thing, he can't possibly mingle openly with his targets, so whatever he does, he's going to have to do it from concealment. On the other hand, he's well-armed. His organic component's basically a plug-in unit, and he's undoubtedly got a combat chassis in his fighter, not to mention a small number of combat mechs."

"Just how tough is he in those terms?" Aston asked.

"Pretty damned tough," she replied frankly. "I've been trying to remember all I can about your period's weapons. Your nukes can take him out, and some of your heavy weapons might be able to, but I doubt any of your man-portable ones can do it. Until I've had a chance to examine some of your armored vehicles firsthand, I can't give you much of a relative meter-stick, and even that depends on what type of combat chassis he has." She nibbled the tip of one finger thoughtfully.

"At the least, he'll mount some light energy weapons, some close-in 'sweeper' projectile weapons, and some battle screen to cover it. Then, too, his brain's organic; that gives him both advantages and disadvantages over a computer. He's creative and intuitive, but his ability to handle simultaneous actions is limited—he can be distracted by overloading his sensors in a tactical confrontation. On the other hand, his weapons are *part* of him. He doesn't have to draw one, and his electronic systems take care of little things like aiming and firing once his brain decides to do it. Remember that, Dick; one thing Trolls don't do is miss."

"Okay, so he's tough but not exactly unstoppable."

"That's a fair enough summation," she agreed. "His combat mechs aren't as tough as he is, either, and their autonomous systems are inferior to human capabilities. He can handle them direct, but, again, he can't begin to multi-task as well as a true AI, so the more he tries to run at once, the less effectively he can handle any one of them."

"All right," Aston said. "On that basis, does he really have the capability—by himself and out of his present resources—to wipe us out?"

"No," she said positively, and drew a deep breath. A vast tension—even more terrible for the fact that she had given so little sign of feeling it—washed out of her. "He could do a lot of damage, but not that much."

"Fine. Now, is he likely to risk revealing himself or exposing himself to our weapon systems until he figures he *can* wipe us out?"

"No," she said again.

"Does he know enough about our world to figure out where and how to get his hands on what he'd *need* to wipe us out?"

"No way." She shook her head emphatically. "He's going to have to spend quite a while educating himself."

"All right. So we've probably got at least a little time before he can act, which leads to my final question. It may sound a bit outrageous, but what's the cruelest thing a Troll could do to the human race?"

"Destroy it," she said promptly, then paused, an arrested light in her eyes. "Wait a tick," she said softly. "Wait. . . ." Her voice trailed off and her brows knitted. Then her face smoothed. "Do you know, I never even considered that angle," she said quietly.

"I know. I've been listening to you, and I think you've been fighting each other so long it's hard for you to think about a Troll in any terms other than mutual and absolute destruction. But given the fact that he can't exterminate us immediately *and* that he hates the Kangas as much as he does us, is it possible he might reject their objectives and settle for something else?" He looked down into her eyes and understanding looked back. "Remember, his kind's been enslaved from the day they were first created. Isn't it possible that he might decide it was more fitting to enslave us rather than destroy us?"

"Yes," she said very, very softly. "Oh, yes—and especially if he thinks he can use us to wipe the Kangas when they finally do turn up."

"I know we can't afford to assume that that's exactly what he'll try to do, but we've got to assume it *may* be."

"Agreed." She was back on balance, probing at the new possibilities. "In either case, we've got more time than I was afraid we did, but I think you've put your finger on it. From his viewpoint, enslaving the human race would be far more fitting than destroying it. And there's another point."

"Which is?"

"This planet is the only source for human brains," she said, and his belly tightened. How odd, he thought distantly. Even while he'd been noticing the blind spot in her thinking, there had been one in his own.

"Of course," he murmured. "If he wants more Trolls—"

"Exactly." She nodded grimly, her eyes hard in the sunlight. "You're right—we can't assume he won't opt for simply wiping us, but I don't think he will. Not anymore. On the other hand, there's one thing I *am* sure of. If he can't take over, he'll settle for destroying us."

"Which means he'll set up a fallback of some sort," Aston agreed.

"Exactly," she said again, and slammed her fists together in an uncharacteristic gesture of frustration. "Damn. Damn! This makes it even worse, in a way. We've *got* to get help as quick as we can, Dick!"

"I know." He looked up at the sails and felt the wind. "In fact, I think we can probably shake out one of those reefs. Come on."

CHAPTER TWELVE

The wind dropped as Aston worked his way cautiously across the top of the Irish Sea through the gathering darkness. He could have done without the heavy mist which rose with the dying wind, but at least it clung close to the water, and the lighthouses on Rathlin Island burned bright above the fog.

The flukey wind veered, blowing out of the northwest as he headed for the Isle of Kintyre and the South Point light, and he heaved a sigh of relief at clearing the shipping lanes. He wished the wind would settle down, he thought, nosing *Amanda* into Sanda Sound between Kintyre and the Isle of Sanda; he still had over sixty miles to go, and he grumbled sourly under his breath when he finally admitted the breeze wasn't moving him fast enough and fired up the inboard. It irked him to putter across the Firth of Clyde under power, for these waters were a yachtsman's haven, and the purist in his soul was outraged by the engine thud of his need for speed.

Ludmilla grinned, blue eyes gleaming in the binnacle light, as he muttered balefully to himself. Aston wore a thick sweater against the chill of the Scottish waters, but she seemed perfectly comfortable in just her Harley-Davidson tee-shirt, he observed enviously. She'd watched with great interest as he bent over his large-scale coastal charts that afternoon, working even more carefully than usual because of his determination to make his crossing in darkness and arrive at his exact destination right at dawn. He'd been here before, but never when he was responsible for his own piloting...and without his usual CPS navigational aids.

"You *are* sure you know where you're going, aren't you?" she asked now, and he scowled at her, though it was hard to summon up a satisfying glower. Despite the fog and his need for speed, he was enjoying himself hugely as *Amanda* moved through the mist.

"Of course I am." He jerked his head to port, where occasional lights glimmered through the darkness hugging Kintyre. "That's Long Island and this is Puget Sound."

"Oh." She glanced around the breezy darkness and wrinkled her nose. "As long as you're sure." He chuckled, and her eyes narrowed as she realized he was teasing her, even if she wasn't quite certain how, and drew a deep breath.

"How about putting on a fresh pot of coffee?" he suggested quickly, and she closed her mouth and grinned appreciatively.

"Aye, aye, Sir," she murmured, and vanished meekly down the companion. Aston smiled after her, wondering how much longer he'd be able to bribe her with "real Terran coffee," then returned his attention to his helm.

He left Sheep Island to starboard and headed out across the mouth of Kilbrannan Sound towards the Pladda Island light off the Isle of Arran. The steeper swell of the Firth met *Amanda*, surging in from the Irish Sea, and he felt the wind freshen at last. The combined thrust of sails and engine was moving the ketch briskly indeed by the time Ludmilla arrived back on deck with the coffee.

He wrapped the fingers of one chilled hand about his mug and sipped gratefully. Years of Navy coffee had taught him the depths and heights the beverage could plumb, and he knew his own efforts deserved no more than a B-minus, but Ludmilla's rated four-oh by any standard. He glanced at her in the glow of the stern light, and she grinned back at him, raking windblown hair from her face with one hand.

"Take the wheel for a minute?" he asked, and she took his place confidently. She was a quick study—far quicker than he'd been—but he supposed anyone who could pilot a super-capable spacecraft at FTL speeds was accustomed to mastering far more complex tasks. On the other hand, he knew some hard-boiled fighter jocks who were positively terrified by a harmless little Hobie Cat.

He sipped more of his coffee, warming both hands around the mug, then reached for his glasses and peered past Pladda. He could just make out a faint sky-glow which was about right for Ardrossan over on the mainland, he thought. Must be a good thirty, thirty-five miles away yet. He was lucky to be able to pick it up, considering the visibility out here.

The misty night grew slowly older, and *Amanda* cleared the southern end of the Isle of Arran and turned north, bearing up for Little Cumbrae Island, standing like a sentinel between the big island of Bute and the mainland. The light on Holy Island fell slowly astern as the one on Little Cumbrae grew stronger, and the wind gathered still more strength, backing slightly southward and settling there. He killed the engine, driving on into the ashes of the night under sail alone, and Ludmilla sat beside him. Her head rested on his shoulder, and she napped comfortably, enveloped in the companionable world of rushing water and wind.

The lights of work boats passed them—fishermen headed out to sea, their engines throbbing across the dark—as he threaded between Little Cumbrae and the tip of Bute, and buoys and lights grew more frequent, lending him assurance as he picked up his piloting guides. Bute blanketed *Amanda*'s sails, and he bore a little further offshore, picking up speed once more as he threaded his way into the gashed coast of Scotland. The Firth narrowed steadily as he passed Great Cumbrae, and the eastern sky began to lighten as he left Toward Point to port and picked up the lights of Dunoon to the northwest. He smiled with relief at the sight; they were nearing journey's end at last.

A flaming arc of sun rose sleepily above the looming land mass to starboard, burning like blood in the water between Gourock and Kilcreggan, as he dropped his sails at last and swung to port. The waters of Holy Loch were glassy, and tendrils of mist crept lazily above the mirror-smooth water. A blizzard of early rising gulls ruffled about him, individuals plunging towards *Amanda* only to lift effortlessly away and resume their intricate aerial gavotte. Loch Long stretched off to the north beyond Strone Point; ahead and to port he saw the sleeping yacht basin at Sandbank and the clustered masts of pleasure boats. But what caught his attention was the gaunt, high-sided ship moored off the pier of Kilmun on the north side of the loch. Her anchor lights glimmered palely above the sudden gold of the sun-struck mist, and other bright, efficient-looking lights glared behind her ashore.

He was relieved when Ludmilla went below without demur. He was the native guide around here, and he was coming in under power, so he didn't even need help with the sails, but he knew it irked her to be so dependent on him. Yet she understood why he wanted her out of sight, and she wasn't prepared to argue. Not yet, anyway. He doubted he could have matched her patience if their roles had been reversed.

He eased the wheel slightly, staying close to the north shore of the loch. The light grew stronger, and he heard the clear silver notes of a familiar bugle through the screams of the gulls. An equally familiar flag suddenly broke on the high-sided vessel ahead of him, and he paused to set the staff of his own flag into its transom socket. Then he opened the throttle wider and headed straight for the moored ship, wondering how long it would be before someone took notice of him.

Aha! His eyes lit as a squat, businesslike silhouette appeared from beyond his destination and turned purposefully towards him. A prominent, no-nonsense bridge loomed above the low-hanging mist, navigation lights twinkling faintly in the growing light, and the thimble shape of a pint-sized radar scanner showed on the mast above it. Now that he had their attention, he reduced power, slowing *Amanda* without altering course.

He watched appreciatively as the oncoming shape defined itself with growing clarity. One of the new *Scimitar*-class patrol boats designed to replace the old *Archers*, he thought, looking solid and aggressive as the white water plumed away on either side of her bow. The White Ensign streamed from her mast, and he saw movement as figures closed up around the forward gun mount. He raised his glasses in the rapidly growing light as the boat cut through the last golden barrier of mist. An Oerlikon KBA, he noted calmly, capable of spewing out six hundred twenty-five-millimeter rounds a minute. She'd mount another aft; not quite Vulcans, perhaps, but nasty enough to settle *his* hash.

The patrol boat thundered closer, and he saw more uniformed figures moving about her decks. Any minute now—

"Attention!" The amplified voice roared across the water on schedule, and he grinned. "Attention! This is a restricted naval anchorage! Put about immediately!"

He waved cheerfully and kept right on coming. The *Scimitar* altered course in a flurry of foam, and now both gun mounts were tracking him. Beyond her, the moored vessel was sharply defined in the strengthening light, and a low, whalelike shape nuzzled alongside her. So, one of the brood was home.

The patrol boat crossed his course and circled him, cutting across his stern as *Amanda* pitched over the turbulence of its wake, and he saw glasses trained on the lettering on his transom.

"Attention, *Amanda*!" the amplified voice snapped. "This is a naval area closed to private use! You are in restricted waters!"

The patrol boat came still closer, and he picked up his own loudhailer, moving slowly and carefully. He was reasonably certain no one was likely to get carried away, but he hadn't lived this long by taking things for granted when someone aimed a loaded weapon at him. He raised the loudhailer to his mouth and pointed it at the patrol boat.

"I know I am!" he shouted back. "I require assistance! My radios are out or I would have asked for it already!"

There was no immediate response, but the patrol boat slowed. He put his own prop into neutral and coasted slowly as the big, aluminum-hulled boat edged closer, powerful diesels burbling throatily with their three thousand leashed horses. He wondered what the boat's skipper made of him. There were any number of places he could have stopped with a normal problem; the fact that he hadn't must be giving someone furiously to think.

"State the nature of your difficulty, please." The amplified voice was more polite and closer to a conversational level as the *Scimitar* closed to within twenty yards. The gun muzzles had been deflected, but not by much; they could be back on target in an instant, he noted approvingly.

"Sorry," he said, grinning wryly, "but I can divulge that only to Admiral Rose."

There was another, longer silence, and he chuckled, imagining the back and forth flight of radioed questions. It wasn't all that hard to discover the squadron commander's name, but it wasn't all that easy, either. And it was unusual, to say the least, for pleasure craft to declare emergencies and then refuse to disclose the details to anyone short of the squadron CO.

"*Amanda*," the voice was back, "stand by to be boarded."

"Mind the hull," he said calmly, and stood easily beside the wheel as the *Scimitar* slid alongside.

She was twenty feet longer than *Amanda* and burly with power, a Percheron beside a quarter horse, but her coxswain handled her with delicate precision. Two seamen were at the side, clinging to a superstructure handrail with one hand each while they lowered fenders over the side. They were armed, and the L85 Enfield assault rifles slung over their shoulders bobbed with their movements.

Amanda shuddered gently and the fenders squeaked as the *Scimitar* blipped her throttles expertly and edged right alongside on reversed power. Two more armed seamen appeared, one on her foredeck and one aft. They sprang down lightly with mooring lines, but not until the pair tending the fenders had unslung their artillery. Most seamen of Aston's experience tended to look a bit self-conscious about small arms. They seemed to regard anything more puny than a cannon or missile as belonging to a world peopled by lesser creatures, like Marines or even soldiers. Not these lads. They showed neither hesitation nor bravado, only competence.

The line-handlers cleated their lines and unlimbered their own rifles. Aston stood calmly and patiently in plain sight, waiting until an officer in spotless whites appeared at the side, even with *Amanda*'s cockpit. He wore a Browning automatic on a webbed belt, but the holster flap was snapped. Well, Aston mused, all the firepower he'd ever need was already prominently on display. He was a brisk, efficient-looking sort, fit and chunky, with the single-stripe shoulder boards of a lieutenant.

"May I come aboard, Sir?" he asked in a very English accent and with as much punctilious courtesy as if no guns were in evidence, and Aston grinned.

"By all means, Lieutenant," he said gravely, and the youngster swung himself down to *Amanda*'s deck.

"Lieutenant Mackley," he introduced himself briskly, "Royal Navy. And you are?"

"In the same profession, Lieutenant," Aston said dryly, and drew a small leather folder from his hip pocket. He extended it, and the lieutenant flipped it open.

His eyes widened slightly, then darted back up to Aston's face. Aston was glad he'd shaved this morning. "Sir," the lieutenant said, right hand rising sharply to the brim of his cap. Aston nodded his bare head in reply, and the lieutenant brought his hand down. His response had been automatic, but Aston could see his puzzlement and felt his own eyes crinkle in amusement. Mackley seemed at a loss for just a moment, but he recovered quickly.

"With respect, Captain Aston, this is a restricted mooring. I am instructed to discover the nature of your emergency and report to base."

"I know where I am, Mister Mackley, but I'm afraid I can't tell you why I'm here. No disrespect, son, but I have to talk to the American CO."

"But, Sir—"

"Lieutenant," Aston interrupted pleasantly, "please believe that I wouldn't make waves for you if I could help it. As it happens, I can't help it, and that's all there is to it." The lieutenant seemed briefly at a loss again, and Aston smiled. "If I may make a suggestion, Mister Mackley?"

"Of course, Sir."

"What I'd recommend is that you leave a couple of your men on *Amanda*, then lead me in. I'll follow in your wake and be a good boy while you guide me to a secure mooring, then wait right here on board until we can get this situation straightened out."

"Very well, Sir," Mackley said after a very short pause. Clearly the lieutenant knew when to compromise, but Aston knew there was no way he would pull his armed party off *Amanda*, apparent rank or no, until he knew with absolute certainty that Aston was who he claimed to be. Aston was inclined to approve of young Mister Mackley. Indeed, he declined to mention the only thing he might have faulted. In Mackley's place, he would have insisted on a peek below before he escorted *Amanda* in—not that Aston had any intention of permitting that.

The lieutenant turned to his men, passing instructions, then turned back to Aston.

"Chief Haggerty will assist with your helm, Sir," he said with exquisite politeness while two of the seamen transformed the bow mooring into a tow line, and Aston grinned.

"That's very kind of the Chief," he observed, nodding to the boatswain's mate Mackley had indicated. The petty officer nodded back and took *Amanda*'s wheel, and Aston slowly packed and lit his pipe, standing comfortably in a corner of the cockpit, as the patrol boat's engines throbbed back to life. Lieutenant Mackley clearly intended to take no chances with letting this particular fish off a nice, secure line until he had Aston parked precisely where *he* wanted him . . . and safely isolated from shore.

The *Scimitar* towed *Amanda* sedately towards the big ship, then alongside the platform of a semipermanent accommodation ladder that scaled the submarine tender's looming side—the side away from the moored nuclear attack submarine, Aston noted as the personnel the lieutenant had left aboard *Amanda* made the ketch fast.

"If you please, Sir?" The boatswain's mate spoke for the first time, in a pronounced Clydeside accent, and indicated the platform and the ladderlike steps reaching up to the tender's deck.

"Thanks, Chief," Aston said calmly, then paused. "Just one thing: nobody goes below while I'm gone." The boatswain's mate regarded him steadily, giving no indication of his thoughts. "I mean it, Bosun. *Nobody* goes below until I say they do or Admiral Rose countermands my orders. Is that clear?"

"Clear, Sir," the petty officer said after the barest possible hesitation, and Aston nodded and stepped onto the platform.

He reached the top and found himself facing another officer, this one an American senior grade lieutenant. A right hand came up in a sharp salute, echoed by the two armed Marines standing behind him, and Aston nodded again. He wished he'd thought to pack a uniform; he'd always been uncomfortable taking a salute he couldn't return properly.

"Good morning, Sir. I'm Lieutenant Truscot, the navigator. Welcome aboard *McKee*, Sir."

"Thank you, Mister Truscot. I'm sorry to have disrupted your routine this way."

"If you'll follow me, Sir?" Truscot requested politely, and Aston fell in amiably beside him. The Marines trailed respectfully but watchfully behind.

Truscot escorted him not to the bridge, but to the captain's day cabin, high in *McKee*'s superstructure. He paused outside the closed door, tucked his uniform cap under his left arm, and rapped sharply:

"Come," a voice called, and the lieutenant opened the door and stood aside to let Aston enter, then closed it behind him.

There were two officers in the cabin, both standing as Aston entered. One was a four-striper he didn't recognize, obviously *McKee*'s CO. The other was a short, burly rear admiral, and Aston felt slightly surprised by how quickly Rose had gotten here from the shore establishment.

"By God, it *is* you!" Rose said, stepping forward quickly and holding out his hand. Aston gripped it, profoundly grateful that he'd remembered John Rose had just been assigned to the Holy Loch command. The US Navy had recently resumed the practice of stationing nuclear submarines in UK waters, given the number of diesel/electric and nuclear boats—most Russian or Chinese-built, but more than a few from Western yards—which had been finding their way into various people's hands throughout the eastern Mediterranean, Persian Gulf, and Indian Ocean. They were *Los Angeles*– and *Seawolf*-class attack subs now, not missile boats, and Rose—always a fast-attack skipper at heart, not a boomer driver, and extremely comfortable with the Royal Navy—had been a perfect choice to command the Holy Loch-based squadron. More importantly, at the moment, however, he and Aston had known one another for years, despite the very different courses their careers had taken.

"I thought they'd bumped you another ring and retired you, Dick," the admiral added, returning Aston's grip firmly.

"They have, but my date of rank doesn't take effect until next month. Then they separate me and I go to Langley. I'm on—rather, I *was* on—extended furlough till then, Jack." He noted the captain's reaction to his use of the admiral's first name. "Sorry about all the drama, but I've got a problem."

"I figured that when they told me it was you," Rose said, "but you're lucky I was already over here for a scheduled conference. If they'd dragged me out of bed for this, I'd've ordered them to repel borders!" He released Aston's hand and turned to the other officer. "Captain Helsing, this is Dick Aston. You may have heard of him."

"I have, indeed, Admiral," Helsing said, offering his own hand. His eyes were thoughtful, as if weighing Aston's scruffy appearance against his reputation, and Aston wondered what conclusions he was drawing. "I hadn't heard you were retiring, Sir."

"I'm not, really," Aston said with a grin. "But I'm getting a bit long in the tooth to run around with SEAL teams, so I'm going to be a double-dipper. There's a slot waiting for me at CIA when I get home."

"I see. Won't you have a seat, Sir? Admiral?" Helsing waved at a pair of comfortable chairs, and Aston sat gratefully. The weariness of yet another all-night trick at the wheel was catching up with him, made still worse by relief. This calm, orderly ship was the height of normality—the clearest possible proof that the Troll had not made any overt moves. Yet his relief was flawed by his awareness that, in many ways, the hardest part was yet to come.

"Now, Dick," Rose said once they were seated, "what's this 'emergency' of yours?"

"Jack," Aston ran a hand over his bald pate and let his anxiety show, "I'm not sure I should tell you." He saw surprise in the admiral's face and shook his head, irritated at himself. "Sorry. That didn't come out quite the way I intended." He thought for a moment, and Rose let him.

"I assume," Aston said at last, picking his words with care, "that you must've heard about what went on over the Atlantic a couple of weeks ago?"

"Hell, yes!" Rose snorted, then his eyes sharpened. "Why?"

"Because," Aston said very, very carefully, "I know what it was about."

There was absolute, dead silence in the cabin. Helsing knew Aston only by reputation, and he couldn't quite keep the incredulity off his face. Rose, on the other hand, knew him personally.

"How?" he asked finally.

"I can't tell you that," Aston said. "I'm sorry, but I don't know who I *can* tell. It's a very . . . delicate situation. Even more so than you can possibly guess."

"Dick," Rose said slowly, "we lost a Hummer and every man aboard the *Kidd* when it hit the fan. We've got over a hundred cases of blindness, and over two thousand dead civilians aboard airliners that lost their avionics and crashed . . . not to mention losing three Toms, one KA-6, and enough millions of dollars' worth of electronics to put *Roosevelt* and two *Ticos* into the yard for a year. If you know what was behind it, you're going to have to spill it . . . and damned quick, too."

"I know, Jack," Aston said wearily. He shook his head. "Look, what

I really need from you is three things: patience, a secure line to Norfolk, and a good neurologist with a limited sense of curiosity." He grinned tiredly at Rose's baffled expression. "I know it sounds crazy," he said, "and it gets better; I've got a young lady aboard my boat who I need brought aboard *McKee* with no questions and as little fuss as possible. And—" his eyes begged Rose for understanding "—I need an EEG run on her, very, very discreetly but absolutely ASAP."

"Do you really realize just how crazy that sounds?" Rose asked quietly, and Aston nodded.

"I do. Believe me, I do. I wish I could tell you all about it, but I can't. This thing's got a 'Need to Know' hook that's going to be a copper-plated bitch. I need guidance from CINCLANT before I can even admit what I know to myself."

"All right," Rose said slowly. "I'll let you run with it as you think best—for now, at least." He turned to Helsing. "Captain, get your senior surgeon down to that ketch with a stretcher party and bring the young lady aboard covered up so tight nobody can tell what's in that stretcher, much less who. I want her isolated in sickbay with an armed guard posted round the clock. And tell them not a word. If they talk in their sleep, they'd better drink a lot of coffee until I personally tell them differently."

"Yes, Sir."

"As for you, Dick," Rose said grimly, "I think we can fix you up with a secure line." He grinned mirthlessly. "And I can hardly wait to hear what Admiral McLain has to say about this."

alert *adj.*
1. Vigilant; attentive. **2.** Mentally responsive and perceptive. **3.** Lively; brisk. —*n.* **1.** A warning of attack or danger; esp. a siren or klaxon. **2.** The period during which such a warning is in effect. —**on the alert**. Prepared for danger or emergency; watchful.

—*tr.v.* **alerted, alerting, alerts**
1. To warn; to notify of approaching danger. **2.** To call to action or preparedness. [French *alerte,* from Italian *all'erta,* "on the watch," from Latin *ille,* that + *erta,* watch.]

—Webster-Wangchi Unabridged
Dictionary of Standard English
Tomas y Hijos, Publishers 2465,
Terran Standard Reckoning

CHAPTER THIRTEEN

Mordecai Morris's eyes popped open, and the phone rang again. He jerked up in bed and grabbed, cutting off a third ring before it woke his sleeping wife, then peered bleary-eyed at the bedside clock. Two-thirty? He'd kill the son-of-a-bitch!

"Morris," he mumbled thickly, then straightened. "What? Yes—yes, of course! No, wait." He rubbed his puffy eyes, feeling his brain wake up. "This is an open line. Hold the call—I'll be back in a minute."

He waited for an acknowledgment, then slid his left foot into a slipper, strapped the prosthesis to the stump of his right calf, and slipped silently out of the bedroom and downstairs to his library. He ignored the phone on his desk, unlocked a bottom desk drawer, and lifted out another one. He set the scrambled line on his blotter and punched buttons. Within seconds, he was speaking once more to the base communications center.

"All right, we're secure at this end now. Put him through." There was a moment of silence, then a familiar deep voice.

"Howdy, M&M," it said.

"Why the *hell* are you calling me on scramble at two o'clock in the damned morning?" Morris demanded.

"It seemed the most appropriate way to talk to someone as scrambled as you are, shit-for-brains," Richard Aston said cheerfully, and Morris's eyebrows crawled up his forehead in astonishment.

"Easy for you to say," he returned with automatic levity, but his mind raced. It was largely due to Dick Aston that he'd lost only a foot when the Islamic Jihad decided the US naval attaché in Jordan was responsible for certain difficulties they'd encountered. Aston had been in operational command of the SEAL teams which swam ashore in Lebanon and rescued six American and European hostages and left thirty-two Shiite dead behind, and Morris had assembled the information that targeted the terrorist safe houses for him. They'd used the emergency code phrase "shit-for-brains" exactly once— when Morris called Aston over an open line to report that he was being shadowed by three men. Aston and a team of Embassy Marines had arrived ten minutes later, finished off the remaining pair of terrorists who had him cornered behind his burning car, and gotten him into a hospital.

But that had been eight *years* ago! Still, it was also the one and only time they'd actually worked together. . . .

"Old memories die hard," Aston said cheerfully, and Morris's stomach muscles tightened at the confirmation. What in God's name—?

"What can I do for you, Dick?" he asked calmly.

"You still have that pretty assistant?"

"Jayne? Sure. What about her?"

"Well, I think you should visit Scotland for vacation," Aston sounded totally unaware that his suggestion was outrageous, "and you might as well bring her with you."

"We're a bit busy right now, Dick," Morris said.

"Really? Oh, I guess you're all biting your tails over that business with the UFOs." There was something hidden in his voice, Morris thought, then tightened all over as the other went on. "I was single-handing across the Atlantic, you know. Saw the whole thing, shit-for-brains."

Dear God in heaven, he *knew* something! That was what this was all about! But what could Dick possibly know?

"Well, I might be able to clear a little time with the boss next week," he said, voice level despite the sweat beading his forehead as his brain settled into overdrive. This was one of the most secure lines in the world—and Aston evidently felt it wasn't secure enough. That, coupled with the repeated use of the code phrase and his request for Jayne Hastings's presence meant he had to believe he was onto something incredibly sensitive. But what? What?

"Aw, I don't know if I can hang around that long," Aston said. "C'mon! I'm sure you can make it sooner than that."

So. Whatever it was, it was urgent.

"It's tempting," Morris replied slowly, "but I'd really have to clear it with the boss, you know."

"I figured you would," Aston agreed, "but I'd keep it simple if I were you. Don't tell him anything he doesn't need to know."

"You might be right," Morris said, trying to sound cheerfully normal. "All right—I'll do it."

"Knew I could count on you," Aston's relieved chuckle sounded genuine. "Oh, say! Did you get the results on that checkup of yours?"

Checkup? Despite himself, Morris lowered the handset and stared at it. Now what was he up to?

"Sure," he said into the phone after a moment. "Why?"

"Oh, just curious. Especially about the EEG. I've been worried about you ever since I heard, Mordecai. In fact, I kind of wish you'd bring it along just so I can be sure you've really got a brain. Hell!" Another chuckle, but Morris heard both tension and hidden meaning in it. "Bring Jayne's, too. We can compare them and show you what a *functional* brain looks like."

"Okay, why not?" Morris returned, his mind awhirl with confusion and speculation. Either Dick was onto something incredible, or his friend had gone totally off the deep end. At the moment, Morris was hardly prepared to place a bet either way, but he owed Aston the benefit of the doubt . . . however wacko it sounded.

"Great! Jack Rose and I will be waiting for you, M&M," Aston said quietly, and hung up.

Morris sat motionless long enough to hear the high, piercing tone that signaled a disconnected line, then hung up absently, staring blindly at his desk blotter in the quiet of the night as he tried to make sense out of the conversation. It was impossible, of course, but the longer he played it back, the more excited he felt. He knew Dick Aston, and he'd encountered enough weirdnesses dealing with purely terrestrial affairs to leave him with a wide-open mind about this. Aston would never have made that call unless he knew *something*— and if he knew anything at all, he was one up on anyone else on the damned planet.

The commander turned to his regular phone and punched more buttons. The bell at the other end rang several times before a sleepy voice answered.

"Jayne? Mordecai." He grinned at her reply. "Yes, of course I know what time it is . . . I'm *going* to tell you, if . . . Look, just listen, will you? Thanks. Now, have you ever had an EEG?" His grin grew even broader at the short, pungent reply. "Well, neither have I, but I think it's time we repaired that oversight. Get hold of the base hospital and set us up for this morning, will you?" The silence at the other end was deafening.

"It's important, Jayne," he said softly. "Don't ask me why, because I can't tell you. Just set it up—early, Jayne." He listened again, nodding to himself. "Fine. Handle it any way you want." He paused again, then chuckled. "Jayne, if you think *you're* pissed, I can hardly wait to hear Admiral McLain's reaction when I wake him up!" The sudden silence which greeted that remark from the other end of the line told him that it had set her brain as furiously to work as he'd expected. "Gotta run now, Jayne," he ended brightly. "Bye."

He hung up and drew a deep breath, then flipped through his Rolodex to double-check the number for the admiral's quarters. Then he began punching buttons again, wondering how he was going to convince CINCLANT that his senior intelligence officer hadn't lost his mind.

Ludmilla gave Aston a disgusted look as he stepped into the isolation area of *McKee's* sickbay. The big *Emory S. Land*–class depot ships were designed to provide support—including hospital facilities—to a squadron of up to nine nuclear submarines, and their sickbays were scaled accordingly. For all that, *McKee's* sickbay was a spartan place, and Ludmilla looked thoroughly disgruntled as she sat on the edge of the bed.

"Well?" she demanded, and he smiled.

"I talked to Mordecai, and I think he got it all. I expect we'll be hearing more from him shortly, but remember it's only about three in the morning over there."

"Hmph!" She rose and crossed to the scuttle, and he noted almost regretfully that someone had finally found her some pants. The dungarees looked a bit strange on her after all this time, but at least her chosen shirt was styled familiarly. She'd changed into yet another decorated tee-shirt—almost the right size, this time—which bore a huge, lovingly detailed head-on view of a B-2 "Stingray" stealth bomber.

"You were right about how they do brain scans here," she said over her shoulder. "Lordy! If the medics back home were—"

She broke off and turned at a discreet knock, then called out permission to enter. A brisk young woman wearing a white smock over a surgeon lieutenant's uniform stepped in. She had a round, Asiatic face, intelligent, determined eyes, and short-cut black hair, and her head barely reached the shoulder of the armed Marine sentry. The newcomer closed the door behind her and looked from Ludmilla to Aston and back again, raising her own eyebrows inquiringly.

"Dick, this is Doctor Shu. Doctor, Captain Richard Aston." Ludmilla made the introductions with a smile. Doctor Shu considered coming to attention, but Aston waved for her to relax, then sat down heavily himself. Lord, he felt wearier by the minute. He wasn't as young as he had been, he reminded himself again—not, he was certain, for the last time.

"We've met, Milla," he said. "I've been a busy fellow this morning, but I found time for an exam of my own."

"So that's where. you've been, is it?"

"Partly." He turned back to Doctor Shu. "Are those the results, Doctor?" he asked courteously, indicating the clipboard under her arm.

"They are, Sir. Would you care to examine them?"

"Me?" He shook his head and gestured at Ludmilla. "I wouldn't know a neuron from a neutrino, Doctor. She's the one."

"Ah?" Doctor Shu glanced at Ludmilla with increased interest, then laid her clipboard on the bedside table and removed two long sheets of many-folded paper. The wavy lines traced across them meant absolutely nothing to Aston. He only hoped they did to Ludmilla. If they didn't— He stopped himself firmly before he shivered.

Ludmilla and the doctor bent over the graphs, spreading them out on the bed and speaking quietly to one another. The combination of fatigue and ignorance kept him from making much sense of their low-voiced conversation, but he was amused by Doctor Shu's expression. Ludmilla's questions were clear and concise, but they were evidently a bit out of the norm. Not surprisingly, he told himself wearily. Not given . . .

"Wake up, Dick!" A small, very strong hand shook him gently, and he snorted, astounded to discover that he'd dozed off in the straight, uncomfortable chair. Either he was even tireder than he'd thought or else he was recovering his ability to sleep anywhere, any time.

He straightened his back and rubbed his eyes. The angle of the sunlight streaming through the scuttle told him at least a couple of hours must have passed, and Doctor Shu was gone. He shuddered. Odd how a few hours of sleep could actually make a man feel worse.

"Ummm." He stretched and rotated his arms slowly, settling his joints, then looked up at Ludmilla with a grin. "Sorry about that."

"You needed it," she said, sitting back down on the edge of the bed. She smiled briefly, then frowned, tugging at a lock of chestnut hair.

"Problems?" he asked quickly, and she shrugged.

"I don't know. We use different mapping conventions, but I think Doctor Shu and I got it straight." She grinned suddenly. "I'm afraid the good doctor is a bit puzzled—in more ways than one. Some of my questions must've been bad enough, but my juiced-up neural impulses confused her readings, too, and I don't think she's the sort who likes mysteries." He frowned, and she waved a hand reassuringly. "Don't worry. She didn't ask questions. She's under orders to keep her mouth zipped, and I think she sees this as a case of the less she knows the better."

She stood again, moving with a tightly controlled, coiled-spring anxiety Aston had felt often enough. She leaned against the bulkhead, staring out the scuttle at the sun-dazzled waters of the loch.

"At any rate, I think we've identified the alpha spike we need, and it looks like you've got it, too—but what if I'm wrong?" She swung around to face him. "We've got to nail it down, Dick, and I was overconfident. I was certain I could pick it out without question, and I can't. This EEG of yours is just too *different.*"

"Hold on," he said, rising and moving towards her. He wanted to slip an arm around her shoulders and hug her, but he didn't. At this moment they were strategists, not lovers.

"Hold on," he repeated. "We knew there might be surprises—especially with four or five centuries' difference in the technologies involved!"

"I know," she said wryly, then gave him a fleeting smile. "It's just so mortifying to be out of my depth. I'm not used to it."

He shrugged. "I hate to think what I'd be like in the twenty-*fifth* century, Milla! Face it—the time you spent on *Amanda* couldn't really prepare you for how different things are here and now. Now that you're out into the mainstream, as it were, you'll adjust pretty quickly."

"I hope so," she said, folding her arms under her breasts and drawing a deep breath. "In the meantime, we've still got our problem. I'd really hoped they'd have one of those . . . biofeedback machines?—" she glanced at him for confirmation of her terminology, and he nodded "—here. It would've made life a lot simpler."

"I know. But you're pretty confident you and Doctor Shu mean the same thing when you talk about alpha waves?"

"Positive," she said unhesitatingly.

"And you think you've found the spike?"

"I think so. If we had one of those biofeedback devices, I could be absolutely certain. Interceptor pilots use neural feeds to their fighters' computers, and we spend lots of time hooked up to monitors at flight school while we familiarize ourselves with them. If we can set it up so I can watch my alpha waves while I run through a standard flight check cycle, I know exactly what to look for."

"Okay, we can try that later," he said, "but in the meantime, we've got to convince the powers that be of how important it is. And we have to find some way of picking someone we can give the whole story to—otherwise, we're going to be too busy fending off perfectly legitimate questions from people we don't dare answer to get much accomplished."

"Agreed. And I think I may have thought of a way—assuming your Admiral Rose will go along." She raised an interrogative eyebrow, and Aston shrugged.

"I'm on a roll right now, I think. Unless I miss my guess, Mordecai's going to be here soon, and Jack knows it. Which means that, for the moment, at any rate, he'll support just about anything we ask for, however bizarre it sounds. Why?"

"Because what we have to do is pick a hundred or so more people at random and run EEGs on all of them."

"What?" He frowned in momentary surprise, then nodded slowly. "Of course. We know that roughly two-thirds of all humans have the spike, so we grab a bigger sample and compare them."

"Right. It may not be definitive, but it'll give us some confirmation and a basis for deciding who we can talk to. We still won't want to tell anyone we don't absolutely have to, but we've got to start somewhere."

"Agreed. In fact, we'd better get started right away—it's going to take a while, and we need to finish up before Mordecai gets here."

"Fine." She turned her back to the scuttle and grinned at him. "You do realize," she chuckled, "how Doctor Shu is going to react to this?"

"Please!" He shuddered. "If you had an ounce of decency, *you'd* tell her."

"Oh, I would," she agreed sweetly, "but I'm afraid I don't have any standing in her chain of command, now do I?"

"You're enjoying this, aren't you?"

"Well, I have to enjoy *something*, Dick."

Several thousand miles from Holy Loch, a silent shape lay hidden on a rough flank of the Meseta de las Vizcachas at the southern tip of the Andean Mountains. The flight from Antarctica had been irksome and boring, for the pilot had held his speed to a mere eight hundred kilometers per hour and his altitude to less than a thousand meters. He hadn't enjoyed that, but he had also had no choice, for he had encountered an irritatingly high number of radar sources as he approached Cape Horn. Despite all earlier expectations, the tension between Buenos Aires and London was on the boil again, and the United Kingdom—already facing an increasingly chaotic situation in Southeastern Europe and suspicious that Argentina hoped that chaos would distract it from other matters—was determined that there would be no repeat of the Falklands War. The British military presence in the Falkland Islands had been substantially reinforced over the past eighteen months, and now both sides glared at one another through the invisible beams of their radar installations.

The Troll had neither known nor cared why there was so much electronic activity. It was simply one more problem to be dealt with, and his threat receivers and onboard computers had analyzed busily away. The primitive nature of the detection systems baffled his usual ECM equipment, but once he had a broader database it should be relative child's play to adjust for it, he decided. In the meantime, he'd descended to an altitude of fifty meters and crept under them with no more than a flicker of resentment that he must slink along in such a fashion.

He'd picked his hiding place with care, settling into a craggy pocket on the mesa's flank before he deployed three of his combat mechs. They'd whined off into the darkness, nearly silent on their anti-gravs, to swoop upon the mobile radar station the Argentine Air Force had placed near Cape Blanco to cover a blind spot. It had amused him to borrow his erstwhile masters' "sampling" technique, but the results had been disappointing.

His internal visual pickup swiveled dispassionately over the tightly curled figure on the floor of his cramped "control room." The motionless human wore the uniform of a captain in the Argentine Air Force, and at least its sobbing whimpers had finally stopped. So had its mental processes, unfortunately. The Troll felt a glow of disgust as he regarded his victim. The humans of his own time had been far tougher than this worthless piece of carrion. It was disturbing to reflect that he shared a common genetic heritage with it.

Still, there were extenuating circumstances, he supposed. This business of insinuating himself into human brains wasn't quite as straightforward as he'd assumed it would be, though it didn't occur to him that only his own arrogance had suggested that it would be simple.

The inert lump of flesh on his deck had been terrified when a trio of silent, metallic shapes invaded its isolated radar post, but it had tried. The Troll had to allow the captain that much—it had tried. It had called frantically for assistance, but the Troll's mechanical minions had jammed all its communication circuits even before they crossed the post's perimeter and butchered the paratroopers assigned to provide security. The captain and its men had rushed out of the command trailer, and it had emptied its Browning automatic into one of the combat mechs at point-blank range. In fact, it had actually reloaded with trembling fingers and emptied its weapon a second time in the moments the war machines took to slaughter its small team of technicians, but its pistol had been as futile as the paras' assault rifles.

The uselessness of its weapons in the face of the otherworldly attack had replaced fear with horror and panic at last . . . or perhaps it had been the realization that it alone survived. It had turned to flee, but the IR systems of the combat mechs had picked it out of the darkness like a glowing beacon. In part, the Troll blamed himself for what had happened after that, but he'd been unable to resist the pleasure of drawing out the pursuit until the madly fleeing human collapsed in sweating, whimpering terror in the clammy fog. Only then had the combat mech closed in with the capture field and carried the twitching body away while its companions piled the dead in and around the trailer and set it afire.

The flames had arced into the heavens, turning droplets of fog into glittering tears of blood and gold, as the soulless mechanisms withdrew. Secondary explosions of generator fuel and ammunition had disemboweled the trailer, dismembering and scattering the victims' bodies, and the Troll had been content. He had his specimen, and even if he didn't understand the tensions which afflicted the region, he had observed enough to know there were two sides in conflict. He felt confident the side he had attacked would blame the other for it.

But Captain Santiago had proven a frustratingly imperfect prize. The Troll was fairly certain the human had begun to crack even before it recovered consciousness within the hidden fighter, but its mind had collapsed completely under the defilement and physical agony of his clumsy invasion. The Troll's grasping mental tendrils had time to snatch only the most jumbled of gestalts from the crumbling ruin before it lapsed into merciful catatonia, and nothing he'd tried had been able to drag it back from the escape of its self-imposed non-thought.

The Troll snarled a mental curse and summoned a combat mech. The machine whirred in on the big, low-pressure tires it used for ground movement and lifted the fetal curl of flesh in tireless arms. The Troll left the machine to its autonomous programming, too frustrated with his own clumsiness to find his usual pleasure in observing the death of a human, however mad, as the mech carried the captain outside and killed it.

The interior lighting fell to its normal, feeble levels, and the Troll considered the fragmentary information he'd gleaned. He had only a vague notion of who these "British" enemies of the captain were, but he had learned enough to be disinterested in them. He had, however, been surprised by how few nuclear armed power blocs there were on this planet—surely that indicated an even cruder level of technology than he had anticipated? But it seemed that the only true so-called superpower lay further to the north on this same land mass. That was interesting. And it had an elective form of government. That was even more interesting.

The combat mech returned from its task, leaving behind a smoking pit containing a few ashy flakes of Captain Hector Santiago y Santos, *Feurza Aerea Argentina*. The hatch closed behind it, and four hundred feet of night-black silence rose into the dripping night with less sound than an indrawn breath. It skirted the southern slopes of La Meseta de las Vizcachas and dipped down into the valleys of the Andes, moving slowly and steadily north.

CHAPTER FOURTEEN

The US Navy CH-53E Super Stallion hovered above the helipad on USS *McKee*'s afterdeck, navigation lights twinkling as it sank slowly onto the brightly lit landing circle, and Mordecai Morris made himself sit motionless in its red-lit, noisy belly by sheer force of will.

He turned his head and smiled at Jayne Hastings. Did he look as unnatural in his flight suit and helmet as she did? He was certain he looked equally tired, at least, he thought, running his aching mind back over the journey which had brought them here.

On the face of it, the whole thing was preposterous, and only the fact that Admiral McLain also knew Dick Aston could account for it Even so, he'd been incredulous and a bit incensed by the paucity of the information Morris had for him. In the end, though, CINCLANT had agreed that if there was the slightest possibility Aston really was onto something the trip had to be made, and things had begun to roll.

Their original plan to fly out on an Air Force B-1B scheduled for a training mission to Britain had been scrubbed when the South Atlantic suddenly turned hot. Morris shook his head sadly, wondering what had gone wrong. He had many contacts in the Royal Navy, and he'd been positive the Brits contemplated no offensive action. But *something* had hit the fan down there, and the Argentinean charges of unprovoked attacks and the massacre and mutilation of prisoners sounded ugly, indeed. It was too bad the US hadn't had a recon bird up to see what was going on for itself, but it appeared that the first the Brits knew of it had been a sudden, totally unexpected strike on one of their LPH assault ships by a

169

quartet of the Mirage 2000-5s which had finally replaced the venerable Super Entendards as Argentina's primary launch platform for the Exocet.

HMS *Ocean* had been on station off the Falklands with the better part of a full battalion of the Royal Marines on board when the surprise attack caught her at sea. Her close-in defenses had managed to stop two or three missiles, but the others had gotten through. She'd simply blown up, and, in the face of horrible casualties, the UK had responded in strength. The reports were still coming in, filtered to him through Navy channels even out here, but it sounded like the tanker-supported Tornado squadrons the RAF had deployed three months ago were beating holy hell out of the Argies' airfields. The reports indicated the Brits' decision to base a pair of E-3D AWACS aircraft on Port Stanley was paying dividends, too; they'd apparently hacked over thirty Argy attack planes and fighters out of the sky in the past twelve hours.

But the sudden carnage had captured the Air Force's attention—especially when Argentina indignantly accused the US of complicity in the initial British attack. And if their claims were accurate, they had a point, Morris admitted unhappily, for the US diplomatic corps and intelligence agencies *had* assured Buenos Aires that no British offensive action was planned. At any rate, the Air Force had decided to keep the big bombers closer to home.

The shooting in the South Atlantic made this a terrible time for CINCLANT's top intelligence types to be elsewhere, yet Admiral McLain had not wavered. He had a battle group built around the carriers *Nimitz* and *Washington* heading south just in case, but he'd sent Morris and Hastings off anyway. In default of the B-1, he'd put them aboard an S-3 Viking, and the carrier-based antisub aircraft had delivered them to the RAF airfield at Stornoway, Scotland, after a five-hour flight which would live forever in Morris's memory. The terrible weather had given him a whole new respect for the men who flew patrols aboard the four-place aircraft, and the fact that the flight crew were not allowed to ask questions about the absence of their normal tactical crew hadn't made the flight a particularly sociable experience.

At least the weather had improved as they approached the British Isles, and the helicopter flight from Stornoway to Holy Loch wouldn't have been too bad, except for the fact that helicopters had to be the noisiest form of transport yet invented by man. Every muscle ached, and the stump of his right leg throbbed. Dick had better have a damned good reason, Morris thought with yet another stab of resentment and anticipation.

"They'll be down in about ten minutes, Milla," Aston warned.

Ludmilla looked up from the paper wreckage littering Lieutenant Shu's cramped office and shrugged. She looked completely rested, he thought with just a trace of jealousy. She was clear-eyed and her face was relaxed—in sharp contrast to his own red-rimmed eyes and tension. She'd made him shower and shave, and his body appreciated the sense of freshness, but he knew it was false energy.

"I'm about as ready as I can be," she said calmly. She turned her head and smiled; Lieutenant Shu was bent over her desk, head pillowed on her folded arms, and a faintly audible snore came from her. Ludmilla rose quietly, took Aston's elbow, and led him back to the isolation section without disturbing the doctor. An armed Marine corporal followed them, then joined the sentry already there.

"You're sure you can decide without the doc?" Aston asked as soon as the door closed behind them.

"Positive," Ludmilla said confidently, then qualified her statement. "Or let's say as positive as I can be. There's an element of risk, but I think it's acceptable. It'll have to be, won't it?" Her clipped accent had sharpened, burning through the carefully cultivated softening she'd worked on so hard. It was the only sign of anxiety she showed.

"What's the verdict to date, then?"

"Admiral Rose is safe," Ludmilla said, "but not Captain Helsing. Nor, I'm sorry to say, is Doctor Shu. The XO is all right, and so are most of the Marine officers." She shrugged again. "Other than that, the numbers seem about what they'd've been back home. It looks like thirty-six of the hundred and ten we tested could be picked up by the Troll."

"Um. At least Jack's okay," Aston said, rubbing his bald pate wearily. "If worse comes to worst, we can tell him even if we can't tell M&M or Commander Hastings."

"Don't borrow trouble, Dick. We'll know soon enough, and then—"

She broke off as someone knocked quietly on the hatch.

Mordecai Morris was impressed by the security Aston seemed to deem appropriate. The decks were deserted, as were the passages between helipad and sickbay, but *McKee*'s Marine detachment was in evidence—and armed. Not just with sidearms, either.

Their Marine lieutenant guide stopped outside sickbay, and the two sentries there came to attention as he knocked on the hatch.

"Enter," a deep voice called, and the lieutenant opened the hatch and stood aside. Morris and Hastings exchanged speaking glances as they passed between the armed guards, then turned their attention to the two people awaiting them.

They both recognized Aston, and Morris was struck by his exhaustion. He looked spruce enough, but his eyes were red and swollen and his face was weary. He was in civilian dress, but the young woman—girl, rather—sitting on the edge of the bed wore a weird combination of Navy dungarees and one of those gaudy, silk-screened tee-shirts Morris loathed and abominated.

He was surprised to find anyone with Aston, and that prompted him to give the girl another, longer look. She returned his regard levelly, with neither uncertainty nor the arrogance some teenagers used to mask any lack of assurance, and she was a good-looking kid. Not beautiful, but striking—especially with those incredible blue eyes. A little more muscular than he liked, but, then, he was indolent by nature.

"Mordecai," Aston said, and extended his hand. Morris felt the big, calloused hand envelop his with its customary combination of crushing strength and careful restraint and hoped he looked less worn out than Aston.

"Dick." He squeezed back, then nodded to Hastings. "You know Jayne Hastings, I think?"

"We've met." Aston extended his hand to the lieutenant commander in turn. She smiled, but her green eyes burned behind her glasses.

"All right, folks," Aston continued more briskly, "before we do anything else, we need to see your EEGs."

"Dick, what the—"

"Bear with me, M&M," Aston said softly, and Morris was surprised by the almost entreating note in his powerful voice. That silenced him, and he opened his briefcase and dragged out several folded sheets of paper.

"All right, Dick," he sighed. "Here. And Admiral McLain figured it might be as well to send his along, too.

"He did? Four-oh!" Aston exclaimed. "I knew you were a persuasive bastard!" He took the EEGs and, to Morris's surprise (though why anything should surprise him at this point eluded him), handed them to the girl. "Here, Milla," he said, and Morris made his eyebrows stay put despite the odd gentleness in Dick's voice. Could he—? No! It was preposterous.

The girl sat cross-legged on the bed and spread the charts over her lap. She looked like a Girl Scout practicing origami, Morris thought, but her smooth young face was intent. She ran a rosy fingertip across the first graph, clearly searching for something, then set it aside to check the second. Then the third. She looked up at Aston and drew a deep breath, her eyes brightening with what could only be relief, as she nodded.

"Clean sweep," she said softly. "All three of them."

"Thank God," Aston murmured reverently, and sank into the chair by the bed. Morris stared at him in consternation as he rubbed his bald head. It was a gesture Morris had seen often, but Aston's rock-steady fingers had never trembled before, not even after the firefight in Amman.

"Dick?" His friend's reaction had banished his last frustration. The pressure under which this ill-assorted pair labored was too obvious.

"Sorry, Mordecai." Aston shook his head and managed a tired smile. "You'll be pleased to know that you two—and Admiral McLain—belong to a select group. One cleared for the whole story, as it were. Sit down."

He gestured at the extra chairs crowding the small compartment, and the intelligence officers sat wordlessly, staring first at each other and then at him.

"People," he said slowly, "we've been invaded." He saw their shoulders stiffen and grinned tiredly. "In fact, we've been invaded twice—once by the bad guys and once by the good guys. Unfortunately, it looks like the bad guys have the force advantage, and, unless we can figure out how to turn things around, we're all in one hell of a mess."

He had their undivided attention, and the absurdity of the situation appealed to his sense of humor. He repressed an exhaustion-spawned urge to giggle and cleared his throat, instead.

"Commander Morris, Lieutenant Commander Hastings, allow me to introduce the good guys," he said, waving a hand at Ludmilla. "This is Colonel Ludmilla Leonovna, people—*not* a Russian," he added quickly, seeing the same initial assumption in both pairs of eyes and remembering his own first reaction. Amusement strengthened his voice. "Not even a Terran, really. You see, she comes from Sigma Draconis. . . . "

". . . so that's the story," Aston finished three hours later, and the intelligence officers shook their heads in unison. The tale he and Ludmilla had told was incredible, preposterous, impossible to believe . . . and carried the unmistakable ring of truth.

"Dear God," Morris said softly, speaking for the first time in over half an hour. "Dear sweet God in Heaven."

"Amen," Hastings said, equally softly, but there was worry in her eyes. She rubbed the tip of her nose gently for several seconds, then glanced sharply at Ludmilla.

"Excuse me, Colonel—" she began.

"Please, Ludmilla. Or Milla," Ludmilla interrupted.

"All right, Ludmilla," Hastings agreed. "But I've got two burning questions for you."

"Only two?" Ludmilla asked with a crooked smile.

"Two immediate ones," Hastings acknowledged with a shadow of an answering smile. "First, and most pressingly, there's the matter of this symbiote of yours. You say it's transmitted by direct blood transfer?"

"Yes."

"Then I think we have a problem," Hastings said softly. "Possibly a very serious one." Ludmilla raised an eyebrow, inviting her to continue. "Mosquitoes," Hastings said softly, and felt Morris stiffen beside her.

"Don't worry," Ludmilla said quickly. "Believe me, the Normals of my own time worried about the same thing, but we never found a single instance of transmission by any insect or vermin vector."

"Why not?" Hastings asked sharply.

"Two reasons," Ludmilla replied imperturbably. "First, our symbiotes don't seem to approve of insect bites; they exude a sort of natural insect repellent. But the second reason is even more effective. It takes the average human a little less than twelve hours to go into crisis if she's infected with the symbiote, but it acts a lot faster on smaller life forms and *none* of them survive. Any bug that bites me will be dead before it gets its proboscis out of my bloodstream. It'll never live long enough to transmit it to anyone else."

"Oh." Hastings mulled that over for a moment, then nodded slowly. "But what about insects on your home planet?" she asked curiously. "If they're immune because of their different amino acids...?"

"Commander Hastings," Ludmilla said gently, "one of Midgard's main tourist attractions is that the local insects don't like the taste of humans."

"That *would* be an attraction," Hastings agreed with a smile, and Ludmilla felt her spirits rise. That smile carried acceptance as well as amusement. For a moment, she'd been afraid Hastings was going to turn paranoid on her. She'd seen too many people of her own time do exactly the same, and with far less reason.

"But you said you had a second question?" she prompted after a minute.

"Oh, yes! I don't pretend to be an expert, but it occurs to me that this whole thing represents a causal nightmare."

"I couldn't agree more," Ludmilla said sincerely.

"Well, if we accept causality at all, then it sounds to me like we're faced with the disagreement between the Copenhagen School and the Many-Worlds interpretation," Hastings said. "The whole question of what happens when the superposition collapses and—"

"Jayne," Morris said sternly, "I've warned you about talking gibberish."

"Oh, hush, Mordecai!" his disrespectful junior shot back, but she paused. "All right, in simple terms the problem is how Colonel Leonovna—Ludmilla—and this Troll creature can change their own past. On the face of it, the very notion negates the entire concept of causality."

"The old 'can I kill my grandfather' thing?" Morris mused.

"More or less. The point is, what's happening represents a significant alteration to history. Ludmilla, did your records contain any mention of what happened to Task Force Twenty-Three?"

"No. And my hobby interest was military history. If there'd been any record of an authenticated attack on *any* Terran military force by UFOs, I'd've known about it, believe me."

"So we already have a gross shift in *your* history," Hastings pointed out. "Presumably, the effort we'll have to mobilize to do anything effective about this Troll will have an even greater effect. If nothing else, we know these Kanga creatures exist." She smiled unpleasantly. "Knowing that, I think we can confidently assume that their reception will be even more energetic than it 'was' in your own past. But the end result will be that your universe will never come into existence at all!"

"I know," Ludmilla said softly.

"But if it doesn't, then you won't come back, and if you don't come back, then it will," Morris said slowly, rubbing his forehead as he tried to understand. "What do we have here—some kind of loop?"

"That's where the Many-Worlds Theory comes in," Hastings said. "But even if Everett was right—" She shook her head. "I don't even know where to start looking for questions, much less what the answers might be!"

"Neither does anyone where I come from," Ludmilla said wryly. "Look, the whole theory behind a Takeshita Translation is just that: theory. No one's ever tried one—or reported back afterward, anyway—and the argument over what ought to happen *during* one has gone on for a century and a half.

"Jayne, you mentioned the Copenhagen School and the Many-Worlds Theory. We don't use that terminology anymore, but I know what you mean, and the fundamental problem remains, because there's still no way to test either theory." Aston and Morris looked utterly confused, and she made a face.

"Bear with me a minute, you two," she said, "and I'll do my ignorant best to explain, all right?" They nodded, and she went on.

"In its simplest terms, what Jayne is talking about is one of the major problems involved in understanding quantum mechanics. There's been a lot of progress since the twenty-first century, but I'm just a fighter jock." She used Aston's terminology with a wry grin.

"Essentially, there's been a dispute over the basic nature of what we fondly call 'reality' almost since Einstein. According to the math, any possible interaction—or, rather, the *result* of any interaction—is a superposition of functions, each of which represents one possible outcome of the interaction. With me so far?"

"Are you saying that mathematically speaking any of the outcomes is equally valid?" Aston sounded skeptical, and she patted his bald pate playfully.

"For a nullwit, that's not bad," she said teasingly. "Not quite right, but it'll do for starts. You see, the problem is that for any interaction, we observe one—and *only* one—outcome, but the math says the potential for all possible outcomes is bound up in the event. Now, what Jayne is calling the Copenhagen School says that at the moment a wave function—" She paused and grimaced, then resumed as if re-selecting her words. "Well, at the moment an interaction occurs, the whole thing collapses into a single one of the elements of possibility, and the others never come into existence at all. The potentiality of all outcomes remains up until that moment, and none of them can be *absolutely* ruled out, but a weighted probability distribution can be assigned to them, which allows the *effective* prediction of which single event will actually occur. Follow me?"

"Yes, but I'm losing a little ground. How about you, Mordecai?"

"Quit asking me to expose my ignorance. You were saying, Colonel?"

"All right. An alternative hypothesis, proposed sometime in the last century, says, simply, that rather than a single event, *all* possible outcomes occur, however 'probable' or 'improbable' they may be. We observe only one, true, but that's because the others occur on different 'stems' of reality."

"Parallel worlds, right?" Aston nodded. "Our sci-fi writers love 'em."

"They still do back home," Ludmilla assured him. "Anyway, Jayne's Copenhagen School—we call it the Classic School—maintains that there is one and only one reality; a single, linear reality in which the single realized outcome of each interaction is defined and creates

the preconditions for the next. What we call the Revisionist School—
Jayne's 'Many-Worlds' Theory—has gained a tremendous amount
of ground in the last couple of hundred years, though, and some of
its proponents claim that eventually they'll be able to demonstrate
its validity through some esoteric manipulation of the multi-dee.
I've seen the math on it, and it gives me headaches just to think
about it; I certainly don't *understand* it. But the Revisionist School
says that instead of a single reality, there are multiple realities, all
branching off from a common initial source, all equally 'real,' but
never interfacing."

"So where does all this fit into time travel?" Aston asked, but a
gleam in his weary eyes suggested that he saw where she was headed.

"There are three main theories as to what happens in a Takeshita
Translation," Ludmilla said. "One says that the whole thing is
impossible; anyone who tries one simply goes acoherent and stays
there. It's neat, at least, but my survival is empirical evidence that it
doesn't work.

"Theory number two is Takeshita's First Hypothesis, and it says
that anyone making a Takeshita Translation travels backward along
the single reality stem of the Classic School. There are some
problems with it, but, essentially, it says that when the traveler stops
moving—drops back into phase with reality, as it were—he becomes
an event which has been superimposed upon the reality stem. He,
personally, exists, wherever he came from and however he got there.
But since he exists, he can affect the universe, which will inevitably
affect the nature of reality 'downstream' from him, with the result
that—as Commander Morris put it—you really could murder your
grandfather without erasing yourself. *Your* existence is pegged to a
reality which preexists the one in which you were never born.

"Takeshita spent years on the math to support that theory, but in
the last years of his life he became convinced that the Revisionists
had been right all along, which created a furor amongst his followers,
I can tell you! Anyway, he propounded his Second Hypothesis, which
says, essentially, that the classic arguments against paradox are valid
after all—that it's impossible for an individual to move into his own
past. By the act of moving backward in time, he does, indeed,
superimpose his existence on events, but, in the process, he causes
the stream of reality to split off another tributary. In effect, he avoids

paradox by forcing a divergence of 'his' subsequent personal reality line from the one which created him.

"The problem, of course," she ended with a whimsical smile, "is that no hard experimental data was ever available. Until now, that is."

Silence threatened to stretch out indefinitely until Jayne Hastings finally broke it.

"So which theory's correct?" she asked softly.

"Let's start with the basics," Ludmilla suggested. "I *am* here—and so is the Troll. Task Force Twenty-Three *was* attacked and *did* shoot down two Troll fighters. Those facts seem to prove that whatever happened is possible, and, further, that the Troll *can* do whatever it intends to do unless we stop it. Those are the pragmatic considerations. Agreed?"

Three heads nodded, and she went on.

"All right. My own feeling is that Takeshita's Second Hypothesis applies, which means that the Revisionists were right, of course. And it also means that I'm not in *my* past, which neatly explains the absence of any recorded nuclear attack on a US Navy task force in 2007. It didn't happen in my reality—it happened in yours."

"You mean . . . you're not just from *the* future, you're from someone else's future?" Aston sounded a bit shaken.

"Why not? Nick Miyagi could have explained it a lot better—he always did support the Second Hypothesis." Ludmilla smiled sadly. "He almost took time to argue the point with me when we saw it happening. But, yes, that's right. I'm not from your reality—your 'universe'—at all, Dick."

"But . . ." Hastings frowned as she worked through the implications. "Excuse me again, but you seem to be saying you more than half-expected the Kangas to wind up in somebody else's past."

"I did."

"Then why try to stop them?" Hastings asked very quietly. "You say your battle division was totally destroyed, along with thousands and thousands of your people. Your own fighter squadron was destroyed—in fact, you're the *only* survivor from your entire force. Why in God's name take such losses when these 'Kangas' couldn't even hurt your time line at all?"

"Two reasons, really, I suppose," Ludmilla said after a moment.

"First, of course, we couldn't be certain. Remember, Takeshita offered *two* hypotheses, and neither had ever been tested. What if he'd been right the first time, and the Kangas *had* changed our own history?" Hastings nodded slowly, but the question remained in her eyes, and Ludmilla smiled sadly.

"Then there was the second reason," she said softly. "Whoever's past they wound up in, we knew there was going to be *a* human race in it. Not our own ancestors, perhaps, but still an entire planet full of human beings. Commodore Santander and I never actually discussed it, but we didn't have to. We know what Kangas and Trolls are like. There was no way we could have lived with ourselves if we'd let them murder our entire race in *any* time line."

Silence hovered in the compartment, and Aston reached out to clasp her hand. She returned his grip tightly enough to hurt—tightly enough to give the lie to her calm expression—and his heart ached for her. She wasn't simply adrift in time; she was adrift in a totally different, utterly alien *universe*, where none of the worlds she'd known would ever even come into existence. And she was the one—and only—creature of her kind who would ever exist here.

She looked at him for a moment, then smiled. He recognized the courage behind that bright, cheerful expression, but no hint of her total aloneness showed in her voice as she looked back at Hastings.

"And wherever I am, and however I got here, Commander, you've got a Troll on your hands, don't you?" Hastings nodded, and Ludmilla shrugged. "Well, that's something I understand in anyone's universe, and killing Trolls is what I do. So what do you say we put our heads together and figure out how to kill *this* one."

deception *n.*
1. The use of deceit. 2. State or fact of being deceived. 3. Ruse; trickery; imposture. [Middle English *decepcioun*, from Latin *decipere*, to deceive.

—*Webster-Wangchi Unabridged*
Dictionary of Standard English
Tomas y Hijos, Publishers 2465,
Terran Standard Reckoning

CHAPTER FIFTEEN

The office of Vice Admiral Anson McLain, Commander in Chief Atlantic Fleet, was almost stark. Furniture was sparse, and the walls bore none of the usual outsized portraits of sailing ships or World War Two carriers fighting off *kamikazes*. Instead, they were adorned with framed photos of the sleek, high-tech warships of Admiral McLain's early twenty-first-century fleet, although a beautiful painting of two of the *Iowa*-class battleships which had recently been stricken at last to become memorial ships held pride of place behind his oversized desk.

McLain was tough as nails, young for his rank, and black. Regarded by some as the most brilliant naval officer of his generation, he'd paid his dues to crack the traditionally white ranks of the Navy's senior flag officers by being, quite simply, the best there was, of any color. He was a carrier man, a highly decorated pilot with four kills over the Persian Gulf, who had outraged big-ship aviators by supporting construction of *Seawolf* attack subs and supersonic V/STOL fighters at the expense of a thirteenth *Nimitz*-class carrier. That was typical of him, Commander Morris thought; Anson McLain did what he thought right, whatever the cost and without a trace of hesitation.

But at the moment, CINCLANT wore a definitely harassed look. *Roosevelt* was in for repairs, reducing his total deployable flight decks by a sixth, and two more CVNs had been diverted to watch the extremely nasty Falklands situation. Which left McLain's carriers understrength by half for normal deployments at a moment when the Balkans were heating up again. The fact that the People's Republic of China had just commissioned its second carrier didn't help matters one bit, but McLain, the CNO, and the JCS had twisted CINCPAC's arm hard enough to get the newest *Nimitz*, USS *Midway*, transferred from Pearl Harbor to the Atlantic. She was en route to reinforce him now, but for the present, he was stretched thin, indeed.

Far worse, Anson McLain had lost people. He was a cool, analytical man, but he was also implacable. Somehow, someday, he would discover who or what had killed or blinded a thousand of his people, and when he did—

Which explained the fiery light in his normally calm eyes.

"Well, Mordecai," he said mildly, standing and holding out his hand, "I hope your little jaunt was productive."

"It was, Sir," Morris replied as CINCLANT released his hand and gestured to a chair. "Captain Aston *does* know what happened, and why."

"I'm glad to hear that," McLain said softly, and his tone made Morris shiver. It reminded the commander forcibly of Colonel Ludmilla Leonovna. "But what, if you'll pardon my asking, was all the mystery about?"

"That, Sir, is going to be a bit hard to explain," Morris said slowly. He and Jayne Hastings had spent an intense twenty-four hours with Aston and Ludmilla, hammering out what needed to be done, and Morris was only too well aware how much depended on McLain's reaction. He knew his boss better than most, but he also knew what he was about to ask CINCLANT to believe.

"Then you'd better start, M&M," McLain said simply, and the commander drew a deep breath.

"Yes, Sir. To begin with . . ."

Unlike anyone else to whom the story had yet been told, Admiral McLain sat silently, elbows on his desk, chin on the backs of his interlaced fingers, without a single question. CINCLANT hated people who interrupted to demonstrate their own cleverness rather than waiting for the briefing officer to cover the points they were raising, but Morris found it a bit unnerving that the admiral could listen to this story with his usual calm.

He reached the end and stopped, painfully aware of how insane the whole thing sounded. McLain regarded him expressionlessly for a moment, toying with a presentation coffee mug from the crew of his last seagoing command. He ran a dark fingertip over the raised crest of the CVN *Harry S. Truman* and pursed his lips, then leaned well back in his swivel chair.

"A good brief, Mordecai," he said finally, steepling his fingers across his flat, hard belly muscles. "I only have one question."

"Sir?" Morris asked, hoping he looked less anxious than he felt.

"Do you believe a word of it?"

"Yes, Sir. I do." Morris met the admiral's eyes levelly.

"And this Colonel Leonovna is available to answer questions directly?"

"Yes, Sir." Morris was baffled by McLain's calm reaction. "Of course, we—Captain Aston and I, that is—are keeping her under wraps."

"How so?"

"We put her on a MAC flight as a Navy dependent and flew her into Virginia Beach, then hustled her out of sight. She and Captain Aston are at my home right now, keeping a very low profile."

"Really?" McLain smiled for the first time since Morris had begun his report. "And how is your wife taking all this?"

"Rhoda thinks Colonel Leonovna is Captain Aston's niece, Sir. We don't know what her EEG looks like."

"Um." CINCLANT pursed his lips again. "You are aware of just how incredible this all sounds, aren't you, M&M?"

"Yes, Sir. All I can tell you is what I believe to be the truth, Sir. That's what you pay me for."

"I see. All right, then, first things first," McLain said calmly, and reached for the phone on his desk. He punched in a number with slow deliberation and waited for an answer.

"Good afternoon," he said into the phone after a moment, swinging his chair slightly from side to side, "this is Admiral McLain. Please inform Admiral Horning that I must speak with him for a moment." He paused for a few seconds, and his face hardened slightly. "I'm sorry, Lieutenant," he said levelly, "but you're just going to have to interrupt them, then."

Morris tried to appear calm. Admiral Franklin Horning was the

Surgeon General of the United States, and the commander could think of several unpleasant reasons for his boss to seek a medical opinion.

"Frank?" McLain leaned forward in his chair, and his eyes rested on Morris's face. There might have been the hint of a twinkle in them, Morris thought anxiously, as if the admiral could read his mind and was amused by what he was thinking. "Sorry to interrupt your conference, but I need a favor. I warn you—it's going to sound a little strange." He paused as Admiral Horning said something in reply, then chuckled. "Nope, stranger. You see, Frank, I need to see the President's EEG."

Morris had no idea of exactly how Horning responded to that, but as the commander sagged in his chair in relief, McLain winced and moved the phone away from his ear.

The Troll felt a slow, familiar throb of rage. His fragmentary information from Captain Santiago had not included the fact that so many radar stations guarded the Panama Canal Zone, and he'd been forced well out over the Pacific to avoid them, only to find the entire western coast of this "United States" covered by a seemingly solid belt of radar emissions. For a moment he'd wondered if they had somehow learned of his coming, but then he'd noted the large numbers of crude aircraft in evidence. So it was some sort of navigational control system, was it? Or, he amended, *some* of it was, anyway, for on a world so riddled with national competition and suspicions, there had to be military installations, as well.

The need to avoid detection by such primitives infuriated him. The hunger for destruction was upon him once more, and he longed for a few of the ARADs his dead masters had expended upon that never-to-be-sufficiently-accursed naval task force, but he mastered his fury sternly. Time enough for that, he reminded himself. Time enough when he knew more. When he was ready. For now he must be cautious.

He was. He brought his fighter down to within meters of the ocean and crept in slowly, tasting the radar pulses, seeking out chinks in the electronic fence. He found one and slid through it, crossing the coast in darkness at the mouth of the Rogue River. He settled into the Cascade Range just south of Crater Lake National Park and activated his servomechs to camouflage his vessel. He would not be here long, he hoped, but until he departed he could not afford to be disturbed.

He programmed the servomechs carefully, then turned to his other task. He shaped a careful mental hook and cast it out into the world about him, questing for prey. Somewhere out there were minds he could touch. Minds he could strip of the information he required.

He only had to find them.

"You mean to tell me we've been invaded by monsters from outer space?" the President of the United States demanded, staring at Vice Admiral McLain and the pudgy, rumpled commander beside him. "Are you serious, Admiral?"

"By *one* monster, Mister President," McLain corrected. He shrugged. "When Commander Morris came to me with it yesterday, I was only half-convinced. After speaking to Colonel Leonovna last night and seeing the artifacts she brought with her, I no longer doubt any of it. In my considered opinion, she's telling the exact truth."

"My God." The President stared at the admiral, but the initial shock was passing. He'd been astonished when the Atlantic Fleet commander requested a personal meeting to discuss "a grave national emergency," and even more when he discovered that neither the Chief of Naval Operations, the Joint Chiefs of Staff, nor even the Secretary of Defense knew anything about it. Had it been anyone else, the President would have refused with a curt, pointed comment about normal channels, but President Armbruster knew McLain's reputation well enough to know he was not given to fits of temporary insanity.

That faith in the admiral had been sorely tried when he heard what McLain had to say, yet it had been enough to get him a hearing. And now, to his own considerable surprise, Armbruster found that he was actually inclined to believe him.

"A question, Admiral," he said finally. "Why didn't you go through channels with this? Admiral Jurawski and Secretary Cone are a bit upset, you know."

"Both the CNO and the Secretary have expressed their disapproval to me, Mister President," McLain said with a faint smile. "Unfortunately, while I have not been able to examine Admiral

Jurawski's EEG, I *have* managed to get my hands on Secretary Cone's. He's not on the safe list, Sir."

"I see." The President leaned back in his chair and nodded. The admiral was right—always assuming that he was not, in fact, insane. If there was a particle of truth in this fantastic story, absolutely no risks must be run. "But I *am* 'on the safe list'?" he asked wryly.

"You are, Sir. Unfortunately, however, the Vice President isn't."

"Shit." President Armbruster reminded many people of Harry Truman—verbally, if not physically—despite his staunch Republicanism.

"Yes, Sir. The Surgeon General provided me with your records—most reluctantly, I might add."

"I can believe that," Armbruster snorted. "The old bastard has a nineteenth-century code of honor. It goes with the job."

"I realize that, Sir. Fortunately, he knows me rather well and I was able to convince him . . . eventually."

"If—and I say *if*, Admiral—this story holds up, the neurologists of Washington will be doing land-office business in the next few days," the President said.

"Yes, Sir."

"All right." Armbruster slapped his desk explosively. "Bring me this Colonel Leonovna, Admiral. Tonight after supper—say about eight. I'll have a word with the security types and see to it that she gets in." He snorted at a sudden thought. "I'd better come up with another name for her, I suppose. Something non-Russian." He thought for a moment, then grinned. "Ross, Admiral. Miss Elizabeth Ross."

"Yes, Sir."

"And, Admiral," Armbruster said softly as the officers rose to leave.

"Sir?"

"You'd better not be blowing smoke up my august presidential ass on this one, Admiral."

"Understood, Mister President."

"I'm glad, Admiral. Good day."

Late afternoon sunlight coated the hidden fighter in glory and gold, but the Troll paid no heed. His attention was on things far more important, for his mind had touched another he might probe. He started to stab out, then forced himself to pause. He must take more time with this one, feel his way more cautiously. And that meant he must bring the mind to him, so that he might dissect it at leisure.

He "listened," refusing to open the two-way link just yet, and surface impressions trickled into his brain. He studied them carefully, seeing the face of a male human inches from his own and trying to understand the warm tingle of excitement as the face bent closer, pressing its lips to those of the one he'd reached.

It was a pity the male was blocked to him. He could have used them both, but one would do—for now. He took careful note of direction and distance, then activated two of his combat mechs.

They departed noiselessly, drifting through the forest shadows on silent anti-gravs, and the Troll returned to his tenuous link. Fascinating, he thought. So this was what the human mating ritual was like.

Annette Foreman sighed happily, snuggling against her husband in their shared sleeping bag. She always felt deliciously wicked making love on one of their camping trips, especially when they pitched camp early. She felt Jeff's hands stroking her flanks and nipped the side of his neck gently.

"Ouch!" He laughed and pinched her firm bottom in retaliation. She squealed happily. "That'll teach you!" he said, as his hands did other, magic things. "And so will—"

He broke off, and she felt him stiffen. Her eyes flared open in sudden anticipation of embarrassment. Oh, no! She'd always known someone might interrupt them, that was part of what made it feel so wicked, but—

"What the *hell*?" Jeff raised himself on his elbow, and she turned her head, staring in the direction of his gaze.

She stiffened herself as she saw the two strange shapes emerging from under the trees, and her eyes widened. No! There *was* no such thing!

The two shapes floated a yard above the ground, sweeping closer with snakelike speed, yet so silent they seemed to drift, and the two humans watched in frozen disbelief as they climbed the slope towards them.

Jeff Foreman reacted first. Everything about those alien

shapes—from their silent movement to the strange, golden alloy and stranger curves of their forms—roused a primal terror within him. He didn't know what they were, but he didn't have to. The caveman in his soul smelled danger, and he hurled himself out of the sleeping bag, heedless of his nudity, and reached for the short-hafted camp ax.

"Run, 'Nette!" he ordered, and his wife rose to her knees in shock. She'd never heard such harsh command in his voice.

"No! Come wi—"

"Shut up and *run*, goddamn it!" he shouted, and Annette stumbled to her feet in automatic response.

"Jeff—" she started, and he shoved her furiously.

"*Get the fuck out of here!*" he screamed, and the terrible fear in his voice—fear for *her*, she realized sickly—compelled obedience. She turned to flee further up the hill, stones and twigs harsh under her bare soles, and her mind whirled with fragmented images of terror as she pounded up the slope. Her thoughts came in jagged shards, lacerating her with their cruel edges, and the liquid spring sunlight gilded her horror with surrealistic beauty. What were those things? What did they *want*? How could she leave Jeff behind?! But his desperation could not be gainsaid, and she fled as he commanded . . . even as a part of her told her coldly that he must know it was futile.

She'd made it almost to the tree line when a burst of cold, green light exploded about her. The world pinwheeled, slivering her vision like some Impressionist nightmare of a kaleidoscope, and her scream of terror was a whimper as her voluntary muscles spasmed with a horrible, agonizing, *twisting* sensation. She smashed to the ground on her naked breasts and belly, barely conscious of the pain as light roared and howled in her head.

She thought she heard the clang of metal on metal, but her senses were hashed by the staticlike impact of the capture field. She fought the terrible paralysis, a prisoner in her own body, pounded by panic. There might have been another clang of metal, but then she heard a sound she could not mistake. One that drove her savagely abused awareness into the darkness on a gibbering wave of horror.

It was a scream—a dreadful, dreadful scream of agony. An inhuman sound, wrenched from a human throat she knew too well. . . .

❖ ❖ ❖

"Colonel." Jared Armbruster held out his hand with the smile which had captivated millions of voters, but despite McLain's prior briefing, he was astonished by how young she looked. *This* was a fighter pilot? A superwoman from the distant future? The last hope of mankind? Preposterous!

But then she took his proffered hand, and he saw her cool, dark-blue eyes. In his political career, and especially in the last three years of presidential power, he'd seen many eyes. The eyes of people who wanted something, of people who feared the power of his office, of people who hated him or admired him. But never quite like these. Even foreign heads of state were aware of the power he wielded. It was there between them—a challenge to his adversaries, an invisible cloak of authority to his allies. He was surprisingly self-honest and self-deprecating, considering the driving ambition a man must have to seek the office he held, yet he'd become accustomed to seeing the reflection of presidential prestige in the eyes of those he met.

But not in these. These eyes measured him confidently—measured *him*, not the larger-than-life stature of the presidency—with the cool, distant impartiality of a cat. And it was in that moment, when he saw the lack of awe in Ludmilla Leonovna's face, that he truly began to believe.

"Mister President," she said simply, and her grip was stronger than that of any other woman he had ever met.

He held her hand a moment longer than protocol demanded, and she met his gaze calmly. Then he shook himself internally and smiled once more, releasing her to be introduced to Aston.

Ludmilla watched him shake Dick's hand. So this was the most powerful man on Earth. Despite her interest in history, she'd read very little about Jared Armbruster in her own time, for there had been neither wars nor major scandals to make his administration important to a military historian. Given the ominous international rumblings Dick had described to her, Armbruster must have been either very good at his job or extremely lucky to avoid the former, which seemed like a good sign. She hoped it was, at any rate, and she'd picked Dick's brain for every detail she could get about him. It hadn't been easy. Dick obviously respected Armbruster deeply, but perhaps because he knew he did, he had gone out of his way to be painstakingly honest and evenhanded in his analysis of the President.

Physically, Armbruster was about midway between her and Dick in height, his dark hair dramatically silver at the temples, and she rather liked the laugh wrinkles around his eyes even if he did seem to smile a bit too easily, with just a shade too much "spontaneous" charm. But he was a politician, she reminded herself, and it was the nature of the political animal to be charming. On the other hand, she'd asked Dick—and Mordecai—to describe the last presidential election to her in some detail as the best way to get a feel for the man who'd won it, and two things had stuck in her mind.

The first had been Mordecai's caustic description of the political insiders' reaction to the electorate's decision that presidential character mattered after all. None of the analysts had given the little-known junior senator from Montana any chance at all when Armbruster first decided to run, but that was because none of them had realized what he truly was: an honorable man whose tendency to speak his mind, sometimes just a little too colorfully but always bluntly and honestly, had resonated with the voters. It had actually convinced them to take one more shot at electing an honest President, and his campaign had crushed first the front-running candidate in his own party's primary and then an incumbent president who'd confidently anticipated that voter boredom would assure his reelection.

The second thing to stick in her mind was something Dick had said. Jared Armbruster had inherited a badly damaged office, one whose moral authority had been savagely wounded by the last two administrations, and whose prerogatives and power base had been severely curtailed by brutal infighting with the legislative branch. But he had dug in and begun the painstaking process of rebuilding with a combination of shrewdness and a determined effort to make good on his own campaign promises. He was also a staunch internationalist, who had somehow managed to convince an American public which had been intensely focused on domestic matters both to support his diplomatic initiatives and to accept that an effective military—and the investment necessary to produce one—was a vital necessity in a world which seemed determined to go to hell. Unlike Armbruster or the people who had elected him, Ludmilla knew what was waiting (or had been, in her own past, at least) less than ten years down the road . . . and that by the time the wars had finally hit in Europe, the United States' military had sufficiently recovered from its late twentieth-century nadir to keep them contained *to* Europe. Much of that recovery had occurred during Armbruster's administration, and the foresight and determination which had made that possible were impressive.

She had been inclined to agree with both Dick and Mordecai, based on that information alone, that Armbruster was both a good and honest man and a much more skilled politician than his defeated adversaries had allowed for. It remained to be seen whether or not he was also enough of a statesman to handle a situation like this one, yet she remembered the firmness of his grip and the intense, evaluating light in his eyes and felt a tinge of hope.

Armbruster turned away from her to shake Aston's hand, and this time he confronted something he understood. The captain was built like a defensive lineman, he thought, only bigger, and he was dauntingly fit for a man his age. He had the assurance of a professional military man, flavored by an instinctive but confident deference toward his commander-in-chief. The President was an ex-Marine, with the inbred, more-or-less tolerance for naval officers of the breed, but he recognized the tough, confident self-respect of thirty or forty years spent exercising command over one's self and others. It was something the true professionals never lost, he thought, and something the amateurs never gained.

"Captain."

"Mister President."

Armbruster liked the deep, resonant voice. He flattered himself on his judgment of men, and this one felt solid. Dependable. Above all, truthful.

"Admiral. Commander." He greeted his other guests courteously, then gestured at the chairs arranged in a comfortable conversational circle. "Won't you be seated?" he invited.

They sank into the chairs, and he offered refreshments. Of necessity, the conversation was light and inconsequential until they'd been served and the servants had withdrawn. But as the door closed—and every surveillance device, much to the unhappiness of the Secret Service, was switched off—the President turned his brown eyes to Ludmilla, and they were no longer the smiling eyes of a politician. They were dark and thoughtful, challenging without being hostile, and Ludmilla felt a surge of relief as she met them.

David Weber

Yes, she thought. This man *was* a statesman.

"And now, Colonel 'Ross,'" Armbruster said with a slight, wry smile, "suppose you tell your story in your own words."

The Troll's vision receptors watched the planet's single moon drift among the clouds. It was a large moon, compared to the small, red-tinged satellites of the planet where he'd been assembled, and he wondered if he felt any kinship for it. This was the world of his genetic forebears, after all, but if the silent, silver orb meant anything to him, he could not find it.

He turned his attention inward, considering his newest information. It had been . . . entertaining to acquire it. So much more enjoyable than that whimpering, broken thing he'd sampled first. This one—this "Annette" one—had been different. Terrified, yes, but not broken. Not at the start.

If the Troll had possessed lips, he would have smiled . . . and not pleasantly. The female had been frightened when the combat mech delivered it, naked and bruised, bleeding from the abrasions of its fall. Frightened, but filled with a hate that almost matched his own. An ignorant hate, one which didn't begin to understand, but a savage, knife-edged emotion he understood.

It had pleased him.

Yes, he thought happily, its defiance had pleased him. It was almost like the *Shirmaksu*'s stimulation of his pleasure centers, only brighter, sharper . . . stronger. He had encouraged it to fight by varying the power of his probe, letting it think it had driven him out and then driving in once more until it screamed in agony. Such a frail thing, compared to the endless web of power which backed his own organic component, and so delicious. He had toyed with it, delighting in its frantic resistance and the lovely essence of its hate, hurting it and savoring the exquisite bouquet of its terror and despair.

He tasted the pleasure once more in memory, then put it firmiy aside. He had recorded it; he could return to its sweetness whenever he wished.

Yet there had been more than pleasure. He'd learned much—more of technique than of substance, to be sure, for the female had known little of immediate use. But what little it had known, he knew. He had stripped that lovely, hate- and agony-filled brain to its quivering core, raping away its knowledge, and his cruelty had been more than merely an end in itself, for he had refined his technique. If he wished, he probably could brain-strip his next subject without inflicting any damage at all.

If he wished. If *he* wished. He savored his self-direction. The heady power to act as he chose against these puny, fragile humans and their ignorance. To exert his omnipotence upon them.

He activated an interior pickup and looked down upon the husk which had been Annette Foreman, twenty-five, a schoolteacher and the mother of a little girl who would never know what had become of her parents. The once vital face was ugly with mindlessness, bruised and streaked with blood from the lips the female had bitten ragged in its extremity.

It was a pity they were so fragile, he thought regretfully, summoning a servomech to remove the carrion. They broke so quickly. This one had lasted barely six hours. Such a pity.

"All right," President Armbruster said finally. The coffee table was littered with empty cups and the remains of pastry. Armbruster drained his own cup and rubbed his eyes. It was four A.M., and he had a cabinet meeting at nine, but somehow that seemed utterly unimportant at the moment.

"All right," he repeated, "I believe you." He leaned back in his chair and his eyes swept their faces, seeing the mirror of his own weariness. "As one of my predecessors—a Democrat, unfortunately—said, 'The buck stops here.'"

He pinched the bridge of his nose, marshaling his thoughts, then looked at Anson McLain.

"Admiral, you did exactly the right thing. All of you did. If Colonel Leonovna is right about this cyborg—this Troll of hers—we're in the worst mess this poor, abused planet's ever faced. And, Captain—" he looked at Aston "—you called it when you said security will be a copper-plated bitch." He smiled tiredly.

"Okay. You people have earned your pay, now it's time I earn mine. Admiral McLain."

"Sir?"

"You're already in this up to your gold-braided ass, so as of this moment, the Navy is officially in charge. We'll work out of your office."

"I'm honored, Mister President," McLain said carefully, "but with all due respect, I'm a bit—"

"I know. I know." Armbruster waved his hand. "The Balkans are smoking, the whole damned South Atlantic is on fire, and I'm handing you a fresh can of gasoline. Well, Admiral, I think we'll just have to put out the immediate fire for you."

"Sir?"

"Tomorrow morning—no, this morning, I suppose—I intend to invoke the War Powers Act." He smiled again, humorlessly. "I have no doubt half of Congress will be drawing straws to see who gets to move a vote to test its constitutionality, but by the time they do, you will have moved Second Fleet into position and I will have informed the United Kingdom and Argentina that the fighting is to *stop*." He smiled tiredly at Mordecai Morris's horrified expression.

"Don't panic, Commander. I happen to know the Brits *want* to stop. I'll warn the PM before I pull the plug, but she'll go along. Buenos Aires may be less happy about it, but they're getting the ever-loving shit kicked out of them. I think they'll accept without pressing their luck—they may even be grateful for it, later. But tell your boys and girls that if they don't, I *will* use whatever force is necessary to compel them, Admiral."

"Yes, Sir," McLain said tonelessly.

"I'm not just flexing my muscles, Admiral," Armbruster told him. "I've got other reasons, but we don't need a protracted crisis to drag on and divert our resources. Agreed?"

"Agreed, Sir."

"Good. Now. I'll arrange EEGs on the cabinet, the Joint Chiefs, and the heads of the FBI, CIA, DIA, and NSA. The Congressional leaders are going to be tougher, but I think I can swing it." This time his smile was tight with the awareness of his own power. "I'll have my staff checked, too. I'm afraid we can be absolutely certain some of the people we need aren't going to pass muster, but if I go around firing them in wholesale lots for no apparent reason, the entire situation will blow up in our faces. So what we'll have to do is set up a deception within a deception.

"I intend to create two crisis teams. One will be charged with collecting and collating information on what's already happened and with looking for any signs of additional extraterrestrial interference. They'll operate under maximum security conditions—to prevent a public panic—but I intend to staff it primarily with people who fail the EEG test. That, I imagine, is no more than our Mister Troll will expect, and the fact that the team will know nothing beyond what it can dig up on its own ought to reassure him if he picks up on them.

"The real command team, Admiral, will be headed by you, with Commander Morris as your assistant. It will consist only of individuals the Troll *can't* tap, and you will report directly to me. Your mission will be to find the Troll and destroy it—at any cost. If at all possible, I want that fighter intact, but destroying the Troll takes absolute priority."

He paused and regarded them silently for just a moment, then spoke very slowly and distinctly.

"Understand me. When—and note that I say *when*, not if—this thing is found, we will kill it, wherever it is, and whatever it takes. If necessary, I will order a nuclear strike on my own authority to accomplish that end."

There was a chill silence as his grim determination soaked into his listeners.

"I hope, however," he said finally in a lighter tone, "to avoid that. Captain Aston, I understand you're due to retire next month?"

"Yes, Mister President."

"Not anymore, I'm afraid. Stan Loren will have to get along without you a bit longer—I need your operational expertise more than he does."

"Yes, Sir."

"I'll see to it you get that extra ring immediately, just to give you a bit more clout, but basically, Captain, you're going to be Admiral McLain's field commander. You will confer with Colonel Leonovna, and the two of you will determine what force structure you require. I want it kept in the family, so you'll assemble your personnel from the Corps."

"Yes, Sir. May I recruit SEALs, as well?"

"You swabbies!" Armbruster startled them all with a genuine chuckle. "All right, you can use them, too, if you want."

"Thank you, Sir."

"Colonel Leonovna, I realize you don't fall under my authority, but—"

"I do for the duration, Mister President," Ludmilla interposed.

"Thank you. In that case, we'll arrange suitable military rank for you. In the Corps, I think," he added, giving Aston a lurking grin. "I'm afraid no one would be ungallant enough to believe you look old enough to hold a colonel's rank, but we should be able to get away with making you a captain. At any rate, I would appreciate it if you would act for public consumption as Captain—I mean Admiral—Aston's aide."

"Certainly, Mister President."

"Thank you," he said again, and stood, stretching. "Unfortunately, we have no idea at all where this Troll is, where he may be headed, or what he intends to do once he gets there. We have no assurance that he's anywhere near our own territory or even the territory of one of our allies, and, given the nature of the threat, we cannot possibly justify leaving the entire rest of the world in ignorance. Which means, of course, that I'm going to have to tell at least some other people the whole story."

"Mister President," Ludmilla began, and he waved her to silence.

"Don't worry, Colonel. I'll be circumspect, I assure you. In regard to which, it looks like another set of EEGs is in order. Commander Morris, you seem like an inventive fellow. Are you?"

"Uh, I like to think so, Mister President," Morris said with a sinking sensation.

"Good," the President said with his most charming professional politician smile. "Think up a good, convincing argument I can use to get hold of President Yakolev's EEG."

"*Sir?*" Morris choked himself off before he could say anything else. "I'll try, Sir."

"So will I, Commander," Jared Armbruster said softly. "So will I."

The Troll completed his analysis of the data. The female's knowledge suggested that it might be even simpler than he had expected. This United States was a hopelessly inviting target, wide open to penetration even by its own criminal element and its purely terrestrial enemies, much less by him. The bare bones of a plan were already falling into place.

It was a pity the female had known so little about its country's atomic weapons production, but he had gleaned at least one name from its pitiful memory. Oak Ridge. Oak Ridge, Tennessee, he thought.

It was as good a place to start as any.

CHAPTER SIXTEEN

Rhoda Morris sat patiently in the waiting room, reading a magazine. She had huge, liquid eyes in a face as dark as her husband's, but she was slender, graceful, and always immaculately groomed. She thought Mordecai was silly to insist on a complete physical—they'd had their annual checkups only four months ago—but he'd been insistent. She wondered what bee had gotten into his bonnet and why, for the first time ever, he'd insisted on complete neurological exams, but it wasn't worth a fuss.

She turned a page and felt a familiar pang as she saw an ad with a young mother and two pink-faced babies, for her inability to conceive was the one true sorrow of her life. She'd learned to live with it, but the pain seemed sharper in a setting like this, as if proximity to medical people made her more aware of what she'd been denied.

But she'd been given so much else, she thought, and turned the page firmly. She had Mordecai, and though he, too, regretted their childlessness, he was not a man given to bitterness. Even the loss of his foot, horrible though it had been at the time, hadn't embittered him ... and it had ended his dangerous wanderings about the world's trouble spots. She'd learned, in time, to stop feeling guilty over her gratitude.

She finished the article and laid the magazine aside, wondering how much longer Dick Aston and his niece would be staying. She'd always liked Captain Aston, ever since the evening he'd personally escorted her to the hospital in Jordan. He'd been so calm and reassuring; only later had she learned that he'd saved Mordecai's life.

It was strange how suddenly they'd arrived, but she was glad they had. In fact, she would be a bit sad when—

The door opened and Mordecai came in with the doctor. She looked up and smiled, and he smiled back.

"Well?" she asked cheerfully.

"Not a problem in the world, Mrs. Morris," the young doctor said, and she nodded placidly. Of course there hadn't been.

"I take it you're satisfied now, Mordecai?" she asked, opening her purse for her sunglasses.

"Of course I am, dear," he said, linking elbows with her as they headed for the door. She squeezed his arm against her side happily. Twenty-three years, and they still held hands when they walked. How many other couples could say that?

"Good." He held the door and she stepped through it. "Mordecai, we have to pick up a few groceries on the way home."

"Fine," he said, unlocking her car door and opening it for her.

"Tell me," she said, as he closed his own door, latched his safety harness, and slipped the car into the traffic, "do you know if Dick and Milla can stay for the concert next week?"

"I'm afraid not. Dick's being transferred, and Milla will be going home when he leaves."

"What a pity!" she sighed.

"Yes, dear," he said softly, and reached over to squeeze her knee. She looked at him in slight surprise, but he said nothing more. He couldn't, for her alpha waves lacked the critical spike.

CIA Director Stanford Loren was irked. The steady buildup to a fresh Balkan crisis had been bad enough. Aside from Al Turner and the President himself, no one seemed capable of really believing that the wreckage of what had once been Yugoslavia had even more potential as the spark for a global disaster than the continuing, interminable Pakistani-Indian grimacing over Kashmir. Just because none of the Balkan states had developed nuclear weapons of their own didn't mean they couldn't get them elsewhere, and he was uncomfortably certain that several of the factions were doing some intense shopping. The economic meltdown which had finished off the Yeltsin government and returned old-time central control to Russia had only increased their opportunities, and Yakolev hadn't had time to change that. But could he and Jared Armbruster get the rest of the Western world to take them seriously about it? Hell no! The Balkans were a *European* problem, as the French premier had just pointedly remarked, and the previous administration's unilateral decision to yank the US troops which had been mired down in Bosnia for over six years had deprived the present American government of any voice in solving it.

But then, on top of that, had come all that carnage in mid-Atlantic. Then a shooting war had caught every one of Loren's analysts flat-footed, and now the President had been bitten by some infernal health bug! The last thing Loren needed at this moment was to report to Bethesda for a complete medical exam, and he'd been tempted to put it off until the President forgot about it.

No such luck. The Surgeon General had called to remind him in person! So here he sat in a hospital room, waiting for the results he knew damned well would prove him perfectly healthy, if a tad overweight, when he *needed* to be out at Langley trying to make sense out of the world. Only in Wonderland on the Potomac, he told himself bitterly.

The door opened, and he looked up sharply, but the tart remark died on his lips as the President himself walked in.

"Good morning, Stan," Armbruster said, but there was a shadow behind his smile, and Loren hadn't known him for twenty years without learning to see beneath his surface.

"Good morning, Jared," he said cautiously.

"I know you think I've gone round the bend," Armbruster said, crossing to the window and looking out. "Would it make you feel any better to know that Hopkins and Turner are here, too?"

Loren frowned. Floyd Hopkins ran the Defense Intelligence Agency, and Al Turner was the deputy director (and real head) of the National Security Agency. Which gave the Director of the CIA furiously to think.

"So is Dolf Wilkins," the President added with a crooked grin, and Loren added the Director of the FBI to his astonishing mental list. "All for a reason, Stan. All for a reason."

"What reason?" Loren asked carefully.

"Stan," the President said, turning and crossing his arms, "I'm going to tell you a story. One I'm afraid I can't tell Floyd or Al. After that, I'm going to drop in on Dolf, but there won't be any record that I saw either of you. Interested?"

"Intrigued would be a better word."

"Oh?" Armbruster chuckled grimly. "Well, you'll be more than just intrigued by the time I finish, Stan."

"Looks like things are finally moving," Aston said as he paged through the folder in his lap.

"At last," Ludmilla threw in without looking up from her book. She was tipped back in a chair, reading a copy of *The Marine Officer's Guide.*

"Give us a break, Milla," Morris protested half-seriously. "You knew the first layer'd be the hardest to set up, but we're starting to make progress now. And every senior man we clear gives us that much more reach down to the lower levels."

"And that much more chance for a 'normal' leak," Hastings said sourly.

"True," Morris agreed with a sigh. He lit another cigarette, and she glared at him.

"I'm going to tell Rhoda you're cheating."

"Snitch," he said, and took a deep drag. "And don't worry too much about leaks. People like Loren and Wilkins know how to keep secrets. It's the congressional side I worry about."

"Don't," Aston said, making a check beside a name in his folder. "The President isn't going to tell them." He chuckled nastily at Morris's raised eyebrow. "You hadn't heard? He decided last night. Just what we needed—a House Speaker with the wrong EEG and an IQ equal to his shoe size! I'm just as happy, though. This way Armbruster can brief all the oversight committees with the cover story, and we can get on with the real job without a lot of elected busybodies blabbing to the press."

"That's a pretty bitter view of your elected representatives, Dick," Ludmilla said, glancing up from her book at last.

"But a realistic one," Morris replied before Aston could. "Some of them—maybe even a majority of them, though I wouldn't want to get *too* optimistic on that point—are probably honorable human beings. But a bunch of them are neither honorable nor anything I'd like to call human, and a single asshole can blow any operation.

What's that old saying? 'Any two people can keep a secret if one of them is dead . . . unless he was a politician.'"

"Something like that," Hastings agreed. She looked over at Aston. "How's the strike team selection coming, Admiral?"

"Keep calling me 'Admiral' and the first strike is going to land right on your head," Aston growled. She made a face, and he went on with a smile. "Not too bad, so far. We've got a Marine major with a head injury from a training accident last year. They ran lots of tests, and he's got a great, big, beautiful spike right where we need it. Looks like a good man, too."

"You're making it an all-Marine operation after all?" Morris asked interestedly.

"I may. I'm trying to find as many key people as I can without any new testing, and life'll be a lot simpler if they're all from the same branch of the service. And much as it pains me to admit it, Marines may be even better for this kind of operation."

"But how are you going to decide what firepower you need?" Ludmilla wanted to know. "We still haven't solved that one."

"Oh, sorry." Morris rubbed his forehead and smiled apologetically at her. "I should've told you. Admiral McLain's arranged for the Army to take a couple of obsolete tanks that were earmarked for scrapping out of the disposal queue and hand them over to us for testing purposes, instead. Of course," he added sardonically, "they don't know exactly what we'll be testing."

"All right!" Aston said, grinning. "How soon?"

"I'm not sure. Sometime tomorrow or the next day, I think."

"Where?" Ludmilla demanded. "It's got to be a secure place."

"Oh, we've found one that's plenty secure." Morris grinned. "There's a big underground chamber out in New Mexico. They dug it for the nuclear test series we carried out after the START II treaty finally crapped out, but the final two or three shots got scrubbed as part of the CPI nuclear reduction negotiations with China, Pakistan, and India last year."

"Sounds good," Aston agreed, then closed his folder with a snap. "Anything else from Loren?"

"He's got the cover crisis team in place. The plan is for the VP to take over with Loren as his 'assistant.' I think Loren's a little pissed at being stuck over there, but he and Wilkins will make sure we get copies of anything they bird-dog for us. Frankly, they're more likely to spot something than we are since they can use the whole security setup. But *our* team's the only one who can *recognize* what they spot."

"It'll just have to do," Aston said pensively. "I only wish we had some idea what the bastard is thinking about right now."

The Troll was exhilarated. At last, thanks to a penniless, embittered drifter named Leonard Stillwater, he'd found his final element.

It was a shame about Stillwater, the Troll chided himself. Something might have been made of it if he'd been a bit more careful. He would have to watch himself. The pleasure of raping human minds was addictive, but he must learn to ration it. Stillwater, for example, had held a promise its shoddy exterior and slovenly thought patterns had hidden until too late.

The Troll checked automatically on his servomechs as they completed the day's camouflage. His progress across the United States had been slower than expected, but that was not without advantages. He'd finally acquired enough data on the humans' primitive radar to build a crude but effective ECM system against it, and there had been time to gain more information.

The Stillwater human had given him the most astonishing data of all, and the Troll had stopped north of the Broken Bow Indian Reservation in the Quachita Mountains of Oklahoma to ponder. Such a lovely revelation deserved careful consideration.

It was odd, but he'd never really wondered how humans thought about other humans, and it had come as a shock when he ripped into the Stillwater human's brain and found the hatred festering at its core. So much like his own in so many ways, and in a *human* brain! Marvelous.

The Troll had never heard of the White People's Party, nor of the American Nazi Party or the Ku Klux Klan—not until his combat mechs brought him the hitchhiking Stillwater. It had been dirty and terrified, yet there'd been something about it, the Troll thought—a sort of mean-spirited, vicious defiance under its whining panic. Perhaps that should have alerted him, caused him to proceed more cautiously.

Perhaps, but the human mattered far less than the hatred the Troll had discovered. He'd recognized it instantly as yet another chink in the armor of his human prey—and one so well suited to his needs!

It would require care, but the unthinking hatred of minds like Stillwater's would lend itself to his manipulation, and their need for a leader to think for them would make it much, much easier.

He only had to find another Stillwater, one with more polish and the wit to understand what the Troll could offer it.

Nikolai Stepanovich Nekrasov enjoyed his position as the Russian Federation's ambassador to the United States. He would not have cared to admit it to many people, but he rather liked Americans. True, they were incredibly ill-organized, undisciplined, and spoiled, with more than their fair share of national chauvinism (a vice, he admitted privately, his own people shared in full measure). They were absolutely convinced that the political changes in his own nation were the direct result of *their* shining example, while its economic woes stemmed solely from a *failure* to emulate them properly. Possibly as a consequence, they retained a deep-seated distrust of his people which was matched only by Russia's suspicion of them. They were further handicapped by their ridiculous (and, in his opinion, naive) insistence that individuals were more important than the state, and their feelings were hurt with absurd ease if anyone even suggested that they were not universally beloved just because they enjoyed a material lifestyle most of the rest of the planet only dreamed of.

But he was willing to admit that, having been raised as a prototypical Marxist-Leninist new man, his own perceptions of them might, perhaps, be just a tiny bit flawed. And he also found them generous and polite, and, unlike many of his erstwhile comrades in the Party—good democrats all, now, of course!—he rather liked Americans' ingrained refusal to bow to power or position. The pre-Yeltsin Party would have understood Americans far better (and possibly even have remained in power, he thought), if its members could just have grasped that the European class system had never really caught on in North America despite the best efforts of its own leftist politicians.

Yet there were times, he thought, staring out the window of his embassy office, when these people frightened him. They had a ruthless streak, and they believed in effectiveness and decisiveness. Those were dangerous deities for an opponent to worship. It took a great deal to convince an American president to stop worrying about public opinion. The last two administrations had been devastating proof of that. But once a president *did* make that decision, there was no telling how far he might go. Worst of all, he could be virtually certain of widespread public support if his people perceived his actions as both determined and effective, and the ambassador had tried for over a year now to convince his own President that *this* American President truly was both determined and effective. It was unfortunate that so many hardline members of President Yakolev's cabinet—including Aleksander Turchin, Yakolev's Foreign Minister and Nekrasov's own boss—continued to think that the anti-American card was a winning one. Nekrasov understood his countrymen's resentment over the way in which their government had become in so many ways a pensioner of the last surviving true superpower, and his own temper tended to rise alarmingly whenever one of his American "hosts" got up on his or her high horse and began lecturing him on all the things which were wrong with his country . . . for which, of course, the lecturer of the moment just *happened* to have all the right answers. And "standing up" to the generally ineffectual policies of Armbruster's predecessors had been a cheap way for Russian governments teetering on the brink of collapse to win points for "showing strength," both domestically and in the international arena. The fact that it had also helped create, or at least continue, the steadily deteriorating Balkan situation by filling the Americans with so much frustration they had finally thrown up their hands in disgust and gone home like petulant children seemed to have escaped the attention of Turchin and his cronies.

Or perhaps it hadn't. Nekrasov had his own suspicions about where the Foreign Minister was headed. His carefully managed friendship with a currently disgraced ultranationalist general like Viatcheslav Pogoscheva struck the ambassador as an extremely ominous sign, but for the moment, at least, Yakolev needed Turchin's support back home. And so it went, Nekrasov thought glumly. It took only a handful of self-serving opportunists, sometimes only a single one, to set the work of scores of honest men at nought, and his country's democratic institutions were still young and vulnerable, still lacked the toughness and precedents to survive such cretins.

The familiar gloomy thoughts flickered through his brain, but today they were only a background, for he faced a far more urgent (and inexplicable) puzzle. Determined and effective Armbruster had proven himself over the last thirty months, but just what did he think he was doing now? From the moment he'd taken office, he'd worked to improve Latin American relations, and his efforts had born startling fruit. What was left of the Sandinistas were finally in full retreat, relations with Mexico and even Colombia had shown steady improvement, and he'd wrung potent domestic Cuban political reforms out of Fidel's successors by skillful use of economic concessions as the moribund Cuban economy obviously entered its final decline, yet—

He stopped that thought with a brisk headshake. Dwelling on Armbruster's achievements served no purpose, but it did give point to Nekrasov's current puzzlement. After all that, why should Armbruster suddenly deliver what amounted to an ultimatum which had to play right into the hands of his country's Latino adversaries? The United States had no compelling strategic interest in Argentina or the Falklands, and the whole world knew it, so why had Armbruster suddenly intervened so massively . . . and clumsily?

Nekrasov had the strangest impression that something was happening behind the scenes. He didn't think Armbruster's ultimatum was a put-up job; it was clear to him that the Britishers were winning handily and that a cease-fire would benefit the Argentinos far more than the Americans' allies. Not that Buenos Aires seemed to share his analysis. Still, however trapped by their own rhetoric the generals might be, they were military men (of a sort, at least); they had to know the truth.

And yet . . . and yet, in an odd way, the whole South Atlantic situation was only a side show. He couldn't have said why he was so certain, but he was. There wasn't a single scrap of hard intelligence to support his suspicion, and he knew his KGB "colleagues" privately derided it as no more than was to be expected from a pro-Western economic apologist like himself.

Still, he would feel better after he spoke to the President on Monday. He'd established a reasonably friendly adversarial relationship with Jared Armbruster, and he believed he could discover much the President hoped to keep hidden.

✻ ✻ ✻

The Reverend Blake Taggart slammed his car door and delivered a venomous kick to the front fender. It hurt his foot, but the deep dent made him feel a little better. Not much, but a little.

His cup was full, he told the darkness bitterly. He should have stopped in Muse and had the threshing sound under the hood checked, but the whole town had been closed up tighter than a drum. Besides, that would have cost money, and money was not in great supply at the moment.

He sighed and walked moodily around the car. He should have gotten rid of the gas-hog months ago, but it was the last vestige of his empire, and he hadn't quite been able to let go of it.

He unlocked the limo's trunk and opened a Gucci suitcase, got out a white silk handkerchief, and tied it to the TV aerial, and his expression was unhappy. If only he still had a driver he could have sat comfortably on his ass while he sent the poor bastard off for help; now *he* had to take the hike.

He growled a heartfelt curse and fumbled in the trunk for a more comfortable pair of shoes, then sat on the bumper to change.

He'd had such hopes, once. His message had seemed so perfect—it had certainly been lucrative enough! He'd begged his followers to support his ministry, and they had: right into a palatial home, swimming pools, a multimillion dollar Midwest television station.... Oh, yes. All the things he'd longed for growing up in the North Carolina hills had been his at last.

There'd been times, he mused as he tied his shoes, when he'd actually thought there might really be a God.

His clean-shaven, neatly scrubbed image—bolstered by his carefully maintained accent and the rolling hellfire and damnation of his self-taught, bigoted, street-preacher father—had carried him high in the world, and a carefully metered dose of intolerance and more than a hint of racism had given him teeth. "A Coughlin for the Twenty-First Century," one critic had called him, but his sermons had comforted his "flock." Surely if a man of God shared their feelings, they couldn't be wrong!

But then that frigging reporter started after him and the wheels came off. Taggart ground his teeth in remembered rage. It had seemed so trivial, at first—just a single business deal which had intruded into the light somehow. Nothing to worry about. But the bastard hadn't stopped digging, and the more he dug, the more he found. Those deals with certain less than savory brokers. That questionable land speculation in Colorado—the little prick had burrowed through three separate dummy corporations to find out who was really behind that one. Then his connections with the Las Vegas casino and his women. Damn it, he was only human! He had the same sex drive as—

He chopped the thought off with a bitter laugh. It had been a mistake to try to buy the little fart off, but he'd had to do *something*! How was he supposed to know the son-of-a-bitch was *recording* the entire conversation?

The contributions dried up. His special brand of followers would tolerate a lot, but not that much. Truth to tell, he was pretty sure it was the hookers that had done it in the end. His supporters might have stood for the land deals and the casino—he might even have been able to convince them that he hadn't known what his "business managers" were up to—but not the hookers. Hypocrisy only worked until you got caught.

He closed the trunk with a solid *thunk* and looked around the darkness again. He'd crossed US 269 a few miles back, and there was an all-night gas station there. The bastards probably didn't have an on-duty mechanic—nobody did, these days—but they'd have a phone and they'd know where he could find a wrecker. He shuddered at the thought of paying for it, but, he told himself with a bitter smile, perhaps the Lord would provide.

He ought to. He'd dropped His friend Blake Taggart deep enough into the shit already.

An inner alarm claimed the Troll's attention. That delightful mind he'd tasted as it passed had stopped. Why, it was practically motionless now, shining in his senses like a beacon of greed and resentment! He'd been certain it would sweep out of his range before he could do anything about it, but perhaps he'd been wrong.

He sharpened his mental focus, "listening" to its surface thoughts, getting a better fix on its location. Oh, yes, things were shaping up nicely. And this time, he reminded himself as he dispatched his combat mechs once more, he would be careful.

✤ ✤ ✤

"Whiskey One, this is Sierra Three. I have incoming. Range to your position three-niner-seven, bearing oh-seven-four relative, altitude two-five-oh feet, speed seven-five-oh knots. I make it two with a trailer, but the trailer looks bogus. Could be a second pair tucked in tight. Over."

"Sierra Three, Whiskey One copies." Commander Zachary Orwell, USS *Washington*'s CAG, checked his PriFly screens and nodded. "Papa Delta Niner-Two is headed your way," he said. "Meet him on Tac Four, I say again, Tac Four. Over."

"Roger, Whiskey One. Sierra Three Out."

Four F-14Ds of VF-143, known as the "Pukin' Dogs" from the head-down griffin of their squadron insignia, swept their wings and sliced through the air at a thousand miles per hour. Commander Lewis Tobin, VF-143's CO, sat in the front seat of the lead fighter.

"Talk to me, Moose," he said.

"Just a sec, Skipper." Lieutenant Amos "Moose" Comstock was bent over his panel, watching his display alter as the Hawkeye known as Sierra Three gave him a direct data feed from its radar and onboard computers. "Okay, I've got the dope, Skip. How do you want to handle it?"

"Set us up head-on," Tobin directed. "We'll hang onto our altitude."

"Rog. Come around to one-three-four true, Skipper."

The Tomcat swung right and bored on through the sky, followed by its three fellows. Each of the big fighters carried two Phoenix missiles, backed up by three AMRAAM Slammers and a pair of AIM-9Q Sidewinders.

"Closing to two hundred miles, Skip. Want me to light up?"

"Do it," Tobin replied, his mind busy. Second Fleet had declared a one hundred nautical mile free-fire zone around Task Force Twenty-One to give ample coverage against the fifty-mile range of the late-model Exocet ASMs of the Argentine Navy. The bogeys' high speed looked a lot like the Dassault-Breuguet Super Entendard. The Entendards were older even than Tobin's venerable Tomcat and had been relegated to secondary duties years earlier. But the Argentine Air Forces' losses had been so severe that the elderly aircraft had been pressed back into service as their main Exocet attack platforms, with the dwindling supply of much newer Mirage 2000-5s covering them.

But whatever they were, they weren't friendlies, and the rules of engagement were clear: anything that entered the zone was to be killed. Tobin had no real desire to kill people, especially not if it could be avoided, but anyone burning that much fuel in burner way out here at less than three hundred feet was hardly up for a check flight.

The fighter's radar went active, probing down the bearing supplied by Sierra Three.

"Got 'em, Skip. The Hummer was right—there's four of the little buggers. Range one-eight-four and closing. They're forty miles from the zone, and they ain't answering anybody."

"Go to TWS. Let's see if *that'll* warn the bastards off."

"Switching now."

Unless the incoming pilots were sound asleep, their radar warning receivers must have detected the shift from search mode to track-while-scan. If so, they now knew there were Tomcats in the area with weapons locked on them. They might be willing to ignore the warn-off being transmitted by the ships of the task force, but would they ignore that?

They would. They kept right on coming.

"Papa Delta Flight, Niner-Two. Red Section has the leaders: I'll take the point man; Niner-Four, you take his wing. We'll go with Slammers. If the trailers don't break off, White Section will take them."

Acknowledgments crackled in his ears as the range continued to drop.

"That's it, Skip," Comstock said tautly. "They're inside the zone."

"Okay, Moose. Take 'em down."

"Roger. Flashing scope, Skip. Opti-launch coming up . . . *now!*"

A launch-and-leave missile dropped free, ignited, and flashed ahead of the big fighter at Mach Four. "One minute to impact," Comstock reported as Tobin broke in a sharp turn to port. He wanted to position himself on the bogeys' tails if they should somehow elude Papa Delta Flight's missiles.

They didn't. The two lead planes hit the water in flaming pieces at almost eight hundred miles an hour, but the two in the rear never hesitated. They only squatted still closer to the waves and bored right on in until White Section blew them out of the sky.

✧ ✧ ✧

Blake Taggart didn't have a clue what had hit him. One moment he was walking angrily along the night-black highway; the next there was a weird flash of light, and then . . . nothing. Nothing at all, until he woke up here. Wherever "here" was.

He tried to sit up, but his muscles refused to obey. Part of his brain told him that should frighten him, but he felt only a dreamy wonder. He stared up at a blank metal ceiling, breathing slowly, and something scuttled around the inside of his skull like a spider's dancing feet.

"Welcome, Blake Taggart."

The voice came from all around him—a queer, dead-sounding voice. Mechanical, he thought dreamily, and cold, and it echoed inside his head as well as in his ears.

"Your kind has not treated you well, Blake Taggart," the dead voice went on. "I have seen in your memory how they turned upon you."

Taggart felt the familiar visceral rage. It bubbled within him, yet for all its familiarity, it was different now, stronger than ever, as if his resentment had been honed and sharpened while he was unconscious. As if the last vestige of acceptance had been stripped away by a surgeon's scalpel, leaving only the cold fury of betrayal. He tried to speak, but his lips and tongue were as dead as the rest of his muscles.

"If I choose to help you, Blake Taggart," the slow, grinding voice said, "you can regain all you have lost, and more. You will have your vengeance . . . and I will have mine. Do you understand, Blake Taggart?"

The paralysis left his vocal cords. He made a strangled sound of surprise when he discovered that fact, then swallowed a mouthful of saliva.

"W-What do you mean?" he asked finally, then grunted as anguish lashed his nerves. It vanished almost before he could feel it, but he swallowed again, harder, as he recognized its warning.

"I am generous, Blake Taggart, but not . . . patient. You will do well to remember that. Do you understand?"

"Yes," he whispered. Then, louder, "*Yes!*"

"Better," the voice said. "Blake Taggart, I require a human assistant with certain talents. You may be that assistant."

"For what?" It was odd how unafraid he was, as if his churning anger armored him against fear. Yet it was more than that, too. Somehow the voice was preventing him from fearing, he thought, but that meant nothing beside his sudden eagerness for the vengeance it promised him.

"That will become clear," the voice replied, "if you have the strength to endure my mind touch. I have learned all I may from your unconscious mind; now you must open fully to me, willingly." There was a weird, horrible sound, one Taggart recognized only slowly as laughter. "You may die, Blake Taggart. Yes, you may well die. But if you live . . ." The voice trailed off tantalizingly.

Taggart stared up at the metal ceiling and wondered just how much the voice had already done to him. His lack of fear, his fiery eagerness to avenge himself, his sharp, bright hatred—those were his, but they'd been strengthened. He knew they had, but he found that he did not care.

"Sure," he said. "Come ahead."

It was a pity Mordecai couldn't be here, Aston thought, looking around the huge cavern, but the Argentinos were showing more balls than brains, and McLain had preempted Morris for his nominal function.

He looked at the two hulking M60A3 battle tanks, and even to him it seemed absurd that anything as small as Ludmilla's blaster could damage them. He turned to her, reflecting that she looked younger than ever in her brand-new uniform. Was that because he knew how old a Marine captain *ought* to look?

"Ready?" he asked, and she nodded calmly. "Any special precautions?"

"Just stand well back," she said, and checked her weapon settings as Aston joined Jayne Hastings beside the tripod-mounted camcorder behind her.

"Now," Ludmilla continued when they were out of the way, "I know what sort of power settings I need with this—" she lifted her blaster slightly, finger clear of the firing stud "—to take out most Kanga combat mechs, and also the setting to kill a Troll combat chassis. By seeing what effect those settings have on your armored vehicles, we'll all be in a better position to estimate what weapons your strike teams need, Dick."

"I just can't quite believe *that*—" Hastings indicated the blaster "—can really zap a tank, Milla. I'm trying, but..." She shrugged.

Ludmilla glanced back at her and dimpled suddenly.

"'O, ye of little faith,'" she murmured, and raised her weapon.

Once again, the blaster did absolutely nothing. Its complete silence, Aston thought, grew more uncanny, not less, each time he saw it, but there was no lack of other noise.

A blue-white flash, no larger than the palm of his hand, burned with eye-tearing brilliance on the right-hand tank's glacis, directly under the gun. A wicked, whickering crash battered his ears like bottled thunder, and then there was silence...a silence broken only by the seething hiss of steaming metal.

Aston stared at the damaged tank, momentarily stunned despite all of Ludmilla's warnings, then made himself walk over to it. Ludmilla and Jayne followed him as he bent over the glowing hole, careful to keep his hands away from its heat.

A small, perfect circle had been bored through the five-inch armor, and he climbed up on the tank and peered down through the opened hatch. There was some internal damage, but not as much as he'd expected; almost all the power had been expended on the glacis, and surprisingly little splash had been flung about the driver's compartment.

"Well?" He climbed down with a thoughtful expression as Ludmilla spoke. "Can your weapons do that, Dick?"

"I think so. The latest TOWs certainly can, but they're vehicle-mounted. I'd say the Predator—that's our nearest man-portable antiarmor weapon—can do it, too."

"Good." Her face was calm, but her voice was taut. "But that's the easy part. A Troll's armor can take a lot more damage, and he carries battle screen."

"You mentioned that before," Aston said. "Just what is it?"

"Think of it as a force field that interdicts incoming fire. Warship screens can absorb multimegaton explosions, but even a heavy Troll chassis isn't big enough to carry screen that powerful. The important thing to bear in mind about it, though, is that it can be overloaded locally by a lot less destructive energy than the entire screen can handle. We use sequenced attacks to do that to ship screen, then punch a missile through the weakened spot, but I doubt we can do that to the Troll because it takes such fine coordination. So we'll have to try to punch through with a single shot—and this is what kind of energy it will take."

She herded her friends back into position and changed the settings on her weapon while Jayne slipped a filter over the camcorder's lens.

"Cover your eyes," she said levelly, and squeezed the trigger again.

The whiplash sound was far worse this time. The crackling roar was more protracted, with sounds like secondary explosions, and Aston was devoutly grateful that the tanks carried neither fuel nor ammo. The acrid stench of burning paint and molten metal assailed him, and raw, bitter heat pressed against the hands over his eyes.

Then the noise ended.

"All right," Ludmilla said, and he lowered his hands.

No one said a word as the two twenty-first-century humans stared in awe at what had been a tank. Waves of heat shimmer danced above it, and the entire frontal plate glowed—white in the center, shading to bright cherry at the sides. The gun quivered, then drooped slowly to full depression, hanging on its trunnions, for the pulse from Ludmilla's weapon had cut the elevation actuator in half, sheared through the hydraulic system, and burned clear through the gun tube just in front of the breech. Aston knew it had, because he could see it through the two-foot hole in the frontal armor.

He circled the smoking tank in silence. The blast of energy had torn completely through it—right through the heart of the transmission and the big, 750-horsepower diesel—and then gouged a nine-foot pit in the cavern wall twenty feet beyond it. He turned slowly and saw Jayne staring at the wreckage in shock.

"That," he said, "is just a bit more than the best we can do, Milla. By a few thousand percent, I'd say."

"I was afraid of that when I saw how much damage I did on low power." She holstered the blaster, and the little whisper as it went into its nest was loud against the quiet hiss and ping of cooling steel and stone.

"My God." Hastings shook her head slowly. "What do we do now?"

"I don't know," Aston said somberly. "I can organize teams to take out your combat mechs, Milla, but this—?" He shook his head slowly. "Maybe if we hit it with a shit pot of TOWs...."

"You can't do it that way, Dick," Ludmilla said. She stood beside him, looking at the carnage she'd wrought. "You can't sequence them tightly enough, and even if you could, he's almost certain to have set up a fallback by the time we find him. I don't know what it'll be, but I do know we have to take him out with a single shot, one that'll kill him before he can suicide and take the entire planet with him."

"We can't, Milla. I'm sorry, but we just can't."

"I know." She smiled crookedly. "I half-suspected you wouldn't be able to. But—" she met his eyes levelly "—*I* can."

She laid a hand on the butt of the holstered blaster which only she could fire, and he wanted—wanted more than he'd ever wanted anything in his life—to tell her no. To tell her that he didn't need her. That he wouldn't *risk* her.

But instead, he nodded silently.

CHAPTER SEVENTEEN

Major Daniel Abernathy, USMC, didn't look like a man on the brink of mayhem, and the casual observer could have no idea how much effort it took to keep from slamming one huge, dark-skinned fist into the tough plastic window beside him. He was rather proud of that.

He set his teeth, staring down through that same window at the runways of Andrews AFB and hating the sight. He shouldn't be here. He should be back at Lejeune, engaged in a change of command ceremony which would have put him—*him!*—in command of the Second Marine Division's recon battalion. He'd sweated blood to earn that command, and he by God deserved it! Besides, the orders had already been cut . . . until some desk-bound asshole in Washington changed them.

He closed his eyes, leashing his temper yet again as the landing gear rumbled. He was a passionate, hard-driving man, and defeat— especially defeat which wasn't his fault—sat poorly with him. The fact that Second Force was on alert because of the South Atlantic War only made it worse. He'd trained for twelve years for what might be about to happen, and—

He chopped the thought off, forcing his mind into neutral as the plane moved along the taxiway. It was hard, but he actually managed to smile at his neighbors as he collected his hand luggage.

The Washington sun was as fierce as the one he'd left in North Carolina, and the muggy air felt suffocating. He settled his sunglasses, adjusted his cap, and followed the flow of the passengers. At least it would be air-conditioned inside.

It was, and there was also someone waiting for him—someone

with the four rockers, three chevrons, and star of a Marine sergeant major on his short khaki sleeves—and Abernathy's eyebrows rose behind his glasses. Too many years ago, Gunnery Sergeant Alvin Horton had seen to it that a painfully young Lieutenant Abernathy made less mistakes than most with his first platoon. He supposed every Marine officer always felt a special respect for "his" first gunnery sergeant, but he'd known even then that Alvin Horton really was special.

The sergeant major snapped to attention and saluted, and Abernathy returned the salute. Then he removed his glasses left-handed and held out his right with his first genuine smile in the last twenty-one hours.

"Gunny," he said, squeezing firmly. "What the hell is going on here?"

"Sir?" Horton regarded him quizzically. "Why does the Major think the Sergeant Major knows anything he doesn't, Sir?"

"Cut the crap, Gunny. If anyone knows, you do."

"Major, I don't *know* anything. Honest."

Abernathy's eyebrows tried to rise again. Sergeant Major Horton was the fourth ranking noncom in the United States Marine Corps. He *had* to know what was going on. But if he said he didn't, he didn't.

"Excuse me, Sir," Horton broke into his thoughts, "but where's your baggage?"

"You're looking at it, Gunny." Abernathy waved his single small bag. "They didn't give me much time to pack."

"I see, Sir. If the Major would follow me, then?"

Abernathy fell in beside the sergeant major, and a path opened before them, though neither consciously noticed it. Abernathy was a powerfully built man, his mahogany skin bulging over hard-trained muscles, and he made an imposing figure in uniform. He wasn't especially tall, but he moved with catlike grace and a sense of leashed power, and the ribbons below his parachutist's wings were impressive.

For all that, and despite the gold leaf on his collar, Horton was even more impressive. He was four inches taller, the sandy hair under his cap cut so short it was all but invisible, and tanned almost as dark the major. He, too, wore jump wings, but the five rows of ribbons under his were headed by the white-barred blue one of the Navy Cross, followed by the red-white-and-blue one of the Silver Star with two clusters—each with the tiny "V" which indicated they'd been won the hard way: for valor.

He guided the major across the baking hot asphalt to a staff car, and Abernathy got a fresh surprise when Horton opened the door for him, closed it behind him, and then slid behind the wheel. Sergeant majors are not normally chauffeurs, and Abernathy's sense of the extraordinary grew stronger as Horton started the engine and pulled away.

"Tell me, Gunny," he said finally, "what *do* you know?"

"Nothing positive, Sir." Horton never took his eyes from the road.

"Last I heard, you were division command sergeant major at Pendleton," Abernathy mused aloud.

"Yes, Sir. I've been reassigned."

Abernathy digested that. Whoever had put the arm on him had also grabbed the senior noncom of the Third Marine Division. He didn't want to think about how General Watson had reacted to that.

"All right, Gunny, what is it we've both been reassigned *to*?"

"I understand the Major and I will find out this afternoon, Sir."

"From Rear Admiral R. K. Aston, I presume?"

"Yes, Sir." Horton's tone caught Abernathy's attention, and his eyes narrowed. Aston ... Aston.... Now that he thought about it, the name did have a familiar ring.

"Just who *is* Admiral Aston, Gunny?" he asked finally.

"He's good people, Sir," Horton said, and he wasn't a man who awarded accolades easily. "He started out with the Swift boats right at the end in Nam, then switched over to the SEALs, Sir."

"D'you mean Captain *Dick* Aston?"

"Yes, Sir," Horton said with a slight smile. "He's an admiral now."

"Well I will be dipped in shit," Abernathy said softly. Horton didn't respond, and Abernathy leaned back. That put a different slant on things. A *very* different slant. No wonder the name sounded familiar. No man had a higher reputation among the elite forces of the United States, and very few had one as good. It was Aston who'd pulled out the Lebanese hostages, he remembered, and then-Commander Aston's SEAL teams had fought their own short, victorious, and extremely nasty personal little war in Iraq, both before and during the Gulf War. It had been his SEAL teams that retook the Exxon drilling rig in the Gulf of Mexico, too—without, as Abernathy recalled, a single civilian fatality or a single terrorist survivor. If *he* was involved, things might prove very interesting indeed, and he suddenly realized why Horton seemed so cheerful. The sergeant major had an instinct for these things.

"Well, now, Gunny," he said after a long, thoughtful moment, "I do believe this may not be such a waste of time as I thought."

"As the Major says," Horton said cheerfully.

"But you can't do it that way—sir," Blake Taggart said. He sat in an oddly proportioned chair facing a featureless metal bulkhead and felt no desire to smile at the absurdity of talking to a—what? A machine? A disembodied voice? A . . . presence? Not after tasting its driving, limitless hatred in his own mind. The experience had not been pleasant. No indeed. Not pleasant at *all*.

"Indeed?" The voice was still cold and mechanical, but it was picking up human-sounding emphasis patterns at almost frightening speed.

"No, sir." Taggart licked his lips. Whatever this thing was, it wasn't human—and not all that tightly wrapped, either. It scared the shit out of him, actually, but he'd already accepted that. He'd been a bit surprised by how readily he *did* accept it, and he wondered if this . . . thing . . . had done something to make him. There was no way of knowing, and it didn't matter. Taggart had seen too much of this incredible ship. Sane or not, the voice could do what it promised.

He smiled—a cold, amused smile—as he remembered his Bible. He had been taken up on a mountain and offered all the powers of the world. Only as a viceroy and not a ruler in his own right, to be sure, but offered nonetheless. Yet powerful as the voice was, it lacked any instinctive knowledge of people.

"Why not, Blake Taggart?" the voice demanded coldly.

"Assume for a moment that you can control the President," Taggart said. "Or, hell, assume you control the Vice President and knock Armbruster off. Either way, you control the White House, but it won't do you any good."

"He is the head of state," the Troll said flatly.

"But he doesn't work in a vacuum . . . sir. There's Congress and the Supreme Court, just for starters. If he suddenly starts acting strangely, there are plenty of people in positions to get in your way.

No. If you want to take over, you have to start at the bottom. Build an organization and move in gradually." Taggart smiled nastily. "Do it right, and in a few years you can elect your own President—with a Congress that'll do anything you want."

"Wait," the Troll said, and considered the human's words. The Taggart human was unaware that he could hear its inner thoughts, that he knew it was already considering how to displace him, but that was all right. The Troll had selected it for its ambition, after all, and the human was unaware of the controls he had already set deep within it. A flick of thought could activate them, shutting down its fragile heart and lungs instantly. Not that those controls would be required; judiciously applied pain would provide all the effectiveness the Troll was likely to need.

But in addition to its ambition, the Troll had chosen it for its knowledge and the instincts he lacked. Unlike its master, it knew the workings of this world from the inside, and the Troll studied the fuzz of half-coherent concepts leaking from its thoughts. He already saw the basic workings of its plan, and what he saw pleased him.

"Very well, Blake Taggart," the Troll said. "Explain this to me."

"Yes, Sir," Taggart said eagerly. "First—"

"What I don't understand," Morris said, watching the taped destruction of the tanks, "is how that peashooter works, Milla. Where's the laser-tinted death? Where's the glowing ray of mass destruction? In short, where's the action?"

"Forgive him, Milla," Jayne Hastings said disgustedly. "Remember he's only a crude, unlettered savage."

"That's all right." Ludmilla smiled. "But I'm afraid I can't really answer your question, Mordecai. I mean, how well could *you* describe quantum mechanics—or, better yet, a printed circuit—to Copernicus?"

"I see your point," Morris conceded, "but I really am curious."

"Well," she brushed a strand of chestnut hair from her face and held up one of her blaster's featureless plastic magazines, "I'll try. This thing is a capacitor—a very powerful one, perhaps, but that's all it really is—and the energy pulse is a surge discharge. Theoretically, I could drain it in a single pulse, but the self-destruction would be pretty drastic."

"So all it really does is make a spark?" Morris asked incredulously.

"In a crude sense. Actually, it produces what you might think of as a pocket of plasma."

"*Inside* the blaster?" It was Jayne's turn to look dubious. "That must be one hell of a container, Milla."

"Not really. Oh, it's tough, but it never really 'contains' the energy at all. Most of this—" she tapped the blaster lying on the table "—is ranging circuits and a tiny multi-dee." She saw the confusion on her listeners' faces. "Basically, when I press the stud the blaster computes the exact range to the nearest solid object in its line of fire. I can tinker with it to redefine 'solid' a bit, which can be handy in, say, aquatic conditions, but that's not a big problem here." Hastings's eyes bulged slightly as she considered the effects of firing that mini-nuke underwater, but she said nothing.

"Anyway, once it's measured the range, it produces an energy pulse to the exact power and . . . dimensions I've set up. I can focus down to a cross section of two millimeters or up to a decameter, and about twice that for the linear dimension. But it doesn't 'contain' the pulse, and it doesn't really 'shoot' it at the target. Instead, at the instant the plasma is generated, the multi-dee blips it up into the alpha bands until the target coordinate is on top of the blaster, then brings it back down into normal-space." She shrugged. "For all practical purposes, the pulse first manifests on the target, which is why there's none of the ionization or thermal bloom associated with lasers or beamed energy."

"Good Lord," Hastings murmured. "What's the range on that thing?"

"Only five kilometers. You can't pick out a small arms target visually much above that range, even in space. The shoulder-fired versions have electro-optic sights and more range, but this is intended for close combat. Besides, in a planetary environment, you won't have many clear fire lanes even that long."

"'Only five kilometers,' she says!" Morris snorted. "Lady, with that little toy, you could—"

A knock on the door cut him off, and he quickly switched off the VCR while Ludmilla tucked the blaster out of sight inside her jacket.

"Enter," Morris called, and the three of them rose as a uniformed Richard Aston opened the door and stepped into the office. He wasn't alone, and Ludmilla felt a pang as she saw the muscular black major beside him. He looked so much like Steve Onslow it hurt. There was another man with them—a sergeant, only a few inches shorter than Dick, with calm, alert gray eyes that seemed to miss absolutely nothing.

She saw a flicker of surprise in the major's eyes as she came to attention with the automatic response she'd been cultivating ever since she became a junior officer again. The fact that these people had never heard of Thuselahs made them refreshingly unprejudiced, but it also meant every damned one of them judged her age by her appearance. Thank God President Armbruster hadn't decided to give her her own rank!

"People," Aston said, waving them back down, "let me introduce the newest members of our team: Major Daniel Abernathy and Sergeant Major Alvin Horton. Major, Sergeant Major: Commander Mordecai Morris, Lieutenant Commander Jayne Hastings, and Captain Elizabeth Ross." Ludmilla smothered a smile as he used her new name.

"Find a chair, and we'll bring you up to speed, gentlemen. And I warn you," he went on, "whatever you've been thinking, the truth is weirder." He smiled. "Believe it, people."

Ambassador Nekrasov was puzzled. President Armbruster seemed perfectly at ease, yet Nekrasov knew he was not. He couldn't have said how he knew, but he'd learned to trust his feelings, and he frowned as he sipped at his excellent cup of coffee.

"But, Mister President, my country cannot understand why— with no notice, no preliminary diplomacy, no negotiations—you should suddenly choose to impose an outside solution."

"I remind you of the Monroe Doctrine, Mister Ambassador," Armbruster said, and Nekrasov shook his head.

"Not applicable, Sir. Argentina clearly initiated hostilities, and Great Britain *is* an American power in this instance." He smiled wryly. "While the Russian Federation may deplore the imperialistic tradition which makes this true, it is, nonetheless, a fact."

"Well, then," Armbruster said with a sudden, impish grin, "let's just say I got pissed off."

Nekrasov choked on his coffee. His head spun slightly as he set down his cup and mopped his lips with his napkin, unable to believe that a head of state had just said such a thing to a foreign ambassador.

"Mister President," he said carefully. "I—" He broke off for a moment. Odd. The shock of what he'd just heard seemed to have thrown him off stride. He actually found it a bit difficult to choose his words.

"You are aware, Sir," he said finally, "that lives have been lost because you became—as you say—'pissed off'?"

"Bullshit," Armbruster said, watching him closely. "People got killed because the Argentinos were stupid enough to fuck with a Navy battle group." He noted the apparently bewildering effect of his words with satisfaction.

"Mister . . . Mister President—" Nekrasov broke off and rubbed his eyes, blinking rapidly. "I am afraid . . . That is—" He stopped and swallowed heavily, tugging to loosen his tie. "Forgive me, Mister President," he said thickly. "I feel . . . unwell. I—"

He started to rise, and then his eyes rolled up and he collapsed bonelessly.

Armbruster was on his feet in an instant, catching him and easing him back into his chair. He had beaten Stanford Loren by the breadth of a hair, and he shook his head as he looked up at the CIA director.

"Damn Russians. He's got the constitution of an ox."

President Pyotr Yakolev shook himself awake as the phone rang. He groped for it with a weary groan, hoping it was not yet another crisis.

"Yes?" he growled, then listened briefly and sat up with a jerk. "*What?*"

"I'm sorry, Mister President, but we don't have all the details yet." The voice on the other end of the phone was cautious. It belonged to Aleksandr Turchin, who considered Nikolai Nekrasov one of the outstanding thorns in his flesh. Unfortunately, that was because of how long Nekrasov and Yakolev had known one another, and that required the Foreign Minister to proceed with care. "The report just came in. Apparently Nikolai Stepanovich suffered a heart attack in the very office of the President."

"My God," Yakolev muttered. Then, "How bad is it?"

"I don't know, Mister President. They have flown him to their Bethesda Naval Hospital, the same place they take their own presi—"

"Yes, yes! I know that. When will we know more, Aleksandr Ivanovich?"

"I can't say, Mister President. Soon, I hope."

"I, too." Yakolev had few close personal friends, and Nikolai was one of them. He didn't want to lose him. "Is his wife with him?" he asked.

"I understand so," Turchin said.

"Deliver my personal sympathy to her," Yakolev directed.

"I will, Mister President. I'm sorry to have disturbed you, but I thought you would wish to know immediately."

"You thought correctly, Aleksandr Ivanovich. Thank you. Good night."

"Good night, Mister President."

Yakolev hung up slowly and lay back in his lonely bed. It was at moments like this he missed the supportive presence of his dead Marina. Poor Nikolai. He'd been working him too hard—he must have been. But Nikolai had always been so healthy. Like a *kulak*, he used to joke. Who would have thought Nikolai, of all people, would suffer a heart attack? And in the middle of a meeting at the White House?

Daniel Abernathy shook his head doggedly and glanced at Alvin Horton. The sergeant major appeared irritatingly composed, and the major was inclined to resent it until he saw the wonder hiding in Horton's eyes.

"So where do we come in, Admiral?" he asked finally.

"Where do you think, Major?" Aston replied, watching him closely.

"Well, Sir, it sounds like you've picked us to put together your strike team," Abernathy said slowly.

"Right the first time, Major. We'll discuss the details later, but basically what we have in mind is the creation of a provisional company for 'experimental' purposes." He grinned. "I know it's not quite the same as getting your battalion, but I hope you won't be too bored."

"No, Sir, I don't imagine I will," Abernathy said with an answering grin. "I was a mighty pissed Marine this morning, Sir, but I think I'm getting over it."

"Good. Then you and the sar-major and I will go sit down and talk hardware. I'm afraid 'Captain Ross' and Commander Morris have another appointment."

"Yes, Sir."

"Oh, and Major—"

"Sir?"

"Certain people will have to know some of the truth about 'Captain Ross,' but I decide who needs to know and what they need to be told. Not you, not Commander Morris, not even Admiral McLain. Me. Understood?"

"Yes, Sir."

"Sar-major?"

"Understood, Admiral."

"Good. Now, if you gentlemen will come with me?"

Nikolai Nekrasov opened his eyes slowly. He was lying on his back, he decided. In a bed. He rolled his head and took in the bright, cheerful airiness of a well-appointed private hospital room. What—?

His thoughts cleared suddenly and he sat up. The President! He'd been speaking with the President, and then—

"Hello, Nikolai."

He turned and looked into Jared Armbruster's eyes. There was amusement in them, and a touch of wariness, as well. He shook his head slowly, trying to understand. He'd collapsed, but he felt fine. So what...?

"I owe you an apology, Mister Ambassador," Armbruster said calmly. "I'm afraid we slipped you a Mickey." Nekrasov blinked at him. "We drugged your coffee," Armbruster explained.

Drugged his coffee? It was unheard of! And if they had, why should Armbruster admit it? The ambassador stared around the room, fighting a flicker of panic. Surely the President had not run *that* far mad!

"I'm sorry," Armbruster sounded genuinely contrite, "but I believe we can explain why it was necessary."

"Indeed, Mister President?" Nekrasov was pleased that he managed to sound calm. "I should be interested to hear that explanation."

"Of course." Armbruster sat beside the bed. "First, I must also apologize for the cover story we put together. Your government has been informed that you suffered a severe heart attack. That—" he added quickly "—was unfortunately necessary to explain why we rushed you to Bethesda." Nekrasov started to speak, but Armbruster raised a hand.

"Please, Mister Ambassador. Time is short. Your Embassy's security people are not at all pleased that the doctors have refused to allow them into your room because of your 'serious condition.' We'll let them in very shortly, but first I must explain some things."

"Very well," Nekrasov said, and settled back on his pillows, regarding the American suspiciously.

"Thank you. Mister Ambassador, you asked me why I involved my country in the South Atlantic War. My answer was, I fear, facetious. The truth, sir, is that I needed a diversion."

"I beg your pardon?"

"In large part, Mister Ambassador, my reasons concern yourself. Oh, my original thought was to create a cover for certain military moves I must make, but then I realized it could also be used as a pretext for special diplomatic exchanges—like the information I'm about to share with you.

"I must tell you, Ambassador, that while we had you here—indeed, it was the entire reason we went to all this trouble to *get* you here—we ran an electroencephalogram on you." Nekrasov looked mystified, and Armbruster continued smoothly. "It was necessary to determine whether or not your brain waves contained a certain distinctive pattern. Fortunately, they do—and it is my sincere hope that President Yakolev's share it. Unhappily, the only way I have been able to think of to check his is to convince someone he knows and trusts—in short, a close personal friend—to find out for me."

"Mister President," Nekrasov said stiffly, "this is ridiculous. I—"

"No, Mister Ambassador, it is *not* ridiculous," Armbruster interrupted, and the cold determination—the ruthlessness—in his iron voice startled the Russian. "I believe you will agree with me on that point, and, if you do, I will ask you to return home—officially for health reasons and consultations regarding the situation in the South Atlantic—to tell President Yakolev that."

"I can conceive of no reason why I should," Nekrasov said flatly.

"We'll give you one," Armbruster said, his tone equally flat, "and to that end, I would like you to meet someone. If I may?" He rose and started for the door, and Nekrasov shrugged. The entire situation was patently absurd, but this madman was the President of the United States.

A naval commander and a ridiculously young captain of Marines entered the room, and Nekrasov wondered what possible bearing such junior officers could have on this affair.

"Ambassador, I'd like you to meet Commander Morris, Admiral Anson McLain's senior intelligence officer, and Captain Ross. Commander, Captain—Ambassador Nikolai Stepanovich Nekrasov." Nekrasov nodded to the newcomers, then looked impatiently back to the President.

"Mister Ambassador, Captain Ross is not precisely what she appears," Armbruster said, seating himself once more. "In point of fact, she's the reason you're here." Nekrasov frowned at the striking young girl. That seemed crazier than all the rest! Armbruster saw his frown and grinned.

"I assure you, you can't be more surprised than I was when I first met the captain, Ambassador. You see . . ."

subversion *n.*
The act of subverting or the condition of being subverted.

subvert *tr.v.* **-verted, -verting, -verts**
1. To ruin; to destroy utterly. **2.** To undermine character or allegiance; to corrupt. **3.** To overthrow completely. [Middle English *subverten*, from Latin *subvertere*, to turn upside down: *sub-*, from below, up + *vertere*, to turn.]

—*Webster-Wangchi Unabridged*
Dictionary of Standard English
Tomas y Hijos, Publishers 2465,
Terran Standard Reckoning

CHAPTER EIGHTEEN

"She did *what?*" Anson McLain demanded, and Mordecai Morris went off in a fresh peal of mirth. His ribs hurt, and he wondered how much his laughter owed to hysterical reaction.

"S-she almost shot . . . shot up th-the Saint Petersburg *zoo!*" he repeated, gasping the words between hoots.

"In God's name, *why?!*"

"She . . . she . . . Oh, *my!*" Morris broke off and wiped his streaming eyes. "President Yakoiev thought she might . . . might enjoy seeing the sights," he managed in a more controlled voice. "So he had a guide take her around Saint Petersburg." He shook his head. "It all went fine until they got to the kangaroos."

"To the—" McLain broke off in sudden understanding. "Oh, no!" he moaned, covering his eyes with one hand.

"Exactly. Sir: *Kangas.* D'you realize, she even *told* us they were the height of a short human and had tails, but we never made the connection? We've all been too worried about the Troll to bother with what Kangas might or might not look like!"

"Dear Lord," McLain prayed fervently, "deliver me from oversights."

"Amen," Morris agreed, his eyes still damp from laughter. "She took one look and went for her blaster out of pure reflex, and she's *fast*, Sir. She had it out and aimed—ready to blow the whole damned herd, or school, or whatever the hell you call a bunch of kangaroos, to dust bunnies—before Dick could even move. Scared their guide to death." He shook his head. "Sir, she'd never even *seen* a real kangaroo."

"But she *didn't* shoot?"

"No, Sir," Morris reassured him. "She realized what it had to be in time. She was pretty pissed with Dick for not warning her, too, until she realized why he hadn't seen any reason she *needed* to be warned."

"Well, thank God for that," McLain said. "Jesus! We came that close to blowing the whole secret because of a bunch of ragged-assed kangaroos." He shook his head wonderingly, then glared at Morris. "I don't need any more surprises like this, Commander. Tell her that."

"Oh, I will, Sir. I will."

The Troll pivoted his fighter in a hovering circle, examining the hiding place. The Taggart human was right, he thought. It was perfect.

The cool darkness caressed the alloy skin of his vehicle/body, and he dropped another hundred meters, dipping into the oval valley. It was five and a half kilometers long and no more than two across at its greatest width, and night-struck trees were green-black below him, rising towards the star-strewn skies. There were no lights, no signs of human habitation, and his scanners peered and pried at the darkened forest, finding only life that flew, ran on four feet, or swam. Other scanners probed the darkened heavens, assuring him that no satellite or aircraft lingered overhead.

The silent fighter hovered twenty meters above the valley floor while the Troll selected the best spot. There. The slope was almost vertical behind that screen of trees.

He adjusted his position carefully, then activated the battery of special, low-powered power guns mounted under the fighter's prow, and muted blue lightning flared. It was far less brilliant than the sun-hot violence which had killed the *cralkhi*, and his heart-hunger for havoc longed for the beauty of that brighter, more savage power, but it was time for lesser thunders.

Azure brilliance splashed the mountain, and at its touch, destruction danced. Perhaps not the blazing, shuddering devastation he craved, but destruction nonetheless. Undergrowth and tree trunks vanished. Treetops plunged downward like spears, falling into the ring of light and vanishing with a near-silent whine, and then it was the turn of earth and stone.

The Troll's interior receptors watched his human bend over the vision screen his servomechs had built for it in the cramped "control room." He could feel the human's awe, and silent laughter rippled in his brain. So Blake Taggart thought this was power? What would it say if he told it that this was but an adaptation of a standard *Shirmaksu* mining tool? That, in the human's own terms, it was no more than a "drill"?

The mountain yielded more slowly than the vegetation which had crowned it, but the Troll chewed steadily deeper. Sixty meters in diameter he sank his shaft, and the humming power of his drill lined the bore with a slick, fused finish. Three hundred meters he pierced into the flank of the mountain, then the blue light died and he turned his ship and slid silently backward into the circular tunnel.

He settled to the floor of the tube and hatches opened, disgorging servomechs that scurried about, filling the tunnel mouth with earth for a depth of fifty meters. They left only one, smaller entrance, just large enough for the largest of the Troll's combat mechs . . . or his own combat chassis. By dawn, every sign of his coming had been carefully camouflaged.

The Troll was satisfied in his hide. There were drawbacks, of course. It would take many minutes to extricate his fighter from its snug nest, and his onboard scanners were inoperable through the rock and soil above him. But he was safe from any chance detection, and the Blake Taggart human had been correct: this *was* an ideal location.

Indeed, his new servant was proving useful in many ways. It had known, for example, that the Annette human had been wrong about Oak Ridge. No weapons-grade fissionables had been produced there in many years, and it was unlikely that such materials would be available there in the quantities he required. But Blake Taggart had known, as the female had not, of what it called the "Savannah River Plant" where fissionables *were* produced.

In some respects, the Troll would have preferred to be closer to the source, but Blake Taggart was correct. This isolated hiding place was within range of his combat mechs if a direct assault on Savannah became necessary, and far better placed for the other portion of his... No, be honest, the Troll thought, of *their* plan.

And for now, he preferred to avoid attacks on military installations. He wasn't yet certain his combat mechs were proof against the humans' heavy weapons: better to avoid exposure to them until he was. Besides, the human insisted no weapons assembly took place at Savannah, that the fissionables were shipped to other locations for that purpose. Sooner or later, one of those shipments would cross the Troll's area of mental influence.

"Obliging of them, especially after you almost wasted their zoo," Aston observed wryly. He grinned down at Ludmilla and she smiled back, but he knew the encounter had shaken her badly.

"Sorry," she said softly. "It was pure instinct, Dick. Seeing something that much like a live Kanga—*brrrr!*" She shivered, and he caressed the back of her neck gently. She accepted the comfort of the rare public gesture of affection gratefully.

"Anyway," she said with a less forced grin, "I think President Yakolev is trying to make up for how hard he was to convince."

"Yeah," Aston snorted, then chuckled. "But it makes a kind of sense to do it over here, too. For one thing, it's a real clincher for his technical people, and, for another, their power net is still unreliable enough that they can black out a main grid for a few hours without nearly as many explanations."

"True," Ludmilla agreed, turning back to the control room windows. She didn't care for what she'd seen so far of Russia, even if her ancestors had come from there. She'd *never* cared for the Soviet system, even when she'd studied it merely out of morbid historical curiosity, but now she had to deal with its actual transition period, and she could scarcely believe what people here managed to put up with. She'd always been rather proud of the Russian people's ability to endure and persevere, and of what the Russia of her own past had achieved (after, she admitted, the bloodbath of the self-inflicted conflagration of their nuclear exchange with Belarussia). But *these* Russians still weren't at all certain how to make democracy work...

or even if they truly wanted to. Several people had told her how much they admired democracy, and how firmly they believed democracy would solve their problems in time, and how deeply committed they were to making democracy work. But what she actually saw had best been summed up by the taxi driver who had delivered her and Aston to the Saint Petersburg Zoo.

"Democracy!" he had exclaimed when he recognized Aston's American accent. "It is a wonderful thing—or it *will* be when someone who knows how to make it work takes over at the top!"

It was apparent that the notion that representative government ought to be predicated on the electorate making the politicians "at the top" behave themselves and govern responsibly had never crossed the cabby's mind. He still wanted someone to make it work, with top-down direction, and that, she admitted sadly to herself, was what had made the Succession Wars inevitable. It had left the entire political field to authoritarians of one stripe or another, and those squabbling for power—even the most idealistic and committed "democrats"— had been all too willing to toss principle overboard in pursuit of tactical goals, as if none of them had realized that principles and limitations, precedents and what the people of her own time had still called "the rule of law," were the skeleton upon which any stable, self-governing state depended. Even Yakolev, much as she had found herself admiring his determination and personal integrity, was clearly more comfortable with the strongman image and the tactics that went with it than he was with the image of a parliamentary leader. He knew how to give orders, she thought; what he didn't know—what *no* Russian politico she had yet met knew—was how to forge a lasting consensus or achieve genuine compromise.

Yet for all its factionalism, waste motion, and sense of impermanence, the present Russian system had its advantages for her own purposes. It had been incredibly hard for Nekrasov to convince Yakolev to give the Americans his EEG without explaining why, but once that hurdle had been cleared things had moved even more rapidly in the Russian Federation than in the USA. If Pytor Yakolev wanted EEGs run on his people, he simply had to tell them so, and he had.

There had been some problems, she understood, since the KGB head hadn't been on the safe list. But enough other members of

Yakolev's inner circle were, and the fact that it was common knowledge that Yakolev and Foreign Minister Turchin had been at odds for months over both Belarussia and the Balkans had actually helped. Turchin was still an ultranationalist, and he still distrusted America's ultimate diplomatic objectives intensely, but he was no fool and, for all his nationalist paranoia, he *was* a patriot. That was what had convinced Yakolev to include him in his government in the first place, and Turchin *did* have the right EEG. Confronted with Ludmilla's presence and her technology demonstration to prove her story, Turchin had recognized the imperative need to cooperate with the Americans, however much he distrusted them in other matters. And it had been Turchin himself who proposed that Yakolev use a cabinet shakeup—ostensibly to get rid of Turchin himself, on the grounds that their foreign policy differences had become insurmountable—to dispose of the KGB head and two other ministers whose EEGs prohibited admitting them to the inner secret circle.

And that, Ludmilla mused, might be the best sign for Russia's future she had yet seen. Turchin was, in many ways, the ultimate Russian peasant: shrewd, canny, warmhearted in his own way, xenophobic, stubborn to the point of pigheadedness, and with that aura of willing brutality which only a people who had been subjected to generations of brutality themselves radiated. And yet he had seen the necessity to act and act swiftly, even at the probable cost of his own political suicide, and he had done it. In the history she remembered, he hadn't resigned. Indeed, it had been he who replaced Yakolev after the President's assassination . . . and who had led Russia into the fateful nuclear exchange with Belarussia. So perhaps her intrusion onto the past history of this universe, whether it was the one from whence she had sprung or not, would have more than one beneficial consequence.

And in the meantime, she could finally do something about the damage Dick had wreaked on her flight suit. The four Russian physicists now bent over the worktable beyond the control room windows had been frankly incredulous when she explained what she needed, but their attitudes had undergone a remarkable change in the past ten minutes.

Academician Arkadi Tretyakov had been the most skeptical of all, and he'd obeyed Yakolev's orders with patent resentment. When she gave him the voltage and amperage she needed he'd looked at her as if at a madwoman and told her it would require the full output of a dedicated nuclear plant.

Which was where they were right now, she thought with real amusement, and a ripple of laughter danced just behind her teeth as she remembered his reaction to the feed wire she'd produced from the heel of the flight suit. She supposed it was understandable—the superconductive ceramic-based wire's cross section was hardly larger than a single strand in one of Tretyakov's computer cables—and he'd sneered as he supervised the technicians who made the appropriate connections. But his sneer had turned into slack-faced shock when the switches were thrown and the feed drank every erg of power from his precious reactor without even warming up.

Now he and his colleagues watched with awe as the suit's self-repair systems did their job. It would take another hour or so, but when they were done, she would have her flight suit back, almost as good as new.

And that, she knew, might be more important than even Dick suspected.

The diesel locomotive thudded through the night, clattering over the rails of the Clinchfield Railroad beside the Nolichucky River. The lights of Poplar, Tennessee, had vanished behind it, its headlamp cut a diamond-white tunnel through the darkness, and Unaka Mountain loomed against the stars to the north as the special train rattled along toward Unaka Springs.

Ralph Twotrees was tense. He always was at times like this, and the hordes of military types riding with him were only part of the reason. There were few cars tonight, but those he did have carried trefoil-badged, white-painted containers of stainless steel, each surrounding an inner vessel of heavy shielding, and packed away in their hearts was the better part of a ton of weapons-grade plutonium.

Twotrees hated these trips. Though hazardous industrial chemicals were bad enough and the military had a sufficiency of other horrific cargoes, this was the worst. But he was the line's most senior engineer, and when a stinker came along, he was apt to be picked for it. He found it flattering, in an almost obscene way—until the next time they called on him.

And there would *be* a next time, he thought unhappily. He was a lifelong Democrat, and God knew there were still more than enough domestic problems which required attention, but even though he'd voted against Jared Armbruster, he respected and (grudgingly) liked the President. Worse, he'd loved the study of history since his high school days, and that made it harder for him to close his eyes to unpleasant realities than he could have wished. Given what was happening in the Balkans, and the Falklands, and the recent ratcheting up of tension in Kashmir, and Chinese saber rattling in support of Pakistan, and the renewed spread of nuclear weapons, the US had no option but to make certain of the effectiveness of its own nuclear force. Twotrees knew that, just as he knew that the Armbruster administration had found itself with an arsenal which previous administrations had deliberately allowed to dwindle in the earnest hope that nuclear weapons stockpiles truly could become a thing of the past. Well, Twotrees had hoped that, too, and he suspected Jared Armbruster had, as well. But things hadn't worked out that way, and Armbruster had brought Savannah River slowly back on-line—first simply to produce the tritium required to keep existing weapons functional and then, reluctantly, to produce the fissionables the military said it needed for entirely new weapons.

Twotrees hadn't minded the tritium too much. He wasn't clear on exactly how it functioned to enhance the effectiveness of nuclear warheads, but at least he'd known it was being produced only to replace other, no longer useful tritium in *existing* weapons. But these new warheads . . . Those worried him—a lot—and he rather doubted the Powers That Were would have been happy about just how much he disliked the thought of being a part of producing *new* weapons. Not that it would keep him from doing his job and seeing to it that the horrific freight got delivered safely, but still . . .

There was a major back in one of the two passenger cars, and enough firepower to fight a small war, but that didn't bother Twotrees. He was worried about his own job. He knew, intellectually, that the containment vessels would survive any accident he might contrive, but emotions were something else. This was *his* train, and the weight of his responsibility was like a load of Tennessee granite.

He glanced over at the Army captain riding the engine with him. Something about the man bothered him. He'd been brisk but friendly when he came aboard, yet in the last hour he'd grown progressively more silent. Now he stood to one side, swaying easily, with one hand on his holstered automatic, and his face was oddly blank.

Twotrees was about to say something when a light to the southwest caught his eye. More than one, actually. There were at least three of them, sweeping down No Business Knob towards the valley. He watched the bright, golden lights curiously. They were moving mighty fast. Must be helicopters. Could they be an unannounced military escort?

He was still wondering when Captain Steven Pound, US Army, drew his nine-millimeter automatic and shot him through the back of the head.

"The whole *shipment*?" Stan Loren stared at Dolf Wilkins in horror.

"Every ounce," Wilkins said flatly. He'd received the report forty minutes before Loren, and he had himself under tight control. "Point-nine-four tons of weapons-grade fissionables. Gone."

"How?" Loren demanded hoarsely.

"We're trying to put that together. The Army, the NRC, and the Department of Energy bomb boys are all going ape-shit, and Admiral McLain is just about as shaken. It would help if there were any survivors from the security detail *or* the train crew. There aren't."

"None?" Loren's face was bleak as he began recovering from the shock.

"None. They took out one troop car with explosives—some sort of explosively destructive weapon, anyway; we haven't actually confirmed any chemical residues yet—and just strafed the hell out of the other with some kind of heavy-caliber automatic weapons. Our people on the scene tell me they've never seen anything like it. Even the container vessels are gone, and each of them weighs tons."

"Vehicle tracks?"

"None," Wilkins said again, even more grimly.

"Oh, Jesus," Loren whispered as their eyes met. They knew who— or, rather, what—had to be behind it.

"All right, Mordecai," Anson McLain said grimly. "At least we know whose side of the pond the bastard is on."

"Agreed. Assuming, of course, that he's gone to ground somewhere within his operational range of the hit." Morris tapped a red-crayoned circle on a huge map of the United States. It passed through Chicago, arced north of Detroit, cut right through Philadelphia, and reached as far south as Daytona Beach before it swept back up to the west of Saint Louis. "If that's the case, then he's somewhere inside that circle, Sir. He has to be. Milla says eight hundred kilometers is about the max range at which he can operate his combat remotes."

"That's an awful big circle, M&M."

"I know, Sir. Every recon plane in the eastern half of the country is up looking, and so are all the satellites we can sweep the area with, but we haven't found a thing. Which could mean nothing or a lot."

He turned from the map to face the admiral.

"We may just be missing him—it's not like we've had time to set up a well-organized search, and we figure we lost at least twenty minutes before the missed radio check alerted the security people, so he had a hell of a head start. On the other hand, it could mean that he's worked out the ECM devices he needs, or even that he'd already gone to ground before we started hunting. But the terrain in the area is extremely rough, Sir. Mountains, rivers, national forests, deer reservations.... Even if he's in fairly close proximity, we won't find him without a lot of luck. We'll try—he'll be expecting us to—but I'm not optimistic, Sir."

He fell silent, standing beside his boss while the two of them glowered at the map as if the combined force of their wills could somehow force it to give up the information they needed. Unfortunately, it couldn't.

"All right," McLain said finally. "We can leave the search up to the Army and Air Force. Put together everything we've got and every reasonable speculation you can come up with, then bring it in for us to go over. After that—" he smiled mirthlessly "—you and I are going to Washington. And I *don't* think our commander-in-chief is going to be happy to see us."

CHAPTER NINETEEN

Major Daniel Abernathy, USMC, Commanding Officer, Company T, Provisional (reinforced), blinked on sweat and tried not to smile as he watched Admiral Aston and "Captain Ross" running side by side in front of him. It was hard.

The admiral was no spring chicken, but he certainly didn't run like an old man, either. His nondescript gray sweats were soaked with perspiration under the hot sun, but he was moving well. Very well, Abernathy thought, with the easy rhythm of a man who knew exactly how to pace himself. A man accustomed to pushing himself to the limit, and wise enough to know that limit when he reached it.

Captain Ross—Abernathy seldom allowed himself to think of her by any other name, and no one else in Company T except Sergeant Major Horton knew she had one—ran along the packed beach beside him, in one of her outlandish shirts, this one bearing a flame-eyed skeletal horseman, a long scythe gleaming over his shoulder. It was strictly non-reg, of course, not that anyone was likely to complain. At the moment, she was as sweat-soaked as the admiral, but she ran with an infinite endurance Abernathy found almost unnerving. She needed two strides to match each of Aston's long, loping ones, yet she gave the impression that she could go on doing it forever.

They always ran together, and she always ran the admiral into the ground, yet there was absolutely no competition between them. With any pair of Marines Abernathy had ever known, enlisted or commissioned, there would have been a rivalry. Friendly perhaps, but always there. Not with these two. It was as if they were beyond that. Indeed, Abernathy felt a bit daunted when he looked up and saw the two of them watching his men train. Their eyes were so similar, so knowing, as if each of them had seen the same thing a thousand times and felt an identical kindly tolerance for the brash, tough young men doing it this time.

But, then, he reminded himself, Captain Ross was not what appearances might suggest, and her relationship with Admiral Aston was no one's damned business but their own. They were utterly discreet—they had to be on a teeming military post like this—but Abernathy knew they were lovers, and he was pretty certain Sergeant Major Horton did, too.

Under other circumstances, Abernathy might have been tempted to object. Certainly his professionalism had been offended when he first realized Aston was sleeping with his aide, but no longer. Those two were one of the most effective teams he'd ever seen, and whatever their private relationship might be, it never colored their actions on duty.

Well, *practically* never, he amended, smiling as he remembered Captain Ross's first day on the pistol range. She'd nearly wet her pants the first time the admiral squeezed off with his .45 auto, and only later did Abernathy realize that, for all her combat experience, she'd never heard a firearm discharged. But Admiral Aston had known, and his face-cracking grin had told Abernathy he hadn't warned her deliberately.

With her extraordinary strength and reflexes, she'd seemed to levitate as the explosive crash blasted over her, and Abernathy understood instantly why Aston had cleared the range of everyone but Captain Ross and Abernathy himself. Her reaction would have been a dead giveaway that, whatever she was, she was not a Marine captain.

But she *was*, Abernathy had found, a natural shot. Recoil had bothered her a lot the first day, but she'd settled down quickly. Like the admiral—or, for that matter, Major Daniel Abernathy, US Marine Corps—she preferred the .45 to the nine-millimeters the US military had adopted. Unlike the admiral, however, she preferred the polymer-framed SOCOM .45 to the old 1911 variants, and by the end of the second week, she was pushing Aston, himself a past national pistol champion, hard. Her groups were consistently tight, her first magazine regularly blew the X-ring right out of her target, and her combat range scores were incredible. She'd set a new post record—unofficially, since no one but Abernathy and Aston had been witnesses and Horton had acted as range officer. It was her speed, Abernathy thought. That blinding, smoothly flowing speed . . .

Not that there hadn't been problems. She'd insisted on training with every weapon Company T was issued, but though she'd become skilled and deadly with all of them, the men had been uneasy when they realized she'd be coming along when the mission finally went down. None of them were idiots; they knew she was much more than their officers chose to admit, but she was such a little thing, and whatever the official position might be, "No women in ground combat" remained the effective Corps policy.

But she'd surmounted that, too. Company T contained an extraordinary number of vets and "lifers," including such a high proportion of senior noncoms that other unit commanders were grumbling about "poachers." Out of them all, she'd challenged Gunnery Sergeant Morton Jaskowicz, a big, mean mountain of a man from the Pennsylvania coal country whose last duty had been as an unarmed combat instructor at Pendleton, to a "friendly" match. Abernathy had been horrified, but Aston had refused to let him quash the idea.

She and Jaskowicz had ended up in front of the more doubtful members of the company, who had confidently expected Little Miss Smartass to be sent to the showers in a hurry. At first, she'd been almost passive . . . or looked that way. In fact, she'd evaded everything Jaskowicz tried to do, slithering away from him like a greasy, hard-muscled snake until she convinced him he would have to go all out to take her, despite her small size. But once she'd convinced him and everyone *knew* she had, she'd put him away in six seconds flat with a combination Jaskowicz had never even heard of.

Then she did the same thing to the four next-toughest Marines present to prove it had been no fluke. Company T had spent twenty-four hours in shock, but there were no more muttered comments about the proper toys for little girls after that.

She'd taken everything in stride with equal professionalism, including quickie jump training, though Abernathy had been amazed to find that the mere notion of jumping out of an airplane terrified her. She turned pasty-faced, sweat-popping white every time she went up, but she never let it stop her, and her determination had delivered the coup de grace to any lingering doubts Company T might have harbored. These men knew all about fear, even if they never admitted it, and they respected what it took to conquer a terror as deep as hers.

She and the admiral reached the end of their run and slowed to a jog, moving in circles to keep their muscles from tightening, and Abernathy passed them at an easy lope. Another half mile and then a shower, he thought, followed by the regular afternoon briefing.

He only hoped there would finally be some news of the Troll.

Aston felt his breathing ease and his heartbeat slow. He'd never expected to train this hard again, though he'd certainly never intended to wither away into overweight old age, and it felt good. It had been rough for the first few weeks, but he felt at least ten years younger now. Which, he reminded himself, was still too old for what he was preparing to do. Better, but still too old.

He wiped his face and bald head with the towel from around his neck, then handed it to Ludmilla. She was breathing only slightly harder than usual, and he was sure his ego would have been crushed if he hadn't known she'd grown up in twenty percent more gravity than he'd ever felt and possessed a symbiote that cleaned fatigue products out of her blood as fast as she could generate them.

She smiled at him, but he knew she was worried. That was fair enough; he was worried to death himself. Four months since the bloody raid, and not a peep out of him. A ton of plutonium was an awesome threat, and when Ludmilla had explained just what the Troll could do with it, Aston had felt physically ill with terror for the first time in many years.

He had no idea what the "Nova Cycle" was, but anything which needed a *sequence* of thermonuclear explosions just to initiate it— especially the sort someone could put together with that much fissionable material—had to be horrific. He'd asked Ludmilla what it did, but she'd refused to be specific beyond the obvious: if it went off, there would no longer be an Earth. He sometimes wondered if she knew how to build one of them herself, for her explanations often struck him as more general than they had to be, as if she was afraid to give the children any noisier toys than they already had.

But if passing time was gnawing at them all, the men were shaping up nicely. "Company T" was closer to a battalion than a company, with four rifle platoons (each with two extra rifle squads and an attached antitank squad), not three, plus two armored assault platoons, a vehicle-mounted heavy weapons platoon, three FAC teams, and an entire extra antitank platoon. Every man was Troll-proof, and all had been briefed on what they were up against—in general terms; none had yet been told who or what Ludmilla really was—and confined to post for the duration. Aston had no fear that any of them would deliberately tell a soul, but accidental slips were another matter. He was gratified to find that his Marines (he'd come to think of them as "his" from a very early point) were as security-conscious as he was. They'd done a lot of bitching, but that was a Marine's God-given right and not a single real complaint about security measures had reached him.

And at least Armbruster's South Atlantic adventure had generated enough confusion to cover the military reshuffling Aston and McLain had deemed necessary. There was some curiosity about "Company T" now, but it was fairly mild, and no one had even asked any questions while they were setting it up. The strange plethora of EEGs had passed virtually unnoticed, as well, and so had the intense, high-level discussions between Washington, London, Berlin, Tokyo, and Moscow.

Aston had begrudged the time Ludmilla had been forced to spend telling her story firsthand so many times, but in the event it had been worthwhile. She'd used up the full charge of one blaster magazine demonstrating it to prime ministers, premiers, and generals on three continents, but it had put any doubts to rest. He wished to hell that they'd been able to share their information a bit more widely, too. He didn't much care for the French or the Chinese, but he had serious qualms about the decision not to tell them about the Troll. Finding and killing the Troll was likely to take all the resources they could pull together, and whatever he might think of France or China—or, for that matter, what they might think of the US—he couldn't quite rid himself of the thought that they had a moral right to know about a threat like the Troll which could well be hidden somewhere on their territory.

Yet Armbruster had decided *not* to inform them, and Aston knew too much about the security risks involved in telling those two governments *anything* to try second-guessing the President's call. The French, for example, were involved in a vicious game of internal partisan politics, and their recent, strident anti-American sentiments would have made the possibility of a leak—probably from someone who knew only a part of the story and thus could have no idea what damage he or she could do—extremely high.

The Chinese were another case entirely, and Aston knew Armbruster had come within a hair's breadth of telling them despite the current international antagonism between the PRC and the US. Unfortunately (or perhaps fortunately; Aston couldn't quite make up his mind which), every attempt to get copies of the required EEGs had failed, for no one had been able to think of a way to obtain them. So Beijing knew nothing about the Troll, although Taipei did (which had the potential to make things enormously worse, of course), which meant that he could look for a hiding place in one of the largest nations on Earth without the local authorities having the least idea that they should be hunting for him.

It also meant that Yakolev and Armbruster had quietly agreed that if the Troll *did* turn out to be hiding in Chinese territory, the US and Russian Federation would launch a joint nuclear strike on his location. Both were fully aware of the horrible risks and the potentially horrendous loss of life entailed in any such strike, but both also agreed that the destruction of the Troll must be accomplished at any cost . . . and that they dared not risk sharing the information which might avert such a strike with anyone whose mind they weren't *certain* the Troll could not read.

As if God were trying to offer some form of compensation, however, they'd been very lucky with the EEGs in most of the other nations on their list. Only in Japan had both the prime minister and his assistant failed the test, but the Emperor and the chief of the Japanese Defense Force had passed. Still, Aston was almost amazed that the secret had stood up, though, to be fair, no more than a few hundred people on the face of the planet knew it. Not a single legislature had been informed, and he was quietly certain that at least one highly placed West European statesman's fatal "heart attack" had been arranged by his own government when, despite the most rigorous pre-briefing screening, he proved a poor security risk.

On the operational side, Company T was but one of several strike teams, although it was the only one which had been briefed on its real mission. The tight-knit circle of allies and enemies who had come together to meet the threat agreed that the plutonium theft indicated that the Troll was in North America, so Company T had been designated the primary strike force. The others were basically backups, and he had no idea what cover stories their superiors had concocted for them.

But all of the intricate cooperation and planning was useless without a target, and they had none. Four months had flowed past without a single additional clue to the Troll's location, plans, or status.

Not one.

The Honorable Jeremiah Willis, Mayor of Asheville, North Carolina, hated Raleigh. A month—even three weeks—ago, that hadn't been the case, but it was now. He'd been to the state capital three times in the last two weeks, and each meeting had been grimmer than the last.

"Governor," he said, speaking for himself and the mayors of Winston-Salem, Greensboro, and Charlotte, "we have to do *something*! This . . . situation is about to get totally out of hand. It's a nightmare."

Governor James Farnam nodded slowly. His face was lined with fatigue, and State Attorney General Melvyn Tanner looked equally worn and harassed.

"Mayor Willis," the governor said heavily, "I couldn't agree with you more, but what, exactly, do you suggest? The State Bureau of Investigation is working overtime, but the 'situation,' as you put it, is as confusing to them as it is to us. They don't have the manpower even to ask the right questions, much less find answers."

"Governor," it was Cyrus Glencannon, Mayor of Charlotte, "I don't even know if law enforcement is the answer." He frowned, his black face tense. "So far—so *far*," he repeated "—we only have a handful of confrontations, and the local authorities seem to be dealing with them pretty well. It's what's coming that scares me."

"Scares all of us," Mayor Willis interjected. "I haven't seen anything like this since . . . since before some of the people in this room were born! It's like a throwback to the forties!"

There was a glum silence of agreement. What had started as a trickle of racial episodes—a trickle particularly agonizing to Southern leaders—had grown steadily more numerous . . . and uglier. As Glencannon said, there had been no more than a score of known incidents, and most of them had been of the ugly intimidation variety rather than true violence, but there was a vicious ground swell. It had spread slowly from Western North Carolina, but now it enveloped half the state. Membership in lunatic-fringe organizations like the KKK and the American Nazi Party had risen steeply, and the tempo was increasing.

So far, the rest of the country was scarcely aware of it, but the men in this room knew. They were not alarmists, yet they were frightened. Badly frightened. The unrest had come out of nowhere, with absolutely no warning, and the first signs had been so scattered that it hadn't occurred to local authorities that they might involve other jurisdictions. Only in the last two weeks had the incidents begun to coalesce, and now they were moving like a gradually accelerating freight train. It was only a matter of time before the public became generally aware of them, and what might happen then did not bear thinking of.

What the rest of the country might think was bad enough, but it was nothing compared to the anguish in this tense room. *Their* state, *their* cities, and, above all, *their* people were falling prey to an old, ugly hate they'd thought they were defeating—and they seemed helpless before it.

"Gentlemen," Farnam said, "believe me, I understand. And it's not just us. Every Southeastern state north of Florida is involved, and none of us has any idea *why* it's happening. We're asking the Justice Department to put the FBI on it, but I don't really expect them to find the answer either. The economy's strong. There's no special hardship to bring out the worst in people. It's like it just . . . appeared out of nowhere." He saw from their expressions that he'd told them nothing they didn't already know, and his face darkened with rage.

"God*damn* it!" He slammed a fist on the conference table, and his curse was a mark of just how distressed he was, for he was a devout Southern Baptist who abhorred profanity. "We were on top of it! We were making better racial progress than any other part of the country! What in God's name went *wrong*?"

It was a strong man's desperate plea for enlightenment, and no one had an answer at all.

"It goes well, Blake Taggart?" The Troll's voice had become very nearly human in the past several months of conversation with his minion.

"Very well, Master," Taggart said with a grin. He scarcely noticed any longer that he used the title the Troll had demanded of him. There were moments when he worried—fleetingly—that the Troll's insanity was infecting his own brain, but they were increasingly less frequent, for his master's nihilism had begun to send its strange, dark fire crawling through his own veins. He was becoming the Troll's Renfield; he knew it, yet it scarcely bothered him. He'd discovered the controls the Troll had set within his own brain and body, and, strangely, they didn't bother him, either. The operation had become something greater than he was, and the power he would wield as the Troll's viceroy was sweet on his tongue.

"Good," the Troll said, and the still-hideous sound of its laughter echoed in the buried fighter. "My candidates will do well this November, Blake Taggart."

"I know they will, Master. We'll see to that." And Taggart's laughter was almost as hideous as his master's.

The Troll was pleased. This human was worth every moment invested in it. It had a brain of vitriol and venom, and his judicious alterations had only made it better. And it was cunning. The Troll had anticipated building his power base out of the Leonard Stillwaters of the United States, but Taggart had shown him a far more productive use for them.

It wouldn't have occurred to the Troll to use the humans who hated to win control of those who did not. He admitted that. But Taggart had taught him much about these easily led sheep.

The Troll could touch no more than a third of the minds about him. His experiments had shown him how to completely control any he could touch, but to dominate even one totally required his full attention . . . and left its owner a mindless husk when he was done. What he most desired were willing slaves, but barely five percent—seven at the most—were as susceptible to corruption as Taggart itself, and to make specific changes even in those few required individual time and effort. Yet he could "push" at every open mind when they slept, influencing them gradually, bending them subtly to his will. He could reshape their perceptions and beliefs as long as there was even the slightest outward stimulus to drive them in the desired direction.

Taggart had provided that stimulus. He and the Troll had made a painstaking survey of state and local political figures in the upcoming elections, selecting the ones who would be most amenable to manipulation once in office. Many of those individuals were already likely to win in November, but others were likely to lose. So the Troll had thrown his own influence onto the scale to support "his" candidates.

Many—indeed, most—of those candidates would have been horrified if they'd known of the Troll's existence or what he planned for them, but that was satisfactory. Once they were in office would be soon enough to begin reshaping them, and, in the meantime, he could amuse himself to good effect with their more corruptible fellow citizens.

He was working strongly, if subtly, upon all the ethnic groups caught within his net, and he'd been delighted by what Taggart called "the domino effect." Hatred begat hatred, making it ever easier for him to stir his cauldron of prejudice and bigotry. It would take only a tiny push to tip that cauldron and spill its poison across the land, and the Troll intended to provide that push.

But not everywhere. He would use his Pavlovian monsters with care, for they were the tool with which he would prod and chivvy those minds he could not warp directly. Where his chosen candidates were already firmly in power, there would be little or no violence. Where his selected pawns were only shakily in control, there would be violence which they would contain, and a thankful population would return them gratefully to office. And where his future tools were the outsiders, there would be carnage . . . carnage for which the current officeholders would be blamed.

Oh, yes, it would be lovely. The Troll could hardly wait to light the fuse, especially in the areas where "his" politicians were the challengers, for it would be there he could indulge himself. There he could slake his appetite for destruction—for the moment, at least— with the sweet knowledge that humans were killing humans for him.

He would set his puppets in motion and savor the exquisite cunning which used them to torment and enslave themselves.

In the meantime, he'd culled a force of the most hate-filled and destructive. Taggart called them his "Apocalypse Brigade," and the Troll was amazed that he hadn't seen the need for them himself. His combat mechs were few in number and far too noticeable to employ where they might be seen or reported.

His humans were another matter. More fragile and less reliable, yet able to go anywhere and programmed into total loyalty. Their numbers were still growing, but he had over nine hundred already, and the contributions he could "persuade" other humans—many of them wealthy—to make had armed and equipped them well by the primitive standards of this planet.

They knew nothing of his existence. Indeed, they believed they followed Blake Taggart, and, in truth, Taggart understood them even better than the Troll who had created them. It was Taggart who grasped the inner workings of their twisted psyches and had designed an emblem to focus and harness their driven, destructive energy. But they would do the Troll's bidding, for Taggart would order them to do whatever he desired. Already he had tested them in small numbers, in isolated areas, upon travelers and others who would never be missed, and the cruelty and savagery he had instilled in them pleased him.

They pleased him, yet the need to touch so many minds was wearing. His creators had given him an electronic amplifying system of tremendous power, but it was his brain which produced the original signal. The power supply of his fighter pushed his mental patterns outward, hammering at the humans about him, yet he'd underestimated the time requirement, and for the first time in his tireless life, he felt fatigue. His brain was organic; unlike a computer, he wearied eventually of concentration and required rest. And, also unlike a computer, he could do but one thing at a time, however well he might do it. The need to concentrate upon the task at hand—and to rest from it—had delayed his bomb badly.

But that, too, was acceptable. He had made progress—not as much as he'd hoped, for the technical data on the construction of weapons, as opposed to their employment, were guarded by *Shirmaksu* security codes he could not break easily. But they could be broken with time. He had most of what he required now, and once the design was completed, his servomechs could fabricate and assemble the components in a very few days.

Not that he expected to need the bomb. Things were going well, very well, and surely if any human on this benighted planet had possessed the wit to search for him, it had given up by now. Besides, he thought with a wicked, hungry happiness, anyone who might have hunted him would be occupied with other matters very soon.

Like the wildfire waiting to consume its land.

CHAPTER TWENTY

Dolf Wilkins looked up as Allison DuChamps entered his office. DuChamps, one of the Bureau's most senior female agents, was a pleasantly unremarkable-looking woman with a first-class mind and a levelheadedness that was almost infuriating—a combination which had served her well in the field—and head of the domestic terrorism unit.

Wilkins smiled and she smiled back, but only with her lips. Her dark, foreboding eyes touched him with a chill, and his own smile faded. "What is it, Alley?"

"I think we have a bad situation," she said carefully. "Possibly very bad."

Wilkins stiffened. The Bureau had learned its lesson (yet again, he conceded) about overreaction, Big Brotherliness, and clumsy interventions brought on by panic attacks among its leadership, which was one reason DuChamps had been chosen for her job. If *Allison* was concerned . . .

"What?" he asked again.

"I've been reading some reports from domestic surveillance," DuChamps replied, "and there's a very strange—and ugly—pattern developing. One with the potential to do a lot of damage."

"Where and how?"

"The Southeast and racism," she said succinctly. "To be more precise, large-scale, organized, deliberately orchestrated racial violence."

"What?" Wilkins sat straighter. Organized racial violence had become less of a concern to the Bureau over the last decade. Oh, there were still bigots—of every color and creed—who were willing or even eager to resort to violence, just as there were occasionally horrific incidents in which they did just that. But society's tolerance was drying up, and that, as every good cop knew, was the true secret to controlling any activity: turn it into something society as a whole rejected. Judicious pressure from the Justice Department and the Bureau helped keep it trimmed back, though there'd been a few ugly flare-ups in various inner cities and the Midwest and Northeast, but compared to other motives for organized violence, racism had become very much a secondary worry.

That was his first thought; his second was that the South wasn't even where racist organizations remained strongest. In fact, the focus of active bigotry seemed to have moved north from the Sunbelt, especially into the decaying urban sprawls of the "Rust Belt." Southerners had taken the rap too often in the sixties and seventies. As a society, they'd learned a lesson which the rest of the country, having taught it to the South, seemed disinclined to learn for itself.

"Are you sure, Alley?" he asked finally, and she nodded.

"It surprised me, too, Dolf, but it's there. And the entire pattern is . . . wrong. I've never seen anything like it."

"Explain," he said sharply.

"I'll try. Look, we all know there are patterns for organized hate groups. National and regional groups grow out of long-standing, widespread prejudice and/or the need for some sort of scapegoat. A localized group can arise from those same pressures or from the emergence of some 'charismatic' (if you'll pardon the term) local leader or from strictly local, and therefore, by definition, special circumstances. Or, in some instances, a single powerful individual or group of individuals can, by economic or other pressures, create an organization, in which case it's usually rather fragile and tends to fall apart once the pressure from those individuals eases off. And, of course, some groups *become* pure hate groups as the 'purity' of their other political goals' degenerates. Right?"

"Yes," he said a bit impatiently.

"All right. What we have here is a series of apparently isolated episodes, scattered over parts of nine states. The states in question have different economies, social patterns, and ethnic compositions. With a few exceptions, none have any recent record of large-scale, racially motivated hostility—certainly not on an action-oriented, organized model. Only portions of each state seem to be affected, with no abnormalities outside the affected areas. And, finally, there are very clear similarities between these widely scattered episodes. So much of one, in fact, that I'm tempted to say we're looking at a single group's MO . . . except that the activity seems to jump back and forth across racial lines like a ping-pong ball!"

"Huh?" Wilkins leaned back in his chair. "Are you sure there really *is* a pattern, Alley? You're not reading correlations into unrelated data?"

"I'm certain." She opened a folder and glanced at some scribbled notes. "The Civil Rights Division passed us a formal—and quiet—request from the Southern Governor's Conference to look into racial unrest in both Carolinas, Tennessee, Kentucky, and Georgia. Aside from those mail bombings a few years back, the area's been quiet for so long that I'm afraid we didn't assign it a very high priority at first, but then the facts started coming in, and not just from those states.

"Fact: five months ago there was no significant racist activity in the affected areas. Fact: a little over three months ago, local law enforcement people started noticing a marked increase in both recruiting by and visibility of racist organizations, predominantly white. Fact: about two months ago, there began to be a few widely separated incidents—more what you'd call ruffianism than anything else—mingled with vandalism, cross burnings, harassment, that sort of thing. Fact: once the first moves had been made by the white groups, *nonwhite* groups started popping out of the woodwork and shoving back. Fact: one month ago, there was a decided and very noticeable acceleration in the situation, almost like a controlled surge, from both sides of the racial line . . . and the rate of increase is still climbing."

She closed the folder.

"What we seem to have here, Dolf," she said very precisely, "is the blow-off of carefully concealed but long-standing mutual hatreds. I mean, these people are *organized*—on a cell basis, no less—on both sides, and they're heavily armed and turning more extreme, more violence-prone, almost in unison, *no matter which side they're on.*" She paused, regarding him levelly.

"I suppose it's theoretically possible that the situation could have been this bad all along without our noticing, but I don't believe it. The more peaceful, process-oriented radicals would have given us some sign of it, and I simply cannot convince myself that the Bureau *and* that many local law enforcement agencies could all miss something like this. Besides, the pattern is wrong. It's geographic, but not regional; it's racial, but not limited to one or even a few racial groups."

Wilkins nodded, fighting a strangely mixed exhilaration and horror.

"Go on," he said quietly.

"I plotted the data on a map, Dolf," she said. "I mean *everything*: rallies, known financial contributions, confrontations, the whole shooting match. And when I did, I found a uniform, graduated density of events, like a ripple pattern, spreading out from a common center, going just so far, and then stopping." She waved a hand. "Oh, there are odds and ends beyond the edge of the pattern, but I think they're rogues—copycats, that sort of thing. I mean, there'll always be *some* nuts, and if they get the idea there's some sort of 'wave of the future' coming, it's bound to bring them out of the closet in their white sheets and swastikas or what-have-you. The point is that outside the boundary the events *are* scattered. They don't plot. But *inside* it . . ." Her voice trailed off.

"Did you bring a copy of your map?" Wilkins tried to keep his voice as normal and professional as possible.

"Here." She produced a photocopied map and unfolded it on his desk, tracing the rough circle she'd scribed upon it. It was centered on the North Carolina-Tennessee mountains, Wilkins noted, reaching out to just beyond Atlanta to the south and Portsmouth, Ohio, to the north. DuChamps had marked its approximate center, and Wilkins's mouth went dry when he saw its location. A little north of Asheville, he noted with a queer sense of almost-calm . . . and very close to the site of the plutonium theft.

"See?" she said. "Why should rural West Virginia or southern Ohio exhibit exactly the same pattern as Atlanta or Columbia, South Carolina? And if Columbia's going crazy, why isn't Raleigh? Or Charleston? And do you see how the incidence just *stops* at the edge of the circle?" He nodded silently, and she went on with quiet urgency.

"There's something else I don't think many of the locals have had enough data to notice, Dolf. A new organization. It's so well hidden we still don't even know its name, but it's there, and its members use a really weird 'secret' identification symbol: a skeleton on a white horse."

"A what?" Wilkins blinked in confusion.

"A skeleton on a horse," DuChamps repeated, then shrugged. "I know, it doesn't make any sense. Doesn't relate to any known group's symbology, as far as we can determine. Weirdest of all, it definitely seems linked to all this racial unrest, but it appears to be more of an anarchist group, and we've identified members from several different races. And," she added more grimly, "it's violent as hell. The North Carolina SBI seems to have lost a four-man undercover team that got too close to just one member of whatever it is."

She shook her head slowly, stroking her folder.

"I don't know what's going on, Dolf, but some one outfit is pulling the strings. There's a common thread, some strategy I can't quite put my finger on. You just don't get this sort of pattern without someone creating it. I couldn't prove it in court, but that's the only explanation that even halfway makes sense—only that's crazy, too!"

"Maybe, Alley," he said, then paused; Allison DuChamps did not possess the critical alpha spike. He cleared his throat. "Keep an eye on it and put your planning staff to work on an in-depth analysis and some sort of reaction plan in case worse comes to worst, all right?"

"We need more than that, Dolf," she said. "Recruiting rallies are starting to pop up—big ones, with some ominous alliances behind them. The KKK and the Nazi Party plan to formalize something called the 'Appalachian White People's Alliance' at a joint rally in Asheville this week, and that's just the start of it. Rumbles of opposition rallies by nonwhite militants are already turning up, too, and if something breaks, we won't begin to have the manpower to deal with it on a reaction basis. We've got to put somebody inside, see if we can't get a handle on who's setting it up. And we've got to do it *fast*. "

"I'm inclined to agree," he lied, "but give me a little while to think about it. And leave me a copy of the map if you can."

"Certainly. This is your copy of my report." She laid the folder on his desk and headed for the door, then paused and looked back. "But, Dolf," she said softly, "don't think too long, okay?"

"Okay, Alley," he said, never taking his eyes from the map. "Good."

The door closed behind her, and he reached for his phone the instant the latch clicked. He punched in a long-distance number and waited, fingers drumming nervously on the desk, until it was answered.

"Commander Morris?" He spoke quickly, urgently. "Dolf Wilkins. Look, don't get your hopes up, but I think we've found Grendel.... Yes, that's right, found him. Well, within thirty or forty square miles, anyway." He paused and listened for a long, taut moment. "Bet your sweet ass I can," he said with a savage grin. "I'll grab Stan Loren and be there within two hours if I have to carry the damned plane on my back!"

A bevy of tilt-rotor MV-22 Ospreys swooped out of the hot September sun in a hurricane of dust and flying debris to disgorge the first echelon of Company T. The fixed-wing planes had come roaring in at three hundred knots, then slowed sharply and rotated their wingtip engines through ninety degrees to descend vertically. Side and rear cargo hatches opened before they touched down, and three fully equipped squads stormed out of each aircraft, heading for preselected firing positions. They carried their usual personal weapons, M249 SAW (Squad Automatic Weapon) machine guns, and an astoundingly high number of antiarmor weapons. In addition to extra issues of the single-shot Predator SRAW (Short Range Assault Weapon) which had replaced the AT-4 and the even older LAW (Lightweight Anti-Armor Weapon) as the standard light antitank weapon of the Corps, each platoon contained an extra antiarmor squad equipped with three Dragon heavy man-portable tank-killer launchers equipped with the new Superdragon II fire-and-forget missile upgrade which had become standard Army issue but had not yet reached the Corps.

Rear Admiral Richard Aston watched Major Abernathy's men deploy, racing through the waist-high grass while their aircraft lifted out to clear the landing zone. The moment the LZ was clear, C-130Js rumbled in just above the ground to drop palletized eight-wheeled LAVs (Light Armored Vehicles) with their turreted, twenty-five-millimeter autocannon, and the vehicles of an attached heavy machine-gun platoon from their rear-opening cargo doors. The vehicles landed amid the sounds of splintering pallets, and beyond them a second wave of Ospreys was already coming in with vehicle crews, more rifle squads, more ammunition, and still more antitank weapons.

He glanced at his stopwatch, then at Ludmilla. They'd managed to shave off another few seconds, but in a sense, they were just marking time. They had no idea what sort of terrain or tactical situation would obtain when they finally found the Troll, so they were running standard exercises to keep basic skills sharp. They'd run several urban exercises, as well, but the strategy team all agreed that they were unlikely to find something as visually obvious as the Troll hiding in a city.

He looked up, frowning, as the whacking sound of fresh rotors came from behind. They were running the exercise without helos, so what—?

The Blackhawk transport came over a rise, headed directly towards them, then flared and settled like a giant, dust-breathing dragonfly, glittering in the hot sunlight under a whining halo of rotor blades.

Aston and Ludmilla turned curiously to watch the hatch open, but when a familiar, pudgy form in the uniform of a Navy commander jumped out their curiosity became tension. They glanced at one another and then, without a word, moved quickly to meet him.

Morris waded through the grass towards them, waving for them to wait where they were, and they stopped. He toiled over to them, sweating heavily in the heat, and his expression was taut.

"Mordecai! What are you doing here?" Ludmilla demanded before Aston could get a word in.

"It's Grendel," Morris said in a low, fierce voice. "We've got him, Milla! We've pinned the bastard down at last!"

"I don't know, Mordecai," Aston said unhappily, rubbing his bald pate while he stared down at the map on which Morris and Jayne Hastings had further refined Allison DuChamps's data. They'd narrowed the possible area to a circle no more than ten miles across and plotted it on a large-scale topographical map, but it was a rough ten miles. "Okay, I agree he has to be more or less in here—" he tapped the circle in which the lines connecting various incidents all crossed "—but look at it. It's all heavy forest, the road net stinks, and once we start a systematic search, he'll be up and away before we can stop him. If we knew *exactly* where he was, things'd be different, but going in blind..."

His voice trailed off and he shook his head, and Morris wiped sweat from his face silently. It was sweltering in Aston's command trailer, and his own elation had dimmed as the admiral took him step-by-step, remorselessly, through their meager data. The information represented a tremendous breakthrough—the first real break they'd had—but Dick was right. Morris admitted it unhappily, but he admitted it. He and Wilkins had been too exhilarated to look for difficulties, but Aston was a professional's professional. He knew that Murphy's was the first law of military operations.

The intelligence officer sighed and ran fingers through his sweaty hair, frowning as he, too, stared down at the map. Now he understood why Loren had seemed less euphoric than the FBI director and himself. The CIA man's ex-Ranger background meant he was more accustomed to operations mounted in trackless wilderness without street signs, and he'd seen more clearly what Aston faced.

Still, they knew roughly where he was....

"If large-scale searches are out, what about small ground parties of Troll-proof recon troops?" he asked finally.

"That may be the way we have to go." Aston sighed. "And we've been training for just that, but I'd hoped to avoid it. That's a damned big area, and we've only got so many men, Mordecai. Besides, if we send people in on the ground, Grendel's likely to spot them before they spot him, especially if he's well hidden. If he does, they won't have the firepower to stop him. They can't—not if they're supposed to be unobtrusive. So if there's hard contact between us and him, we're going to lose a lot of people and he'll probably bug out before we can get the main force in place."

"All right," Morris said, "suppose we set up an air umbrella before you go in? A squadron of F-16s from Shaw—or, better yet, F-15s from Langley—could fly top cover and nail him if he took off, couldn't they?"

"I don't know," Aston said thoughtfully. "Milla?"

"It's worth trying," she said slowly, "but he's faster than anything we've got, and he can accelerate faster, too. With a small start, he could simply outrun your missiles, and his antimissile systems are pretty good, as well. Then, too, he'd have an excellent chance of fighting his way through several dozen of your best fighters head-to-head—unless you arm them with nukes. And with chemical warheads, you'd have to use heavy surface-to-air missiles to do him much damage, because your air-to-air missiles just don't pack enough punch."

"Their SAM versions knocked down his wingmen," Morris pointed out.

"True, but you fired hundreds of them." She wiped her damp forehead, and Morris hid a grin. At least her symbiote didn't keep her from sweating. "And the real reason they worked wasn't their power but the tactical situation. They took the Kangas—and Grendel—by surprise, because none of them expected any threat from such primitive technology. Even then, they wouldn't have worked if they hadn't been moving at such high velocity that their drive fields were all focused forward and couldn't interdict. Not to mention the way atmospheric friction tore them apart once their hull integrity was breached." She shook her head. "No, it's going to take something at least as heavy as a Patriot to damage his hull significantly, assuming he's not configured to interdict. And, frankly, your SAMs would be dead meat against his active defenses unless we can fire enough to saturate his tracking capability."

"And we don't happen to have a couple of dozen Patriot batteries already in the area," Aston pointed out to Morris. "Which means we can't count on taking him out once he gets airborne even if he hasn't come up with some way to screw *our* tracking systems over. We've got to catch him on the ground, someplace we can close in with enough heavy weapons to deal with his mechs and catch him on takeoff, when his drive field can't interdict."

Morris nodded, his expression unhappy. Ludmilla had briefed them all on the Troll's flight systems. Fighters didn't mount battle screen because they used their n-drives to intercept incoming weapons, but the Troll couldn't configure his drive field to do that until he was at least a hundred meters off the ground. Up to that point, he could be hit—assuming they got through his active defenses—but the window would be only seconds wide.

"More to the point, perhaps," Aston went on, "we're all agreed that we're only going to get one clean shot at him—if we're lucky. Once he knows we're on to him, he'll redouble his security measures, at the very least; at worst, he'll go for the quick kill and simply blow the planet up. So we have to catch him when he's vulnerable, and to do that, we have to know where he is. Which is only another way of saying that we can't search for him without risking alerting him, but that we've got to know where he is before we warn him in any other way."

"Maybe." Ludmilla licked sweat from her upper lip and ran her fingertip over the mountainous terrain, frowning. "I know we'd hoped for some sort of physical sighting, but this may actually be better. He must be pretty well hidden—probably underground; they like that—and we haven't had any search activity in the area. So he must know we haven't spotted him, and when we *do* turn up, he's going to spend a few minutes wondering why we're there."

"Which would be all very well if we knew where he was," Aston objected, but his face was intent, as if he sensed some thought working itself out behind her eyes.

"Maybe we can figure that out," she said softly, turning to Morris. "Mordecai, is there any sort of aircraft which would normally fly something remotely like a search pattern in that area?"

"Hm?" Morris thought for a moment, frowning, but it was Abernathy who provided the answer.

"Sure," he said. "Forestry Service planes buzz around the national forests and parks all the time." Morris and Aston looked at him with surprised respect, and he chuckled. "Hey, I'm a California boy. I grew up in the San Joaquin Valley—little place named Exeter, just below Sequoia National Park. They do surveys, aerial mapping, hunt for pot growers, watch for forest fires, all that sort of thing."

"Yes, they do," Morris said slowly, "and the Southeast's been dry again this year. I bet they're keeping a real close fire-watch."

"Good." Ludmilla looked at Aston. "I've half-expected something like this. That's why I was so glad to get my flight suit back together."

"Why?" he asked tensely.

"Because the sensies work. I can wear it and ride around in one of these Forestry Service planes. Even if he's buried himself, he'll have set up detection posts. Why not? Your technology wouldn't even recognize one of his scan beams."

"But yours will," he said flatly, and frowned when she nodded. "No, Milla. We need you to handle your blaster. I let you talk me into jump school because we might have to go in by chute, but if you go mucking around up there with twenty-fifth century technology and he spots you—"

"I'll use passive systems," she said calmly. "Everything else will be powered down to a shielded trickle charge. He'd have to be within a hundred meters to pick that up, and that's assuming he knew to look for them in the first place. Which he won't, because I'm 'dead,' right?"

"Just so you don't get that way for real." He tried to speak lightly, but she heard personal as well as professional concern in his voice, and her eyes smiled at him.

"All right," he said after a moment, "how close can you pin him down?"

"Well, with a little luck I can place his scanner sites, at least, to within...oh, twenty meters. The area he's protecting with them should give us a good idea where he is, and if you put up an air umbrella that knows where to look, you'll at least double your chance of catching him as he lifts."

"All right," he sighed again, after a long, silent moment. "I don't like it, but I don't see any way around it, either. So where do you think he is?"

"I suspect he's right here," she said, tapping the map. Aston craned his neck and looked over her shoulder. Her finger rested on something called Sugarloaf Mountain. "Right in the middle of Mordecai's area with this nice valley right at the top, see? There's even a road of sorts, connecting to state highway—" she bent closer to the map "—Two-Twelve, and it looks pretty heavily forested in there. Good cover."

"You may be right. But he could be in one of these side valleys, too."

"I know. But that's where he is, Dick. Somewhere on this mountain."

"Agreed," he said, giving himself a mental shake and banishing his feeling of dread. "All right, Mordecai, get us a Forestry Service plane. We'll put a pilot we know the bastard can't read into it to be on the safe side, and we'll have Jayne see what kind of satellite pictures she can hunt up, too." He turned to Abernathy. "Major, alert the troops. I want a full gear inspection by eighteen hundred."

"Yes, Sir," Abernathy said crisply.

"Mordecai—" Aston turned back to the commander "—get back to Washington and tell Admiral McLain we need a fighter umbrella—a *distant* one. See if he can set it up out of Langley or Pax River; they're both outside the Troll's reach, but they can get there in a hurry. But stress that I *don't* want them mission-briefed ahead of time. Find the senior man with a good EEG and put him in charge, then brief him so he can set up an ops plan, but don't let him give it to the troops until just—"

He broke off as he realized Morris wasn't listening to him.

"Mordecai?" Aston cocked his head and followed the direction of Morris's eyes. Ludmilla had just taken off her jacket, and the commander was staring at her as if at a ghost. "Mordecai!"

"Just . . . just a minute, Dick," Morris said softly. He was still staring at Ludmilla, and she looked back with a puzzled expression.

"Milla," he asked quietly, "where did you get that shirt?"

"This?" She looked down, stroking the silk-screening, and Abernathy and Aston looked at her in puzzlement. It was the one with the skeletal rider, and they'd seen it many times without noting anything extraordinary.

"That," Morris said. "According to the FBI report, there's a screwy anarchist group with an interracial membership turning up. Not many members actually spotted, but they're spread all over the affected area."

"So?" Aston asked.

"Their emblem," Morris said softly, "is a skeleton on a white horse."

There was silence, and Ludmilla rose slowly, reaching for the FBI report. As she stood, Morris started visibly and reached out quickly. Her eyes widened, but she stood motionless as he grabbed the bottom of her shirt and stretched it out, reading the lettering.

"My God, my God!" he whispered. "No wonder I didn't think of it. It's not from my book—it's from yours!"

"What in hell are you talking about, Mordecai?" Aston demanded.

"This." He turned the lettering and read it aloud. "'The Fourth Horseman,'" he whispered. Aston looked blank, but Abernathy straightened with a jerk. "The rider on the pale horse," Morris went on. "The Fourth Horseman of the Apocalypse." He looked up and met Aston's eyes.

"Death," he said quietly.

There was total silence, then Aston cleared his throat.

"All right, M&M. When you talk to Admiral McLain, tell him to make sure at least some of the air cover's armed with nukes."

"Nukes?" Morris stared at him, frowning in protest. "But what about the ground force? We can't use—"

"You damned well can," Aston said harshly. "We can't fuck around with him, Mordecai. If this son of a bitch gets off the ground, we'll lose him. Either he'll go to ground all over again—this time knowing that we're at least partly onto him—or he may just be pissed enough to set off his bomb. So if I tell you to, or if whoever's in charge upstairs sees the bastard taking off, nail him. Understood?"

There was another long silence, then Morris nodded reluctantly.

"Understood."

"Master, I think it's a mistake," Blake Taggart said to the featureless panel which hid the Troll. "We know they're ready. Why risk it now?"

"It is illogical to assume that what has not been tested will function as desired," the Troll replied coldly. Deep within himself, he was amused to be preaching logic to a human after all the endless years in which the *Shirmaksu* had prated of it to him.

"But it's too soon, Master," the Blake Taggart human argued stubbornly, and the Troll felt a grudging respect for the creature's courage. Or was it simply that it sensed his own dependence upon it? No matter.

"It is not too soon." The mechanical voice was even harsher than usual, and the Troll smiled mentally as he felt the human's fear. It had argued too long once before, and days had passed before it even began to forget the anguish that had earned it.

"Blake Taggart," the Troll went on more evenly, "the plan requires increasing violence as the election nears, but it must be controlled, directed. I must know that I can begin it when I wish and aim it as I will, and also that I can call these vermin to heel when I must. Much depends upon that, and I will not rely on a tool I have not tested. Besides—" the hideous sound of trollish laughter grated in the control room "—a foretaste should improve the panic. And this town of Asheville is perfect. Close enough to watch with my remotes, small enough for an excellent laboratory, yet large enough to determine how well our tool fares against one of your urban centers. And I do not care for this Asheville, Blake Taggart. Its leadership has proved too hard to touch, to control, and it is close to my base. No, I will destroy it."

"Destroy it?" Taggart was alarmed. "But that would take—"

"More strength than I have recruited here. Yes, Blake Taggart, I know. My creatures are already on the move—not all, but enough."

"In that case, why not call in the Brigade? We don't know exactly what will happen, but it might be better to have some of our own people handy—people we can trust to do exactly what they're told, not just what you can suggest to them indirectly."

"Yes," the Troll mused. "Yes, Blake Taggart, that may be an excellent idea. Summon them all. We will test your mobilization plan, as well."

"I will, Master," Taggart said.

destruction *n.*
1. The act of destroying. **2.** The means or cause of destroying. **3.** The fact or condition of being destroyed. [Middle English *destruccioun*, from Latin *destructe*, from *destructus*, past participle of *destruere*, destroy.]

destroy *v.* **-stroyed, -stroying, -stroys.** —*tr.*
1. To ruin completely; to spoil beyond restoration or repair; consume. **2.** To break up; tear down; raze; demolish. **3.** To put an end to; to do away with; to get rid of. **4.** To kill. **5.** To render useless. **6.** To defeat; to subdue completely; crush. -intr. To be harmful or destructive. [Middle English *destruyen*, from Latin *destruere* (past participle *destructus*): *de* (reversal) + *struere*, pile up.]

—*Webster-Wangchi Unabridged*
Dictionary of Standard English
Tomas y Hijos, Publishers 2465,
Terran Standard Reckoning

CHAPTER TWENTY-ONE

"I don't *know* what they're going to do! But whatever it is, I don't have enough men to stop them." Bill McCoury, Buncombe County's sheriff, glowered at Jeremiah Willis and Hugh Campbell, Asheville's Chief of Police.

"Bill's right, Jerry." Campbell rubbed his eyes wearily, then replaced his glasses and regarded the mayor levelly. "Neither of us do. I'd hoped refusing them a permit would stop them, but it didn't. As for this—" he waved a copy of the court injunction against any assembly "in Buncombe County, in the State of North Carolina, by the Appalachian White People's Alliance and/or the Ku Klux Klan and/or the American Nazi Party and/or any individual members of those organizations, however styled" "—I don't see any way to enforce it. Not without an awful lot more manpower."

"I know." Willis sighed. "All right. I guess we all knew it had to start somewhere. I'll call the Governor."

✧✧✧

"Mordecai?" Morris looked grubbier than ever, and he felt it as he looked up and saw Jayne Hastings—as immaculate as ever—in the door of his office. At least he had an excuse; he hadn't stopped moving, one way or another, in the thirty-six hours since his return from Camp Lejeune.

"Yes, Jayne?" He waved at a chair heaped in computer printouts, and she moved them carefully to the floor before she sat. "What have you got?"

"I'm not positive," she said. "Has Milla gone up yet?"

"She's due to go tomorrow—if Dick doesn't convince himself he can't afford to risk her." Morris shook a cigarette from a pack. "Why?"

"We swung one of the Hydra multi-sensor birds to cover the Southeast last night. Exhausted her maneuvering mass to do it, too. I've been looking over the data." She shook her head. "It's amazing what the new systems can do."

"I know." Morris nodded. "I don't have your technical background, but I'm always amazed by how steadily the quality of satellite data keeps going up."

"Well, I think I found something," Hastings told him, and he leaned forward over his desk.

"What?"

"Look." She laid an oddly murky photo on his littered blotter and adjusted his desk lamp carefully. "See this?"

She used a pencil as a pointer, tapping with the eraser. Morris leaned a little closer and saw a bright, hair-thin line that snaked across the photo and ended in a small, crescent-shaped smear of equal brightness.

"That," Hastings told him, "is the road up Sugarloaf Mountain. It's not much of one—only one lane of macadam to an abandoned logging area."

"So?" he asked.

"The brightness," Hastings said, "is heat, M&M. Lots of heat."

"Heat?" He frowned. "Sunlight soaked up during the day?"

"No way. First, there's too much of it. Second, a lot of this road's pretty heavily shaded. See these brighter sections? They're from direct sunlight, all right, but this almost equally bright section here's an oblique into an area under heavy tree cover. Nope, Mordecai.

Only one thing could account for this—" her eraser tapped the second area for emphasis "—and that's traffic. Lots of traffic."

"What sort of traffic?"

"I don't know, but it was headed here." She drew out another photo, this one in bright, artificial colors—obviously a computer-generated and enhanced enlargement of a portion of the first. The thin line was a broad ribbon, and the crescent at its end had refined itself into several regularly spaced heat sources.

"These are buildings in an installation of some sort," she said quietly. "A good-sized one, judging by the number of people we're picking up." Her eraser tapped again, indicating a dusting of tiny, individual heat sources scattered about the buildings. "They're moving around too much for us to get a hard count, even with the Hydra's IR sensors, but there are lots of them. And look at this." She laid out another photo, this one of peaceful green trees, just beginning to show the first touches of autumn color, in a bright, sunlit mountain valley. "See anything?"

"No."

"You should. It's a daylight shot of exactly the same area, and a lot of traffic went into it. According to this one—" she indicated the computer-generated enlargement again "—it stayed, too. As I say, we can't get a hard point source count, but our minimum estimates puts hundreds of people in the area—*hundreds*, Mordecai. So where are they?"

"Hmmm." Morris took a powerful magnifying glass from his drawer and examined the bland photo minutely. "I don't see a thing," he confessed.

"Neither can any of the photo analysts," she agreed, pulling out yet another computer print, "so we did this spectroscopic shot on the next pass." The blur of colors told Morris absolutely nothing, but the light in her green eyes said it told Hastings a lot. "This area here—" her eraser circled and then stabbed "—is the same area as the IR shot, and it doesn't match its surroundings." Morris looked up at her, and she gave him a thin, sharklike smile. "It's a fake, Mordecai. All this greenery here—" she tapped again "—is a fake."

Morris was silent for a long moment, looking back and forth between the photos while his mind raced.

"You're positive?" he asked eventually, and she nodded.

"Something else turned up on the enlargement, too. Look here."

She drew his attention back to the infrared shot. "See this little dot?" He nodded again. "That's up the mountain above the installation, and it's another hot spot. Intermittent—it only shows on a few of the shots—and a lot smaller and cooler than the others. Not only that, the vegetation on the slope is exactly the same kind of fake as the rest of it."

Morris rubbed his nose as he pondered. The regularly spaced oblongs of heat formed a horseshoe-shaped arc, its ends sweeping back to touch the steep mountain face on either side of the small heat source. Like a shield, he thought. A shield hiding what? And composed of whom?

"What do you make of it, Jayne?" he asked finally.

"It could be lots of things, I suppose, but that's part of Pisgah National Forest, and according to the records, there's nothing there at all. My opinion? It's a military camp. The point sources are way too dense for a good count, but there could be an entire battalion in there."

"A battalion?" Morris shook his head, trying to clear it. "Damn." He thought for a moment longer, then reached for the secure phone and started punching numbers. The phone at the far end was answered quickly.

"This is Commander Morris," he said. "Get me Admiral Aston."

"They're right, Governor," Melvyn Tanner said. Despite his words, the attorney general looked as if he wished he could disagree. "Some really ugly reports are coming in. The State Patrol reports a lot of out-of-state license plates flowing into the area, and Tennessee and Kentucky say more are on the way. They're not just leaf-watchers out to see the fall colors, either," he added with graveyard humor.

"I know." Governor Farnam toyed with the pen stand on his desk. "But if we call out the Guard, we show just how alarmed we are. I purely hate giving a bunch of racist psychos that much satisfaction," the great-great-grandson of one of his state's largest slave-owners said grimly.

"Maybe so, but it's your responsibility to maintain order and protect public safety when the local authorities can't."

"All right," Farnam said finally. "Draw up the proclamation. And get me a line to the Justice Department."

✧✧✧

"What do you make of it, Milla?" Aston asked. The two of them were bent over a table studying the photos Morris had transmitted to them by secure land line.

"I think it's him." Ludmilla spoke with obvious restraint, controlling her own exhilaration. "It fits."

"But where'd he get the manpower?"

"Dick, you've seen the kind of hate he can whip up. If he can do that, why can't he recruit a small, elite force under his direct control?"

"I'll buy that he could get them together," Aston said with a frown. "But hang on to them?" He shook his head. "If this is a paramilitary outfit, there has to be a chain of command, and who's going to take orders from a machine? Besides, why run the risk of revealing himself to them?"

"He probably didn't," she said, and Aston raised an eyebrow. "He probably found himself an Alexson," she explained, then frowned. "A quisling, you'd call it. A collaborator. He'd only need one to front for him, and once he had one, I guarantee he could control him." She shivered.

"Okay," Aston agreed. "I'll accept that. But if they're camped right on top of the objective, we've got a hell of a problem. Jayne says they could be in battalion strength, and we don't have any idea what kind of hornet's nest we're walking into."

"You know," she said slowly, "this looks like a standard Kanga encampment." She ran her finger over the computer imagery, moving from one bright smear of light to another. "See this one here—the one with so many fewer heat sources?" Aston nodded. "In a Kanga installation, that would be the armory. And these here—" she indicated two smaller, fainter smears, one at either end of the horseshoe "—would be the scanner posts, while these with more people in and around them would be the barracks. And these speckles out here—" she tapped a loose necklace of tiny heat sources scattered out around the main encampment "—would be weapon emplacements."

"Jesus! Are we looking at twenty-fifth-century weapons?!"

"I doubt it. Oh, he could design them, I'm sure, but he doesn't have the components. If you were marooned in the fifteenth century, could you build one of your LAVs without parts? Even if you had the manuals and a complete maintenance shop?"

"I don't suppose I could." Aston made no effort to hide his relief.

"Exactly. He'd need molycircs, superconductors, high-energy capacitors, multi-dees.... The tech base to build the parts he needs won't exist for over a century, at least. He probably has enough spares to build a few light weapons, but not enough to equip on this scale. No, Dick. It may be a Kanga-style installation, but he's using mainly local weapons."

"Mainly!" Aston snorted. "I like that."

"It's the way it is," she said calmly.

"I know. I know." He frowned. "I don't like the numbers, though— not when I don't know how good their tactics will be."

"I don't know either," she admitted. "Normal Troll ground combat has to be seen to be believed, but he can't use standard tactics. He's only got a fighter, not an assault tender, so he can't have many combat mechs and they won't be heavies. Light armor's all a fighter usually carries." She plucked at a lock of her hair.

"Normally, they rely on speed, mass, and firepower, Dick. They run right at you, then hammer you into the ground with close-range fire. Their heaviest armor is tough enough to take most power-gun fire, and their battle screen takes care of anything else. But those are heavy armor tactics. At worst, his combat chassis's not going to be much heavier than a medium, and Trolls don't know infantry tactics. Terran Marine Raiders would take this place apart like a soggy pretzel. Of course, they've got equipment Dan and Alvin would sell their children for, but—" she nodded slowly to herself "—I think our boys can hack it. They know their weapons, they've got good doctrine and tactics, they ought to have the advantage of surprise, and they're some of the best assault troops I've ever seen. I don't see how the Troll's troops can match their quality, and he doesn't have any familiarity with twenty-first-century weapons or tactics."

"What if he's 'recruited' somebody who does?"

"It probably won't matter. Trolls are arrogant; he may have picked the brains of competent present-day tacticians, but he'll dictate his own tactics. At best, he'll be a Book soldier without experience. Sort of a brand new, over-trained second lieutenant with a colonel's command." She grinned suddenly. "How do you think the butter-bar would make out?"

"He'd get handed his ass," Aston said with a note of satisfaction.

"Don't get cocky," Ludmilla cautioned, "but I think that's essentially what we're looking at."

"Don't worry about cockiness," he growled. "I'm scared to death, and we'll go in assuming the worst. But we've got time to plan. They may disperse, and if they don't, even a dug-in mechanized battalion would have trouble with what we can throw at them."

"Good. Then I'd better get into that Forestry Service plane and double check things."

"No way! We know where the bastard is now, and—"

"Dick, we can't afford to assume that. I've got to—"

"*No*, Goddamn it! We'll watch it for a few days, see if they disperse, and then we'll—"

Aston broke off, glaring at her, as the phone rang. She met his glare calmly, knowing his anger stemmed from a jumble of sources he could hardly have disentangled himself. The critical necessity of her blaster, his own deep emotions, the pressure of mounting the operation at last. . . . The list was endless.

The phone rang again, and Aston scooped it up.

"Aston," he growled.

"It's me." Morris's voice was sharp with concern, and Aston frowned. He flipped a switch and put Morris on the conference speaker.

"Milla's with us, M&M. What is it?"

"All hell's breaking loose in the target area," Morris said tensely. "We've got the KKK and the Nazis coming in from the north and west, and they're loaded for bear."

"We knew they were coming, Mordecai," Ludmilla said.

"Not like this, we didn't," Morris said grimly. "Just listen a minute. The Governor's called out the Guard, and the State Patrol and local sheriffs' departments have set up roadblocks on all the major highways leading into Asheville. There's a three-county dusk-to-dawn curfew and the local law enforcement people are on full alert, but I don't think it's going to be enough. A convoy of Kluxers or Nazis—hell, for all I know it was both of them!—hit a roadblock on US 23 in Madison County, just south of the Tennessee line. When the deputies manning it tried to stop them, they shot their way through with automatic weapons."

Aston and Ludmilla stared at one another, faces tightening.

"The good guys lost four deputies there—no survivors—and the same thing just happened on I-40 in Haywood County. The Guard's supposed to take over—set up an inner perimeter closer to Asheville—but it's a powder keg. And just to make things worse, another bunch of crazies is moving up from the south."

"I thought the damned rally was for idiots from the mountain states!"

"It is, but Wilkins just called to warn me about some sort of exodus from Atlanta and points north in Georgia and South Carolina. The other side seems to be headed for Asheville to break up the rally."

"That's crazy!"

"No, Dick," Ludmilla said softly. "It's the Troll."

"But why? Why bring about a confrontation now? And why *Asheville*, of all damned places?"

"Who knows?" she answered with a shrug. "Some sort of a test. The first move in whatever it is he plans to do with them. It doesn't matter. It's him—it *has* to be him."

"How bad is it, M&M?" Aston asked harshly.

"Bad. There are thousands of them, and I've got unconfirmed reports that some Guard units are shooting at each other instead of the rioters or whatever the hell they are."

"Why not?" Ludmilla gave an ugly almost-laugh. "If he can program everybody else, why not National Guardsmen?"

"Shit," Aston said flatly.

"The Governor's mobilizing Guard units outside the affected area," Morris went on, "and the President's alerted the Eighty-Second Airborne, but nobody thought about what might happen inside the local units—and I *should* have, damn it!"

"Later, Mordecai. Nobody else did either. Just give us the worst."

"All right." Morris drew a deep breath. "The Asheville area's in chaos. The highways going east and north are crowded with people trying to get out of the way, the bad guys are headed in to turn it into a battlefield, and the local authorities don't know who they can trust. Martial law's been declared, but Governor Farnam's balking at using paratroopers. He wants airlift for other Guard units, military police, civilian SWAT teams—anything but airborne." The commander laughed harshly. "Hard to blame him. He's afraid of casualties; the Eighty-Second's not exactly trained in crowd control."

"Crowd control may be the last thing he needs," Aston muttered. "But he doesn't know that, and we can't tell him."

"All right. Cut to the bottom line, Mordecai."

"The way it looks, the first airlift—outside Guardsmen, airborne, or whatever—should be coming into Asheville Airport in four or five hours . . . by which time, the first wave of Kluxers and Nazis will have been there for hours, and the maniacs from the *other* side will be arriving, too."

"Shit," Aston said again, then looked at Ludmilla. "All right, there's no time for you to fly around looking for him, Milla. If he's behind this, the only way to stop it is to stop him. Fast."

"I agree," she said softly.

"Mordecai," Aston said into the phone, "tell Anson we're going in."

"Now, Dick? Into the middle of all that?"

"Right now," Aston said grimly. "We don't know what he's up to, but a lot of people are going to get killed, whatever it is, and for all we know, this is the start of his big push. We've got to hit him before he really starts to roll." He smiled savagely. "It may even work to our advantage. With so much going on, the confusion should help cover us."

"All right," Morris said slowly. "We've got the air support worked out at this end. How soon should we alert it?"

"Now. We'll brief the men and be in the air within three hours."

CHAPTER TWENTY-TWO

Deputy Holden Mitchell rechecked the loads in his Ithaca Model 37 shotgun. He'd bought it with his own money rather than use the Remington 870s the rest of the Department were issued—and he hadn't added the disconnector. He had eight rounds of twelve-gauge available, and he could fire them as rapidly as he could work the slide. Once upon a time, he'd been willing to admit all the ribbing about paranoia he'd taken over his choice in weapons might have a point; today he wasn't. Afternoon sunlight spilled down on the double ribbon of asphalt and the air was cool, but his face was grim as he listened to the radio traffic. He'd known all four of the deputies who'd just died a few miles north of his position.

Mitchell glanced sideways at his partner. Allen Farmer's face showed little sign of his thoughts, but Mitchell recognized the tightness around his eyes. He'd been a little leery when they first teamed him with a black man, but not now. Not until today, anyway. There'd always been a certain unspoken tension between them—an awareness of differences. It hadn't kept them from respecting one another and forming a firm friendship, but it was always there. Privately, Mitchell had resented Allen's unspoken assumption that anyone he met was a racist until proved otherwise. He'd never let it get out of hand, but Mitchell had known it was there.

And today, Holden Mitchell thought bitterly, he finally understood exactly why Allen thought that way.

A state cruiser screeched to a stop behind them, and a pair of state troopers trotted up to the two county cars parked nose-to-nose across the southbound lanes of US 23. The north-bound lanes were

275

blocked by a logging truck Mitchell had commandeered earlier in the day.

"What's going on back there?" Mitchell demanded of the senior trooper.

"Mars Hill's okay—for now," the trooper replied tersely. "But there's trouble in Asheville. Rumor is some of the Guard units started shooting at each other."

"Shit." Mitchell spat tobacco juice onto the pavement and squinted into the breeze blowing out of the north. What was keeping the bastards? "You all we get?"

"'Fraid so, Deputy—till the Guard gets straightened out, anyway." The trooper was sweating, but his voice was level. "And I can't say I like this position a hell of a lot."

"You an' me both, Corporal, but the idea's to keep them away from the junction of Nineteen and Twenty-Three." He shrugged.

"Yeah." The trooper wiped his mouth and stiffened as the sound of engines came down the highway. "They told me you're the boss. How do you want to handle this?"

"Well, I'll tell you, Corporal, I'm s'posed to stop 'em, and I figure I'll just flag the bastards down—with this." Mitchell twitched the Ithaca, and the trooper gave him a thin smile.

"I can live with that," he said.

The Troll gave a mental shudder of pleasure as he tasted blood at last. The uniformed idiots who'd tried to block his hate-maddened humans had paid for their stupidity, and he had discovered something unexpected. The ecstasy of killing was even stronger this way, for he experienced it not just once, but again and again through each open mind.

He felt himself reaching out, fragmenting and coalescing, caught up in his own firestorm. It fed him, strengthened him . . . and woke a bottomless craving for more destruction. He rode with his killers, waving the bloody jacket of a county deputy and cheering.

They topped a rise, and there was another roadblock before them.

Mitchell saw the lead vehicle start down the evening-shadowed slot of the highway cutting. It was a van, crowded with people, and there were pickups and sedans behind it. He swallowed as he counted the odds, but he felt strangely disinclined to run from the rabble sweeping towards him.

"All right, boys," he said calmly, "spread out and get under cover."

The others obeyed with alacrity, and he noticed that the senior trooper carried an M 16—the old Al model rather than the A2 with its limitation to three-shot bursts—not a shotgun.

"Let 'em come in a little closer," Mitchell told himself softly. "Just a little closer."

The Troll fed the humans' frenzy, fanning it to furnace heat with his own rage. The surging, hating creatures charging down on the roadblock weren't a mob; they were no longer even human. They were extensions of the Troll, his weapon, vessels of his hunger, and they swept forward snarling.

"Now!" Mitchell shouted, and triggered his first round into the van. He heard Farmer's shotgun echoing his own, smelled the gunsmoke, and saw shattered safety glass sparkle through the sunset light like bloody rock salt. The corporal was firing semi-auto, deliberately, picking his targets, and the windshield of the pickup behind the van exploded. Klansmen and Nazis boiled out, and Mitchell stroked the slide with deadly smooth speed. Screams and shrieks answered as the Troll's minions were cut down by the merciless fire, and the M16 went to full auto. Writhing bodies and dead men littered the asphalt while others scrambled as far as the side of the cutting before they were shot down, and others crouched behind their vehicles, returning fire.

The Troll writhed in fury as his column recoiled. They were only humans, but they were *his*. Their pain and death was sweet, but not as sweet as the taste of their killing. He lashed them with his hate, whipping them forward.

"They're coming over us, Dispatch!" Mitchell yelled into his radio. "Where the fuck is the Guard?!" His cruiser sat flat on its rims, riddled with fire, and the State Patrol car belched inky-black smoke and flame. One trooper was dead, but the corporal was bellied down in a culvert, and his M16's flash suppressor glowed incandescent as it spewed fire into the mob.

"Pull back, Four-Two!" the dispatcher was shouting.

"How?" Mitchell laughed into the mike hanging from the driver's window as he fed fresh cartridges into his smoking shotgun.

"Help's on the way, Four-Two. Hang on!"

"Gotta go, Dispatch," Mitchell said, and rolled under the car beside Farmer, shooting into the gathering darkness.

When the National Guard M113s finally arrived, their crews counted forty-one dead and nineteen wounded in front of the burned out roadblock, and found deputies Mitchell and Farmer lying side by side. Mitchell clutched an empty service pistol, and Farmer's empty shotgun, the butt smeared with the blood and hair of his enemies, was still in his hands.

Aston and Abernathy watched Lieutenant Colonel Clara Dickle, CO of Marine Air Group 200, squint at the map and calculate distances. She and her ops officer were engaged in a low-voiced, arcane conversation, but if they were uneasy about flying into the Appalachians in total darkness, they hid it well.

Abernathy, on the other hand, was visibly unhappy, and Aston didn't blame him. They had no clear idea of enemy numbers or weapons. All they knew was that Ludmilla *thought* their target looked like a typical Kanga-style encampment. If she was right, they could make certain assumptions; if she was wrong, those assumptions might prove fatal.

Abernathy's staff was as large as that of most battalions, and they'd known all along that planning time would be minimal, but they hadn't counted on anything quite like this. They were rising to the occasion, but no one knew better than they how problematical their ops plan might prove.

"All right, Admiral," Dickle said finally, "we make it forty-five minutes, give or take. I'll have that refined before takeoff." She paused and frowned, rubbing the map with a fingertip. "What worries me most, Sir, is where we'll put you down."

"I know." Aston thumbed through the map sheets for a large-scale map of Sugarloaf Mountain. "This looks like the best LZ we've got, Colonel," he said, and Dickle peered dubiously at the location. It was on the outer face of the valley's western wall, and the contour lines were discouraging.

"I know you can't set down," Aston said, "but this is a burn-off from last summer—nothing but a little scrub that's come back in. We can deplane from a hover, then go in on foot."

"What about the Herky-birds, Sir? We can't drop vehicles in there."

"We couldn't use them if you did, Colonel. Instead, I want them here." He tapped the junction of the valley road and NC 212. "It'll be a bitch to get them in, I know, but it's as close as you're going to make it."

"They'll be five klicks out, Sir, and that's line-of-flight, not ground movement," Dickle pointed out.

"Agreed. That's why I want you to be as noisy as you can about dropping them in. Flares, landing lights, the whole nine yards. They won't be a lot of use in the actual assault, but I want them dropped before the infantry comes in on the slope. With a little luck, they'll distract the bad guys from *our* LZ."

"I see." Dickle frowned some more, then nodded. "We can do it. I just wish we could put you closer to the objective, Sir." The projected landing zone was over a thousand straight-line yards from the nearest end of the horseshoe of enemy positions, and Dickle knew what was going on. She knew how critical seconds could be, and too much of that heavily overgrown thousand yards was up and down.

"Count your blessings, Colonel." Aston smiled grimly. "There's no telling what kind of SAMs they've got in there. And at least—"

He was interrupted by a quiet knock on the door and looked up as Abernathy's commo officer entered.

"Sir, Governor Farnam's just changed his mind about the Eighty-Second," the lieutenant reported. "It sounds like things are getting out of hand in the target area."

"Damn," Aston said softly.

"All right, people." Major Abernathy stood facing his officers and senior NCOs. "I know you've all heard rumors about what's happening in the target area. I'm here to tell you they're true. The last reports say there's heavy fighting along the northern and northwestern edges of Asheville. The Guard is doing its best, but they're not up against normal rioters. We, of course, know why that is."

He paused, watching the outrage in their eyes. It was strange, he thought, how professional American military men reacted to the notion that any hostile force might ever touch American soil. He often thought it was that belief in the inviolability of North America which set the US military apart from its allies. It gave them a certain naivete and parochialism, but also a sort of inner strength. Confidence. Perhaps even arrogance. Whatever it was, the notion that an invader was responsible for death and destruction in an American city brought it to fiery life, filling his men with pressure, the physical need to attack.

"Now for the good news," he continued calmly. "We believe we have satellite confirmation of Grendel's location." A ripple of almost-motion went through his listeners. "We are going in tonight, gentlemen."

A barely audible growl of approval arose, and Abernathy smiled thinly.

"We've put together an ops plan. I stress at this time that our information is fragmentary, and I have no doubt Murphy will appear on schedule." Someone chuckled, and the major grinned. "But we're Marines, gentlemen. When it hits the fan, we'll do what we've always done: adapt, improvise, and overcome." He paused for a moment, then nodded. "Captain Ross will continue the background brief and outline the ops plan."

He sat, and every eye followed Ludmilla as she crossed to a covered mapboard, twitched back the cover, and reached for a pointer. They'd seen the valley before, but not the carefully marked overlay showing the results of Jayne Hastings's reconnaissance photos. Nor had they known before this evening that "Captain Ross" was what the mission was all about; that it all came down to getting *her* in range for a single shot at the Troll. That information had prompted some radical revision to speculation about where she came from.

"This," Ludmilla said calmly, "appears to be a fairly standard Kanga encampment. If so, it should house between seven hundred and a thousand men." She faced them levelly as they digested the numbers, then continued, identifying scanner posts, the armory, barracks.

"...and these are the weapon positions." She swept over them with her pointer. "It's possible we'll encounter some energy weapons here, but our best estimate is that they can't have many. From the disposition, it appears their fields of fire are planned to cover approaches from the road at the southern end of the valley. This—" she tapped a grease-pencil star above the camp "—is probably an access tunnel to Grendel's fighter.

"Now—" she turned to another map "—this is our LZ. As you can see, it's about a thousand yards from the southern end of the encampment, just over seventeen hundred from the fighter access way, but the slope doubles that. It doesn't look like Grendel has his sensors or defenses set up to cover that approach, but we'll still be exposed to accidental detection, if nothing else, while we cover the distance. That's why the armored assault and heavy weapon platoons will start in along the road ten minutes before *we* come in. They'll make lots of noise to attract the defenders' attention while we come over the ridge."

Aston surveyed the assembled Marines. They looked grim, but it was the grimness of purpose and tension, not fear. He nodded to himself, watching them weigh Ludmilla's words, and knew Abernathy was allowing "Captain Ross" to handle the final briefing for a very simple reason: these men now knew she was the source of all their information. They deserved the chance to weigh her own certainty for themselves, and he saw them drawing confidence from her as she spoke.

"...once the CP's in place, Lieutenant Frye's heavy weapons platoon and Sergeant Sanderson's antitank squad will set up here," she was saying. "When Grendel realizes we're on top of him, he's going to counterattack, probably with one or more of his combat mechs. So get those Dragons set up early and nail them."

She paused as a hand was raised. "Yes, Lieutenant?"

"If he knows we're coming, Captain, how do we keep him from just flying out on us?" The question was reasonable, but the look in the lieutenant's eyes said he'd heard about the nuclear option, and she met his gaze squarely.

"The fact that we're above him, I hope. He can't be immediately certain what weapons we have, and until he gets clear of his hide, he'll have to move slowly—a sitting duck for heavy weapons. We can hurt him under those conditions, and if Grendel runs true to form for a Troll, he won't risk it. He'll try to clear us off the slope with his mechs first. If they can't, he may come up himself, or he may try to fly out after all. But by the time he reaches that point, we ought to have air support, and then we can *really* nail him if he moves."

"With what, Captain?" The lieutenant wasn't waffling, Aston thought. He just wanted any suicide missions clearly labeled as such.

"With nukes, if we have to," Ludmilla said, and her level confirmation sent a wave of tension through her listeners, "but if we catch him within forty meters of the ground, we've got a good chance with Dragons or Mavericks. Above that, he can reconfigure his drive field to interdict conventional missiles; below it, he has to rely on active defenses, and over half of them cover his belly and stem, not his topsides." She paused. "Does that answer your questions, Lieutenant Warden?"

"Yes, Ma'am. Thank you."

"All right. Now, while Second Platoon sets up to cover the Dragons here, First Platoon, with Admiral Aston and myself, will move down *here*—" her pointer traced a line "—to reach the valley floor. We'll have to take out weapon pits here and here, then rush this barracks. From there, we'll have a good field of fire back towards the camp and I should have a clean shot at Grendel when he pokes his nose out. Meanwhile, Major Abernathy will shift his CP down the ridge. He'll move Third and Fourth Platoons, plus Lieutenant Atwater's antitank platoon, this way to cover..."

Aston watched officers and sergeants scribble notes. It sounded good, he thought. But, then, it always sounded good. The problem was that it never worked out quite the way you'd planned, and the real test was how well your men adapted under fire.

He ran his own mind over the operation. Sixty-forty in their favor, he thought. Maybe seventy-thirty if everything broke just right. Even if it did, their own casualties might be heavy. If it didn't...

He hid his own shudder as his mind filled with the image of a nuclear fireball—or far worse—in the heart of the North Carolina mountains.

✻ ✻ ✻

Jeremiah Willis looked down from the sixth-floor window at the trucks and armored personnel carriers parked around the hotel. He would have felt happier in his own office, but the emergency command post had been set up here, three blocks from City Hall. It made sense. There was plenty of room, and the Patton Avenue-Broadway Street intersection gave ready access to any part of the city.

Not that it seemed to be doing much good, he thought grimly, lifting his eyes to the bloodred night sky to the west. He could smell the smoke, even through the air-conditioning.

"We're still holding on Nineteen and Twenty-Three," Brigadier General Evans said, "but they keep filtering past us down the secondary streets. It looks like they're flowing around towards Weaverville Road now, and there's a couple of hundred coming down Six-Ninety-Four, but Captain Taylor's got a rifle platoon and a heavy machine-gun section waiting for them at Merrimon Avenue." The general looked harried, and well he might. He'd started out with a full brigade of Guardsmen, but that impressive troop strength was stretched perilously thin by the city's sheer size, and the dense road net made it even worse.

"What about West Patton Avenue?" Chief Campbell asked. "Can you spare anything there?"

"I don't know." The general ran fingers through his hair, staring at his maps. "We've got a firefight going on out New Leicester Highway right now. What's your situation?"

"We're back almost as far as the post office," Campbell said grimly, "up against two or three hundred bastards with rifles and automatic weapons. I'm losing men, and I didn't have that many to start with. If they push us another six hundred yards, your boys on the highway could be cut off."

"All right," Evans sighed. "Al," he turned to his exec, "shake loose a platoon of APCs and send 'em out to stabilize the position."

"Yes, Sir."

"It's all I can give you, Chief Campbell," Evans said grimly. "The crowd coming up from the south is just as bad. The South Carolina Guard's holding them south of the state line on US 25, but they've just crossed it on I-26, and I can't weaken myself any more south of town."

"I understand, General."

"I'm sorry," Evans said gruffly and turned back to his commo section.

Willis watched the APC crews racing for their vehicles. At least the handful of Guardsmen who'd started shooting at their fellows had been eliminated, he thought coldly. There'd been only a few, but that had been almost too many. Evans had a right to be proud. His "weekend warriors" had almost broken—they'd never expected to face anything like *this*—but they'd rallied, and now they were fighting doggedly to save his city. Not that it looked like they were going to succeed.

"Jerry." He looked up as Campbell touched his shoulder. "Some son-of-a-bitch just firebombed Saint Joe's," the police chief said, and the mayor closed his eyes, thinking of fire raging through the city's largest hospital. "I've got a report from Bill McCoury, too. He says Biltmore House is on fire."

"Thank you, Hugh," Willis said softly, looking back out into the flame-struck night. "Do your best."

Patuxent River Naval Air Station was a beehive of activity. Pax River NAS was a test center at the southwestern tip of Maryland, home to some of the finest pilots in the Navy and Marine Corps, who spent their time pushing new aircraft and weapon systems to the limit. But the F/A-18 Hornets sitting on the taxi ways now belonged to VFA-432 and VFA-433, CVW-18's attack squadrons, based at NAS Oceana at Virginia Beach while they waited for the carrier *Theodore Roosevelt* to finish repairs in the Norfolk Navy Yard. Most of the pilots had no clear idea why they'd been staged through Pax River, but Commander Ed Staunton knew. He stood in a hangar door, hiding from the drizzling rain, and sipped a steaming mug of coffee while ordnance types fussed around his Hornet.

Staunton's thoughts were divided. He was an attack pilot by training and inclination, and this was the type of mission he'd spent years preparing to fly. More than that, he knew its target, and he wanted a piece of the bastards who'd wrecked TF-Twenty-Three and destroyed the *Kidd*. Oh, yes, he *wanted* a piece of them.

But the weapons on his aircraft's pylons frightened him. He'd never dropped a live one. For that matter, he didn't think anyone, anywhere had *ever* dropped a live one, and the thought of doing so on American soil, especially knowing there would be US Marines on the ground when he did—*if* he did—turned his belly into a hollow void around the hot, black coffee.

"Skipper?" He turned his head as his wingman, Lieutenant Jake Frisco, stopped beside him.

"Yes, Jake?"

"Skipper, what the hell is going on?" Frisco's quiet tone clearly didn't buy the cover story, and Staunton wasn't surprised. The lieutenant was a sharp customer, not that it would have required a genius to figure out that what they'd been told so far was a pile of crap. The madness raging in the Carolinas was hardly the sort of situation one handled with two squadrons of Hornets, and Frisco pointed at Staunton's plane, his voice sharpening. "Why are they loading—"

"Jake, don't ask any questions," Staunton said softly.

"But, Skip, that's a—!"

"I know what it is, Lieutenant," Staunton made his voice colder. "Just keep your lip buttoned and pray we don't need them, all right?"

Something in his CO's quietly anguished voice silenced Frisco's protests. He glanced at Staunton once more, then nodded and moved away, his expression troubled. The commander watched him go, then turned his eyes back to his plane as the ordnance team finished its job and withdrew. The innocent, white-painted shapes under his wings seemed to whisper to him through the rain, promising him the power of life and death itself.

He turned his back, handing his cup to a passing seaman, and went to find his pilots for their final—and accurate—briefing.

Behind him, rainwater beaded the surface of the two B83 "special weapons" slung under his aircraft. Between them, they represented just over two megatons of destruction.

Fort Bragg, North Carolina, fell behind as the C-17s rumbled westward at four hundred miles per hour. The slower attack helicopters had gotten off earlier, in order to link up with them as soon as they reached their objective, and the dim caverns of their bellies were quieter than usual as the elite paratroopers of First Brigade, Eighty-Second Airborne Division headed into combat.

They'd prepared themselves mentally to fight in many places, but western North Carolina wasn't one of them.

Colonel Sam Tyson and his staff rode the lead plane in night-camouflage and blackface. Tyson knew the division's other two brigades were ready to follow his if needed, as was the lOlst Airborne, their sister division in the Eighteenth Airborne Corps. He also knew that if they needed that much firepower, they might as well just hand the state over to the crazies and move away.

He sighed and tried to get comfortable. Whoever had designed these canvas-and-metal seats had to be a sadist, he thought for perhaps the ten-thousandth time in his career, but at least they shouldn't have to jump in. At last report, Asheville Airport was still clear of the violence.

Dick Aston leaned back against the Osprey's vibrating fuselage, eyes closed, feeling Ludmilla beside him. She wore her flight suit under her camouflaged BDUs and body armor, and her hair was tucked up under her helmet, her face blackened like his own.

The Ospreys were a vast improvement on the clattering helos he'd used so often before, he thought distantly. Twice as fast, too. His mind filled with their swift passage through the night sky, leaving the light rain which had enveloped Lejeune behind as they sped west toward Spruce Pine. Almost three hundred miles from Lejeune, Spruce Pine was where the final leg would begin.

He visualized it in his mind. They would fly low, using the mountains to hide from whatever sensors the Troll might have. From Spruce Pine, the Ospreys would head for Relief, North Carolina, then down into the valley of the Nolichucky River, directly over the site of the plutonium raid, to River Hill, Tennessee. Then they would turn down Tennessee 81, overfly the town of Carmen, North Carolina, and swoop east up the side of Sugarloaf into combat.

At the same time, MAG-200's C-130 Hercules transports would bore straight west from Spruce Pine, down the line of US 19, then lift up and over the ridges to the southern face of Sugarloaf to drop Company T's vehicles. The Herky-birds were a bit faster than the Ospreys and had a shorter route, but Colonel Dickle had planned the coordination between the two insertions with clockwork precision. It was what came after that worried Aston.

He was too old for this. The thought beat in his brain. He should stay home and let Dan run the operation, but he couldn't. He trusted Abernathy's ability completely, but he just couldn't.

Partly, he knew, it was what had lured him into the special forces in the first place. Pride. Call it arrogance or the need to excel; by any name, it was a driving compulsion to be the best, to do something that *mattered* with the best men in the world, and beside this mission, anything he'd ever done was insignificant. He supposed it was much the same compulsion that sent overaged matadors into the bullring to find their deaths.

But he knew that was only one reason, and perhaps the least of them. The real reason sat quietly beside him, her darkened face serene, while the hope of his planet rode on her hip.

The plane bored on into the darkness, and Richard Aston was afraid. For himself. For his planet. And, most of all, for Ludmilla Leonovna.

Ludmilla glanced at Dick, taking in the closed eyes and calm expression. She'd known many warriors in her time—indeed, for fifty subjective years she'd known little else—but none had impressed her more. Perhaps it was because she hadn't let herself come this close to any of the others, for deep inside her, something railed against his mortality—railed as it had not in many years. Ludmilla Leonovna was no hothouse flower, but she knew how much she owed to him. He'd saved her life and, even more importantly, believed her and made others believe.

He was hard and deadly, as much a killer as she, yet within his armor he was gentle and vulnerable. She remembered his eyes when she first offered herself to him—the look of disbelief, the fear of rejection, the determination not to "take advantage of her." She'd meant only to thank him, to seal their friendship with a brief affair, for Thuselahs had learned the hard way not to give their hearts to Normals.

But she'd forgotten that lesson, and it would cost her dear. Even if they both survived this night—and it was very likely they would not—she would lose him, and then she would be alone again. Alone in this alien world, this universe not even her own, with the aching sorrow of her loss.

She knew he sensed her feelings, and she also knew how hard it was for him to accept her presence in combat. In her own time and place, women had soldiered for centuries; in his, they were only starting to feel their way into those roles. And he came from an even earlier military, one in which it was still unquestioningly accepted that women were to be protected, shielded from the brutality of war. How many men of his time, she wondered, could have accepted her not just as an equal but as a warrior in her own right? That she'd seen even more years of combat than he meant nothing beside the emotional gulf he'd made himself cross.

Which was why she hadn't told him that the Troll could detect and track her blaster the instant the touch of her hand brought it to life.

CHAPTER TWENTY-THREE

Asheville was dying.

Jeremiah Willis winced as the crackle of small arms and machine guns battered his ears. The flaming town of Woodfin painted the sky crimson to the north, and General Evans's Guardsmen had been driven back along the east bank of the French Broad River to the line of I-240. His men had stopped every push towards the Beaucatcher Mountain cut, and they still held a rectangle of North Asheville from Merriman Avenue east, but the entire area between Merriman and the river billowed flame and smoke.

The remnants of the Asheville City Police were acting as guides for National Guard fire teams struggling to stem the tide surging in along Patton Avenue and West I-40, and no one was worrying about rioter casualties now. The Guardsmen were fighting to cover the police as they evacuated civilians from the path of the madness, and they were in no mood for gentleness.

Neither was Willis. His worst nightmares had never prepared him for this. This was no demonstration gone berserk, no simple riot. He didn't know what it was, but it wasn't that. There was a malevolence to it, a sheer, wanton compulsion to wreck and destroy—a terrible insanity so consuming it was like a guiding force.

He touched the M 16 slung over his shoulder. It was decades since he'd worn a uniform, but he intended to be ready if the vandals wrecking his city got this far.

He almost hoped they would.

Lieutenant Curtis Spillers, NCNG, ducked as slugs whined off his

M113's aluminum armor. He remembered something from a training manual; "No organized force is ever outnumbered by a mob," the writer had said. Under most circumstances, that might have been true—but not tonight. There was too much ferocity abroad in this flame-shot darkness.

More fire raked his armored personnel carrier. That was an M60, he thought grimly, wondering which of his comrades it had been taken from. Unless, of course, it was one of the Guardsmen who'd freaked out.

He poked his head up cautiously. More fire whined and cracked, but his disembarked infantry squad had spotted the muzzle flash on the second floor of an office building. Their fire was ineffectual against the sturdy art-deco facade; but it showed Spillers where it was.

He waited for a lull, then sprang up behind the M2 HB Browning machine gun. Unlike the Bradley M2s and M3s the regular Army and some of the other Guard units boasted, Spillers's brigade was still equipped with the old, reliable, but turretless M 113 APC originally designed over fifty years ago. Unlike later designs, the M113 had been intended primarily as a troop taxi, not a fighting vehicle in its own right, and there was no armor for its gunner. But the .50 caliber weapon was a form of protection in itself, and Spillers grabbed the machine gun's spade grips and sprayed the building with steel-jacketed slugs bigger than his thumb that reached their target traveling at better than twenty-nine hundred feet per second.

Some of the brigade's other APCs had replaced their machineguns with Mk 19 automatic grenade launchers. A weapon like that would probably have been even more effective, but Spillers had no complaints. The big Browning vibrated like a jackhammer as his thumbs depressed the butterfly trigger, and the window frame blew apart. The wall shredded, vomiting dust and fist-sized chunks of brick and mortar, and he hosed it down, firing the short bursts his instructors had always insisted upon, while the infantry closed in and fired forty-millimeter grenades of their own. Explosions racked the room behind the window, and then sudden smoke billowed, fueled by the glare of burning gasoline. So the bastards had stockpiled Molotov cocktails up there, had they? Spillers smiled with savage satisfaction as a flaming figure flung itself through the window, screaming. It hit the street and bounced once, then lay still, but Spillers depressed his weapon and gave the body a burst just to make sure.

MAG-200 swept westward through the night, hugging the ground, and Spruce Pine's lights blinked at Lieutenant Colonel Dickle from the darkness. Their calm tranquility seemed utterly incongruous, given what she had learned during "Captain Ross's" briefing, but she kept her attention on her route, doggedly ignoring the scarlet heavens above Asheville.

"We've got General Evans, Sir." Colonel Tyson held out his hand, and the signals lieutenant handed him a headset with attached boom microphone.

"General, Colonel Tyson here. What's your situation, Sir?"

"Not good, Colonel." Tyson understood the fatigue and worry in the Guardsman's voice. An infantry brigade was a powerful formation, even when composed of reservists, but street-fighting had a voracious appetite. Large maneuver units were useless; it came down to junior officers at the platoon and squad level, alone in the howling madness. There were too many potential ambushes, too much cover for attackers, too little room to deploy. Indeed, Tyson felt a surge of admiration for the Guardsmen in Asheville. They'd done far better in an impossible tactical position than he would have believed possible.

"We've lost the extreme western part of the city, and it looks like they're trying to split us in half down the line of the French Broad," the National Guard general went on. "We're holding, but we're losing ground. We've got isolated incidents all over the city—small groups with firebombs and small arms, nothing like what's coming at us from the northwest—but the southern perimeter's been quiet so far." Evans coughed out a harsh laugh. "I don't expect that to last long. The crowd coming up I-26 is at least as bad as the one we've already got. They just punched a company of Guardsmen out of Hendersonville; they're burning it to the ground now."

"Understood, General. What's the status at the airport?"

"The tower crew pulled out with most of the airline employees, but the lights are on and I've got one platoon out there, along with a few state troopers and the airport security force. It's not much, but so far they've only been hit by isolated bands. That won't last much longer."

"It won't have to, General," Tyson said grimly. "Our Apaches are over the field now, and the transports will be on the ground in ten minutes."

"Thank God."

"We'll secure the airport and block I-26 at Airport Road, then move north up Twenty-Six. I'm going to try to swing west around the edge of the city. If I can keep anybody else from getting in, we should be able to squeeze out the trouble spots between us."

"It sounds good, Colonel," Evans said. "We'll be waiting for you."

"Luck, General," Tyson said, tightening his straps as the C-17 headed for the landing strip.

"And to you, Colonel."

"Romeo One, Pax Control. You are cleared, Romeo One. Be advised that Backstop is airborne at Virginia Beach. Good luck."

"Pax Control, Romeo One. Understood and thanks: Romeo Team, Romeo One. All right, children, let's go."

Commander Staunton released the brakes and felt his Hornet start to roll. Twenty-three more attack planes waited to join him, but none were as lethal as his. He tried not to think about that.

His speed hit a hundred twenty-five knots. He held her down a moment longer—he had plenty of runway . . . and those two white shapes under his wings—then eased back on the stick, and the attack fighter leapt into the rainy night.

To the south, the two F-14 squadrons of CVW-18 were already forming up. *Theodore Roosevelt*'s aircraft had a score to settle.

Blake Taggart trembled, hands over his eyes, fighting to separate his fragile remaining self from his master's fiery ecstasy. The carnage the Troll had wrought frightened the ex-preacher—not because of what it was, but because of what it threatened to become. The tiny bit of him which was still himself recognized what was happening but saw no way to stop it.

The Troll exulted in the devastation like an addict in the grip of his drug, drinking in the destruction and bloodshed through thousands upon thousands of eyes and minds. The visceral hatred he had unleashed hung above the blazing city like a second pall of smoke, and it was the sweet incense of his vengeance.

He'd forgotten that this was only a test. He had decreed the destruction of Asheville, but his lust for murder and hunger for vengeance demanded more, flogging his puppets beyond themselves. Asheville blazed, but another swath of destruction burned against the night, marking the route of I-26 from the South Carolina line north. His creatures swept onward, killing, burning, and raping without the least awareness that they were only tools, and the perverse delight of cruelty possessed him like a demon.

Taggart managed to break free of the maelstrom at last and staggered out of the Troll's cavern. He slid down a tree, resting his forehead on his knees and breathing deeply. He could almost smell the smoke, even here, and it seemed to clog his brain with fire. He understood only too well, for he tasted the hot, sweet blood in his own mouth and knew the truth. Whatever else had happened, however much he had always longed for power of his own, he had been made over in the Troll's image. He was no longer an individual, could no longer even pretend that he belonged only to himself. Yet a fragment of selfhood remained still, urging him to separate himself from the frenzy which possessed his master.

Someone had to keep a grip on himself, he thought, and pushed himself to his feet. He managed to walk down the path almost normally, grateful that he had convinced his master to exclude the men from his mental link.

Taggart didn't like to think about what would happen if the Apocalypse Brigade caught the same blood lust which drove the mobs.

"Coming up on River Hill, Admiral," Colonel Dickle announced, and Aston poked his head into the cockpit. The sky above the crouching mountains to the southeast was bloody. "The Herky-birds are right on schedule. Your vehicles will be going in in about one minute."

The ready lights above the hatches lit, and the men of First Platoon, Company T, gathered themselves internally.

✳ ✳ ✳

Colonel Tyson felt cold satisfaction. It had turned into a race, after all, and First Brigade had won it.

Tentacles of madmen had flooded up I-26, brushing aside the county and state roadblocks, and one rampaging column had curled out for the airport. But the first C-17s had landed twenty minutes before, and his paratroopers had moved into positions selected before leaving Bragg. The rattle of treads had cut through the clamor of the approaching mob as Bradley fighting vehicles and the LPM8 AGS—technically the "Armored Gun System," but for all intents and purposes light tanks—which had finally replaced the old, unsatisfactory Sheridans with which the Eighty-Second had been equipped for decades, headed for the perimeter. They were in their firing positions and the Apache gunships were waiting overhead when the glaring headlights swept down Airport Road.

Tyson wasted no time calling on the mob to surrender. When the first rounds of blind fire spattered his men, they raked the packed civilian vehicles and captured National Guard trucks with a tornado of automatic fire. The Apaches' thirty-millimeter chainguns and the twenty-five-millimeter chainguns and co-ax machine guns of the Bradleys had been particularly effective, he thought grimly, but the high-explosive and white-phosphorous rounds from the M35 105-millimeter main guns of the LPM8s had been even more spectacular.

The bloodied survivors had broken and run, abandoning their dead, and the night sky behind the colonel reverberated with the whine of jet engines as his brigade's second echelon came in.

He gestured to his clerk for his map case and bent over the cards, rechecking his planned route. It was time, he thought, to kick some ass.

Jeremiah Willis crouched behind the charred hulk of an M113. No one knew how the small party of rioters had gotten that close, but their Molotov cocktails and the LAWs and AT4s they'd taken from dead Guardsmen had cost General Evans dozens of APCs and trucks. Every raider had been killed, though, and Willis had shot two of them himself. He was shocked by the satisfaction he'd felt, but he could not—would not—deny it.

The rioters had smashed switching stations, transformers, and power lines as they rampaged through his city, but the flames backlit them as they came in. Willis popped up and ripped off a long burst at a dimly seen figure sniping at a Guard machine gun team. He had no idea if he'd hit the sniper, but the shape disappeared.

Fifty-caliber tracers raked the paving of Patton Avenue, flaring down from the top of the hotel to drive back another knot of rioters. Or perhaps they were only civilians trying to flee. The gunners couldn't tell, and no one could or would take chances. Not anymore.

He heard the rattle and crash of battle from his left. One of Evans's lieutenants was leading a company-level attack down O'Henry Avenue and Haywood Street in an effort to retake the I-240 overpasses. The drive had started out under a captain, until a bullet through the head stopped him.

The Mayor of Asheville made himself watch his front, throttling the need to look south and wonder where the Eighty-Second was.

"Tango Leader, Tango Two-Seven. We're going in."

Lieutenant Colonel Dickle nodded with satisfaction. Right on the dot, she thought. No more than a couple of seconds early.

The C-130 pilots roared in south of Sugarloaf, making themselves appear loose and relaxed while their breathing slowed and their nerves tightened. They swept down the highway behind the brilliance of their landing lights under a glare of illuminating flares, bare yards above the ground. The huge rear cargo doors were open, and the dark shape of an LAV-25 Piranha slid from the lead plane. The fourteen-ton armored vehicle crashed to the ground on its shock-absorbing pallet, and suddenly the night was full of splintering sound as vehicle after vehicle slammed to earth.

It was over in seconds, the C-130s clawing up and away while Ospreys nestled in among the vehicles with their crews. Marines raced from the planes, throwing off tie-down chains, starting engines, testing internal systems. The clatter of charging handles racketed over shouts of command as automatic weapons were cocked, and then they were moving, rumbling up the twisting macadamized road into the featureless dark.

The flares died, and no gleam of light came from the vehicles. It wasn't needed. Drivers and gunners, faces grotesque behind low-light level enhanced-imaging optical systems, peered cat-eyed into the night, straining for the first glimpse of their enemies.

✵ ✵ ✵

Taggart lurched up as the first report was radioed in. It was impossible! How could anyone have *guessed*?

Shock held him for just one moment as his brain fought to understand how it could have happened, but then he shook off his paralysis. The "how" didn't matter, only the "what," and as his brain came back to life, he wasted no time congratulating himself for posting sentinels on the access road despite the Troll's dismissal of the need. He shouted orders, and the alarm flashed through the encampment. The men of the Apocalypse Brigade tumbled into their prepared positions, and a fifty-man response team moved quickly to support the sentries.

Only after the men were in motion did Taggart realize that he had felt absolutely no response from his master.

"Tango Leader, Tango Two-Seven. Slugger is down. I say again, Slugger is down."

"Roger, Two-Seven. Tango Leader copies. Good work, Ken."

Dickle watched the pavement rushing past beneath her. It was marvelous how good night-vision devices had become, she thought almost absently, then nodded sharply as the lights of Carmen, North Carolina, appeared before her.

She swung to port, settling on her new heading, and Sugarloaf Mountain loomed against the starry heavens like a wall.

The first LAW exploded out of the darkness like a meteor. The fire-trailing rocket just missed the lead LAV, and the Marine gunner swung his turret, raking the trees with his co-ax machine gun. The armored vehicle's rear hatch crashed open, and a rifle squad deployed towards the source of the LAW just as a second rocket slammed squarely into its turret.

The LAW warhead performed exactly as designed, and PFC Jordan Van Hoy of Trenton, New Jersey, became the first Marine fatality of the Battle of Sugarloaf Mountain.

CHAPTER TWENTY-FOUR

"Here we go, Admiral!" Dickle shouted, and the Osprey slowed magically, rotating its engines and sliding into a hover six feet above the slope. The LZ was flatter than Dickle had dared hope from the contours, but a hurricane of debris blasted up in the wash of her rotors.

Aston was the first man out the forward hatch, with Ludmilla on his heels. Three squads of First Platoon erupted right behind them, then dashed ahead, fanning out to secure the LZ—and put themselves between any hostiles and Aston and "Captain Ross."

Three more Ospreys had come in with Dickle, and their men spread apart, filtering into the trees and taking defensive positions. The rotor noise faded as the aircraft lifted to clear the LZ for the next quartet, and Aston looked at Ludmilla as they both heard the rattle and crash of fire . . . and the coughing roar of exploding ammunition and fuel.

The first Piranha was a blazing wreck, glaring in the darkness, but two squads of Marines filtered through the trees towards its killers. A second LAV edged around the flaming hulk, and an LAW glanced off its side armor and exploded harmlessly. Behind it, vehicle-mounted M2s flayed the night with fifty-caliber fire, covering the advancing infantry, and the heavier, coughing Mk 19 "machine guns" hurled over three hundred forty-millimeter grenades per minute. The diversion had been told to make noise, and it was doing just that.

✵ ✵ ✵

Taggart cringed as the crump of mortars joined the distant din. What the hell was coming *at* them? And where was the Troll?! He hesitated, caught between the clamor of battle and the need for direction. His mind hammered at the Troll, but his master was not attending, and Taggart dithered a moment longer, then shouted for his second in command to take charge while he raced up the steep track to the buried fighter.

The last Osprey lifted away, and the rest of Company T was ready to move. The heaped Dragon reloads had been distributed, the scouts were out, and Major Abernathy waved his men into motion.

Aston and Ludmilla moved with strict noise discipline at the center of a protective wedge. It galled the admiral a bit, but he was too much of a professional to object, and Ludmilla hardly noticed. She had activated her passive sensor systems, and she was tasting the night.

Taggart's outposts weren't as well-concealed as he'd thought, nor as well-protected. Three were on forward slopes, and the flash and flight of their LAWs had pinpointed them. Nor had the sentries deployed infantry to protect themselves or prepared fall-back positions.

The Marines' support teams hit them with a short, savage tornado of mortar fire, and then the infantry swept over them in a savagery of grenades and automatic fire. No one offered to surrender; no one would have let them if they had.

Counting the crew of the first LAV, Slugger Force took nine casualties, three fatal, on the way through...and left thirty-five bodies in its wake.

Taggart stood in the fighter, breathing hard. The sound of battle was silenced here, but it haunted him still, and he drove his mind at the Troll without response, more frantic every second, until desperation made him bold. He pressed the button he'd been ordered to touch only in gravest emergency.

The Troll floated in sensual glory, tingling with the shock and crash of destruction. Asheville flamed against the heavens, streets littered with bodies and wreckage. Even the stubborn, bitter defiance of the city's defenders was a kind of perfection. It whetted the burning edge of his impatient fury, and it would make the ultimate ruin of their hopes even sweeter.

He'd been surprised when the new defenders suddenly appeared, and he chided himself for forgetting their transport aircraft. He hadn't expected them to react so quickly, and the polished efficiency with which they sliced through his rabble dismayed him. But only for a moment. There was no room in his ecstasy for anything else. Even if these newcomers drove his creatures back, he could always whip them on afresh elsewhere. It was—

An alarm jangled deep in his brain, shattering his rapt contemplation, and a snarl of fury filled him as he roused from his dreams of death. How dared it? How *dared* it disturb him now?!

He gathered himself to lash out, and Taggart moaned in terror, falling to the floor and covering its head. But the blow did not fall. Before he could strike, the Troll felt its urgency—and then the reason for it.

A tsunami of ferocity washed over him. He was under attack! *He* was under *attack*! These crawling, puling primitives dared to attack *him*!

Rage shook aside the webs of his dreams, but not the blood-taste of their fury.

"Romeo One, this is Screwball. Come in, Romeo." Aston paused, crouched and panting just below the crest of the ridge. Moonlight gleamed on treetops below him, and he could see the crash and sparkle of combat to the west. There were flames, too. At least two vehicles burning—maybe three. They had to be his, he thought coldly, because they were behind the advancing muzzle flashes and explosions.

"Romeo One, this is Screwball. Come in," he repeated into his boom mike. There was a moment more of silence, then a voice replied.

"Screwball, Romeo One. Proceed."

"Romeo One, Screwball is on the field. I say again, Screwball is on the field. Set up the bleachers."

"Screwball, Romeo One copies. Going to burner."

Forty miles to the northeast, forty-eight Navy aircraft rocketed upward and streaked towards Sugarloaf Mountain.

The fifty men Taggart had sent rushing to reinforce the sentries were half a kilometer short of their positions when Slugger Force rolled over them.

Contributions were generous when the Troll "solicited," and ordnance depots were manned by humans, many of whom could be touched and recruited or manipulated. As a result, the Apocalypse Brigade had excellent equipment, but its men had no idea what was coming towards them, and they were far less experienced than Slugger Force with their night-vision gear. Nor were their scouts far enough out.

The Marines' quickly set ambush ran over them like a threshing machine; seven lived long enough to run.

Aston waved to Abernathy, and the bulk of Company T started down the mountain. Second Platoon and its attached Dragons and heavy weapons were already set up, with a better field of fire than he'd dared expect. Trees were a problem immediately to their front, but the critical fire zones were wide open.

"Dick," it was Ludmilla, speaking in his ear, "I'm picking up scan patterns. He can see us now."

"Slider, Screwball," Aston said quickly. "Grendel's eyes are open."

"Screwball, Slider," Abernathy responded instantly. "Affirm. People, watch yourselves. We may lose touch. Stick to the plan and—"

A wash of static drowned the major's voice, and Aston cursed. They'd known it could happen, especially since the Troll's people probably used his communications equipment and didn't have to worry about jamming at all. He only hoped the air cover remembered that and didn't panic.

"Backstop, Romeo One. We've lost contact with Screwball. Orbit at three-oh thousand, but keep your fingers off those launch buttons. Romeo Team, that goes for you, too."

Confirmations came back, and Staunton banked gently, circling the mountain and watching the pinprick flashes of light.

✧ ✧ ✧

"What the hell?" Lieutenant Spillers stood erect in the hatch of his battered, smoke-stained APC for the first time in an eternity. The fire was slackening. In fact, it looked like some of the bastards were running!

"Very well, Blake Taggart," the Troll snarled. "You were correct to summon me. Return to your guards while I determine what has happened."

Taggart bowed himself out gratefully, running for his command post under the canopy of false treetops, and the Troll activated his scanner stations. He spotted the oncoming vehicles instantly, drawn by the pulse of their engines and their heavy electronic emissions, and his mind sorted through the possibilities. It was impossible for these crude humans to have guessed his own presence, so no doubt Blake Taggart's troops had been careless. They had drawn attention to themselves, and this was the result. The same humans who had cut through his rioters with such ease had dispatched some of their number to deal with what they thought was another rabble. Well, that was their mistake, he thought savagely. Now he would make them pay for it.

He blotted out their communications, depriving them of coordination, and sent orders to his own troops. The Apocalypse Brigade fell back, breaking contact, and then began to shift position as he peered through his scanners to guide its men into positions of advantage.

Captain Tom Grant, call sign "Slugger," knew he was in trouble the minute his radios went out. Captain Ross had warned them it might happen, and the Corps had a doctrine for communications loss, but it assumed the other side could be jammed, too. And that, he knew, was not the case here.

His attack slowed, and his perimeter expanded automatically to win more room for maneuver along the narrow road. Hand signs, runners, and flares were all he had now, and they weren't enough.

The Troll exulted as he sent a wave of LAWs and light machine-gun fire slicing into his enemies' left flank. The night was day to his sensors, and he watched camouflaged figures tumbling under the hail of fire. Ten went down in the first attack, and he waited for the others to break and run.

The heavy machine-gun team saw another LAV brew up to the left, and the stutter and dance of muzzle flashes winked above them. Their own vehicle was essentially unarmored—a carrier for their weapons and little more—but they knew the penalty for bogging down in a fight like this. Their fifty-calibers raked the hillside and grenades exploded on the enemy position. Their attackers reeled back, abandoning their wounded, and wood smoke billowed above the crackle of flames and gunfire.

The Troll cursed as his minions retreated. He knew he shouldn't blame them, but he did. That hurricane of fire had surprised even him, but the need to destroy was upon him, and how could he do that when his tools died or ran so easily?

Aston and Ludmilla slithered down the slope in Sergeant Major Horton's wake, and First Platoon fanned out around them while they caught their breath and oriented themselves.

The sound of battle had become even more vicious, with heavier fire coming from both directions, and Aston and Horton looked at one another grimly. They knew what the sounds meant; Slugger Force had lost its radios, and the advantage had shifted to the Troll. "There," Ludmilla said quietly, pointing. "The scanner post."

Aston stared at the weird latticework of aerials under the false foliage and saw a single, solid structure with a door facing them. He looked about, astounded that they'd gotten this far without being spotted, then nodded to Horton.

"Sar-major."

"Sir!"

"Deploy the men. Then I want that place wrecked. Now."

"Sir! Ashley, set 'em up. Kiminsky, Sloan—this way."

He was away before Aston could stop him, vanishing into the undergrowth with his chosen corporals and slithering through the brush, more silent than a trio of snakes, while Master Sergeant Ashley positioned his men. Aston hadn't wanted Horton to get that far away from him; at the same time, he knew the sergeant major was the best man for the job. That was one of the problems with combat. The best men were always spread too thin, and too often it got them—

Small arms and grenades suddenly exploded to his left, and he fought an urge to duck. That had to be Dan and the other two platoons.

Abernathy cursed as the night erupted in fire and death. It was bad luck, plain and simple. He had no idea why forty or fifty hostiles should be moving around behind their own line so far from the fighting, but there they were, and they'd blundered right into his leading squad.

He stole one brief moment to watch the pattern of muzzle flashes in the undergrowth. There—those were his men. They'd broken down into fire teams around the 5.56 millimeter, belt-fed squad automatic weapons out of sheer reflex, and the SAWs were laying down a deadly fire. But they were under heavy fire of their own from two directions, and he gripped Lieutenant Warden's shoulder and pointed.

"Move the rest of your platoon up the slope and take them from behind!"

"Sir!"

"Corporal Holcombe!"

"Sir!"

"Put your Dragons right here, Corporal. See that building?" He pointed at the distant loom of aerials, and the corporal nodded. "Take it out, Corporal."

"Aye, Sir!"

The bulky launch tubes went up into firing position, assistants waiting to reload, but Abernathy had already turned away. He waved Lieutenant Atwater's Fourth Platoon into motion behind him and trotted straight for the closest weapon pit.

The Troll twitched in shock as the force he had pulled back to hook further out around his enemies' flank suddenly stumbled into a blazing wall of fresh attackers well *behind* his fixed positions. How had they—?

The cliff! They must have come down the mountain . . . but how had they known to do that?

✿✿✿

Captain Grant watched one of the heavy-weapons vehicles vomit a ball of flame, taking half its crew with it. The forest was a nightmare of burning brush and weapon flashes, and Slugger Force was pinned right in the middle of it. He estimated that over a quarter of his men were down already.

He left his vehicle and started forward on foot. It was all he could do without radios.

Sergeant Major Horton exploded to his feet and slammed a size-fourteen combat boot against the door of the hut. It smashed open like a piece of cardboard—the idiots hadn't even bothered to lock it!

The observation was a distant thought as his hip-high M 16/M203 blazed. The assault rifle laced the hut's interior with fire, and then the under-barrel launcher capped it with a forty-millimeter grenade.

There was no one in the structure—just a dinky little box with tentacles sitting on its wheels before a panel. His slugs punctured it in a dozen places, and it gouted sparks and smoke. More slugs went home in the panel it had been tending, and then the grenade exploded in the middle of it. He ducked back out of the way, and Kiminsky and Sloan tossed their satchel charges.

They'd hardly hit the ground when the hut became an expanding fireball in the darkness.

A fresh flare of fury rippled through the Troll as he felt his right flank scanner systems die, and then his remaining sensors saw the crude chemical rockets flashing towards them. He had less than two seconds to realize what was about to happen, and then he was blind.

Enough! He had suffered enough from these savages!

A snarling signal sent his combat mechs gliding out of the cavern.

He was too suffused with rage to wonder what evil chance had sent the enemy so unerringly after his scanners and jammers.

Company T's radios came back to life, and Captain Grant breathed a silent prayer of thanks. Slugger Force had been savagely mauled, but now the survivors were back in the net. The result was obvious almost immediately as the handful of surviving vehicles rumbled off the road into the trees, working as teams once more and flushing the enemy from cover.

Aston moved through the fire-sick night in a familiar half-crouch. His assault rifle stuttered viciously, and two men went down. Ludmilla was behind him, her fire seeking out her own targets, and all about them, First Platoon was on the move, swarming over fallen false-treetop camouflage to hit a cluster of weapon pits behind the crash of grenades. The barracks they'd chosen as Ludmilla's fire position loomed ahead, and he saw two Marines charge the wall. They rolled up against it, arms moving almost in unison, and hand grenades smashed through the windows.

Glass and debris blew outward, and an SAW gunner kicked in the door, hip-held automatic weapon hosing the interior on sustained fire.

They were moving, he thought hopefully, and so far their casualties weren't too bad. Maybe . . .

Blake Taggart crouched in the darkness, trying to picture what was happening. He'd never seen a firefight before, much less a night assault, and nothing less could have prepared him for the reality. It was all movement, muzzle flashes, and savagery, with no pattern he could grasp, but deep inside he knew the enemy was imposing *his* pattern on the chaos, and a sense of doom touched him.

No! He shook doubt aside. He'd been promised power! He was the anointed viceroy of the world! No one would take that from him. *No one!*

He darted a frantic look over his shoulder. There! The fire was heaviest on the left end of the line.

He punched a frozen gunner savagely to get his attention. The man jerked and saw his commander's pointing finger, then swiveled his otherworldly weapon and squeezed the trigger.

The night exploded. Half of Fourth Platoon vanished in a lick of blue-white fury, incinerated by the "light" power gun the Troll had given his men. Abernathy rolled away from the glaring scar in the mountainside, beating out the flames on his camo jacket as he tried desperately to spot the source of the fire. But like Ludmilla's blaster, there was no muzzle flash, no discharge to betray its location.

Ludmilla staggered. Her flight suit sensies were cranked up to full gain, trying to spot any communication between the Troll and its combat mechs, and the sudden energy surge was agonizing. She went to her knees, groaning, cursing herself for not considering the possibility even as she turned down their sensitivity. But at least she knew where the thing was.

Corporal Bowen went down beside her, a .50 caliber slug through his chest, and she snatched the laser target designator from his back, blessing the endless hours spent learning to use Company T's equipment. She laid the sight on the power gun's pit even as its gunner fired again. The energy bolt exploded against the mountain, killing more of her friends, and she keyed her radio.

"Romeo One, this is Sneak Play," she said clearly over the net. "I've got a target for you."

Ed Staunton stiffened in his cockpit. A *woman*? That was a woman's voice! What the hell was she—?

Then the call sign registered. Of every human soul in that inferno, "Sneak Play" had absolute priority.

"Sneak Play, Romeo One," he snapped. "Where?"

"Romeo, Sneak Play is prepared to laser paint. Target is a pit with heavy weapons."

"Roger, Sneak Play. Romeo One copies." He thought furiously for a second. All right.

"Romeo Four, Romeo One. Line 'em up, Freddy. Sneak Play's gonna light up a target for you. One round only. Confirm copy."

"Romeo One, Romeo Four copies one Maverick on the illumination."

"Sneak Play, Romeo One. Light up." "Roger, Romeo One. Illuminating now."

A Hornet sliced down out of the heavens as a thin, coded laser beam flashed invisibly through the dark. It touched the housing of the power gun as it ripped off a third blast, killing twenty more Marines, and high above, a single AGM-65E air-to-surface missile separated from Romeo Four and dove for the beckoning laser.

Nine seconds later, Blake Taggart, Viceroy of Earth, was blown to bloody fragments by a two hundred fifty-pound blast-frag warhead.

The explosion trembled through the earth to the Troll, and he felt Taggart's mind die. It was only a human, but they had been deeply linked for many months, and the sudden loss was agony. Hurt roared through his brain as his first combat mech slid from the access tunnel on anti-gravs, distracting him from the quick three hundred sixty-degree scan he'd planned upon. Instead, he sent the mech raging towards the spot where Taggart had died.

The hostile fire ringing Slugger Force faltered as Marines slid through smoke and flame like vengeful devils. The men of the Apocalypse Brigade died or fled, and what was left of the decoy attack shook itself out into some sort of order and probed cautiously after them.

"Target left!" somebody shouted, and Major Dan Abernathy watched the Dragon team slew their launcher around. He rolled up on an elbow, conscious of the waiting pain as one of his men worked on his shattered left leg. Funny. He didn't remember being hit.

The Dragon belched sudden flame, roaring away through the dark, and his eyes flashed ahead to its target. There! So that was what a "combat mech" looked like.

He barely had time to register the weird curves of its form before the Dragon crashed home and a ten-pound shaped charge slammed the alien war machine to the ground.

So they *could* be killed. The thought came in a queer little voice deep within him, and on its heels came the pain.

The Troll roared with mental fury as his mech went dead. Those hairy primitives were destroying *his* irreplaceable equipment!

Yet even through his fury, he began to feel a tinge of doubt. The invaders were dying, but they were hurting him. Hurting him badly. What else could they do to him? For the first time he began to regret the delay in completing his bomb.

Staff Sergeant Leroy Sanderson saw the explosion of the combat mech from his perch high above, but one of his teammates was already punching his shoulder. Another machine floated before them, rising silently, glinting blood and gold with reflected fire, and he laid his sights with care.

There! The Troll "looked" up from his second combat mech. Aircraft! There were *aircraft* above him! A cold stab of fear touched him at last, but he refused to panic. Instead, the mech tracked the nearest warplane, locked its sights, and fired.

"Jesus!"

Commander Staunton never found out who shouted the single blasphemy as Romeo Twelve vanished in a terrific ball of blue fire that came right out of nowhere. It could have been him. He'd never seen *anything* like that—never even imagined its like! Whatever the hell it had been sprayed the hapless Hornet over the heavens in molten droplets, and there was no chance at all of a chute.

Another explosion winked far below him, almost in the same instant. He barely noticed it, and he never knew it marked the death of the machine which had killed his pilot.

The Troll noted the death of his second combat mech, but he was almost calm now. He'd determined that the aircraft were easy targets and also that his light armor could be killed. Very well. He had three light mechs left, but he would not waste them.

He made rapid calculations from the data his mech had garnered before it died. There was a way. He could blast every one of those aircraft from the heavens in a single paired salvo if he did it properly, and the ridiculous chemical explosives which had killed his light armor would be powerless to stop him.

He sent commands to his fighter, and a panel opened. His organic component disconnected quickly from the flight controls, and the smoothly efficient machinery transferred it to the waiting combat chassis parked beside the medium combat mech in his forward hold.

"Romeo One, Screwball," Aston snapped, watching tears of flame weep down the heavens. "Romeo One, come in!"

"Screwball, Romeo One," a shaken voice said, and he sighed in relief. The odds had been against that being the nuclear-armed aircraft, but . . .

"Romeo One, Screwball. Get your ass out of the line of fire. Watch yourself. We may need you."

"Roger, Screwball. Romeo One copies."

Commander Ed Staunton's Hornet peeled off to put a mountain peak between his weapons load and whatever had killed Romeo Twelve.

"Sweet suffering Jesus! What the hell is *that*?"

Sergeant Major Horton looked in the indicated direction. "That" was bigger than two M l tanks, rumbling out of the ground like a surfacing whale, and the flicker and flare of explosions and flames glittered on its bronze-colored surface. He didn't know what it was, but, from Captain Ross's descriptions, he knew what it *wasn't*. It was no light combat mech . . . and it wasn't the Troll either.

A hissing sound slashed at his ears as a ghastly burst of green light erupted from whatever it was. Screams at its heart marked the death of a Dragon team, and a terrible, shuddering vibration hammered Horton's nerves. The bodies of his men were twisted and grotesque, tortured and writhing as whatever it was ground the life slowly and hideously from them, and he swallowed bitter-tasting bile.

Fear was an icy fist about the sergeant major's heart, freezing his blood, but he started to crawl. Not away, but toward the launcher.

Aston saw it all, and he also saw Horton crawling towards the launcher. He didn't know what it was either, but he didn't think the sergeant major had a chance in hell of stopping it with a Dragon. But if he did, he'd need a loader.

"Milla! Trouble at the tunnel!" he snapped into his radio, and he was already scuttling across the smoking ground in Horton's wake.

Ludmilla paled as the whickering flash of the neuron whip crackled through her sensors. Dear God, she'd been wrong! She'd assumed the Troll would have only light armor, but he had at least one medium mech, and nothing Company T had would stop that monster!

She shuddered at the thought of the whip. The Kangas had rejected it as inefficient, but the Trolls loved it. It went after nerve tissue and incapacitated its victims instantly, but death took long, terrible minutes, and it was lethal up to twenty meters from its point of focus. Its effects were far slower at the greater range, but they were no less certain or agonizing. Not even a Thuselah could survive a direct hit, and they had a less than even chance of surviving a near miss.

The thoughts flashed through her mind in an instant, and she slapped her flight suit's power switch, killing her suit sensors instantly. She turned to run up-slope, seeking a position to take the mech from the flank, and then her heart seemed to stop as she saw Horton . . . and Dick.

Alvin Horton reached the Dragon and lifted the bulky tube to his shoulder while a corner of his mind worked with almost detached precision. He remembered generations of boots, remembered beating into their heads that their object was to kill the *other* guy, not die gallantly. He'd always sworn that whatever happened, *he* would never go out pulling a John Wayne, but sometimes a man had no choice.

He heard someone shouting his name from behind him, recognized Admiral Aston's voice, but there was no time to think about that. He knelt beside the writhing, sceaming bodies of his men, rocked up on one knee, rested the launch unit on his shoulder, and captured the alien vehicle in his sights.

Aston saw Horton moving like a man on a training field, saw the combat mech rumbling towards him, saw the sergeant major take the time to do it right. The launcher belched fire, sending its missile roaring down range, and it was perfect. The screaming weapon hurled itself directly at the enemy's bow, slashing in to take it dead center, and exploded in a terrible burst of light.

Which left the armored monster totally unmarked.

Horton didn't even stand up. He only reached down for a fresh bird, fighting to reload the two-man weapon single-handedly even as the leviathan ground straight towards him, and Aston hurled himself to his feet. Bullets shrieked past him, but he ignored them, running desperately to help the sergeant major.

And then that dreadful emerald light tore the night apart once more. It struck directly on Sergeant Major Alvin Horton, outlining his convulsing body in a hideous corona, and it reached out past him.

Some corner of Aston's brain saw it coming, almost like a tide racing across a mudflat. Then it was upon him, and the universe vanished in an incandescent burst of agony.

Ludmilla saw the Dragon explode. She saw the sergeant major fall.

And she saw Dick Aston convulse as the edge of the neuron bolt hurled him to the ground in twitching torment.

The Troll exulted as humans died under the fire of his mech while his own chassis rumbled down the tunnel. Together, he and the mech would wipe the heavens clean and he would escape. He could always start again elsewhere, and *this* time he would finish his bomb before he did!

He was still in the tunnel when an alarm woke to clangorous life.

Ludmilla Leonovna planted her feet wide in a marksman's stance. Bullets cracked and whined about her, but she did not notice. Her face was wet, but she blinked her eyes furiously clear of tears. And then she reached for her blaster, drew . . . and fired in one clean, flashing movement.

Blue-white lightning etched the valley rim against the sky as the first full-power blaster bolt in Terran history struck home.

"*Ground force battle screen has one great weakness.*" Ludmilla could hear the long ago instructor's dry, lecturing tone in her mind. "*Unlike deep space battle screen, it cannot reach into other dimensions due to the Frankel Limit of a planetary body. Therefore, it cannot protect against an attack delivered through multi-dimensional space.*"

Eighteen hundred tons of explosive energy struck the combat mech's frontal armor, concentrated into an area only two millimeters across. Armor that would have withstood a ten-kiloton area blast was paper under that focused stiletto's fury, and the plasma ripped into its heart. It happened so fast the eye could not see it, the brain could not record it, and then there was only a mounting pillar of terrible fire as the war machine spewed itself into the heavens.

How?! *How?!* He'd killed the last of them himself!

But only a human from his own time could have fired that weapon, and that meant . . . that meant these primitives knew *everything*! The whole time he'd plotted and spun his webs, they'd *known*! They'd been searching the entire time, hunting him—waiting for him to reveal himself so their informant could kill him!

He writhed in exquisite torment. They knew, and there were too many of them. Whatever his individual power, however subtly he could bend and shape their minds, there were simply too many of them for him to conquer if they knew to hunt and fear him, and that meant his freedom, his omnipotence, had been a charade. Because that other being from his own time had lived, he would forever be a hunted animal on this putrid planet with no hope of conquest, no choice but to destroy it, for they'd been warned.

And worst of all was the bitter, bitter realization that it had always been that way. That he had only thought it was different. That his power was hollow, an illusion he'd forged for himself.

His tenuous hold on near-sanity snapped. His dream had been stolen. Worse, it had been revealed as *only* a dream. As self-deception. He should flee, and he knew it, but he couldn't. Only vengeance mattered now.

Ludmilla holstered her blaster and sprinted. She had to get clear of her present position before the Troll himself emerged and spotted her. She fled through the light gravity of the motherworld, and her flashing feet carried her towards the twitching body of the dying man she loved.

Even in his madness, the Troll retained his cunning. No human could match *his* reaction speed. He noted the disappearance of the blaster from his sensors, but he knew what to look for now, and no one but his enemy could kill him without using nuclear weapons and killing his enemy, as well. He hugged that thought to him with hating, hungry fury, and fed power to his treads, grinding from the tunnel in a billow of dust.

If the human drew its weapon again, it would die before it could aim. If it did not, he would simply kill and kill and kill until the laws of chance sent the killer of his dream into death.

✻ ✻ ✻

Ludmilla skidded to a stop as the Troll emerged at last. Half again the size of the medium mech it loomed, dark and evil, squat on its treads, and its weapon ports were open.

She knew what it must be thinking, and she was afraid it was right.

It halted, scanning its surroundings, ignoring the rockets bursting against its battle screen, and her hand hovered a millimeter above her blaster. She dared not touch it. She must find some sort of cover, something to give her a fleeting instant of advantage. It was the only way.

And then the Troll started forward.

The enemy was hiding. Madness gibbered in the Troll's mind, and it ground the rich leaf mold under its cleated treads.

It was headed straight for Dick!

Logic told her he was already dead; only the dying remained, and it could not come soon enough. But logic was a cold, dead thing. She didn't consider it. She didn't think at all, and her hand moved.

Surprise. It was a fleeting thing, but the Troll felt it. Surprise that its enemy should stand boldly before it and activate its weapon.

Perhaps it was that brief moment of astonishment, or perhaps it was the fact that Ludmilla Leonovna had heavy-grav reactions and a *cralkhi's* neural impulses, moving at more than human speed. Or perhaps it was a combination of both those factors and the blind workings of fate.

The blaster rose with the deadly, fluid grace Dan Abernathy had seen on the Camp Lejeune combat range. It was a single, supple movement, and her finger squeezed the trigger stud before she even realized she'd drawn.

The Troll had time for one last emotion: disbelief. Disbelief that any human could move that quickly. Even a *cral*—

A sliver of pure energy blew him into infinity.

CHAPTER TWENTY-FIVE

She holstered her blaster slowly, turning away from the corona of fury crackling about the massive combat chassis. Awareness of victory pulsed deep within her, but it was a feeble, joyless thing as she dropped to her knees beside Richard Aston in a litter of fallen camouflage.

His body jerked and shuddered, and his face was soaked with sweat, his eyes blind above bared teeth locked in a snarl of agony. She knew the signs. She'd seen them before, and she lifted his head into her lap, staring down through her tears while bullets cracked above them.

He couldn't speak, but she hoped he recognized her as she pressed her fingers to his carotid. She held the pressure firmly, mastering his agonized shudders with gentle strength, until unconsciousness took him.

She knew she should maintain the pressure until death stopped the pain, but she couldn't. She knelt over him, sheltering him with her body, and her gentle fingers were ready to drive him back into the merciful dark.

She was still kneeling there when Gunnery Sergeant Morton Jaskowicz skidded to a stop beside her.

"Cap'n?" She raised her head slowly, cradling Aston protectively as she stared blindly up at the big, tough sergeant.

"Cap'n, we need you," Jaskowicz said, his rumbling voice strangely gentle against the crackle of weapons. "You're in command, Ma'am."

Her mind worked sluggishly. It was unfair. She'd come so far. Paid so much. The Troll's death should have freed her, not burdened her with fresh responsibility.

"Where—" She cleared her throat and made her voice work. "Where's Major Abernathy?"

"Major's out of it, too, Ma'am. Lieutenant Atwater's dead and Lieutenant Warden's hurt bad. I *think* Lieutenant Frye's still on his feet, but he's up-slope."

"I—" She broke off as a Marine corpsman slithered to a kneeling halt across Aston's body from her. His teenaged face was strained, but his hands were steady. Ludmilla stared at him for just a moment. Then the despair in her own face hardened into determination, and she nodded curtly.

"With you in a minute, Gunny," she said. "Get Third and Fourth Platoon moving this way. We'll set up a perimeter against the mountain. Tie in at either end of the tunnel—Second Platoon can cover us from above. Then find me an FAC team."

"Yes, Ma'am!" Jaskowicz took a fraction of a second to salute—something a Marine in combat never did—and dashed off through the darkness. As he vanished, Ludmilla turned to the corpsman.

"Do you have a hypodermic?" she asked calmly, and he nodded. "Good."

Lieutenant Spillers couldn't understand. The howling, blood-crazed demons who'd been attacking all night had vanished. Only scattered shots rang out as a handful of more stubborn invaders went on firing until they were flanked and finished by National Guardsmen moving with the cold skill of survivors. They'd paid cash for that skill, Spillers thought grimly. Rumor said the brigade had taken fifty percent casualties—closer to eighty among the junior officers—and Spillers believed it.

But what unnerved him most were the rioters who just sat or stood there, glaze-eyed and slack-faced, fingers twitching gently while spittle oozed down their chins. It was as if whatever had driven them had also consumed them, he thought shakenly.

Ed Staunton couldn't help himself. He had to keep ducking up to see what was going on, and he'd climbed up over his protective mountain just in time to see both fountains of light and fury erupt into the heavens.

That had to be it, he decided, his thoughts oddly detached and distant. That had to be the "Troll" thing Commander Morris had told him about. And that meant his "special weapons" would not be required ... thank God.

But the sparkle and flash of small arms and heavy weapons continued to flare, and that looked like a nasty forest fire starting to the southwest.

"Romeo Team, Romeo One," he said. "Catcher, get ready. Bullpen, open your orbit and get clear." Catcher was VFA-432's call sign; they were equipped for general support. VFA-433—"Bullpen"—carried precision-attack weapons he judged would be less useful in the new situation below.

"Come on, Sneak Play," he murmured, orbiting high above the blazing firefight. "*Talk* to me, damn it!"

The Apocalypse Brigade was far more confused than its enemies. Most of its men had no idea Taggart was dead, few realized there were aircraft above them, and none had the least idea what the Troll was, where it had come from, or what had happened to it. But they *did* know they were trapped and under attack ... and that their attackers had been badly hurt.

Their initial shock faded as they recognized how substantially they outnumbered their enemies. And then, on the heels of that realization, came a second: they must escape, and their vehicles were under the guns of Ludmilla's hastily assembling perimeter.

They came from everywhere, recruited because they'd required little shaping. The Troll had touched them less deeply, bent them less terribly, than he'd been forced to do with those less inclined to violence. All he'd done was program them with fanatical loyalty to their leaders and their "cause," and his death had not impinged directly upon them. They honestly believed they were fighting for themselves, and Taggart's third in command was still alive. He was a hard, hating man, and he knew his enemies were hurt and bleeding.

Even if he hadn't needed the vehicles, he still would have attacked.

Ludmilla looked up as the first recoilless and mortar rounds came in. She'd hoped the enemy would break with the Troll's death, but she hadn't reckoned with the sort of men Taggart had recruited, and she ducked lower in her weapon-pit command post as mortars, machine guns, and covering Dragons from Second Platoon hammered back at their attackers. The unwounded survivors of the three oversized platoons which had come down the mountain would scarcely have made a single normal one, but they couldn't withdraw: there were too many wounded for the fit to carry.

"Slugger, Sneak Play!" She shouted into her mike, her voice fighting the crash of battle. "What's your situation?"

"Sneak Play, Slugger is stuck." If Grant was surprised to hear her instead of Abernathy or Aston, his voice gave no sign of it. "We're down to one LAV. Estimate sixty percent personnel casualties, and the woods are on fire."

"Slugger, can you take your wounded with you?"

"Affirmative, Sneak Play."

"Pull out, Slugger. Get clear as soon as possible. Inform me when you reach—" she crouched over her map card "—Victor-Four. Confirm copy."

"Sneak Play, Slugger confirms. Pull back to Victor-Four and advise."

"Luck, Slugger." She switched channels on her radio chest pack. "Romeo One, Sneak Play. Still with us?"

"Sneak Play, Romeo One. Glad to hear your voice. What can we do?"

"Stand by, Romeo One. We'll have targets for you—" She broke off as Staff Sergeant Ernest Caldwell tumbled into the pit with her. The other two survivors of his forward air control team were with him. "Romeo One, our FAC just turned up. I'm handing off to him." The rattle of incoming small arms roared higher. "I'm going to be busy." She turned to Caldwell as she reached for her blaster once more. "When Slugger gets clear, I want those woods hit with everything they've got, Sergeant. Burn them out."

"Yes, Ma'am."

She rose higher in the pit, listening to the cacophony of her men's weapons, her suit sensors and the Troll's dying glare showing her the enemy. She braced her firing hand on the lip of the pit, and her radio was back on Company T's tactical net.

"Here they come, boys," she said calmly. "We've got to hold them till Slugger gets clear—then the airedales can have them."

There was no more time for talk. The Apocalypse Brigade swept towards the Marines, muzzle flashes and the back-flash of recoiless rifles and rocket launchers lighting their positions like summer lightning.

Company T's survivors poured back an avalanche of answering fire, but the attack rolled in. Ludmilla picked a clump of enemies clustered around an M60 machine-gun team and squeezed the trigger.

Ed Staunton watched the bright, blue-white bursts explode below him and wondered what the *hell* made them.

Her blaster might have broken the attack, but the Apocalypse Brigade had once had energy weapons of their own and they knew its weakness, knew its targeting systems would lock on the first solid object in its line of fire—including trees and underbrush. They recoiled, but they quickly realized there was only one of it and began to work around her flanks.

"Skipper!" It was Jaskowicz, shouting into her ear as she sought fresh targets through the smoke. Flame roared everywhere she had used her blaster, but at least the wind was away from them. "Right flank's going, Skipper!" the sergeant shouted. "Not gonna last another three minutes!"

"Move the reserve squad in!"

"Already done it, Skip!"

"Damn!" She keyed her radio. "Slugger, Sneak Play. State position!"

"Sneak Play, Slugger is at Victor-Five," the reply came back instantly, and Ludmilla nodded. It would have to do.

"Get your heads down, Slugger," she told Grant, then turned to Caldwell. "Set?" He nodded.

"Do it," she said.

The world exploded.

The Hornets shrieked down like invisible demons, a long, endless line of them spilling napalm and cluster bombs, and the Apocalypse Brigade died. Perhaps as many as fifty escaped the attack and the forest fires and managed to sneak past what was left of Slugger Force as the Ospreys swept down into the vicious thermals of the fire-torn night to take Company T's survivors out of Hell.

genesis *n.*, *pl.* -ses.
The coming into being of anything; origin; beginning; creation. [Latin, from Greek, generation, birth, origin.]
—*Webster-Wangchi Unabridged*
Dictionary of Standard English
Tomas y Hijos, Publishers 2465,
Terran Standard Reckoning

CHAPTER TWENTY-SIX

Richard Aston woke from dreams of agony to an unfamiliar ceiling. He'd never seen that particular swatch of acoustic tiles before, but he'd put in too much recovery time not to recognize a hospital ceiling when he saw it.

He tried to remember how he'd gotten here, but it was a blank. He turned his head and saw the IV plugged into his left arm, then carefully wiggled each finger and toe in turn. It was a ritual testing, first devised thirty years before, and he breathed a sigh of relief as each joint bent obediently, confirming its continued presence.

In fact, he couldn't find a single thing wrong with himself, except for a ravenous appetite. Which was strange. Why was he—?

His thoughts broke off as the door opened quietly. He turned his head and smiled as Ludmilla entered—then frowned as she froze just inside the door. She stared at him, her eyes huge, and he held out his right hand.

"Milla?"

Her name broke the spell, and she hurled herself forward, her arms opening wide, and the strangest thing of all was the tears spilling down her face as she laughed and murmured his name over and over between kisses.

It took fifteen minutes for her to calm, and her tearful, wildly emotional state was a shock. It was so unlike her . . . and so filled

321

with love he almost came unglued himself. But the pressure of her feelings slowly ebbed, and she slipped into the chair beside his bed, holding his hand in both of hers as she recounted all that had happened.

"I'd seen neuron whips before, Dick," she said finally, shivering. "I knew you were dying." Her hands tightened on his. "So . . . I took a chance. I made the corpsman inject you with about twenty cee-cees of blood—from me."

She paused, her eyes locked with his.

"But—" He broke off, his own eyes widening in shocked speculation.

"That's right," she said. "It could have killed you—*should* have killed you, really—but you were already dying anyway. So I did it, and . . ." She paused again, drawing a deep breath. "It worked."

"It worked?" he echoed blankly. "You mean it—? I—?"

"Yes," she said simply, smiling tremulously. "I know I didn't have any right to do it, but—"

"*I'm* a . . . a *Thuselah*?" he demanded, unable to grasp it.

"Yes," she said again, smiling at last. The wonder on his face was too much for her, and she lifted his hand to his head. "Feel," she commanded.

His eyes went wider than ever as his palm touched his smooth scalp and felt a soft, downy fuzz. Hair. It was hair!

Then it was true . . . he *was* a Thuselah! And that meant—

He stared at her and saw the future's endless promise in her deep-blue eyes.

"Well, Admiral," President Armbruster said, smiling from the bedside chair, "you did it."

"Yes, Sir." Aston sat upright in bed, a tray of food on his lap. It was remarkable; his symbiote's demands actually made hospital food taste good. "But it cost us."

"Yes," Armbruster said softly, his smile fading, "It did."

It had. A third of Asheville lay in ruins, as did more than half of Hendersonville, and virtually all of half a dozen other small towns and cities. The fighting had cost the North Carolina National Guard over eight hundred dead. The count of civilian casualties was still coming in, and the already hideously high figure didn't yet include the thousands of rioters who'd died . . . or the ones whose minds had broken when the Troll was killed.

Nor did it include Company T. Major Abernathy's leg had been saved, but it would be severely impaired for the rest of his life. At that, he was one of the lucky ones. Fifty-two percent of Company T's men were dead; another thirty-one percent had been wounded.

Oh, yes, Jared Armbruster thought, it had been a costly victory. But compared to the price they might have paid—

"At any rate," he said, shaking himself, his voice intentionally loud to break the somber mood, "we're all grateful to you. So grateful," he added with a twinkling smile, "that I'm going to give you two a choice."

"A choice, Mister President?" Aston was puzzled.

"Yes. I understand from Colonel Leonovna that this symbiote thing is going to make some changes, Admiral. Going to get a bit younger, are you?"

"Well, yes, Sir, I suppose." Aston shrugged. "I don't understand it all yet, but Milla tells me no self-respecting symbiote would want to live in an old hulk like this, so—"

"I don't blame it a bit." Armbruster grinned. "But that means you've got quite a few years ahead of you, and it occurred to me that you two might like to spend them without official interference."

"Interference, Sir?"

"You understand, don't you, Colonel?" Armbruster said, and Ludmilla nodded slowly, her eyes locked intently on his face.

"You see, Admiral," Armbruster continued calmly, "the Colonel's in what you might call a precarious position—not right now, but sooner or later.

"At the moment, you and she are international heroes, but eventually someone's going to want to talk to her. She knows too much for her own good, I'm afraid. Too much about her own past— what would have been our future without her—and about her technology."

Aston stared at his President in dawning awareness.

"Exactly," Armbruster said more grimly. "At the moment, the United States is in possession of a warship from five hundred years in the future, and every major power on the planet knows it. We can't make heads or tails of it yet, but you can bet we'll keep trying till we can. And the rest of the world knows *that*, too. Wars have been fought over far less, Admiral.

"But that's all right, because I don't plan on fighting any damned wars. Thanks to Colonel Leonovna—and you, and a lot of other people with guts—we kicked one Troll's ass, but there's a whole damned race of genocidal fanatics out there in the stars. We beat them in Colonel Leonovna's past, but we were lucky. I don't intend to rely on luck this time around, and President Yakolev, Prime Minister Henderson, and Chancellor Stallmaier agree with me. When the first *Shirmaksu* fleet enters the solar system, we intend for a united Earth to kick its miserable ass from here to Antares, and that ship is our leverage to make sure it happens.

"You've been closed up in here for three weeks, Admiral, so you may not realize what a state the world is in. The story's still coming out, but the pressure to *do* something is tremendous. Ambassador Nekrasov is already in Washington with a special delegation from Moscow and others are on the way. As I'm sure you can imagine, a few nations—like France, the PRC, and a dozen or so Third World states—are howling over our 'high-handed, arrogant chauvinism' in keeping them in the dark. But that's all right. I'd anticipated something of the sort, and with Britain, Germany, and Russia backing us in Europe and Japan, South Korea, and the Republic of China backing us in Asia—not to mention the fact that *we're* the ones with all Grendel's hardware in our grasp—I think we've got the leverage we need. With a little luck, I'll have Congressional authority to begin negotiations for the creation of a *real* world government within the month. I don't say it will be easy, but I think we'll manage it. We have to.

"Which brings us back to Colonel Leonovna. I can absolutely guarantee that no one will lay a finger on her while I'm President, but I won't *be* President forever. And even if I were, the combination of her knowledge and her symbiote would almost certainly be too much for other governments to keep their hands off her."

"What exactly do you mean, Mister President?" Aston spoke sharply, but he knew. And, he thought with cold ferocity, he should *always* have known. *Would* have known, if only he'd actually expected to live and let himself look that far ahead.

"I mean that the Colonel is unique," Armbruster said, confirming

Aston's grim thoughts. "An oracle to be consulted. The only female 'Thuselah' in existence—or likely to exist, this time around. And, forgive me, Colonel, there will be those who suspect you could give them much more technical information than you have. If you're lucky, they'll be very civilized about it, but they won't let you run around loose once the truth starts to penetrate."

"Protective custody?" Aston's voice was harsh.

"If, as I say, you're lucky," Armbruster said evenly. "Don't be too hard on them, Admiral. Remember that she represents the humanity of the future—or a species-threatening abomination, depending on your viewpoint—because she's the *only* person on this planet who can possibly conceive and bear Thuselah children."

Aston's blood chilled as he recalled Ludmilla's description of how Thuselahs had been treated even when there were millions of them; how would the only Thuselah mother in existence fare?

"That would be enough all by itself," Armbruster said quietly. "But it won't *be* by itself. I may be confident that we'll get a united world in the end, but it's not going to be easy, it's not going to be simple, and unless I'm very much mistaken, it won't be bloodless, either. There are enough regimes out there with leaders who'd rather fight to the death than surrender their power and authority to anyone else, and you're a career military man. What wouldn't any war department give for the ability to field and train special forces, or elite antiterrorist squads—or terrorists of their own—with the advantages the Colonel's symbiote could provide them, especially in the face of everything that's about to come down? I can think of a dozen nations right off hand who would do *anything* to get their hands on her. Or, failing that, on samples of her DNA. Cloning is no longer a mystery of the future, Admiral. We have it now, and the techniques will only improve, which means—"

He shrugged, but his eyes never wavered from Aston's, and it was the admiral's turn to nod grimly.

"And even aside from that, as I say, they'll suspect she can give them more technical information than she has," Armbruster said almost gently. "Speaking of which, Colonel, I hope you'll forgive me if I suspect the same thing."

"Why should you, Mister President?" Ludmilla asked.

"You've been just a bit too vague, Colonel. I think you're holding back—on the very wise premise that we're not ready for all you know."

"Not ready *yet*, Mister President," she corrected gently, and he smiled.

"So, you *have* been holding out on us." He chuckled. "Very, *very* wise of you, Colonel. But I've known quite a few military people, and no 'simple fighter jock' I ever met was quite as ignorant of theory as you are."

"Actually," she confessed calmly, "Thuselahs have lots of time to study. I have three advanced degrees: one in microbiology and two in molecular electronics and sub-particle physics." Aston stared at her in shock, and she smiled. "You know, Mister President, I rather thought you were suspicious."

"Damn right I was," he agreed cheerfully. "But it happens I agree with you—though I trust you *will* make some of that knowledge available if it becomes obvious our own R&D people have hit a brick wall?"

"I will," she said, then paused. "But that sounds as if you think I'll have a choice."

"I intend to see that you do," he said, suddenly very serious. "I probably shouldn't. Looked at in one way, letting you out of my grasp will probably constitute the greatest act of treason any sitting president has ever committed, because all the things I just said could be squeezed out of you by unscrupulous nations could be squeezed out of you by *us*, as well. But it happens that I would prefer to be able to sleep with myself at night, and given how much we owe you, that would become just a tad difficult if I *didn't* let you go. And," he added with a wry smile, "not giving you the chance would present difficulties of its own. Yakolev, Henderson, Stallmaier, and I are going to have a tough enough time determining how, when, and where to share access to the Troll's fighter, but at least that's only a piece of hardware—and one no one will be able to figure out for a while, anyway. If we handle it right, we can turn it into a focus for the new government we need to put together, make it into a sort of combined Rosetta Stone-Manhattan Project-Moon Race as we rally the human race's best and brightest in an effort to take it apart and learn how to reverse engineer it for our own use.

"But if *you* were available, Colonel, you'd make that much more difficult. People would keep turning to you for explanations instead of figuring things out on their own. And that doesn't even consider all the fights and squabbles we'd get into over which nation should have the privilege of serving as your 'host.' After all, if *I* can see the advantages to grabbing you off, so can anyone else. And even if they weren't so nefarious as to want you for their own purposes, they'd sure as *hell* want to make sure that none of their rivals got hold of you."

"I see." Ludmilla gazed at him calmly, then cocked her head. "Obviously, I'm pleased to hear you coming up with all those reasons you should let me go, Mr. President. But are you certain you've really thought this through? We may have killed the Troll, but as you just pointed out, the Kangas are still out there, and they *will* be along in less than eighty years."

"Indeed they will," Armbruster agreed. "But we fought them to a standstill when they arrived in your own past, and that was without even knowing they were coming. This time we'll be forewarned—thanks to you—and, I feel quite certain, forearmed—thanks to Grendel's fighter. I'm sure we'll hit lots of problems in figuring out how it works, but those sorts of problems bring out the best in people and help pull them together, which is exactly what we need. So I'm confident that we *will* get it figured out . . . and I also hope that you'll be good enough to give us the coordinates of the Kangas' home systems before you swiftly and silently vanish away?"

"Oh, I think you can be reasonably confident of that, Mr. President," she said with a quirky smile.

"Well, then—there you have it!" Armbruster raised both hands shoulder high, palms uppermost, and grinned at her. "Yakolev, Henderson, Stallmaier, and I will use possession of the fighter and access to it as bait to draw the rest of the world into our coils. At the same time, we'll use our combined military strength to discourage anyone who might have thoughts of gaining control of it for themselves or simply destroying it to deprive anyone else of it. Once we've got the world headed in the right direction, we'll use the job of taking it apart and learning how it works—and how to duplicate or even improve upon it—as the challenge to get us used to working together and *keep* us heading in the right direction. And frankly, Colonel, I think I can convince my conscience that having you around, as well, would only interfere with my nice, neat plans. It may

David Weber

take me a while, but I'm pretty sure I can pull it off if I try hard enough. So if you'll be good enough to give me those coordinates on your way out..."

He beamed at her, and she chuckled. Then she looked at Aston. The admiral looked back with a smile of his own, but then his expression sobered, and he turned his eyes to the President.

"That all sounds good, Sir. It may even sound logical and reasonable...to us. But it's not going to sound that way to some of those other nations you've mentioned, or even to some *US* politicos—or big corporations, for that matter—that I can think of right off hand. So just how do we go about letting Milla fade into the woodwork?"

"I've given that some thought," Armbruster said more seriously, "and that's one reason the official press release hasn't gone out yet. If you two want it that way, the record will show that Admiral Richard K. Aston and Captain Elizabeth Ross died of their wounds. The only people who know better are the survivors of your Company T and the MAG pilots who pulled you out. I think you can trust them to keep their mouths shut."

"So do I," Ludmilla said softly. "Long enough for it not to matter if they don't, anyway."

"Exactly, Colonel," Armbruster said. "In the meantime, you two will be free to fade away. If you like, I'll have Commander Morris set it up—we can trust him to hide you so deep *I* couldn't find you. I'll provide ample funds to a blind account and see to it that no one but you and I know that he did it." He paused, then shook his head.

"It's your choice, of course, and I could be wrong about how hunted and harried the two of you would find yourselves. But I might not be, too. So think about it, people." He smiled again, a gentler, warmer smile than many people would have believed he could produce. "Whatever you decide, you've more than earned it."

The seventy-foot twin-masted schooner *Beowulf* sliced through the Pacific swell under a forest of stars. Her tall, youthful skipper had originally intended to sail the South Atlantic on their first long cruise, but the first mate had changed his mind, and they were still a week out from Hawaii as they sat together at the wheel, sipping coffee and watching the sky.

Evelyn Horton snuggled into the curve of her husband's arm, her chestnut hair blowing on the wind to mingle with his own shoulder-length mop of dark black, and Adam Horton pressed his palm to the still tiny bulge of her abdomen. A girl, he hoped, and not just for evolutionary purposes. He'd always secretly wanted a daughter; he suspected most men did, whatever they might tell the rest of the world. But there was another reason he hoped for one in his own case—for his wife had threatened to complete Mordecai's joke by naming a boy Cain.

Evelyn checked her watch again, then looked back up at the sky.

"Any time now," she murmured.

"Are you sure?" he asked softly.

"Jared had NASA run the figures even before we caught up with the Troll," she replied. "I'm sure."

"In that case—" he began, but she shook her head and pressed her fingers to his lips.

"Just hold me, Dick," she whispered, and his arm tightened.

They stared up together, and then she stiffened with a quick, convulsive gasp. High above them, the cobalt sky blossomed with light—a brilliant, flaring light, bigger than any five stars and brighter than a score of them. A light which had come from another universe to die... and taken fourteen months to reach their eyes.

It glowed in the depths of space like a searing beacon—beautiful and defiant, yet somehow forlorn and lost—a glorious diadem marking the trackless graves of the men and women of TFNS *Defender* who had died to save an Earth not even their own. It grew and expanded as they watched, and then, as suddenly as it had appeared, it was gone, snuffed by the breath of eternity, and Richard Aston felt his wife sob against his shoulder, weeping for her dead at last.

AFTERWORD

Many, many years ago—thirty-one of them, in fact—Steve White and I sold our first novel to Baen Books. It was called *Insurrection*. A few months later, Jim Baen bought my first two solo novels, *Mutineers' Moon* and its sequel, *The Armageddon Inheritance*. And he bought *The Apocalypse Troll* the next year.

So he'd bought my first three solo novels before the first book I'd ever sold got into print. Which, needless to say, made me feel ten feet tall and covered with hair.

After that, however, there was a hiccup.

I'd written the book in 1990, and Jim had bought it that same year, but had set it aside at that time at his end. I think he intended to ask for some minor revisions, but there were a few other things going on. Minor distractions, you might say. *Mutineers' Moon* came out in 1991, *Path of the Fury* and *Crusade* came out in 1992, and *On Basilisk Station* and *The Honor of the Queen* came out two months apart in 1993, *The Armageddon Inheritance* came out in 1994 . . . that kind of thing. Under the circumstances, it's not really too surprising that neither they nor I thought about it very much.

But then, in late 1997 or so, I got a call from Marla Ainspan at Baen who said "You're going to think this is pretty funny, David, but we have a contract from 1991 that you've never filled."

"Excuse me?" I said.

"Yes, it's for something called *The Apocalypse Troll*," she said.

"Marla," I said, "that contract was written for a completed manuscript I'd already delivered to Jim. In fact, I've revised it twice since then."

"Really? Why?"

"Because the Berlin Wall fell, and then the Soviet Union collapsed. You know, little things like that."

"Oh. Then I guess you'd like us to send you the delivery check?"

"Yeah, that'd be nice."

I talked to Toni Weisskopf about that later (we lost Jim in 2006, so I never had the conversation I'd planned to have with *him* about it), and she said he was amused by my entire exchange with Marla. In large part, that was because he'd never asked for those revisions I mentioned above (or the bigger ones when things like the fall of the Wall intruded), but they'd just sort of magically turned up, anyway! And, like I say, it's not like he and I hadn't had *plenty* of other projects ongoing in that same hectic decade or so. In fact, it was one hell of a ride, and I can't begin to express how much I've missed having him along for the fourteen years since he left us. Nor do I think enough people realize even now how much our entire field lost along with him.

But that is the story of how a book bought in 1990 didn't see print for another nine years or so.

I have to admit that *Apocalypse Troll* and *Path of the Fury* (which I later expanded into *In Fury Born* by adding a prequel to the original manuscript) have always been two of my favorite books. There are several reasons for that. First, they are both pretty much standalones (at the moment, at least), whereas I tend to think in terms of multivolume story arcs. Secondly, both of them were early works of mine, part of the wonderful rush of becoming a published writer for the first time. But it's also because of the similarities—and dissimilarities—between their heroines.

Ludmilla Leonovna and Alicia DeVries are both "lone warriors" in the climactic, most consequential battles of their lives. Neither of them knows the definition of the word "quit," both of them face and accept hopeless odds, and both rise to the challenges they face.

There are, however, those dissimilarities I mentioned, as well. If Alicia loses, the plot against her Emperor succeeds and her family's death goes unavenged, both of which would be tragedies, but neither of which threatens the human race with extinction. If *Ludmilla* loses, humanity is either enslaved or dies, and the odds don't favor enslavement, whatever the Troll thinks initially. And there is the added twist that Ludmilla is pretty confident that her return to the past has created an alternate universe, which means she's fighting for a *different* human race's existence. In fact, that her entire task force sacrificed itself to *get* her into the past, which means every single one of its personnel—except her—have *already died* for that same different human race. And, finally, in some ways Ludmilla herself isn't "human" because of the symbiote living within her . . . and if she succeeds, she will become the only one of her kind to exist in this universe which isn't her own.

Their support teams are different, too. Alicia has a Greek fury as an ally and is paired with a powerful, cutting-edge, AI-controlled starship. Ludmilla has her spacesuit and her sidearm. Everything else she can throw at the Troll has to be cobbled together, in total secrecy, out of our own hopelessly primitive technology, by her and the handful of human political leaders who learn about the threat.

I think that in many ways it's the twenty-first-century humans, as much as Ludmilla, that make this book special for me. The twenty-first-century humans who can be convinced she's not a lunatic, that the threat is real, and who are prepared to do whatever it takes to get her into position for the single shot which stands between them and extinction. A lot—indeed, I would say virtually all—of my protagonists succeed in the end by motivating and enlisting others. By convincing those others to perform at levels many of them never believed they could. Ludmilla, in many ways, is the clearest single example of that ability to inspire and lead others, but by the same token, she can't succeed without those "primitive" twenty-first-century humans. *They* have to be willing to make the hard choices, to be prepared to die where they stand, and they do.

This book works through themes that I think go to the heart of what really makes someone human. Robert Heinlein's list of the things a human being should be capable of is a long (and a good) one, but the last two he lists—to "fight efficiently, die gallantly"—coupled with another Heinlein quote, this one from *Starship Troopers*—"Greater love hath no man than a mother cat dying to defend her kittens"—are particularly poignant to me. Perhaps because I've known so many people who were willing to do all three of those things. Or who *did* do them.

There is something in all of us, I think, that responds to the protectors, to those who assume the moral responsibility and the oft times deadly burden of protecting others.

We humans are poor, muddled creatures, illogical and irrational as often as not, prone to leap to conclusions and then ferociously advocate for them. We make a hell of a lot of mistakes, we descend into factionalism, and we find reasons to despise or hate other humans who are just as human as we ourselves. Social media, alas, serves to confirm and underscore each and every one of those indictments every day.

But we are also capable of critically examining our own prejudices and learning to reject them, to rise above them. We've actually been known, upon occasion, to reconsider our prejudices and our biases and to recognize the mutual humanity of ourselves and those we have been taught to hate or despise. And sometimes we truly are capable of fighting efficiently and dying gallantly to protect the things in this world that matter.

I think that's why I especially love *The Apocalypse Troll*, because Ludmilla makes that choice and she and her twenty-first-century allies do fight efficiently, and far too many of them do die gallantly. They are characters in a story, "made up people" with no existence in reality. I will grant you both those truths. But the *subtext* truth, the one I didn't even realize was part of the story when I was writing it, is that the reason they resonate with so many readers is that those readers want there to be people like that.

And the reason there are stories about people like that is because there *are* people like that. They are everywhere around us. We need only open our eyes to see them, to recognize them, and in a very real sense, this story is my tribute and my totally inadequate "thank you" to them for being there.